IN SEARCH OF
EDEN

Books by

Linda Nichols

FROM BETHANY HOUSE PUBLISHERS

Not a Sparrow Falls
If I Gained the World
At the Scent of Water
In Search of Eden

IN SEARCH OF
EDEN

Linda Nichols

Minneapolis, Minnesota

Published by Bethany House Publishers
11400 Hampshire Avenue South
Bloomington, Minnesota 55438

Bethany House Publishers is a division of
Baker Publishing Group, Grand Rapids, Michigan.

Printed in the United States of America

ISBN-13: 978-0-7642-0167-7
ISBN-10: 0-7642-0167-0

Library of Congress Cataloging-in-Publication Data

Nichols, Linda, 1954–
    In search of Eden / Linda Nichols.
        p.   cm.
    ISBN-13: 978-0-7642-0167-7 (pbk.)
    ISBN-10: 0-7642-0167-0 (pbk.)
    1. Young women—Fiction. 2. Police chiefs—Fiction. 3. Abingdon (Va.)—Fiction.
I. Title.

    PS3564.I274515   2007
    813'.54—dc22

                                                                    2006037944

For Bridget,

with love.

LINDA NICHOLS, a graduate of the University of Washington, is a novelist with a unique gift for touching readers' hearts with her stories. *Not a Sparrow Falls,* her bestselling debut novel for the Christian fiction market, was a 2003 Christy Awards finalist in the Contemporary category. Linda and her family make their home in Tacoma, Washington.

www.lindanichols.org

Acknowledgments

I would like to thank all my friends, both writerly and not, who have held my hand and encouraged me during the writing process and who have upheld me with their prayers. Readers and friends I've never met have prayed for me regularly, making me realize again what an incredible bond we have in Christ, whether we meet on this earth or later in our Father's home.

Debbie Macomber, Susan Plunkett and Krysteen Seelen have been wonderful, as have Sherrie Holmes, Sherry Maiura, Bob Moffat, JoAnn Jensen, and MaeLou Larson, the Thursday night scribes. My agent, Theresa Park, has seen me through this journey as she has the others. I would also like to thank Sharon Asmus and Carol Johnson for their wonderful editing as well the entire Bethany House staff—pros one and all.

The book would not have been written without the testimony of Lloyd and Joan Brown, two of my heroes.

As always, my devotional life spills over into my writing. To that end, I want to thank all the teachers of grace. Billy Sarno, pastor of Tacoma Foursquare Church, and three other wonderful Christian pastors and writers have blessed me incredibly: John Eldredge, David Seamands, and Steve McVey. I would also like to thank the people at Tacoma Foursquare who have loved me and prayed for me and my family.

Finally, I would like to thank my cousin, Lane Perry, who gave me the inspiration to visit Abingdon and set my story there. I have taken certain liberties with Abingdon's geography and places. Its charm and history are true.

"He will make her wilderness
like Eden,
and her desert like the garden
of the Lord."

ISAIAH 51:3 AMP

Prologue

Eden's hands trembled as she opened the heavy box. She had waited ten years to look at its contents—until the conditions in the instructions had been met. *Wait until you don't need to know what's inside the box to know who you are inside your heart,* the tag had said. So each year on her birthday she had asked herself if the time was right. And each year something inside her had hesitated, and so she had put it away. This year, on her twenty-first, with college and Christmas and applying to police academy, she had almost forgotten about the box. Mom had reminded her, looking at her with a steady, settled smile. So she knew the time was right.

She lifted off the lid and carefully folded back the sheets of tissue paper. She gave a half smile of puzzlement when she saw the contents. It wasn't what she'd been expecting.

It was an artist's spiral sketch pad—a huge one—and with so many things glued to and stuck between the pages that it bowed out into an arc of papery waves. A scrapbook of sorts, but raw and lively, not polished and cleanly edged. The front was covered with a collage of glue-bubbled images: a country road heading off into the woods, babies and mothers, an iceberg. She fanned the pages and saw sketches and tiny watercolors, handwritten and typed entries, and more magazine pictures. She didn't understand. But she would, and she was finally ready. She opened the front cover, and there inside was an envelope addressed to her. Her heart began to beat faster. She opened the flap and slid out the solitary piece of stationery.

Dearest Eden, she read.

Today is your birthday. I don't know if I will see you, or even if I'm a part of your life. But I want you to know that you are in my heart, as you always have been. I think of you every day. I pray for you every day. I pray that your life will be happy and blessed. I pray I did the right thing.

My friend says the luckiest people are the ones who don't walk away. Those words have settled in, and I carry them around with me because, for most of my life, I was what you would call unreliable. It's not that I wanted to be that way. It's just who I became. I have walked away from almost everything in my life at least once. When things became marred, I always thought they were ruined. I was the kind of person my friend would say was unlucky because I floated away from things like dandelion fluff drifts off in the breeze. Almost before I realized it, I let go of people and jobs and promises and just slipped away, the wind lofting me off to someplace new. But I am getting ahead of myself—another one of my faults.

I'm sure you'll see them all for yourself before I'm finished because I'm going to give you the whole unvarnished story. Not the sanitized version. This is another friend's expression, and it was his idea, too. "Gather it all up," he said. "The old parts and the new parts. The parts you're proud of and the parts you're not, and put them all together in your book. It will be your gift to her," he said, "and you will know the right time to give it." So that is what I've done. I have written all of it down just as I remember it and as others have told me they remember. I've told the tale in total honesty, which, I have to admit, is a good quality of mine. I do have a few, I think. But that's up to you to decide.

Anyway, you'll see. I'll tell you all about what happened and then you can see for yourself whether or not I did the right thing. You're the only one who can really judge. I hope you will do so tenderly, for I am now and always will be,

Your Miranda

Eden took a deep breath and smiled, her joy spilling out from the edges of her too-full heart. She supposed a part of her had always known. Had always hoped. She wanted to get up and run to the phone, to the car, but instead, she read the letter again, slower this time and with tears. And finally, when her heart had become calm and steady and she was ready to know the how and why, she turned the page and stepped into the story.

chapter 1

Wanda stifled a yawn. Ever since the hospital had gone to ten-hour shifts, she'd begun feeling her age. It crept up and settled in her back after a long day on her feet. Especially on days like today. She felt another pang of sympathy for her patient. She was just a girl, not quite sixteen, barely past childhood herself. Much too young to be having a baby.

But she had. They had whisked the newborn away so quickly Wanda had barely gotten a look at the child herself. They hadn't wanted Wanda's patient to hold her child or even look at it. They. Dr. Herbert and the baby's grandmother, who reminded Wanda somehow of the wicked stepmother in all the fairy tales she'd read. Oh, she was pleasant enough to look at with her red hair and heart-shaped face, but there was something to the narrowed eyes that gave Wanda a shiver, like feeling a cold hand clamped down on the back of her neck.

"The baby's being *adopted*," Dr. Herbert had said with that same pursed-lip expression. "It's been *privately* arranged." Emphasis on privately. Wanda thought that kind of secrecy had gone out in the fifties, but you didn't argue with Dr. Herbert. Not if you wanted to keep your job. Wanda had a sudden image of some

14

rich socialite buying the baby from that horrible grandmother. She shook her head and closed her eyes. Where had her patient's mother been when her daughter had been crying and frightened out of her wits during her labor? Nobody had sat with her. Wanda had made her as comfortable as she could and held her hand throughout, but it had been a long, frightening ordeal for her. Dr. Herbert had finally done a Cesarean, which had made it easier for them to keep the baby away from her.

The infant was fine, though. Born healthy and squalling, Apgar scores of nine, but Wanda hadn't even been allowed to tell the young mother the vital statistics. Not the birth weight, length, not even the baby's sex.

"The family has decided it would be best if the girl doesn't know," Dr. Herbert had said. The family. Meaning the bride of Frankenstein.

Wanda glanced at the grandmother, now sitting in the waiting room. Every so often she would go outside to smoke a cigarette, and when she returned, she'd pace the room or rearrange all the magazines in that nervous way she had. Wanda shook her head and glanced at her watch. It was a sad situation all the way around. She sighed and felt the weariness again. It was time for her shift to end, but she wanted to check on her patient one more time.

She walked down the hall to the postnatal wing. Here was another cruelty, she thought. Wasn't there any place they could have put her besides here on the same floor as the other mothers and babies?

She found the room—510. At least it was a private room, and Wanda thanked the Lord for small mercies. The door was closed. Wanda opened it slowly. The lights in the room were off, the curtain on the far window pulled shut. It was gloomy and dark. She heard sniffling. Sure enough, the young girl was crying. *Who wouldn't be?* she thought with a surge of anger. Here the child was, not even sixteen, trying to cope with all the emotions of having given birth, the baby's father absent, her own mother absent, not to mention the physical pain she was in from the long, fruitless labor and resulting surgery. Why, just the anguish and fear of going through such a thing by herself at such a young age would be enough to leave a scar on the heart. Not to mention having her baby taken away.

"Hey there," Wanda said gently, approaching the side of the bed. She leaned over and smiled. Her back gave another twinge, but she barely noticed.

The girl opened her eyes, and Wanda saw them light with recognition and then fill with tears. The girl turned her face away, looking ashamed.

"It's okay," Wanda said. She took the girl's hand and stroked it, and that seemed to open the floodgates. Wanda put down the rail and sat on the side of the bed and opened her arms. The girl let herself be gathered in close, as close as she could get with her fresh incision, and she cried against Wanda's chest for quite a while. The shoulder of Wanda's scrubs got wet, but she didn't care. She hugged the thin shoulders and kissed the thick, slick hair and murmured, "Hush, now. It'll be all right. It's okay," just as she did to her own daughter, but somehow those crises seemed minuscule compared to this.

After five minutes or so the little mother seemed to have cried herself out. Wanda handed her the box of tissues and then rose up and filled the plastic pitcher with water, feeling another little spurt of irritation at the nurses on the floor. This child was just a few hours postpartum, postsurgery, and no one seemed to be paying much attention to her. But even as she thought these things, she knew they weren't true. They would be monitoring her closely. In fact, someone would be coming in to check her any minute. She knew her irritation wasn't really toward the nursing staff but toward the situation in general.

"Here, drink this," Wanda said, holding down a plastic cup of water and bending the straw so the girl wouldn't have to raise herself up.

The girl took a sip. Then another. After a minute she moistened her lips and spoke. "I never got to see my baby. They wouldn't even tell me if it was a boy or a girl."

She looked at Wanda with a question in her eyes, and Wanda felt torn between hospital policy and her tender heart.

She was opening her mouth to speak when she heard the patient's mother. She couldn't make out the words, but she could tell from the tone that she was complaining about something. She caught "left me sitting out there in the waiting room" and "went downstairs for some food and took the wrong elevator." The door opened and in she came with a whoosh.

"There you are," she said, her presence, if not her slight frame, filling up the room. Her tone was accusing, as if her daughter had done something wrong. Well, perhaps she had, but Wanda thought this was not exactly the time for blaming and shaming.

"Hey, Mama," the girl said weakly, her voice containing more misery than Wanda could stand to think about.

The woman gave Wanda an accusing look, as well, though she had no way of knowing Wanda really had no official business here. Wanda patted the small hand, now trembling slightly, and left the room. She waited at the nurses' station, feigning nonchalance, talking and sipping coffee until she saw the woman leave.

"There's a piece of work," the charge nurse said, shaking her head in the new grandmother's direction.

Wanda nodded and waited for more. She was not disappointed.

"Adoptive parents are on their way. They're taking the baby home today." Wanda and the nurse both watched Grandma march toward the elevator, heard her heels clicking on the polished floor, saw her cross her arms and wait impatiently, tapping the button several times before the elevator arrived and she stepped inside. The doors slid shut. So she had left without even saying hello and good-bye to her grandbaby. Wanda shook her head and exchanged another glance with the charge nurse, who shrugged, grabbed up a chart, and headed toward the other end of the hallway, leaving Wanda alone.

Wanda hesitated just a moment and then went straight to the nursery, not letting herself think too much about what she was doing. Not thinking about the fact that this could mean the loss of her job, just knowing what she would want someone to do for her if she were in the same situation. She punched in her code, then stepped inside the nursery doors. The attendant was Martha Green, nearing retirement, too. In fact, Wanda had gone to nursing school with Martha back in the dark ages. Martha was busy bathing and weighing a new arrival, the father helping, all thumbs and elbows. She gave Wanda a quick smile and a nod before going back to her task.

Wanda looked across the cluster of Isolettes and found the one she was looking for. Oh my. What a sweet, beautiful baby. Pink cheeks, dark hair, and a tiny pursed mouth. But then, they were all precious. The baby was wrapped in an anonymous white blanket, and she remembered the charge nurse's words: *"Adoptive parents are on their way."*

She had only a minute. She picked up the tiny bundle, opened the door, and headed back across the hall, moving quickly and holding her head high. Acting as if she were on official hospital business and had every right to be doing what she was doing, not as if she were breaking hospital policy and maybe even the law. She went down the hall toward the girl's room and pushed open the door, pulling it closed behind her.

The girl looked up, then dropped her mouth in shock. "Oh," she said before tearing up again. "Oh, thank you!"

Wanda helped her sit up, put the baby in her arms, then went to the door and cracked it slightly. So far, so good. She flicked her eyes back and forth between the scene on the bed and the hallway outside. The girl held the baby gingerly and was saying something too quietly for Wanda to hear. She reached down to touch one tiny hand, bent her mouth to brush the baby's cheek.

Wanda checked her watch and moved to the bedside. She didn't want to interrupt the sweet scene, but she put a hand on the young mother's head and another on the baby's. "Lord Jesus," she prayed aloud, "your heart is loving and forgiving. You said just as a mother would never forget her child, so you would never forget us, for you have engraved us on the palms of your hands. I pray now for these two, that somehow, someday, your love would bring them back together and that in the meantime you would guard and keep them. In Jesus' name. Amen."

The little mother wept and wiped her eyes on the back of one hand, the baby gripped with the other. A noise from the hallway jerked Wanda's attention away. She went to the door and looked out. Someone was coming out of the elevator. It was Dr. Herbert with a couple who looked so excited they could only be the adoptive parents. Oh dear.

"I'm sorry," she said, "but I've got to get the baby back to the nursery. Now."

The girl didn't fight her, but she didn't hand over the baby, either. Wanda gently pried the child out of her hands, and the mother began to cry again. Wanda didn't look backward, slipped out into the hallway, and cut through the medication room just as Herbert and company were rounding the corner. She put the baby back in the Isolette and then, for no reason except sheer panic, went to the sink and began washing her hands. They were shaking so badly she could barely manage the simple task. Dr. Herbert and the adoptive parents came in just then, and there was such a joyful buzz that no one noticed when she slipped out. She went to the nurses' lounge and just sat there, waiting for her heart to stop pounding, thinking about the possible repercussions of what she'd done and trying to calm herself.

The new little family was checking the baby out of the hospital when she passed them in the hallway on her way out. The adoptive mother was a pretty blond woman and in tears herself. She was clutching the baby as if someone might try to take it away from her. The father was beaming, his arm around both of them protectively. What a pleasant-looking man he was! Warm skin and eyes and a soft brown beard. He reminded Wanda of the way some people painted Jesus, and her heart softened a little toward them. Perhaps it would be all right. The baby was obviously going to a good home. That was the important thing.

Still, her heart ached again as she passed room 510 on her way out. She slowed for a moment but didn't go inside this time. She felt cowardly and ashamed, but the truth was, she didn't think she could stand it. Even though she could see that one person's heartache and loss was another's blessing, it hurt too much. It was all just too sad.

chapter 2

DECEMBER 14, 2006
MINNEAPOLIS, MINNESOTA

Dorrie didn't have the heart for making things up and playing games. Not today. It was better when this day fell on a Saturday or a Sunday, because then she could go off by herself, away from prying eyes. She could hide until it was no longer December fourteenth. Although the pain never went away completely, it was better on the fifteenth. More like a dull ache than a sharp, breathtaking drill bearing down on the exposed nerve of her heart.

But today there was no hiding. Today would be sandpaper rubbed across that nerve. The problem was her current job at Good Shepherd Lutheran School. Normally she was the crossing guard and playground attendant. She usually loved being here and dressing in her silly outfits to entertain the children. One day she was Pippi Longstocking with pipe cleaners twisted into her hair to make her braids stand out. Another time she'd been Tinker Bell. The clown was the old standby. Then there was the pirate, the astronaut, the firefighter, the nurse. The children liked to see who she would be each day, and she smiled a little now as she looked out the classroom window and watched them chase one another.

She glanced down at the plain jumper and blouse she wore today. The only thing silly was her Cinderella watch. And her shoes. They were patchwork with an assortment of buttons and bows, and she had bought them just because the children would like them. She checked the time, for today she was not playground supervisor or crossing guard. Today, due to the desperation of the tiny school, and the fact that they weren't governed by the same regulations as public schools, she was pretending to be a teacher. She was pretending to be someone who had set a goal and accomplished it. Someone who had made something of her life.

A nasty flu bug had made the school desperate for teachers. They'd already been hiring substitutes for the substitutes when the kindergarten teacher's children had caught the virus. So she'd been put in charge. Temporarily, of course, and ordinarily she would be thrilled. Ordinarily she would be pinching herself and wondering when they would realize they had made a huge mistake. Ordinarily she would be heartsore that tomorrow was Friday and that on Monday their teacher would return. But today was no ordinary day. Today would be the most painful of places to be on this most painful of days.

The bell rang and the children came in from recess. They hung up their coats with the noisy confusion that was as close to organization as they came, then semiquietly arranged themselves in an uneven half circle with legs crossed and hands on their laps. Crisscross applesauce, the way she'd taught them.

"We're not going to do our story today," Dorrie said brightly in a falsely cheery tone, holding up the fairy-tale book. "I'm going to read to you instead." She hoped the children didn't ask why.

As they received the news that there would be no new installment of Hero, the talking blue jay, their small eager faces were slashed with disappointment they were powerless to hide. And, of course, her own heart wrenched. They were so vulnerable, children. So at the mercy of what the powerful ones decided to do with them. To them.

"We tried to be good, teacher." Roger earnestly pushed back his tortoiseshell glasses and leaned forward, as if the weight of all his noble deeds rested heavily on his back. His small face was knit into a frown of concern. It undid her.

"You *have* been good. Oh, my goodness, there *never has been* a group of children more cooperative and well-behaved!"

Their faces lit with hope, and she, as always, plunged toward it despite her intention to do otherwise. "As Hero was telling me the other day, not all children are as lucky as you are."

Their faces shone with happiness, hope barely saved from being dashed on the rocks, and her own heart eased. They cupped chins in hands, sprawled down more comfortably on their resting mats, and Dorrie grasped something and pulled it down from the air—a gift, as all stories were.

She paused, groping for a plot, catching one from the whirring in her mind. "There was one little girl Hero knew in a town far, far away who wandered away one day and couldn't find her way back home."

A slight rustle, a shift of warm bodies. She heard their quiet breathing, felt the warmth of their bodies and their love, and her heart eased.

It was nearly three-thirty before the classroom was empty. Roger, her favorite, although she tried hard to hide that fact, was the last one to leave. His mother was barely out of her teens, and Dorrie had been suspicious of her immediately. Today she arrived late, in a flurry of hair and exposed midriff under a black leather jacket. Dorrie stood at the doorway and continued to hold Roger's small hand in her own, not realizing what she was doing until she became aware that both Roger and his mother were looking at her in puzzlement. She released him and took a step backward.

"Bye, teacher," Roger said with a squinting grin, pushing those glasses back with his small hand.

Dorrie felt another twist of anxiety. He was so small and vulnerable. She looked at his mother. The woman's bangs hung down in her eyes. She was much too young to have such a responsibility. Who was she really? Who had qualified her for this? You ought to have to pass a test or something in order to raise kids. They were such little souls, children, and so desperately helpless.

"Yeah, thanks," the girl said brightly, and Dorrie had a flash of hope that she was, in fact, an older sister with her platform shoes and short skirt.

"Look, Mom," Roger said, squashing her hopes. He held up his artwork as the two of them walked away. Dorrie forcibly put Roger out of her mind, repeating a familiar refrain. *He is not your child. He is not your child.*

She turned around to survey the room. It was a disaster, as usual, so she took a few minutes to put it in order, then turned out the lights and left the classroom.

She walked the few blocks to the bus stop and paced to stay warm. It was bitter cold. Sometime since recess, it had begun to snow. Tiny, mean flakes hurtled sideways through the frigid air. The bus arrived, warm and well lit inside. Dorrie took a seat near the middle and looked around. Her eyes brushed over the middle-aged men and college boys without thinking, coming to rest on a young girl. She looked about eleven. She was sitting with an older man who looked a little dissolute. Dorrie frowned. She took another look at the girl's face and was somewhat reassured. The child looked happy enough. Yes. She supposed so. She had brown hair and pale skin, and her pink coat looked dirty but warm. She studied the girl's features but looked away before she crossed the line to rudeness.

She deliberately turned her gaze out the window. They passed a bookstore, a few coffee shops, a car dealership, and after a few more turns, the church that had once been a theater. The Father's House it was called now instead of the Rialto. Services Sunday at 10 A.M. and Thursday at 7:00 P.M. Open each morning for prayer. This week's message title was featured on the other side of the marquee. "A Place at Abba's Table," it said. She didn't know who Abba was, but the image captured her at once. It would be a good place. She knew that much.

The traffic slowed. A line of brake lights lit up the gray dusk. There was an accident up ahead. Someone had probably spun out. Maybe a visitor to Minneapolis, someone not used to driving in the snow. She thought of all the places she had lived where winters were serious. There had been that winter in Chicago, a short stay in Bozeman, Montana, and the year in New York City. Yes, she'd seen her share of snow.

The bus wound around a few more streets. She pulled the cord. The bus groaned to a halt. She stood, wrapped her scarf tightly around her neck, and got off.

Dorrie stepped into the dark apartment and tensed.

"Hello, Frodo," she said into the gloom. He was here. She knew he was.

Thump! He pounced at her feet, and she started. She cringed as she turned on the light, but there was no mouse corpse slung over her shoe today, only Frodo himself, bored and a little angry at her for leaving him all alone again. She leaned over and tried to pet him, but he stalked away in a huff.

"You'll get over it," she told him, giving up her attempt at affection. She hung up her coat, put down her book bag and purse, then filled his dish with dried food and replenished his water. Not that he was hungry, for the floor was littered with his breakfast.

She didn't know what she would do with him when she moved to another town, another job, another apartment. For she knew she would. She didn't ever *plan* to leave places, but then again, she didn't plan to stay, either. It just seemed that whenever things started feeling cluttered or marred, she wanted to start over somewhere fresh. It was like turning over a new sheet of paper in her scrapbook.

Her pattern was the only thing regular about her. She would travel, work here and there, then go home to work in the Sip and Bite until she saved up for another six or nine months of travel. She couldn't imagine herself getting married and settling down like some of her friends from high school had done. Not that there was anything wrong with the boys they had chosen. It was just that they were so satisfied to stay in Nashville, working at the Jiffy Lube and bowling every Friday night. She knew that if she joined up with one of those men, she would never go anywhere, either. She would never go to Spain or France or any of the other places in those pictures she'd pasted in her journal. Every now and then someone would come close to convincing her, but then a part of her would become restless and drift away.

"You need to grow up, Dorrie," her mama would say. *"You're twenty-six going on fifteen."* And she supposed Mama was right. Even about her so-called age. Fifteen *was* the year everything had fallen apart, so to speak. She knew that some part of her was still back there, waiting for . . . what? She had no idea, but she wasn't getting any younger, and she supposed she needed to prove, even if only to herself, that she was not going to end up bitter and alone like Mama.

Her life had certainly followed a different course than her mother's, a fact that Mama was prone to point out to her on any given occasion with a definite lack of admiration. Mama was married with a baby by the time she was out of her teens. And here Dorrie was at twenty-six, still rattling around. She would go somewhere and work, sometimes renting a room, sometimes an apartment, sometimes staying in hostels.

She just moved along until she couldn't find another job or her money ran out. And, of course, the destination she had been saving for all her life loomed before her as an unfulfilled dream—

a trip to the Basque country, that small bit of paradise situated between France and Spain high in the Pyrenees Mountains. Her father had come from there, and just the names of the cities gave her a thrill. Vizcaya, Alava, Guipuzcoa. She would go there some-day. She *would*! Maybe she would hunt down her daddy and take him, too, she mused, a slight smile passing across her lips. She poured herself a glass of water and went to the window, watching the silent snow.

She supposed she had gotten her love of wandering from her father. He had loved showing her pictures of his travels, and finally, when life with Mama got too tiring, he had resumed them. He'd sent her postcards for a while. She had saved them all. They were pasted safely in her scrapbook: scenes of Tokyo, the Philippines, London, Tibet. Then they had abruptly stopped.

"He's probably in jail," Mama had pronounced.

Dorrie smiled, remembering how he used to read her his favorite poem. She remembered bits and pieces of it now. "Vag-abond's House," it was called.

When I have a house . . . as I sometime may
I'll suit my fancy in every way.
I'll fill it with things that have caught my eye
in drifting from Iceland to Molokai . . .

My house will stand on the side of a hill
by a slow, broad river, deep and still,
With a tall lone pine on guard nearby
where the birds can sing and the storm winds cry.

She smiled and could see Daddy's handsome face, his dark snapping eyes. He blew in like a wind himself, bringing life and joy, and then abruptly he would be gone. And once he just didn't come back again.

"*Good riddance,*" Mama had said.

Dorrie had grieved for a year. Then, Daddy's DNA asserting

itself, she had embarked on a trip of her own. She'd known Daddy was from somewhere east of them, so she had used her baby-sitting money and had gotten all the way to Sulphur Springs on the Greyhound bus before the police had picked her up.

"Where do you think you're going?" the kind, grandfatherly Tennessee State Trooper had asked her, gripping her hand firmly as he escorted her into the waiting car.

"I'm going to find my daddy," she had said, jutting out her chin.

"Well." He had looked at her sympathetically as he had returned her home, perhaps already having encountered Mama.

She walked over to her Christmas tree now, a pathetic little thing she had dug out from under the fuller, more expensive trees. The man in that poem had a paperweight made of a meteor that had seared and scorched the sky one night. She had loved that part so much that one day Daddy had appeared with a small piece of spiky gray rock.

"Here you are, baby girl," he'd said. *"Now you've got your very own meteor."* This year she had taken it from her jewelry box, tied a ribbon around it, and hung it from her Christmas tree. She picked it up now, let it dangle in her hand, and looked at it. She turned it over and tried to imagine it hurtling through space, never stopping, flaming bright and clear in the sky as people watched, then disappearing as suddenly as it had flared up. A shooting star right here in the palm of her hand.

She felt its cold weight and remembered how that poem ended. The vagabond man remembered a place he had missed, something he'd failed to see. He had left his people and his nice house and had set off again. She wondered if that vagabond man had ever found what he was looking for. She carefully let go of the rock, and it swung gently from the bent branch on her tree, still in motion as she walked away.

She paced restlessly around the small room. She opened the refrigerator, but nothing looked good to eat. She fixed herself a cup of tea, turned on the television, then sat down at the table, pulling her latest unfinished drawing toward her. She was always sketching and scribbling, as her mother called it. This week's project was a Christmas scene, or at least a quick pencil sketch beginning of one. There was a beautifully decorated tree, warm candlelight, children playing on the floor, all viewed from outside the window, framed by the panes. She filled in detail now with ink. She would go back again and do a watercolor wash. She worked for several hours, until the only figures left to draw were the children. She outlined their faces and features, and as she did, the thoughts she'd been evading all day arrived on her with a thud. She felt tears rise up in spite of her resolve. She went to the bathroom, got a tissue and blew her nose, splashed some cold water on her face, then went back to her work, but it was no good. She had lost her concentration. She would finish it tomorrow, she promised herself, pushing the paper away from her.

She sighed, suddenly feeling the weight of life behind her. What did she have to show for all those years? She thought about her life and had a sudden sense of overwhelming . . . litter. She sighed again. Usually when this feeling struck, it forecast a change of address, the only remedy she could come up with.

She went back to the window and stared, her mind going back to the theater marquee with the beckoning words—"A Place at Abba's Table."

After a short walk she stood in front of the imposing building, a huge brick-and-marble monument to Serious Religion. She felt suspicious and wary. She had never found anything but condemnation and rules in the church. Well, she could stand it for a night, she supposed, and she started up the stairs. She opened the heavy double doors, made her way into the sanctuary, and found a spot on the back pew.

The speaker was a fatherly-looking man in his fifties, Dorrie guessed. He was medium height and portly with gray temples. He wore nondescript suit pants and a shirt and sweater. Ordinary in the extreme, except that he had a way of looking out over all of them just as a father would look upon his family. There was a tenderness in his gaze, a gentleness in his voice that made her want to move closer. She shook her head at her gullibility and stayed where she was.

They sang a few songs, the words to which were unfamiliar; then he launched into his sermon. He spoke about someone with a complicated name who was a friend of King David. The child of a friend, actually, who was lame. He was an orphan but had been adopted by the king. He sat at the king's table. Then it seemed to Dorrie as if the speaker was addressing her directly, telling her gently that God wanted to be like that to her. He wanted to be her Abba. Her papa.

"You were made for relationship with Him," he finished now, in that "in conclusion" tone of voice. "He loves you. Just the way you are. You don't have to be perfect or to strive all the time. He wants to give to you," he said, "not take things away. You can trust Him." His eyes were pointed straight into hers, or at least that's how it seemed, and if he had held out his hand just then and beckoned her to come, she might have.

He prayed and she stiffened, waiting for pressure and guilt that never came. He dismissed them with a blessing. The people around her began to rustle, murmur, then chatter. A few people greeted her, but she tried to avoid a conversation. She turned her legs sideways and nodded politely as people clambered over her on their way out. She pretended great interest in the contents of her purse. She looked up front at the pastor. He was standing at the bottom of the speaker's podium, listening as an earnest-looking young man spoke and gestured to him. There were two others milling around, obviously waiting to speak to him. She sat. He patiently worked his way through the people. Still she sat. She had no idea what she wanted to say. Her thoughts weren't coherent enough to formulate a question. Still, she didn't leave. And pretty soon there were just a few clumps of people left talking. The pastor looked at her then. She looked back at him. She should get up and go forward, but she felt as if her rear end were glued to the polished oak pew. Then he smiled and started toward her. She watched him coming, getting larger as he approached.

"You're still here," he said, smiling, softening the impact of what might have sounded like criticism.

She nodded but couldn't seem to move or speak.

He sat down on the pew in front of her. He seemed to hesitate.

"Was there something you wanted to talk to me about?"

She paused for a moment and looked down at her hands. "I don't know what to ask," she said. "It feels overwhelming."

"It can feel overwhelming if you've never heard any of it before. Tell me," he said gently, "where are you on your spiritual journey?"

She felt a tear slide down her cheek, to her mortification. She wiped it away furiously. "I guess my spiritual journey never got out of the starting gate. I think I got on the wrong track. But I'm making good time," she said, lifting her face with the hint of a smile.

He smiled back. "Someone wise once said that if you've made a wrong turn, the best thing to do is to go back to the last time you were sure you were on the right road. Go back to where the mistake was. I think that's what Jesus meant when He talked about repentance. Turning around and going the other way."

She nodded, her thoughts rushing too fast to examine.

"When would that time be for you?" he asked.

She blew a stream of air out of pursed lips and shook her head. She flicked her eyes past his and focused somewhere up near the ceiling. "Back when I was a kid, I guess."

"Was there a fork in the road back there?"

"You could say that."

He waited, obviously thinking she would say more.

"There's no way I can go back and undo it."

He shook his head. "Maybe I used the wrong analogy. I'm not talking about anything *you* have to do. God will take you right where you are. It's not about you getting yourself ready for Him. All you have to do is give yourself to Him. If anything needs fixing, He'll do it."

"What do you mean, 'give myself to Him?'"

He looked past her shoulder for a moment, then smiled slightly. "I think the simplest way to explain it is to tell you what my Sunday school teacher told me when I was five years old. Just open your heart's door and say, 'Jesus, come in,'" he invited softly. "He'll tell you what to do next."

Dorrie's eyes filled with tears. The minister waited quietly. "You don't have to understand everything," he said. "I didn't for many years. In fact, I've done some things I'm not proud of at all, even since I've known Him. But God honored my prayer and I grew in my understanding. And He's a forgiving God. A God of second and third and hundredth chances."

She looked directly into his eyes and nodded; then she picked up her coat and stood. "Thank you," she said. "I need to think."

"Of course," he said. She waited for some kind of ultimatum or pressure, but none came.

"My mind feels too full," she said. "I need to let some of this digest."

"God bless you," he said. He stood and held out his hand. She held out hers. It was a brief, firm clasp; then she turned and went on her way. She looked back once and he was still watching. He held up a hand and she did the same in return.

Dorrie made the short walk home quickly. She had left the television on—she didn't like to return home to a silent house— and reruns of sitcoms were playing. She flipped through the channels and finally turned it off, then back on again after the loudness of her thoughts disturbed her. The talk with the religious speaker had upset her. She had the feeling that something menacing was gaining on her, something she must not face at any cost. She thought about going to bed but knew she would not sleep. She felt a mixture of love and anger and loss and bitterness that was too heavy to dream away.

She went to the table, but she was too upset to work on the drawing. Instead, she took out her book, half scrapbook, heavy on the scrap, and half journal. It was getting thick. And such a mess. The pages were warped with glue, pictures of anything and everything she might someday want to share with . . . someone. They were cut from magazines, taken from her own camera, sketched or drawn by her, arranged around snips of articles, quotes, things she'd read and wanted to pass on someday. And interspersed here and there was an entry written by her. She paged through it quickly.

There was a picture cut from a magazine of a winding road heading off toward green hills. There were a lot of pictures of children, at every age and of every description. And other things, as well, that caught her fancy. An old postcard of huge trees in Oregon ten times the width of a man, proven by the man standing beside it. There was a Christmas card, a black-and-white photo of a park bench covered with snow and a red cardinal perched in the tree behind it. There were pictures of houses where she might someday want to live, drawings she'd made of gardens she might someday want to plant. The cover of an Annie Oakley comic book she had loved as a girl was pasted beside a photo from the fifties she had found in an antique shop of two mothers pushing their babies in strollers. And last, the one she had pasted in yesterday. She had found it in an old copy of *Reader's Digest* in the teachers' lounge at the school. A picture of an iceberg floating in black water, only the tip protruding, the vast mass of it under the dark water, all the more dangerous for its invisibility. She blew her nose, turned to an empty page, and wrote:

December 14
Today is your birthday. You are eleven years old. I don't know where you are, even who you are, but I want

you to know that you are in my heart, as you always have been. I only caught a glimpse of you, and even that was stolen, for you belonged to someone else already. You were dressed in white, so I don't even know if you are a boy or a girl. I touched your hand, and your fingers opened and closed around my own. The hardest thing I have ever done was to let them go.

I have thought about you every day since then. I pray your life is happy and blessed. I pray you can find it in your heart someday to forgive me. . . .

She kept writing, the tears flowing and wiped away while barely noticed, the pressure in her heart easing as the words flowed onto the page.

By the time she had finished writing, she knew, of course, the remedy for what ailed her. It was the usual cure. The one she employed whenever things like this came up. She would reinvent herself again. After all, as her aunt Bobbie was fond of saying, a change was as good as a rest. And that was what she needed. A change.

She needed to forget about kids. To put them all out of her mind. It was taking the substitute teaching job that had brought all this up again. That and the silly decision to go and hear the religious speaker.

She would not go back to being playground attendant and crossing guard at the school on Monday morning. She thought of Roger and the others and felt her usual steam-rolling regret. But she could not do it. She would call and leave a message that she would not be back.

She felt a little better once she'd made the decision. It always took pressure off to change the scenery.

She began reading the want ads. She would find another job. One that had no small people to tug at her heartstrings. No warm little hands slipping inside her own, no small faces to leave such a gaping hole in her heart when the inevitable parting occurred.

There would also be no one religious telling her she needed to change her life. What had she been thinking? She began getting ready for bed, putting the pastor's kind, earnest face out of her mind.

chapter 3

D avid Williams was lost. He held the directions from the church in Maplewood where he had delivered his seminar back to the Minneapolis/St. Paul airport. The street names were a blur in the meager illumination from the map light in the rental car. He shook his head. He had never been good at directions. But there was hope ahead in a familiar sign. He pulled into the Starbucks, got a cup of coffee and reorientation, then found his way back to the highway. Sure enough, the landmarks the clerk had described were just where she'd said they would be. He leaned back, relieved. He was on the home stretch now. There were only a few more miles to the airport, and he was making good time. It ought to be fine unless there was a crowd at the car rental counter. He patted his lapel where his electronic ticket confirmation was tucked along with his picture ID and the car rental agreement. He took out his cell phone and called home. It was sweet to hear his wife's and daughter's voices. He'd been gone only a week, but he missed them. He checked his watch. He would be back in Virginia in a little less than three hours. He would sleep in his own bed tonight.

He turned his attention back to his driving. The roads were

icy. A flurry of snowflakes pelted the windshield, their rhythm relentless and hypnotic. He thought about the book he was writing, about finding the heart and keeping the heart. All that remained was the last chapter, but it would be the summation, the charge, the call to battle, the map to the entire quest. He thought of his own journey toward that goal and remembered with regret the wrong turns he had made. Would he do any differently, he wondered, if he could turn back the clock, or would he still take what he wanted and leave others to pick up the pieces? He thought of his brother. The distance between them seemed as vast and cold as an icy continent. He did not know how to begin to span it. He prayed and felt the comfort and assurance of forgiveness he always received. He sighed, turned on the radio, and found the local classical station. His troubled thoughts eased, and his mind became a comfortable blank as he drove, the only sound the rhythmic thump of the wipers, the snowflakes mesmerizing as they floated down.

He came out of his reverie suddenly, attention focused but puzzled. It was an odd sensation, for one part of him was still listening to violin music and planning the last chapter of his book, and the other part was trying to understand what it meant that a set of eastbound headlights was coming toward him in the westbound lane.

Why did people say there was no time to stop? he wondered. There was too much time, stretched-out time. You could live an entire life in the seconds it took a small sedan to slide, brakes locked, across a hundred feet of slick highway. He was experiencing that lifetime pass now with an odd sense of objectivity, as if things were not real. He had the strange sensation of time hanging motionless, suspended, and in that drawn-out space David watched everything. He saw his coffee tipping from the cup holder, saw the white cardboard cup, the mermaid logo, the dried brown dribble marks down the side, all in vivid detail. He saw the amber liquid arc through the air, and as if from very far away, he felt the searing heat join his other bodily sensations—the tense pressure of his leg upon the brake pedal and the stiffening of his arms against the steering wheel. There had been no warning. Another incongruity. No horn sounded. No siren. Nothing at all but this event now unfolding. His car began to spin as he stood on the brakes. The movement was oddly graceful, and he noted things passing by—the dented metal guardrail streaked with tire marks, the hillside covered with snow-frosted trees, the staggered line of matched headlights, which had once been following behind him but was now coming toward him in that same slow-motion dance. Life should have sirens, he realized. *Oh, Jesus, oh, Jesus,* and suddenly, as the grill of the oncoming vehicle met the driver's side of his car, the seconds became seconds again instead of hours. Events piled atop one another in a crushing heap, lights too bright, screeching, roaring, tearing screams of metal upon metal, metal dragging on concrete, metal into flesh, jagged glass, searing pain, then nothing at all.

chapter 4

NEAR ABINGDON, VIRGINIA

The Baby Ben alarm clock by Joseph's bed went off, the shrill ring jarring the morning stillness. He reached across and turned it off. He had awakened without it, as usual, even though he set and wound it faithfully every night in case he should oversleep. He shunned the electric models. He didn't like to depend on batteries or electricity. There was no reason for him not to be at his post just because the power went out, and that was not an uncommon occurrence up here on the mountain in winter. He was prepared. He had a woodstove for heat and plenty of lanterns and kerosene lamps. And his truck could drive through anything.

He set down the clock, got up and pulled on a pair of jeans and a warm shirt, then went to the kitchen. He measured out a generous portion of coffee and filled the metal coffeepot with water. Flick emerged from his bed beside the banked woodstove and greeted him with a few swishes of his tail. The wood planking under Joseph's feet protested as he went about his morning routine. It was simple and rarely varied. There was no newspaper here; indeed, the mailbox was a mile beyond, where the lane met the graveled road, all but impassable in the winter except by four-wheel drives. Then he picked up his mail at the post office. There

39

was no television. His nearest neighbor was five miles down the mountain. He didn't know if he was lonely. There was the dog. And he saw plenty of humans every day as he worked. Besides, he didn't think along such lines anymore. He did his work and then drove the winding roads to his home. It was quiet here. He could rest.

Not everyone approved of his isolation.

"It's your choice if you want to live out there in the backside of nowhere," Susan Cummings, the mail carrier, had sniped. *"But I don't have to drive to your doorstep every living day."*

"It's not the end of the world," his mother had complained, snug in her house in town, *"but you can see it from there."*

Joseph turned on the burner under his coffee. Leaving it to brew, he shrugged on his jacket, pulled on his boots, and went outside. The wind cut at his cheeks and his hands. It blew hard and moaned between the empty branches. He guessed the temperature was somewhere in the twenties. The snow clouds were gray and low and looked like dirty cotton.

He walked toward the river's edge, Flick bounding along beside him. The ground was frozen hard under his feet. He stopped at a place he had always intended to plant a garden, a little flat spot that got good sun and was near the river. Maybe someday. For now, his mother kept him supplied with vegetables. In fact, she was expecting him for supper tonight, and that thought along with the responsibilities of the day began to line up like patient children waiting for a word with the teacher.

He went to the riverbank, squatted down, and looked out over the river. It was swift here but not deep. The water was frozen along the banks and out in the middle by the log snag. Most of the trees along the bank were a gray tangle. There was something about winter out here that let a little hope remain. He supposed that was why he chose to live here. Even though the bareness was more stark, at least here he could see the first promises of thaw, the first swelling of buds.

He stood and walked a ways into the woods. The air was

heavy and still. He smelled earth and mulched leaves and pine. He could see the scuffs and scat from the deer he had spotted yesterday. He followed the signs of crushed leaves and broken twigs and found the spot where the animal had bounded off into the brush. There beside it were old prints in the frozen ground that looked like a small dog's. No doubt from the red fox he had spied crossing the road last week during the warm spell. He raised his eyes a little higher and saw a possum's nest in a hickory tree. Higher still and there was the gray sky again, the blanket of clouds low and heavy. He turned and made his way back to the river.

He tossed a stick absently across a smooth deep spot and watched the ripples meet the white current along the shallows. Flick bounded in after it, despite the cold. They played their game again and again. Finally Joseph put his hands in his pockets, the signal to Flick that the game was over. He turned and headed back toward the cabin while Flick ran in circles, shaking himself.

He had built this house for Sarah. It was to have been their home together, but he well remembered how that had ended. He could still close his eyes and call the whole pitiful scene back. He could see his brother, guilty and miserable, unable to look him in the eye; his mother, grief-torn and swollen-faced at this rift between her sons. And Sarah, the one who had caused it all, had hidden from him. He had been reduced to searching her out, but when he found her, he had seen the evidence himself. On her face. In the wide eyes, guilty and half afraid. On her hand, the glinting diamond his brother had given her winking slyly at his pain. And he knew what he could not see: she had given the hidden places of her heart and her body to David, and she carried his child. His brother's face flashed before his eyes. His handsome, happy brother and his beautiful wife, their happy marriage and fulfilling ministry, and their lovely daughter, whose very name bespoke perfection.

He felt the hard lump of iron that his anger had become and touched its familiar shape, much as a person will run their tongue over a broken tooth they have long since learned to accept. The weight of that anger, though familiar, was heavy and had shaped him over the years. It had pressed him into someone he hadn't been before. The fight to forgive his brother and his wife was a battle he had given up as lost, and he understood what love became when it turned.

They had seen each other only a handful of times in the years since that first good-bye. David had taken his wife and budding family and moved up north, just west of D.C. Up to the big city where their daughter went to private school, and David and Sarah hobnobbed with fancy people.

Joseph had left home, as well, after Sarah had left him for his brother. The marines had been a good distraction. Within hours of his arrival at Parris Island, his aching heart had been the least of his worries. He smiled wryly, thinking about it, and turned to go inside. He left his boots by the door, hung up his coat, then fed some wood to the banked fire as Flick settled in beside the woodstove to dry off.

He had fled heartache for chaos. First in Somalia, then in Haiti. Initially it had seemed to be just what he needed. For at least during war there were weapons at his disposal. There was a plan and a well-defined mission. Good was good and evil was evil. He remembered a kid in his company—a boy, only nineteen or so—who had taken a bullet to the head from a sniper in Mogadishu, and Joseph had wondered why it hadn't been him instead.

He didn't want to accuse God of doing wrong, but really it would have made more sense for him to have been taken. Oh, his mother would have grieved, of course, but she'd have healed. Sometimes he looked around at the beautiful scenery, the peaceful-looking town where he worked, and he knew it was an illusion. He had wondered if he was just being pessimistic, but he'd remembered a Scripture, and finally he'd taken down his long-forsaken Bible and looked up the verses. They had resonated with feeling as he read them. *Nature itself will be set free from its bondage to decay and corruption and gain an entrance into the glorious freedom of God's children.* He imagined what it would feel like to step into a place where the pinpoint of light would become wide and full. But now even the pinpoint seemed covered over, blocked by an invisible hand. Here in this world. Below.

He suddenly felt the pressure of his mother's unanswered prayers on his shoulders. He had always been grateful for her prayers before, and he wondered what had changed. When he'd been in the desert fighting, they had felt like a shield covering him.

He played again with the idea of leaving this place. He had first thought of it when he had left the marines. He'd thought about moving to New York City. He could have joined the police force there, but in the end, home had called him back. But if he had thought simply being here would heal what ailed him, he was sorely disappointed.

He thought of his great-grandmother, who had been able to feel the weather changing deep down in her bones. He felt an ache like that nearly all the time, and he knew it had more to do with the state of the world and the state of his soul than with the falling barometer. He felt a cold shrug of fear and wondered if grace had a limit. Was there a time for repentance and after that the door quietly closed? Was there a window for reconciliation, but after a season it sealed shut? Would there be a penalty for the coldness of his heart?

He checked his watch, then showered and dressed for work, looking at himself in the mirror as he combed his hair and brushed his teeth. He was thirty-five. His hair was lighter around the edges, not gray yet, but the sandy pigment was slowly fading. His face had changed, as well. It still had the firm leanness of a young man, but when he looked closely, he could see lines where trouble and sorrow and weariness hadn't quite covered their tracks.

He finished dressing, then glanced toward the leather Bible on the dresser. A few old habits still called to him, but he did not pick it up. He did pray the Lord's Prayer, though. He had done it since he was a boy, and though he wondered if his prayers were answered any longer, he still formed the words with his mouth if not his heart. "Deliver us from evil," he said, the one sentiment about which he was fervent, and when he was finished he strapped on his gun.

He drove in slowly, as he always did, and surveyed the town. Inside its demarcations the generally kindhearted and peaceable citizens of Abingdon lived, eight thousand or so souls at last count. He made his rounds every morning, driving slowly around his territory, beginning in the heart of town.

Abingdon was idyllic in its own upright way, not changed all that much from the days of its founding when it was a fort, an outpost in enemy territory. It still was, Joseph supposed, and at the heart of the outpost were the churches he passed now, the four old mains, he thought of them, and they reminded him of the four chambers of a heart. Across from each other on opposite corners were St. James and St. John, the sons of thunder, as the town called them.

St. James was the Methodist church, built of old red brick with tower, steeple, and spires, and surrounded by a tidy hedge of boxwood. Legend told that it had been visited by the Wesley brothers themselves soon after it was established by the same circuit-riding preacher who had first brought the gospel to the town—or so the Methodists claimed, outraging the local Baptists, who had been here since dirt and *sent* missionaries, not the other way around. St. James Methodist was led by the Reverend Hector Ruiz, and a more lionhearted father in the faith could not be found. Hector had ministered to youth in his youth, and now that those days had passed, he tended his flock with love and fierceness. Joseph knew firsthand that he pursued the lost sheep with a gentle tenacity. He was generous, prone to speaking his mind, and would give away the altar candlesticks to the first desperate beggar to cross his doorstep. Then he'd come to the city council and try to get someone to donate their replacements.

St. John Episcopal Church was across the street, a bit more

ornate in Vermont granite with intricate stonework, and a rectory beside it. The Reverend Dr. E. Julius Stallworth presided and had come to them only lately—twenty years ago or so. He was continually outraging his parishioners with some blunt statement or another. A few of them would be angry enough to cross the street to the Methodists, whereupon Pastor Hector would promptly send them back, only to have the favor returned when a group from his flock strayed. Not an uncommon occurrence, since both pastors were staunch believers in speaking their minds.

On the third corner was the Catholic church, Shepherd of the Hills. Father Leonard was nearly seventy but showed no signs of slowing down. He organized the hospital chaplaincy and had begun Catholic Community Services of Abingdon, which had been thriving for over thirty years. They ran four group homes for foster children as well as programs for pregnancy counseling and adoption. He was busy and always on the move. Joseph saw Father Leonard every morning at the Hasty Taste, where the priest ate breakfast, read the *New York Times*, the *Washington Post*, and the *Roanoke Times*, jotted notes in his Day-Timer for the next week's homily, and made nonstop calls on his cell phone.

Abingdon Presbyterian was on the fourth corner. It was a plain wood-frame structure and had been led for the past thirty years by Pastor John Annenberg. He was the soul of gentleness but passionate about defending his understanding of doctrinal truth. The only time anyone ever remembered him raising his voice was during a skirmish with Pastor Hector. The two of them had begun discussing predestination in the city hall after a town meeting, and the only thing that had saved the entire event from becoming a conflagration was the intervention of Pastor Mike, the young Foursquare minister who had established himself on the front lines out along the interstate with a strategically placed outpost of independent churches. They were the young folks, ecclesiastically speaking, and their houses of worship could be anything from a Quonset hut to a sheet-metal hangar and generally looked much like a warehouse grocery store.

The four old mains were silent sentinels, guarding their corners in the center of town. A few blocks down was the Barter Theatre, so named because when it was begun in the Great Depression, admission to a play was forty cents or livestock or produce of corresponding value. Across the street was the Martha Washington Inn with its red brick, white columns, and black wrought-iron fence. A little farther east Joseph crossed the creek that ran through town on his way to the Virginia Creeper trailhead. There were a few runners out already. He turned around in the parking lot and headed west. Past the Visitors' Center, the museum, the library, the post office, the historical society. He passed the police department. All was still, the windows still dark. The grass in the ball field across the street was frozen and spiked with hoarfrost, the trees alongside so bare he could almost hear their branches clicking together in the wind.

He drove past the homes, the attorneys' offices, the tourist shops all adorned with wreaths and garlands. Later on today there would be banners flying, twinkling lights in the windows, inviting smells and sights, but now things were dark. The bakery was the only lighted storefront. He slowed and could see the warm beads of condensation on the window, and in the back he glimpsed yellow light and movement. He rolled down the window, and sure enough, the yeasty smell of baking bread rushed to meet him. It gave him a brief surge of well-being.

He sent the window back up with a flick of his finger and continued on his way, past the motels and fast food restaurants on the edge of town, past the elementary school.

He drove a bit farther out because it gave him peace to do so. He loved to see the farms and fields, spread out wide and green but neatly marked off with well-mended fences. He felt a warmth that he played a part in keeping his people safe and shielded. He stopped his car just past Herman Pfaff's farm, stepped out for a moment, and looked around. The Amish had been coming down from Pennsylvania in search of good land and welcoming people. They had found both here. The fields were frozen and fallow now, but come spring they would be crumbling with life and ready to sow.

His territory ended here. Beyond this line was the county sheriff's jurisdiction, but from here in he did his part. He fulfilled his responsibility. The souls within this boundary depended on him and others like him to be able to carry on in peace and innocence, and he took up that responsibility again today as he did every day.

He drove slowly back to town and stopped in front of the Hasty Taste. The seven-o'clock regulars were there. He could see their familiar cars parked in the side lot. He parked the truck and stepped inside the restaurant to the jingling of bells. It was bright and warm with wood flooring and pies in a glass case. It smelled like breakfast.

Henry Wilkes, the county sheriff and his late father's best friend, was already there. Joseph walked over and slid into the vacant side of the booth. Their breakfast together was a daily ritual, as it had been when his father was police chief and Henry sheriff. Everyone, including the current chief, had expected Joseph to make a bid for his father's job, but he had surprised them all. Politics frustrated him, especially office politics. He had no desire to kowtow to the town manager and the city council, and why on earth would anyone sign up for more paper work? He liked staying busy, moving, and being where real events impacted real people. He liked running things to the ground, but Ray Craddock, the police chief, always suspected Joseph was after his job. Joseph knew it burned him like acid that he and Henry breakfasted together. He had long ago decided not to let that fact bother him. Henry was the closest person he had to a father and was his best friend. He was not likely to give that up just because his boss had an insecure temperament.

"Good morning," Henry said, greeting him with a smile.

"Back at you," Joseph replied, sliding into the booth and turning his cup right side up. He glanced toward Elna, who read his mind and came toward him with the coffeepot. She was sixty-five and plump, with hair that was brilliant red down to a quarter inch above her roots, where it turned cotton-batting white.

"How's the back today, Elna?" Joseph asked her.

She tilted her head to one side but, as usual, gave a stoic reply. "I'm sitting up and taking nourishment, as my granny used to say. Menu?" she asked, filling his cup expertly with a swift swoop down and then up. Not a drop spilled or splashed.

"No need," he answered. "I'll have two eggs over easy, bacon, and a short stack."

She gave a nod of approval. Elna liked a man to have a hearty appetite.

"And you, darlin'?" she asked with a wink toward Henry.

"The usual," Henry sighed. The doctor had told him his cholesterol was sky high. He was on a breakfast diet of oatmeal, bran muffins, and skim milk. Elna patted his shoulder sympathetically.

Joseph grinned and looked Henry over. He was nearly seventy. His hairline was a little farther back and a little whiter than it had been ten years ago when Joseph had come back from the marines. His neatly trimmed mustache was salted with gray. His face was weathered and lined, but his uniform was crisp with starch, and though the pale blue eyes were perhaps getting a bit faded behind the stronger lenses, they still missed little. Nothing got by Henry. Joseph supposed he would be retiring someday. He didn't like to think about it. He took a sip of his coffee. It was scalding, black as a bat's cave and strong enough to stand up and walk away, so the saying went.

Henry handed him a sheaf of papers, the report from the county's night shift. Joseph read, shaking his head at the things Fred Early, the shift commander, thought worthy of mention.

A suspicious incident was investigated on Crooked Creek Road. At 1:15 A.M. a passing motorist reported a noose hanging from the porch of a residence. Upon investigation it was discerned that the residents were not victims

*of a hate crime, but the rope in question was a swing util-
ized by the minor children at the residence.*

*At 2:14 A.M. a call was received from Albert Johnson
of 215 Old Mill Road reporting two juveniles standing on
the Dry Creek overpass throwing projectiles onto vehicles
passing below. Upon investigation the projectiles were
determined to be horse excrement. The perpetrators were
taken into custody and their parents called.*

He smiled and handed the papers back, then sobered when
he thought about the real crimes they had to deal with. At one
time Abingdon had been a place removed from the world. Not
anymore. Domestic abuse had always been around, as had
alcohol-related offenses. But now drugs were more and more of
a problem, methamphetamines especially. He felt a familiar pressure to *do* something. He wouldn't have his town invaded by evil.
He would do whatever it took to stop it.

Elna brought the food, interrupting his grim thoughts. Joseph
buttered his pancakes, drenched them with syrup, and dove in
enthusiastically.

"What's up for today?" Henry asked, eyeing his own oatmeal
with a frown.

"Oh, just the usual. Whitley has to testify at a trial today.
Redding's on vacation. I guess I'll just hold down the fort."

Henry nodded with understanding.

The weeks before Christmas had bare-bones staffing. It
should be all right, though. They weren't exactly a hotbed of
crime. Not yet, anyway.

"Think the storm will amount to much?" Henry asked.

Joseph glanced out the window and nodded. "A foot or so at
least and starting soon."

Henry smiled. "Is that from the weather forecast or from
swinging a dead cat around your head in the graveyard during a
full moon?"

Joseph took the ribbing. Henry liked to rattle his cage, but he had been right often enough to make Henry a little more respect-ful. His father had taught him the weather signs, saying half were hogwash and half were science, and it was up to him to sort the two out. Joseph thought of his father again and missed him. Both men ate their breakfasts in peaceful silence.

Joseph was just finishing his second cup of coffee and prepar-ing to leave when his cell phone rang. He looked at the number and didn't recognize the area code.

He flipped it open. "Lieutenant Williams," he said briefly.

It was a woman's voice, poorly transmitted and trembling. It took him a moment to realize who it was, much less to under-stand what she was saying.

"Sarah?" he asked, not quite believing it.

Henry sat up and paid attention. Joseph barely noticed. He plugged his free ear, and his body tensed.

"Yes, it's me, Joseph." Her voice bounced hollowly off the satellite and thinned as it streaked through the cold, cloudy sky. He hadn't heard that voice for nearly twelve years.

He braced himself, for just the sound of it cranked up the adrenaline levels in his blood. Sarah wouldn't be calling just to say hello. Not now. Not after all this time and space. Something ter-rible must have happened, and he braced himself.

"There's been an accident," she said.

He had the odd sense of his brain rising above his pounding heart and quickened breath.

"Last night David was hit by a drunk driver," she said.

Pain and cold shock spread through him. He had always known this might happen. That he and his brother would wait too late to get things right. "Is he dead?" He tried to moisten his dry mouth.

There was a pause that seemed to last forever.

"No. But they won't promise anything. His spinal cord is injured. They don't know how badly."

He closed his eyes, then opened them immediately and switched modes. He could feel the emotions, dangerously close to the surface, and he forced them to recede back down to safe levels. His heart slowed by sheer force of will. "How are you? How is Eden? Where are you?" he asked, remembering the unfamiliar area code. He was back in charge again, an officer taking stock of his troops after an attack.

"I'm at the airport in Minneapolis. Eden's all right. She's . . . she's being taken care of." She sounded disjointed and confused.

"Where is David? Where did the accident happen?"

"Here. He was here doing one of his seminars. He was on his way to the airport."

An irrelevant detail right now. He was annoyed with himself for asking. "Do you have the best doctors? Do you know who to ask about things like that?" He didn't know, but he could find out.

"Yes, Joseph, all of that is under control. He's at Hennepin County Medical Center. It's the best trauma center in the area."

"What can I do? Do you need me to come?" Even as he was asking, he knew what she would say.

"No. I don't know. . . . If I thought the two of you could—" She broke, paused, tripping over the old familiar barrier. "He isn't conscious," she finally said. Her voice choked then.

His pain rose up. This had been the black outcome he had feared when he had let the silence rise between them like a great wall. What if the story ended before it was resolved? He had thought about that eventuality every now and then. And now it had happened, just as he had feared.

He brought himself back to fact taking. "How did it happen?"

"What?"

"The accident. How did it happen?"

"A drunk driver in an SUV crossed the median on the freeway. He hit David head on."

Anger flushed Joseph's face and raised his voice. "What exactly are his injuries?"

He noticed Henry was leaning forward, his knuckles white on the coffee cup.

A sigh, a tremulous breath from Sarah, then a litany he could hardly bear to hear. "Crushed pelvis, broken leg and arm, crushed vertebrae. He's already been in surgery once to have something called an external fixator put on his pelvis. His leg needs more surgery, but they're waiting on that. Right now they're just trying to keep him alive."

"I understand." But he didn't. How could he understand? His light, bright brother was lying near death a thousand miles away. His brother.

A pause. Another tremulous breath.

"What can I do?" he repeated again, hearing a note of demanding desperation in the echo of his voice on the poor connection.

"Could you tell Ruth? I didn't want to tell her over the phone."

"Of course. I'll go right away." He thought of his mother beginning her day, suspecting nothing, not knowing that evil had once again invaded her world.

"And, Joseph—"

He waited, poised for another direction, something, anything, to *do*.

"You could pray. You still do that, don't you?" she said, wistfulness rather than criticism in her voice.

"Of course I do," he lied. He heard pain in his echo.

"Pray for him, then, Joseph," she repeated. "Pray for us all." She disconnected.

He closed the phone and sat there for a second or two before he grabbed his hat and jacket and slid out of the booth.

Henry stood with him. "Is it David?" he asked.

Joseph nodded and gave him the brief facts.

"Oh, God," Henry breathed, and Joseph knew it was a prayer.

"I'm going to tell Ma."

Henry nodded. "I'll let them know at your office. You do what you need to do."

Joseph nodded, tossed a ten-dollar bill onto the table, and said an abrupt good-bye with one last glance at Henry's worried face.

The wind was sharper and biting when he stepped outside, the sky darker and lower. His premonition had been right. The first flakes of snow began to fall. He looked up and saw them rushing down, hard, fast, and inexorable.

chapter 5

Ruth Williams padded into her quilting studio in her slippers and flannel robe, a cup of steaming coffee in her hand. She had spent some time with her Bible but wasn't quite ready to launch into the day yet. She stood before the window near the heat vent and looked at the sky with a practiced eye. It was dull gray and low and promised snow. In fact, as she looked closely, she could see that the first flakes had begun to fall.

She took a mental inventory of her readiness. All was well due to Joseph's almost compulsive need to make sure she was prepared for any eventuality. There was firewood stacked nearly ten feet high just outside the back door, and the cast-iron Papa Bear stove in her basement was piped into her ductwork and full of kindling, newspaper, and wood, ready to be fired up. That had been her son's contribution the last time he had visited.

The pantry was full of candles and cans of lamp oil, and her kerosene lamps were full with fresh wicks, neatly trimmed. Joseph had even checked her cupboard to make sure it was well stocked with canned goods and matches. What he saw had apparently satisfied him. She also knew that the rooms she customarily rented out to bed-and-breakfast guests were freshly dusted, with clean sheets on the beds. And her closets were packed with quilts and blankets in case some of her neighbors weren't as well equipped as she. She glanced once again at the clouds and the more rapidly falling flakes and verified her prediction. The storm was here. But she was ready.

She looked out the frosted window onto the town. It had the idyllic Christmas-card look of a mountain village. The streets rose and gently fell, following the curves of the Blue Ridge Mountains they nestled against. The buildings were old red brick, the trim paint fresh, lights warm and welcoming. It was a Thomas Kinkade picture, a Norman Rockwell scene, and some, on seeing it, on being here amidst the peaceful faces and gentle accents of its people, might think it a place where no spiritual battles of consequence were won or lost.

They would be wrong.

She used to be involved in that battle. More so than now, she realized, fighting back a familiar feeling of uselessness, a well-worn lie that she was too old and irrelevant to be of use to God any longer. She was only sixty-seven, but she might as well be a hundred and seven for all the impact she made on anyone's life.

She had closed the campground when the family fell apart, and once again she wondered if she had done the right thing. But John had died, and David and Joseph had their split, and it had seemed as if she were the only one, struggling alone. Not alone, for her two most faithful friends had helped her run the camp for the rest of that year, since churches had already booked and made deposits, but she hadn't felt free to impose upon their good graces forever. Carol Jean had her quilt shop and Vi her artwork. So after struggling through the winter, she had finally closed down the camp. She had moved into town, into this place, her husband's family home. The campground was to have been her retirement. *"Sell it,"* a few friends had urged. *"You'd get a pretty penny for that land. Lakefront, mountain view. You'll be a wealthy woman."* But how could she sell a piece of her life? The place she and her husband had poured their hearts into? The place she had raised her boys?

But that part of her life was over now, she told herself. Which brought her back to her initial complaint. The truth was, she was bored.

Oh, she stayed plenty busy. She went to church three times a week and served on the Threads of Love group and the altar guild. She did hospital visitation, taught quilting classes at Carol Jean's shop, took classes at the college, taught a women's Bible study, rented out rooms to tourists, bought season tickets to the Barter Theatre. She had taken a trip to England one year with David and Sarah and Eden, but what wouldn't she give to be once more ringing the gong for breakfast and seeing a hundred mismatched, gawky campers pour or straggle out of their cabins and gather around the long wooden tables. She remembered making vats of French fries, piles of hamburgers and hot dogs, and buckets of slaw.

But more than that, she had seen lives change at that camp. She knew that for a fact, and she impatiently brushed at her eyes as she recalled the cardboard box full of letters and pictures she had collected over the years. She sighed and looked out the window, the depressing thoughts taking on a life of their own, rewinding and preparing to replay.

"Wait just a minute," she said out loud. "I'm not having this." Somebody needed an attitude adjustment, and today it wasn't one of a throng of children or one of her own boys. It was she, herself. "Forgive me, Father, for being so hopeless and negative. You are the God of all hope."

She dropped the curtains, bowed her head, and started the day over again by putting on her armor, piece by piece. Beginning with her shoes. "Thank you, Jesus, that I stand forgiven and cherished, firm and secure in the peace I have with you," she breathed softly. "Thank you that the belt of your truth holds me together. That the body armor of your perfect righteousness covers and protects me. Thank you that the filter that protects my mind is the truth of my salvation, of who I am in you. I pray your Word would come against every scheme of the enemy in my life and in those of my loved ones today, Jesus. And I thank you for the powerful shield of faith. I pray you would help me to stay under it. Strengthen my arms to lift it up. Put your angels around me, Lord. Help me to pray in the Spirit today, and lead others to pray for me."

She took a deep breath and, remembering the tears and fractures in her own family, again brought that pain to the Lord. She closed her eyes once more, seeing at once the gentle shepherd and the captain of the heavenly armies. He would see to it all. She prayed for David and Sarah and Eden. She prayed for Joseph. She prayed that God would heal the rift.

"In the mighty name of Jesus," she finished. "Amen."

She turned from the window and finished her coffee in one long swallow. There were things needing to be done. She set down her cup and brushed her palms together, as if finishing off the self-pity and sorrow she'd been visiting. She checked her watch. Seven-twenty. Carol Jean and Vi would be here at nine to pray. She wondered if the snow would stop them and decided it probably would not. They both lived within spitting distance, and if anyone got stranded, they knew she would call on Joseph to drive them home in his truck. She went down to the kitchen to see what she could throw together for refreshments.

She rummaged through the fridge and dug out a few oranges, a sack of cranberries, an apple, and grapes. She took out flour and sugar and set to making orange-cranberry muffins. She was glad her late-season bed-and-breakfast guest had departed the day before. It was her policy to leave the two weeks before Christmas free for holiday preparations, and she had always done so except for the year that Homer Dawkins had asked to rent a room, even though he had a perfectly good house just over on Randolph Street. She shook her head at the foolishness of men. She had said yes because he hadn't a soul in the world, his wife having died just months before, and Joseph had immediately pitched a fit. Not just because some silly old man was willing to pay a hundred dollars a night to make cow eyes at his ancient mother, but because he said it just wasn't *right*.

Joseph was always concerned about the *rightness* of things, and she feared sometimes that it got in the way of his seeing the *goodness* of them. A fine distinction, but she felt it was important, somehow, and she worried about her son's inability to see it. But, of course, in this matter, he'd been absolutely right. She couldn't have the two of them staying in the house all alone together, what with Homer's own place merely a stone's throw away. There was the appearance of evil to think about, even at their age. The solution she'd come up with had satisfied her quite well, but Joseph still fumed whenever anyone referred to it. She had prevailed upon her son, and he had moved back into his old room, now done over in pink and green with lace curtains. He had spent two weeks glowering while Homer had a fine time helping her hang Christmas lights and wrap packages. The man hadn't wanted to leave when the holidays were over, but she had sent him packing on January second, bright and early. Joseph had left the same day, and she smiled with a rueful sigh. Having her son sit at her supper table every night, even with the frowns and grunts that replaced polite conversation, had been a blessing. Her spirits sank when she thought about Joseph, but she took herself in hand. There was no time for melancholy today. There were preparations to make. Besides, the story wasn't over yet.

She checked her watch again and switched on the radio. The local station was playing Christmas songs from Thanksgiving until New Year's. She greased her muffin tins while Johnny Mathis crooned and was just softening her butter in the microwave when she heard a commotion on the porch. The front door opened and Joseph called out. She smiled in pleasure and walked out to meet him, her hands dusted with flour. She stopped cold when she saw his face, for it was gray, simply gray, as if all life and hope had been drained from it.

She felt a flutter in her chest and a dryness in her mouth. "Who is it?" she asked quietly, hands suddenly dangling by her sides.

He didn't answer, just came toward her and reached his arms out, and that was when she knew.

"It's David," she said.

He nodded, and it was a good thing he had a hold on her, because her legs gave out and she had to sit down on the stairs.

chapter 6

Sarah looked at her hands lying helpless in her lap and thought how odd life was. Her hands had been busy just hours ago. She sat now amid the calm but urgent activity in the intensive care unit and felt a sense of bewilderment. There were four nurses in David's room and one doctor, each doing things to her husband. At least they said it was her husband, but if she hadn't seen the discolored thumbnail from a baseball accident when he was twelve, the tiny scar above his left eyebrow, hadn't had his wallet and wedding ring handed to her in a brown manila envelope, she would not have believed it. She certainly would not have recognized him. She had expected to see him broken and bleeding, but she had not expected the hugely swollen state that distorted his features and made him seem like a stranger lying naked there on the bed. He was covered with just a sheet, and she was reminded of Jesus in the hour of His extremity. They had told her the swelling had something to do with his injuries, something about intra- or extra-cellular fluid, but all she knew was that he did not look like someone she knew, someone she loved, and irrationally, she held the wild hope that the man there on the bed was not her husband at all but someone else's husband. That her own husband would come walking through the door any minute now. He would calm her fears and stroke her hair and hold her and comfort her. Because that's what David did. He ministered to others. He helped others. But what happened to the sheep if the shepherd was cast down? It made no sense, and the bewilderment returned. She tried to pray again, opening her mouth but making no sound, gaping like a landed fish gasping for oxygen. Her need was too deep for speech, and she thought of the groanings of the spirit that were too deep for words.

His hair was the same, she told herself, and she focused on his hair. His beard was the same, as well, but if she looked at his beard, then she must look at his face, and she couldn't bear to look at his face. Even his hand, when she held it, caused her pain, for it, too, was grossly swollen and unfamiliar. But it didn't matter, for she couldn't touch him at all just now. They were working on him and had sent her out again. They allowed her near only once an hour for a few minutes. The rest of the time she waited here in the hall or out in the waiting room. She had pulled a chair near the glass window, and no one had stopped her, so here she sat. She looked once more toward David, then down at her hands again.

It amazed her that everything could change so suddenly, that life was so fragile when it had seemed so fixed. Just yesterday evening she had been making soup and worrying about their daughter. It seemed so trivial now, but then she had been browning meat and slicing onions, watching the knife slice cleanly through the outer papery layers and peeling them away swiftly and wondering why everything couldn't be as simple as cooking. Follow the directions and things would turn out as you expected. A cup of this, a pinch of that, cook at the prescribed temperature, and the end product was assured. She had been comforted in the rituals of measuring and chopping and stirring. In knowing that there were some realms in which actions had predictable results. If meat was put in a pan over high heat it would turn brown. If you added baking soda to a bowl of batter, it would rise. She had even enjoyed washing her dirty dishes, squirting in the soap and rubbing it around with the bubbly cloth, then seeing pots and bowls emerge from the steaming hot water clean and squeaking. Why couldn't life be as straightforward as that? she had wondered. More particularly, why couldn't raising children work the way it was supposed to? Why couldn't you do the right things and say the right things and have them turn out right, like a pot of soup or a loaf of bread?

She had sighed as she worked, the day's energy already spent in her never-ending mission to turn her daughter into something other than a wildcat.

Eden was not the child she had imagined.

She had imagined a little girl who would wear pink. Who would adore coloring and making scrapbook pages adorned with tinsel and glitter, who would want to play dolls and dress-up. Well, the dress-up part had come true, she thought wryly, thinking of Eden's disguises. Once she had decided that the mean girls at school were plotting against her friend, and she had dressed up like a bag lady and lurked in the park, listening to their conversations and writing everything down in that spiral notebook she carried everywhere. Then there was the night disguise—a set of dark clothes and dark face paint she had put on so that she and the girl next door could spy on the neighbor's older brother. And of course it had all begun with the cowgirl outfit she had worn at age five. It was still a treasured possession.

Sarah had imagined cozy talks with her daughter, the two of them sitting on a ruffled canopy bed, slowly turning the pages of a fairy story, watching *Little Women* together, and having tea out of china cups. Instead, she spent half her time trying to *find* her daughter, or having found her, to find out what she was up to. She could picture Eden's dark hair, freckles, and squinty-eyed stare, that pretty little rosebud mouth a straight line, chin jutting forward, jaw clamped as tight as a pit bull's.

A little princess she was not.

In fact, as Sarah frequently bemoaned to David, who persisted in being amused rather than concerned at his daughter's antics, they were well on their way to having a hellion on their hands. She sighed· again in aggravation. Eden needed a firm hand. And both of hers were completely exhausted. Tiring did not begin to describe the state motherhood had become for her. She felt a familiar guilt. It was probably all her fault. She shook her head resolutely and stirred the vegetables with vigor. The solution wasn't to pile onto the sofa in frustration. It was to try harder. She picked up the notepad on the table and made herself a note— *Sign up Eden for soccer lessons tomorrow*—telling herself guiltily that she was not simply shifting her daughter to someone else for a few hours. Eden would learn a new skill and burn off some energy. And what would she do while Eden ran and played?

Sleep. She had eyed the sofa hungrily.

Then the telephone rang. Wearily, she had moved to answer it, and as she heard the unfamiliar voice and the heart-stopping words, she sensed a sharp knife running down through all their lives. No, a guillotine blade, forever severing what had been from what was to come.

They had all stepped into the *After* when that telephone had rung, and they'd left *Before* forever behind.

She felt guilt now as she remembered Eden's pleading to let her come with her to Minneapolis. She had said no and wondered again whether it had been from a genuine desire to spare her daughter or a knowledge that she couldn't cope with all this and Eden, too. But Eden just wanted to be with her father. Sarah knew Eden loved him best, and that was all right. That was just fine, because she wanted Eden to have what she needed, and who wouldn't need David? Who wouldn't love David best? He was a rock to both of them.

She squeezed her eyes shut, as if she might will them all back in time. She tried again to pray, but all that would come was *Help him, Jesus. Help him, Jesus. Help him, Jesus.* A hand on her shoulder startled her back to here and now.

"Mrs. Williams?" It was the volunteer from the waiting room.

She nodded.

"There's a family member to see you out in the foyer."

Ruth. She rose quickly and fairly ran through the wide halls lined with carts and machines. The double doors to the waiting room took forever to open after she tapped on the square button. Then there was her mother-in-law, standing in the middle of the hallway, wearing her pretty red coat and clutching the handle of her purse with both hands. Her face was red and swollen with grief and distress. She looked older and tired.

Sarah flung herself at Ruth. The arms opened and the two of them clung together and wept.

"Where is he?" Ruth finally asked when most of their tears had been spent.

"This way," Sarah said and punched open the door. "He doesn't look like himself," she started to explain, but she realized how futile the words were. Nothing spoken could prepare her. *Help her, Jesus. Help her, Jesus. Help.*

The crowd had thinned in David's room. She could see just two nurses in there now, one adjusting intravenous lines, the other charting. Sarah introduced Ruth to the charge nurse, and her mother-in-law went inside. Sarah waited in the hallway. Only one allowed in at a time. She watched for a moment as Ruth took David's hand and smoothed his hair, and then it was too hard to watch any longer. She sat back down in her chair, lowered her head again, and closed her eyes. *Jesus, Jesus, Jesus* was the only thing she could think of to say.

chapter 7

J oseph drove to Fairfax and followed the directions his mother had given him to David's house, then let himself inside after retrieving the key from the neighbor, as he'd been instructed. It felt strange being in his brother's home. He had never been here before. Not once in twelve years, and he looked around with a sense of unreality. It felt as if he were watching something on television or at the theater. He felt a little guilty, as if he'd done something wrong, but he was only waiting for Eden to be returned from another friend's house so he could take her back to Abingdon.

He looked around slowly and felt himself slip into cop mode—gathering evidence as to what kind of people David and his wife had become.

Someone was artistic. He knew it was Sarah. She had always had a flair for making things beautiful. The walls were deep colors—the living room red, the kitchen gold. He wasn't well versed in interior design, but the furnishings and decorations looked expensive and had been put together with care. Everything was either red, gold, or dark green, with flashes of purple here and there. Something about it reminded him of royalty.

The house was decorated for Christmas, but with excruciating care. The tree was artificial and done completely in purple and gold. Even the presents underneath were all wrapped in the same gold foil with purple bows. He couldn't help remembering his mother's Christmas tree, a live, noble fir covered with mismatched ornaments—evidence of thirty years of teaching elementary school and twenty summers of running a camp. Ma had a homemade quilt underneath it, and the presents were covered in a motley assortment of wrappings. He turned away and walked back into the kitchen.

He lifted an eyebrow at the scattering of something on the kitchen floor. He bent closer and examined it. Seed husks. He looked up. There was a hook in the ceiling. So there had been a bird. It was gone. Neighbors were taking care of it, most likely. And Sarah had left in a hurry, so there'd been no time to sweep the floor.

He went near the photo wall in the front hallway. There were studio stills and black-and-white candids, all tastefully matted and framed. Sarah's handiwork again, he supposed. He scanned the pictures. There was Eden as a baby. Pretty eyes, button nose, pink mouth, and a thatch of dark hair. He looked at the photograph of Sarah holding her in the next shot, looking blond and tanned and happy. There was a set of what seemed to be mother-daughter pictures taken each year, probably on Mother's Day or some such. Sarah wearing a pink dress and holding Eden as a baby. The passage of years was evident mostly in Eden as she progressed from drooling infant to toddler to child. He calculated how old she was and then realized with a familiar flood of emotion that he didn't have to calculate. He knew. The day his brother had taken Sarah and left plus nine months, give or take six weeks or so.

He felt his jaw clench but released the tension when he thought of Eden the person rather than Eden the symbol. For the real flesh-and-blood child had wrapped him around her heart from an early age. He'd called her Annie Oakley since she was five. He talked to her weekly. She phoned his mother every Sunday night without fail, and he just happened to be stopping by most of those nights. She e-mailed him twice a week or so. She was in the midst of writing detective stories now and frequently would post her latest installments to him via e-mail. He recalled yesterday's missive. It was a fast-paced whodunit, liberally salted with exclamation marks and parenthetical asides. *"Do triggers click?"* she had asked.

He'd sent back his reply last night, not knowing he would see her before she read it.

Dear AnnieO: Your bad guy is most likely using an automatic weapon, in which case the trigger does not need to be pulled back to fire. However, the sound the daring investigative reporter might hear is the release of the safety catch. Would that work? Keep me posted. Uncle Joe.

She was a bright spot in his life, which was funny, since he had been determined not to love her.

From the time she was small, David and Sarah had let her come every summer to visit his mother. He had managed to avoid her for the first five years of her life except for pats on the head and brief drooly encounters. He remembered the day that had all changed. Eden had been five years old.

"You're baby-sitting," his mother had announced, leading his niece into his office. *"I have a hair appointment I can't miss, and this is just plain silly."* She gave him a glare that said, *"Don't you dare ask what I'm talking about."* With that, she had left.

Joseph had sighed and sized up his adversary. About forty-two inches tall, with no tattoos or visible markings except the brown freckles dusting her nose. Dark hair cut in a bowl shape with crooked bangs. *"She won't hold still! It's like wrestling an alligator!"* Maisy at the Beehive had complained to his mother. She was small and quick—too quick, it had been alleged. She was prone to running off. She had small hands with chipping red fingernail polish, at that moment planted on her hips. She was wearing rolled-up jeans, the cuffs showing the red plaid lining. A red plaid flannel shirt, a gun belt complete with two western pistols, and a cowboy hat.

"*These shoes ain't right,*" she'd said, looking with disgust at her pink tennis shoes.

"*No. I can see that,*" he had agreed.

In the end he had taken the small hand and led her down the block to Larry's Western Shop. There just happened to be a pair of size ten Tony Lama boots, black with black stitching, just like his. They had been fast friends ever since.

She had come to the office every day after that. She drank Dr. Pepper out of a chipped white coffee mug on which he wrote her name with black permanent marker. He put her to work separating Wanted posters from crime reports and shrugged off his mother's objections.

"*She can't read the gruesome stuff,*" he said. "*Besides, it keeps her busy.*"

They had lunch together every day at the Hasty Taste. Elna knew to bring Eden a grilled cheese sandwich and chocolate milk, and after that she spent the afternoon at the office. He returned her to his mother's for supper. They had done it every summer for six years now. The visits had gotten longer, too, from a few weeks to a month or two.

He got a kick out of her.

Now, at eleven, she was still feisty and funny and not afraid of anything. Her hair was still short with crooked bangs. She had a cowlick that never lay straight. She still had the freckles and so far had disdained covering them up with makeup. She was still prone to running off.

She sent her stories off to *True Crime* and *Ellery Queen's Mystery Magazine.* They always came back with printed rejections, which she cheerfully threw away. She seemed immune to discouragement.

He barely remembered whose child she was, and when he

did, he put it out of his mind. She was his buddy. That was all. Besides, you couldn't blame the child for the sins of the father. Or the mother.

The doorbell rang. He started guiltily. The door opened and he saw Eden, followed by a woman and another girl. She ran for him and threw her arms around his waist. He smoothed her hair, nearly covering her head with his hand. He realized again how very small she was. Introductions were brief. He barely listened. Murmurs of condolence were made, and the friends left.

When the door closed behind them, Eden pushed herself away and glared at him with a defiant expression, a poor cover for the fear he could see in her eyes.

"What's going on?" she said. "Nobody will tell me anything."

He frowned and looked at her with confusion. "What do you mean?"

"I mean Mom left and just said she'd be back as soon as she could. She said she had to go meet Dad and that you would come and get me. I know something bad's happened, and everybody knows but me."

He felt a flush of anger, followed quickly by one of bitterness. Sarah had never liked to deal with messy emotional situations. It looked as if nothing had changed. He reached down and took Eden's hand. It was bigger than the day he had first clasped it, and there was no chipped red fingernail polish today. The nails were small and rimmed with white and tipped slightly upward. She wore a bracelet of braided thread, a hooded purple sweatshirt, and jeans. Her dark hair still flew every which way. Her pretty blue eyes were worried, the freckles standing out sharply against her pale face.

"Tell me," she ordered.

"It's your dad," he said gently. "He's been hurt."

She cried a little while, and he held her. She dried her eyes, went into her room to pack, and came out with a backpack, a small suitcase, and her notebook. He had to suppress a smile at that. She never went anywhere without her writing utensils.

She stood there in front of him, backpack and suitcase in hand, and lifted her chin. "Uncle Joseph," she said, "I want to go see my dad. Will you take me?"

Joseph hesitated. His instructions had been explicit. Take her back to Abingdon, and Sarah would.decide what arrangements to make before Christmas vacation was over. Suddenly it made him angry that Sarah had walked out on someone else who was left holding the sharp-edged pieces.

He sighed. "I'm supposed to take you to Abingdon."

She jutted out her chin.

He softened. "If we go, it will only be for a day or two," he warned.

Eden's face lit with hope, for she knew the battle had been won. "All right. I won't argue. I promise."

She had a right to see her father, he told himself as he booked the tickets and drove to the airport. They climbed onto the 6:20 flight from D.C. He called Sarah when they were irrevocably committed. She sounded upset at first but quickly lapsed into passivity. He remembered that about her, that tendency to let go too easily.

"How is he?" Joseph asked.

"Holding on," she answered briefly.

They arrived in Minneapolis not long after eight and took a cab to the hospital. They found the Trauma Intensive Care unit after a few minutes of wandering.

Joseph didn't go into the waiting room with Eden right away after seeing Sarah there with his mother through the doorway. He sent his niece in alone, saying he would be along in a minute. He felt guilty, as if he were not doing the right thing, as if he were focusing on trivialities of the heart while a life hung in the balance, but somehow he could not make himself go into the room. At least not without preparing himself first by getting a look at who she had become. Eden gave her mother a quick hug, threw herself at her grandmother, then gestured toward the hall. He saw his mother nod and knew they had asked about him. Then Sarah faced him and he was forced to walk toward her.

She looked smaller than he remembered, or maybe it was the oversized sweater she was wearing. It looked like one of David's, and he wondered if it was. She hugged herself as if she were cold. Her face looked thin, the angles of her cheeks standing out in sharp relief. Her blond hair was chin length, not long, as he remembered. There were dark circles under her eyes, and suddenly he felt ashamed of himself, hovering like a lovesick schoolboy while his brother—yes, even as Sarah—was suffering. It was wrong, this hesitation, and he quickly covered the remaining space between them before he could think further.

He expected her to take stock of him, but she didn't, just stepped toward him in a brief hug, then stepped back quickly and draped her arm around Eden, who looked miserable and small. His mother came and took his hand, and he wasn't sure if she was trying to draw strength from him or impart it.

"Nothing has changed in David's condition since I spoke to you," Sarah told Joseph briefly.

"I want to see him," Eden said, and Joseph saw Sarah hesitate.

"He doesn't look like himself, honey," Ruth soothed. "Why don't you wait a day or two?"

"I want to see him!" Tears threatened; her voice tightened.

"Let her see him," he said, surprising himself and the rest of them, as well. Eden looked at him with gratitude, and oddly, so did Sarah, who seemed relieved to have someone make the decision for her.

"Will you come with me, Uncle Joseph?" she asked.

He looked at Sarah, who nodded permission. So the three of them went to the desk outside the ICU and waited while Sarah called. Permission was given for him and Eden to come in for five minutes. "Room 910," Sarah said, back to hugging herself.

Joseph hit the button on the wall, and the doors opened slowly. They walked through. Joseph looked for the numbers above the doors. They were headed in the right direction, and he couldn't help but glance inside as they passed each room. This was the Trauma ICU, and each bed looked like a morgue slab with a limp sprawled body snaked with tubes and crowded by machines. Man or woman, all were ground down to the elemental here, and he wondered if he had been wise to advise that Eden see her father like this. Maybe his mother and Sarah were right. If David should die, maybe it would be better if his daughter did not remember him in this state. He glanced down at her face. It was set, and her eyes were frightened. He felt compassion for her.

He had steeled himself, but even he, who had seen so much in war and crime, was shocked. They stood in the doorway at first, neither one of them moving in. There were three nurses in the room, one adjusting lines, the other punching buttons on the IV machine, the third typing into a computer and talking on the telephone. His brother was swollen to nearly twice his normal size. His head was as big as a basketball, and Joseph wondered how his skin kept from splitting. Eden moistened her lips. Joseph felt profound pity for David and for his daughter. He stepped closer to the bed, moved toward the head, and looked at the face on the pillow, searching for something recognizable. It had been twelve years. He had not expected to meet again like this.

"You can talk to him," one nurse said. She was tall and lean with washed-out blond hair and features. "He may be able to hear you."

He kept silent. The sound of his voice would not be welcome to his brother and would probably only confuse him. He looked toward Eden. She came forward slowly, stood beside Joseph at the bedside, reached out her hand, and gingerly touched David's arm. He was covered with a sheet, his arms and legs and head exposed. Some sort of contraption jutted under the sheet over his pelvis— the external fixator Sarah had talked about, most likely. The air in here felt tenuous and unclear, as if life actually hovered and hung, like an image coming into focus and then fading out. A vapor, a mist, kept present only by their magic and machines.

"Hi, Dad." Eden's voice trembled. She stroked his arm with one finger. "I love you." A tenuous rise on the last word, a phrase that expected a comforting reply, but there was nothing from David, just the steady hushing sound of the ventilator, the beeping of the monitors, the hum of their machines. Eden withdrew her hand. She suddenly looked very small and frail, and Joseph reached down and took her hand in his. She stepped closer to him. He covered her with his arms. She was frightened, just a scared little girl.

After three days David's condition was still critical, and all of them were tense and brittle. None of them had slept much since the ordeal had begun. Sarah was staying in a room near the ICU, with Eden sleeping on the floor beside her on cushions. She had insisted over Sarah's objections. Joseph hadn't heard the conversation, but Sarah's voice had risen in tension as she had argued with her daughter, and he had watched Eden's face grow closed and cold. He and his mother were staying at the Holiday Inn nearby. Joseph ferried them back and forth in his rented car. David had survived the first onslaught of injuries and surgeries, but now a secondary wave of troubles had attacked. His kidneys were in distress, overwhelmed by the waste products of devastated muscle.

"We may have to do surgery to remove the damaged muscle," the doctor—one of the myriad—said briefly.

Sarah shook her head helplessly and looked even more fragile than she had the days before.

They did the surgery. David survived. They waited to see if the kidneys would regain function or if dialysis would be necessary. Sarah was not doing well, and he remembered now that she had always hidden from disaster. He wondered if she would leave, but she did not. She was trembling and tense, wouldn't eat, and haunted the hallways. Eden stood at the doorway of the ICU, looking through the rectangular glass. *Look at your daughter*, he wanted to urge Sarah. *Be strong for her.* But somehow he knew even if he spoke the words, they would do no good. It would be like urging a lamb to fly. So it was his mother and he who comforted Eden.

The days were a strange dance of creeping in and out of David's room and up and down the stairs, of pretzels and soda and vending-machine coffee, an endlessly droning television, the same clumps of families growing increasingly familiar, and an endless parade of doctors and specialists giving Sarah updates. They did the dialysis. After another three days, the report was guardedly hopeful. His kidneys had begun to function again. After another two days he began to wake up.

There was a giddy joy. *Unrealistic,* Joseph thought, exchanging glances with the resident on duty while his mother and Sarah and Eden hugged.

"This is where the real pain begins," the young doctor told him quietly. "Up until now you've been the ones who suffered. From now on he will suffer, as well."

Joseph did not go in. His brother was barely conscious, still on the ventilator and in severe, unremitting agony. He would wait until later to see him. Their reunion would be traumatic enough then. He did not want to burden his brother with it now. Better he see faces that would bring comfort.

The days and surgeries blurred together. They took David to the operating room almost daily to do wound care. He finally had the surgery to set his broken leg and arm. Joseph began to realize this would be his brother's life for the foreseeable future. It was time for him to return home. He needed to be back at work, yet he was hesitant to leave. He knew his mother could cope with Sarah and Eden, but it seemed a lot to ask of someone who had her own griefs to bear.

David's awakening seemed to have caused Sarah more pain, as well as relief. He understood. It hurt him terribly to see his brother suffering. He could only imagine how Sarah felt.

"I don't know what to do." Sarah stood in the hallway, looking gaunt and tense. The cup of coffee in her hand shook as she raised it to her lips.

"About what?"

"Eden."

"What about her?" Joseph asked, feeling suddenly defensive for his niece.

"She can't stay here," Sarah said bluntly.

Joseph stayed silent.

Sarah began spilling words. "I can't cope with her and David, too. It's too much. And I can't leave David."

"No. Of course not." He forced himself to focus on the present words, their present meaning. "What are your options?" he asked.

Sarah took another swallow of coffee and visibly pulled herself together. She ran her hand through her disheveled hair. "She could board at her school in Fairfax. Or she could stay with friends and continue as a day student, I suppose. My parents would take her if I asked, but they're in retirement mode since they moved to Gatlinburg. The doctors say David will be in the hospital for six to nine months."

"I suppose you could get a place here," he offered. "An apartment. She could go to school here, and you could all be together."

Sarah shook her head. "I can't do it right now, Joseph. I just can't."

"Have you asked her what she wants to do?"

Sarah shook her head. "I know what she'll say."

Joseph raised his eyebrows.

"She'll want to stay here with David." A slight smile. "She adores him."

He nodded, then after a pause suggested the obvious. "Let us take her."

Sarah's expression showed she had considered it. "It would mean a new school," she pointed out.

"But she'd be with people she knows who love her."

"She adores you, too," Sarah said.

He heard a hint of bitterness. It must be a sour pill to know that the daughter of her betrayal loved the one betrayed. He felt ashamed that it pleased him. "I'll take her back with me," he offered simply.

Sarah sighed, then nodded wearily. "Fine," she said.

He saw lines of exhaustion on her fine features.

"I just can't deal with her here," she repeated. "She wears me out when everything is normal. I can't imagine what it would be like trying to keep track of her and deal with all of this, too."

"She's no trouble," Joseph said. "We're glad to have her." And then he saw her standing not ten feet away, listening to their conversation. Sarah followed his gaze and half turned, sloshing coffee when she saw her daughter. Joseph wondered how much Eden had heard. He wondered if she had heard her mother say she was too much trouble.

"Oh, hi, honey." Sarah smiled at Eden with the guilty face he remembered well.

Eden didn't answer and would not look at her mother. So she had heard enough.

Joseph excused himself to leave the two of them alone. Sarah gave him a panicked look as he passed by her.

"I won't be any trouble," he heard Eden say as he walked away, and his heart stretched out in pain toward his niece. Oh, how well he knew what it was like to stand in that place. He couldn't hear what Sarah answered, but the following day he and Eden boarded a plane for home.

"She doesn't care where I go. As long as I'm out of her hair," Eden said bitterly.

"That's not it at all," Joseph argued, but Eden turned her face away and he, out of his element, didn't know what to do.

After arriving in D.C., they drove to Fairfax and spent the night in David's house before filling the backseat of Joseph's car with Eden's clothing and belongings. They made the drive back to Abingdon the next day in silence, Eden staring out the window.

The town seemed unnaturally cheerful with all the Christmas doings. Carolers strolled; tourists shopped. The promised storm had dumped nine inches of snow, which still adorned everything with a clean sugar coating. He stopped at the Hasty Taste and bought Eden a grilled cheese sandwich and chocolate milk.

"My place or Grandma's?" he asked. She shrugged, so he picked his mother's. She was all set up for visitors. They drove there, unpacked the car in silence, and then he settled her in her old room, the nursery/playroom, still full of toys and things she had reveled in the years before.

He went downstairs and made himself coffee, then returned to check on her. She was asleep on the bed, clutching a stuffed dog, and her face looked very young and vulnerable. He unfolded the quilt on the foot of the bed and covered her up, but he left a light burning. He remembered she didn't like the dark.

chapter 8

D oes *repellent* have one *l* or two?" Janelle asked, tapping her cigarette butt into her empty Coke can.

"Two," Dorrie said. She looked back down at the handwritten notes she was transcribing and read the sentence aloud. "'If your home doesn't have mice and rats, they are just waiting to get in.' Who writes this stuff?" she asked in amazement.

Janelle grinned. "Don. He gets a kick out of it."

Dorrie pictured Don, the head exterminator, a pleasant, heavyset man who reminded her of Hoss on *Bonanza*. He didn't exactly seem the threatening type, but then again, everyone had a living to make. She sighed and went back to her typing.

"This is truly disgusting," she said after another minute. She leaned back from the computer screen and read aloud again. "'Mice have no bladders. They trail urine at all times. Therefore, any time a mouse walks through your home, he leaves a trail of urine, and the scent invites other mice to follow.'"

Janelle shrugged and took a drag of her cigarette in defiance of Minneapolis's "No smoking anywhere in the entire city" policy. "That's the business, kiddo," she said, flicking another ash. "It pays our salary."

"Grossing people out is our business?"

Janelle grinned. "You want them to sign up for the twelve-month-guaranteed contract, don't you?"

Dorrie continued reading. "'A typical infestation pattern is mice followed by rats.'" She looked doubtfully at Janelle. "This isn't true," she said. "Is it?"

Janelle gazed toward the ceiling as if in fond reminiscence. "I had nightmares my whole first year in the business," she mused. "Mice at the windows. Rats coming up the drain. Mice in the cupboards. For months I wouldn't sit on the toilet without looking first." She shrugged and took another draw. "After a while you get used to it, though," she said, exhaling a delicate little lick of smoke. "And I'll tell you something, it beats cleaning sewers. Now, *that* I couldn't abide. My brother-in-law cleans drains. You should hear him tell about some of the things he's snaked out of people's sewer lines."

"No thank you." Dorrie went back to her typing. She could see Janelle watching her, amused. She concentrated on the brochure. She typed another sentence, this one about the reproductive habits of rats. She closed her eyes for a minute, then resolutely went back to her typing. She had a moment of yearning for the kindergarteners at the Lutheran school. She had thought about going back to visit, but she hadn't done it.

This was the worst job she had ever had. In her life. Worse than the dry cleaners in Santa Fe with all those toxic chemicals. Worse than the dog groomer in Los Angeles. After that one there were dog hairs on everything she owned. This was definitely worse, but it was the only thing the employment agency had open on such short notice. The Mice B Gone Exterminators were the bottom of the barrel. The end of the line.

She felt something ominous building up behind her discouragement. It was that full-to-the-brim feeling that came over her whenever she'd had all she could take of something. She had awakened this morning and looked at her small apartment with distaste. She had known every single thing she was going to see today before she even opened her eyes. She knew there would be the small quarter-moon-shaped stain on the ceiling from the leaky sink upstairs. She knew there would be dark green loop carpeting and Danish modern furniture in the small living space. She knew there would be an unfriendly cat and a bus ride into town and another day spent typing about rats and mice and then another bus ride home, and oh, she was bored. She was tired of it and sick of it and disappointed.

Yes, that was it, she realized. She was disappointed. She saw that now. The city that had seemed so gleaming, so promising and full of hope when she'd arrived was now familiar and dreary. She didn't see the sparkle anymore, only the dingy spots. As she had so often found, the longer she looked at things, the less appealing they became. And really, what was holding her here? She didn't need to answer the question. Nothing. Absolutely nothing and no one.

The empty feeling that came with that knowledge was accompanied by a little pulse of excitement at the thought of going someplace new. Who knew what people she might meet or what she might do? Where would she go? She thought of the possibilities.

What was she in the mood for? Long, lonely stretches of wilderness? Montana? Wyoming? She shook her head with a shudder. Somehow her loneliness here in Minneapolis ruled that out. She thought of crowds and bustle and decided she wanted a large, friendly city. Maybe she would settle in Little Italy in New York. No. Not in the winter. Too much cold and snow. L.A., then? No. Too much smog. San Francisco? San Francisco! Now *there* was an idea, and for a moment she thought of cable cars and sunshine and Rice-A-Roni and a book she'd read about a single woman who lived in San Francisco and fell in love with a carpenter. Yes! San Francisco! She stared into space as she filled in the details of the daydream. Her apartment would be in one of those Victorian row houses on the hilly streets. Yellow with white trim, like the one in that movie she'd seen where Chevy Chase played a police detective who's protecting Goldie Hawn. A batty old man lived downstairs, and Goldie worked in a library and drove a sports car along winding highways that hugged the ocean. There were marinas and vineyards, and she remembered a commercial she'd seen with a handsome man sipping wine, and in the background were long, rolling acres of grapevines. She remembered seeing dappled sunlight and happy people sipping jewel-colored liquid from fluted glasses. They'd been eating pasta. Well, she liked pasta. The spokesman had been handsome and sturdy looking, with a nice beard, and she became lost for a moment in the pleasant story she told herself.

She looked up. Janelle was watching her. "It's been nice knowing you, kiddo," she said with a kind smile.

"I'm not gone yet," Dorrie said, feeling somehow ashamed. She went back to her typing with vigor, but in a way she knew she was lying. She was as good as gone, and she could tell that Janelle knew it by the wise and oddly pitying look in her eyes.

The apartment was silent and empty when she arrived back home, and for a moment Dorrie hoped Frodo had managed to escape and run away. She had left the bathroom window open a few inches. No such luck. He jumped at her feet, as usual, and as usual, she startled. She fed him, tried to pet him, thereby subjecting herself to more of his ill treatment, then put her frozen dinner in the microwave.

She turned on her cell and saw two missed calls with her mother's familiar number. Odd. Dorrie checked for messages, but there were none. She frowned, trying to remember the last time her mother had called her. It had been last March, on her birthday, in fact, and she still remembered the message. *Just called to see how you're doing, but you're probably out with your friends.* Loud sigh. *So you're twenty-six today. When I was your age I had a husband and a child and two jobs. Talk to you later.* There had been no good-bye, just the decisive click of Mother disconnecting.

But Mama was consistent, at least. There had been a check in the mailbox that day, as there was every birthday. For twenty-five dollars. The same every birthday and another one at Christmas, along with a generic card, both signed in her mother's firm, unadorned handwriting.

She thought about calling Mama back but decided to eat her supper first. She then fussed around the apartment for a while, and just as she had steeled herself to make the call, her phone rang. She went to answer it, feeling a sudden foreboding.

It was Mama, and she didn't mince any words. After a perfunctory greeting, she delivered her message.

"I've got cancer," she said. "Breast, and it's growing like kudzu."

Three days later the apartment was cleared of Dorrie's belongings, which had been dispersed to various places. Frodo had gone to the old lady upstairs, who already had four cats. Dorrie wished her luck. She hadn't exactly been sorry to quit at Mice B Gone Exterminators, but she would miss Janelle. She would catch the 5:50 bus to Nashville, but first she had one last thing to take care of.

Good Shepherd Lutheran School looked strangely different today, even though Dorrie had been away less than three weeks. Class had just dismissed for the day, and children were streaming from every door. She felt oddly self-conscious as she headed down the hallway and had a sudden image of a small vine tugged out of the soil before the bud could flower and bear fruit.

She took a deep breath and wondered if she should continue on, but the decision was taken out of her hands. For there down the hallway was Roger, standing in the doorway of her old classroom, holding today's artwork, blinking behind his glasses. A tired-looking middle-aged woman, obviously another substitute, stood behind him.

"Teacher!" Roger's face lit like a candle, and Dorrie felt her heart lurch, coming precariously unbalanced. He came toward her and held out his arms, and before she could think, she was on her knees beside him, feeling his sturdy warmth.

"Where were you?" he asked solemnly, hug completed.

His round cheeks and earnest expression made her feel inexpressibly sad.

"I had to be somewhere else, Roger," she said, giving one of those meaningless explanations that probably do not fool children in the least.

"Will you be here tomorrow?" he asked.

She paused and her heart felt too heavy in her chest. Everything in her wanted to lie.

"No," she said, the truth landing like a rock on her heart. "I came to tell you good-bye. I have to go home and help my mother." She wondered if that was the only reason she'd been able to come today. Because she had a real reason for leaving instead of just her usual whim.

"Will you come back again, teacher?"

"I hope so," she said. "Maybe." A lie. A bald lie, but she had to tell it, as much for herself as for him. She would, she promised herself, but knew she would not. She knew it because of the fierce pain she felt right now. It was as persistent as an ache, as sharp as a knife thrust.

Roger frowned and looked desolate. He glanced over his shoulder toward the new substitute with an expression that would have made Dorrie laugh if she'd been able to feel beyond her own emptiness. *He is not my child,* she told herself. *He is not my child.*

Roger's mother came then, in her usual whirlwind of jacket and cell phone and purse sliding off her shoulder. Today she was wearing tight jeans and a blouse that didn't quite span the distance between midriff and hips. Roger greeted her, his face lit up again, and Dorrie was stranded somewhere between relief and dis-appointment.

"Let's go, honey," his mother said. "Carl's waiting for us."

Who was Carl? Dorrie wondered with a twist of concern that Roger didn't appear to share. He put his hand into his mother's and followed her out the door, then turned and faced Dorrie again.

"Good-bye, teacher," he said solemnly.

Dorrie held up a hand and waved. She couldn't answer.

This, she reminded herself, sniffing back hot tears, is why you should never say good-bye.

chapter 9

D orrie had been home for a month now. She had found Nashville still the same and Mama still—well, Mama was still Mama.

She glanced up now and saw her mother coming out from the doctor's office. Dorrie set aside the book she'd been reading— an old Perry Mason novel she'd found in the glove compartment. She should bring something of her own to read when she chauffeured, but Mama was always in a hurry to go and impatient over any delays but her own.

Mama opened the door, *harrumph*ed as she flumped down on the seat beside her, and pointed forward—Mamaspeak that Dorrie should start the car and leave. Dorrie obliged, driving a mile or so before she had the nerve to ask the results of the latest scan.

"What did the doctor say?"

"It's spread to my lungs and liver." Mama delivered the news in a tone of outraged irritation more than shock or grief, as if the paperboy had skipped their delivery or she'd been overcharged at the grocery store. She seemed personally irritated at the doctor, the clinic, and now especially at her. Mama glared at her with those sharp granite eyes piercing her own, as if daring her to express any emotion. Dorrie half expected to again hear her say, *"Don't you dare cry, or I'll give you something to cry about."* So she stifled whatever jumble of emotion she was feeling and drove her mother to the supermarket, the pharmacy, and then home. And Dorrie did not cry.

Things seemed to be progressing fast. Mama had taken to lying down every afternoon and actually using on occasion the portable oxygen they gave her—an indication of how her equilibrium had been upset, a fact she would rather die over than admit. Dorrie shook her head at the wry irony of the thought. For die she would and probably soon. Mama's cancer had metastasized, and there was nothing they could do now but wait for the end. Mama was not dying particularly well but with the same demanding energy she'd lived.

Dorrie helped her mother out of the car, into the house, and upstairs to rest. She then checked her watch. She had taken the whole day off to take Mama to the doctor, and it was already one o'clock. There was no point in going into the Sip and Bite, since her shift would end in an hour. She had applied for a job as a teacher's aide at a local school, but Mama had discouraged the idea. Her mother hadn't approved of the idea of her going to college to begin with and had been triumphantly vindicated when Dorrie's half-finished teaching degree fell victim to her impermanence.

"You should have just gone to work at the Sip and Bite," she had reproved. She knew Myra Jean needed help at the diner and thought it was ridiculous that her daughter would think herself qualified to teach. If Dorrie pursued any higher education, Mama wanted it to be at Françoise's School of Beauty, her own unfulfilled dream. One of many. She heard her mother's voice scolding her. *"Surely you don't think you're qualified to see to children, Dorrie? They have their teachers. They have their mothers."* *They don't need the likes of you,* she might as well have added. Dorrie shook her head. Not only was she talking to herself, she was answering back. She wondered if Mama's voice inside her head would outlive Mama's

life on this earth, and suddenly she felt a desperate fear that it would.

She looked around at the house. It was immaculate, as usual. Nothing had changed for as long as she could remember. Off-white carpet, shampooed on schedule every six months for the last thirty years, gold-and-green sofa and chair set, with matching pillows artistically scattered about. Well, Mama was consistent. You knew what to expect from her, and Dorrie supposed that was worth something.

Dorrie sat down in the recliner, feeling a little rebellious for usurping her mother's chair. She looked around. There was the clear plastic placemat protecting the Formica end table. Her mother's nail file, pencils, and pens were handy in the small vase she set beside the remote control for the television set, and a new addition—a little cluster of pill bottles on the polished tabletop with Noreen Gibson's name on each one. Take as needed for pain. There was her crossword puzzle book, neatly folded back and held in place with a rubber band, beside the novel she was reading. Dorrie knew without looking that it would be a lurid romance with a pink and scarlet cover and a bare-chested gorgeous man bending back a nearly bare-chested gorgeous woman in a passionate embrace. She smiled a little at her mother's taste in literature, out of character as it was. But who really knew who lived behind Mama's stern façade? Dorrie certainly did not, and she wondered again who her mother might have been if her life had gone a little differently.

She hadn't had it easy, that was for sure. Dorrie knew that much, even though Mama never talked about her early life. She thought back to when the recorded history of Noreen Gibson began and tried to remember what her mother had looked like on her wedding day. She vaguely remembered the photograph that used to sit right there on the brick mantel beside the china figurines. She'd worn a simple white dress, and her red hair fell in lush waves. She was tiny, curvy, and beautiful with her gorgeous dark blue eyes, her pretty mouth curved into a smile beside her husband, who was dark and handsome in his roughshod way. His people were Basque, he bragged, proud and mysterious, and even his name was flashy and vaguely dangerous. Thomas Orlando DeSpain. And he had bestowed an equally dashing name upon her. *"We'll call her Miranda,"* he'd told her in one of his endless repetitions of the story. *"Miranda Isadora DeSpain. A name fit for a princess."* Apparently Mama had balked, but Daddy had been one person she hadn't been able to push around.

But she had been able to push him away.

After he'd gone, Mama had cleansed the house of any of his footprints, including Dorrie's name. *"You can use your middle name,"* Mama had declared. *"And my last."* So she had become Dora Mae Gibson, the only Dorrie in a flock of Lindsays and Hayleys and Jennifers. And so Daddy's last gift to her had been taken away along with his presence. He was gone. Long gone, and though Dorrie had longed for him often, sending her thoughts to him as if by sheer force of will she could make him appear, he had not. She had gone looking for him two times and had found him on the second try. She stared at the far wall, at the framed poster she'd given Mama for Christmas the year it had happened. She stared at the picture of the dancing girls in the pastel gauzy dresses and saw herself. Fifteen, riding the Greyhound to El Paso, the place where her father's sister said he was living.

Mama had gone to work the evening shift and left her at home a few days after they had given away her baby. She had been half sick, her breasts sore, hard lumps leaking milk. She could go back to school in a week or two, the doctor said, depending on how she felt. A different school, though. Mama had seen to that.

"Why?" she had wailed. *"They already know."*

"Don't be ridiculous," Mama had snapped. *"It's not about saving face. I've got no face left to save, thanks to you and your father."*

"Then why?"

"You don't need to be around that boy anymore. He's got you into

trouble once. *You need to tend to your business and let him tend to his. Besides, I don't want any complications,"* Mama had said, giving her a threatening look before going out the door.

Mama didn't know the half of it. Dorrie had been sneaking out to see Danny throughout her pregnancy. They were going to get married. As soon as he graduated. She'd also been saving her money from the job at the Sip and Bite. She had gone to the telephone book and called a lawyer as soon as Mama left. The same lawyer who had done the adoption. He wasn't in, but his secretary was really nice, and she had listened to Dorrie sniffle and cry and told her, *"Honey, don't worry, no matter what your mama made you do, you can revoke an adoption if you speak up within twenty-five days."* That had cheered her up. Once she told Danny, he would help her. She hadn't done a thing after that phone call to the lawyer but get dressed and go to Danny's house to tell him.

"He's not at home." His mother was a little cool but not unkind. *"Honey, you need to go on home now."*

She hadn't gone home, though. She had walked to his school, and there she'd found out what everyone else had probably known. He was there, just leaving football practice, his arm around some girl wearing a cheerleading uniform.

He had been shocked to see her, had murmured something to the girl, who had given her a look that was both smug and pitying before she'd walked away.

"What is this, Danny?" She'd been simply confused, the obvious explanation being unthinkable.

His ducked head and shamed tone answered her question even before his words confirmed things. *"I'm sorry, Dorrie,"* he had said. *"I don't want the baby. I'm only seventeen. I'm a senior. I'm sorry. I never meant . . ."*

She had begun walking away before she even heard the rest of what he had to say. She remembered, oddly, how cold she had been on the long bus ride home. She'd been wearing a warm coat, but she had been so cold her teeth had chattered.

She had gone home and, almost in a panic, called everyone

she had known to borrow money to get her baby back. She called Aunt Bobbie, who told her to mind her mama and after that didn't answer the phone. She called Daddy's sister, Aunt Weezy. She wasn't home, but her cousin Robert said she was at work and would be home at nine.

Finally Aunt Weezy called back. She had said she couldn't pay for a lawyer, but she gave Miranda her daddy's address and phone number in El Paso. So Miranda had taken her two hundred dollars of savings out of her dresser drawer and gotten on the bus. She had prayed all the way. It had taken seventeen hours, and after she got to El Paso she had to take a cab to Daddy's house, and she had been flat broke then.

Her breasts hurt. The incision hurt. Her head hurt. She felt nauseated and sick. She felt hot, as if she had a fever. The cab pulled up to the curb in front of Daddy's house. *Please let it be his house,* she prayed. *Please let him be home.* It was dingy and small and looked just like all the other houses they'd lived in when Daddy had lived with them. There was a dog in the front yard, short and muscular looking, and he barked as if he'd like to eat her alive. A little boy and girl had come out and seen her standing at the gate, swaying slightly, and they'd run back inside. Then Daddy had stepped out onto the porch, with them hanging on to his legs.

He looked about like she remembered. Kind in spite of the hard lines etched onto his face. He had dark hair and eyes. Long and lean, he was wearing cowboy boots and jeans, just as she remembered his always doing. He stood on the porch for a minute and looked down at her.

"Mirandy?" he asked.

She was too relieved to do anything but cry.

And he might not have wanted her, but he brought her inside, and within an hour she was in bed, and some woman named Rita with big hair and red fingernails had come in and seen to her. Rita had a baby, too, her daddy's baby, she supposed, and she remembered lying there listening to Rita's baby cry, her own breasts leaking milk.

"You're sick," Rita had said, bringing her a 7-Up and a bowl of Top Ramen. Daddy had driven her to the hospital emergency room, and the doctor said she had a breast infection and was dehydrated and gave her some medicine and an IV and some more medicine to dry up her milk, since the first dose hadn't worked so well. Then the doctor and Daddy and Rita and Rita's baby had gone into the other room, and Dorrie had gone to sleep. She supposed she had known then how it would end, so she hadn't been surprised when Daddy never showed up again.

"He had to go to work," Rita said, the baby on her shoulder. *"And you've got to go home."* Not unkindly, just stating a fact. Rita had put her back on the bus with her medicine and a sack lunch and ten dollars, and when she got back to Nashville, Mama was there to meet her.

She had said things to Dorrie all the way home. Dorrie had tried to hold her ears shut, but every word Mama said met with one inside her that agreed. She said that Dorrie was irresponsible and this just proved it. That she would have been a no-account mother, that she should stop being so hardheaded and accept the facts: *"That boy doesn't want you, and that baby is gone. Your daddy doesn't want you, and you ought to be grateful I'll still take you home. I'm so disappointed in you, but I knew it. I knew it from the beginning, because you're just like him."* Somewhere during the barrage of words, Dorrie let go. She just let go and realized how foolish she had been to even think things would turn out any other way.

She had felt something in her break loose then. It pulled loose like an unraveling knot that was keeping her moored, and she felt herself break away and drift. She felt herself float out into the middle of the ocean, so far she couldn't even see the land anymore.

"Listen up," Mama had said. "Here's what you're going to do just in case you're *considering* your *options.* You're going to get yourself on the bus and go to the school every day and get your high school diploma. And then you're going to get a good job. And you're going to forget about Danny Loomis, and you're going to forget about that baby. I won't have you throwing your life away. I came after you once, Dorrie. If you run off again, I won't be coming after you, and don't expect to come home."

She supposed that's when she had been pulled into Mama's orbit, for she had just caved in after that. Whatever spit and vinegar she'd had left after the ordeal of the baby had been drained right out of her when she'd seen Danny and his new girlfriend and then Papa and his new family. She had realized then that whether she wanted it or not, this was her lot in life and her place. Here with Mama. No. The preposition was wrong. *Under* Mama. Under her care and control, and she accepted the truth then, that she wasn't capable of making good decisions. She realized that whether she'd meant to or not, she'd brought someone into the world for the sole purpose of hurting his or her little soul, and she would not do that again. She, of all people, understood that mistakes had consequences and nerve endings, and they cried and hungered.

All she'd ever wanted was a family. Someone to love her that she could love back. She hadn't planned on getting pregnant, but neither had she avoided it. She had no plan, no ideas about the future. She didn't think God had made her for anything special. Having the baby was the most special thing she'd ever done.

She'd read one time that there were times when you could be shown a partial picture or told a series of words with some left out and you saw things as whole because your brain wanted to. Your brain filled in the blanks. She could see now that that's what she'd done in her life. About everything.

She remembered watching her newlywed cousin Claudia in her tiny apartment, putting away groceries in the tiny open shelves, making dinner on the tiny stove, washing dishes in a tiny sink. The apartment had been like a playhouse. Dorrie's imagination had filled in the details of love and peace and joy. That's what she'd always done, she could see now. Someone would give her a little piece of a story, and she would fill in the blanks. She'd been doing it with Daddy for years. He would show up and say, *"I love you,"* and she would fill in the blanks. She took a sketchy life, a little bit of love from Daddy and Mama and filled in the blanks. That's how she had believed Danny Loomis when he had said he loved her. She gave a rueful shake of her head now as she thought of what had finally happened to him. He'd gotten the cheerleader pregnant, and his parents had shipped him off to military school where there weren't any girls.

Hope had bobbed up once or twice in the ensuing years. She had gotten up every morning and done just what Mama had said, but every day of her life she had wondered who her baby was and where he or she was. She'd made up stories. Fantasies about the baby's home. About their future reunion. She got a job and started saving her money to go to the lawyer. She got up to five thousand ninety dollars before Mama found out. She had been furious.

"You're nothing," Mama had finally said. *"You don't have what it takes to raise a child. Who do you think you are? Look at you. You're trash."*

Now she thought that Mama had been talking to herself more than to Dorrie.

She had wanted to keep that baby, she thought now, with a strange lack of passion. Well, she had finally healed up from it. But even as she thought about that, she had the idea that rather than healing, something had been buried alive. And she thought of the nightmares she had every so often. Of hearing a baby crying, and the cry was coming from down there, under the earth. She supposed she would go to her own grave and never know what happened to that baby.

She'd picked up her life then, determined to make the best of it, but somehow she could never quite manage to stay at any one place long enough to do anything. Her feet started itching as soon as the dust settled.

She knew the adoptive parents had given Mama money for

her college education, but Mama had commandeered that early on, afraid Dorrie would use it to finance another escape. She had grudgingly let her use some of it for the community college and offered to dip in again to finance Françoise's when Dorrie quit her teaching degree, ever hopeful for a lifetime of free perms, but Dorrie hadn't wanted to go to school anymore. She had wanted to leave.

So she had. Again and again and again. She left. She came home. She left. She came home. She would start over and regroup, proving Mama was right about her after all. She didn't know why, she just didn't seem to be able to settle down. She knew she was constantly dreaming of things she would do some-day and the places she would go, but somehow, when the time came to take the steps to make her dreams come true, she would find she had run out of gas. Oh, she left for various places, sure enough, and started new adventures, but whenever reality began to tarnish the perfect image of her dreams, she would come drag-ging back home to the backside of Nashville to move back in with Mama, work at the Sip and Bite, and regroup.

The first time she'd returned home, she stayed with Mama for a week, then looked for her own apartment. Mama had said, *"Why pay rent somewhere when you can live here free?"* And for just a minute Dorrie thought she saw something flash in her eyes that looked like fear. So she had stayed. Until she left again.

She had made a serious attempt to find that baby one other time. When she'd turned eighteen, she had gone back to the attorney who had handled the adoption. His eyes were sad and old, and he told her he couldn't give her any identifying infor-mation on the child or the adoptive parents. Her only hope was to sign on to a registry, and if the child inquired after turning eighteen, they would give out Dorrie's contact information.

She had gone back to the hospital where her baby was born, but all of the nurses looked young and new. She had asked about the one who had helped her, but all she could remember was the woman's first name. No one knew her. They had sent her to personnel, but personnel had said they couldn't release any information about employees. She had gone back to find Dr. Herbert, who had delivered the baby, but met another stone wall. Dr. Herbert said it would be against her ethics to disclose information about the adoption. She had recommended calling a registry, which Dorrie had done, but there wasn't much chance of a reunion coming from that avenue for a long, long time. The child was gone, and she had finally accepted it.

The living room clock struck two, and Dorrie came back to the here and now. She did a few chores, then went into the kitchen and started supper, but Mama came down, lugging her portable oxygen and obviously sick, decided Dorrie wasn't seasoning the pork chops right, and took things over. Dorrie finished setting the table and then went out onto the porch. It was cold for Nashville in February.

A plane came in on the approach to the airport and created a racket for a minute or two. This had been a nice neighborhood once, and it still was, in Dorrie's mind. The yards were neat and tidy and the flower beds weeded and kept, but Mama didn't like the skin tone of the neighbors who had moved in around them. Mama would have moved if she'd had the money, but she didn't, so she just kept to herself and considered herself better than her neighbors.

"Good afternoon, Miranda." Mr. Cooper emerged from his house, and he nodded in his courtly way. He was tall, dark, and lean, but his face had worn and his hair faded in the years she had known him. He refused to call her Dorrie. *"Miranda was your name when your daddy brought you over and introduced us when you were three days old, and Miranda you'll stay,"* he'd said. She liked Mr. Cooper. Sometimes she went over and sat and visited with him, and he fixed her a cup of coffee or a glass of sweet tea. She usually went when Mama was at work or, lately, when Mama was resting. His wife had died a few years back, and the occasion of her death was one of the few times she had openly defied her mother.

"You're not going to that colored church," Mama had said.

She hadn't answered but had marched right out the door and to the funeral and even back to Mr. Cooper's house afterward for the wake. Mama had pouted for a week, and to tell the truth, Dorrie had been surprised at how few consequences Mama really had to wield on her. She supposed she obeyed now more out of habit than anything else. That, and a lack of any better ideas.

"Hello there, sir," she answered back to Mr. Cooper now. "Are you staying warm?"

"Oh yes, ma'am," he assured her. "How is your mother these days?" Always generous and polite in spite of Mama's meanness.

"About like you'd expect," she said simply.

He nodded, face grave. He was probably remembering his wife's suffering. "I'm off to prayer meeting, where I'll remember her. Come on and go with me."

Dorrie smiled. She could imagine what prayer meeting at Mr. Cooper's church was like. It was the Holiness Revival Pentecostal something or other, and even the funeral she'd attended there had been more lively than her usual Sunday experience with the Methodists. The preacher at the Methodist church Mama belonged to was a burdened man who spent hours describing historical detail and translations and Greek tenses. His idea of application was a list of instructions delivered with the resigned air of someone who knew his flock would be defeated even before setting out. It was a sorry affair, and as soon as she'd turned eighteen, she had stopped going.

"I guess I'll stay on here," she said with a smile.

"Well." He tipped his hat and got into his car, an old Chevy Impala that he washed as religiously as he read his Bible. His wife's ancient Cadillac was still lovingly parked beside it.

She held up a hand as he drove away; then she huddled on the porch and watched the cars stream by until Mama called her in to supper.

It was a quiet meal. Mama seemed to have lost a little more of her starch. Dorrie guessed it was taking all her grit just to take the next breath. She ate the pork chops, seasoned very well indeed, the rice, sticky the way Mama liked and made it, the green salad, and the butterbeans and politely declined banana pudding, earning a frown from Mama. But her mother would be equally critical if she gained weight.

"What are you saving your appetite for? Got something better coming up?"

Mama was always hoping she would have a date. She shook her head, and Mama didn't disappoint.

"You need to find yourself a man, Dorrie, and settle down," she said, and oddly, instead of the usual aggravation she felt, Dorrie was touched. Suddenly she didn't see Mama's interfering as pushiness but as one more way of ordering things before her departure. Proof that Mama must care for her in her own strange way.

"I know," she said.

"You know I'm dying." Mama lifted her face up to Dorrie, and all Dorrie's glib reassurances died on her lips.

She nodded. "I know."

"If I knew you were taken care of, I could go to my grave in peace."

Dorrie wished she could finally do something to please her mother. She had meandered around her life long enough. Wasn't it about time she put down some roots and bore some fruit? She thought of children then, of warm, sticky babies and chubby toddlers and gangly boys and long-legged girls with missing teeth and freckles. They could be hers. She would do it. Why shouldn't she have a life? Why shouldn't she? She wasn't trash, and the fact that Mama wanted this for her proved it.

The only sound was Mama's labored breathing, and she was somewhat surprised that her thoughts were not making shuttered little clicks the way a camera or a slide projector will do, for she was seeing her future flash before her, and it was not an altogether bad thing. Oh, it was not the grand adventure she had thought her life would be, nor the endless romance, but whose life turned out like that, after all? It wasn't a perfect world. This was reality, as she had been so often reminded. This was lesson one in the school of hard knocks. Take what you can get and be happy to get it. After all, it's probably more than you deserve.

She got up and began clearing off the table. She scraped the dishes, then put the food away while Mama washed. Mama stood there at the sink and washed every one of those dishes, even though Dorrie knew she must be tired. Dorrie tried to take over the job, but nobody but Mama could wash the dishes well enough. Dorrie could hear her breathing, a slight wheeze as her hands moved efficiently, rubbing the rag across every visible surface of every dish, bowl, and glass.

"I need some time alone tonight, Dora Mae," her mother finally said.

Dorrie looked at her in surprise. "I can stay in my room," she said.

"No. I mean really alone."

"Okay. I'll call Aunt Bobbie and see if I can stay with her." She had a horrible thought. "But why?" she asked, a tone of suspicion creeping into her voice.

Her mother's mouth tightened in anger. "Since when do I need to explain myself to you?" She pulled herself up and glared at her daughter. "Don't worry," she said, looking annoyed. "I'm not going to take all my pills and be dead on the sofa when you get home. I *despise* a coward."

What would life be like without her? Dorrie wondered as she went to call Aunt Bobbie. She felt a little surge but would not, absolutely would not, call it hope. She shoved the feeling away quickly, guiltily, feeling as if she had somehow hastened her mother's demise by thinking these traitorous thoughts.

chapter 10

Noreen worked through that night with an energy some might say was unnatural. She supposed it *was* flying in the face of nature for a woman with stage four lung cancer to be tearing things up and washing things down, but it gave her a grim satisfaction and eased her anxiety to do so. She had never been one to think much about the past, but lately she'd been feeling like something big was bearing down on her, something that wanted to grab her and make her admit to things. She felt fear, almost panic when she thought of looking it in the eye. Once you started admitting to things, there would be no end to it, would there? That's how things came unraveled. That's how people lost control.

She shook her head as she squirted Windex on the pane of glass in the front door and rubbed it until it squeaked. She had never been one to go weepy and regretful, and she wasn't about to start now, she vowed with grim fierceness. And all this cleaning and sorting and throwing things out was making her feel better, so she went to it with a vengeance.

Halfway through scouring the bathroom walls she had a strange thought, and it slowed her down for a minute. She was put in mind of those criminals they always showed on *Forensic Files* or *CSI* wiping down the scene of the crime. She thought about that as she scrubbed out the inside of the medicine cabinet and threw away old prescriptions and half-used tubes of ointment. She tore into the shower grout with Clorox and a stiff-bristled brush and felt like some murderer scrubbing away fingerprints so that no trace—none whatsoever—would be left behind.

But there were no police after her. She had been scrupulous all her life about obeying the law, she thought with pride. No, the thing that spurred her on was not some detective seeking out bloodstains or hidden bodies but the thought of her daughter, dark head bent in concentration, scrutinizing her life after she was gone and passing judgment on it. She tightened her lips with a simmering anger and set to work again. She would not have it. She had never allowed criticism in life, and she would not abide it in death, either.

She finished with the bathroom, then went through her old bank statements and canceled checks—still saved from the days when they sent them to you every month. They went into the pile for the burning bin. She sorted through her clothes and dispatched most of them to the porch for the Salvation Army pickup tomorrow. She set aside her nicest cream-colored suit and pinned a note to the lapel saying that she should be buried in it. She put her pearl earrings and necklace in a Ziploc bag and pinned it underneath the note, found a Wal-Mart bag and put in it a new package of panty hose, her new bra and slip and panties and her beige pumps, but only after checking to see that there were no scuffs or nicks in the leather. She left her purse on the floor beside it. Were people buried with purses? She wasn't sure, but she'd never gone anywhere without her pocketbook. She went through her dresser drawers and threw out all the old slips and nylons, all the old panties with their pulled elastic.

She sorted through each room of her small house in that fashion. The kitchen, the dining room, the living room. She sorted through the bookshelf. She set aside the three or four romance books that had been her favorites and got rid of the rest. *I didn't know Mama was interested in history,* she could imagine Dorrie saying to some neighbor or friend of hers as her Civil War histories and World War II books went out to the Salvation Army pile. As if she was ignorant just because she'd never finished school. *Look at this half-finished dress,* she imagined Dorrie saying as she sorted through her sewing closet. She gathered up the pieces of material with the patterns still pinned on and packed them in boxes for the pickup, along with the rest of the patterns and yards of fabric she had never managed to make anything from.

She sorted through her towels and linens. Got rid of all the recipes and cookbooks. Dorrie had never bothered to learn to cook. There was no reason to think she ever would. She halted briefly when she came to the photographs in the den but finally saved the ones of Dorrie when she was a baby and the one she had of her mother. She got rid of everything else—the few from her girlhood. She'd long ago thrown out her wedding photos and the pictures of herself and Tommy.

She had already cleaned out the basement and the storage closets. She had thrown out bushels of old paper work, everything but her insurance policy, the deed to the house, and the title to the car. Now she made an envelope for Dorrie and put her birth certificate and old school report cards inside it. All her assets were in the First National Bank, and when she was gone Dorrie would get it all. Not that she would appreciate it. She had never appreciated any of the sacrifices Noreen had made for her or realized all the pain she had caused. Why should she start now? Noreen threw away her marriage license and the divorce decree. Heaven only knew why she had saved them in the first place.

She found Dorrie's violin and sheet music and felt her mouth hardening in anger. She couldn't look at a fiddle without thinking of Tommy. He played the fiddle like he'd been born with one in his hands. He could make it sing and cry, and she had loved that about him, she realized with a burst of pain she had thought she was incapable of feeling. It was he who had taught his daughter to play. He'd enrolled her in lessons from the time she was big enough to stand and had carried her clear across town to some woman who taught children too young to read. He'd had to put in eight hours of overtime every month down at the garage to pay for them, but he'd bragged on her and set her out in front of whoever came over.

"Play your violin, baby," he would say over Noreen's objections that he was spoiling her and swelling her head.

But even Noreen had to admit Dorrie had been talented. She probably could have played concerts or in some orchestra, but when Tommy left, the lessons had stopped. Noreen was certainly not going to pay for them. She had all she could do to keep bread on the table. Not one penny did she see from Tommy. Not one dime, she told herself, feeling a little better. Dorrie had cried and taken on at first, but finally she'd stopped. The violin had sat here with the old sheet music and the pictures of the recitals. Noreen felt a little twinge of something but quickly smothered it with a load of blame. It was his fault for leaving. She had done the best she could. She hesitated for a minute but finally left the violin and music alone, although her fingers were itching to add them to the burning barrel.

When she finished sorting through everything, she unhooked her oxygen line, left the tank inside, and hauled out the last sack of papers and photos to the burning barrel. The sky was just beginning to lighten, giving her familiar backyard a gray overcast look. Even here things were in order. Last week she had paid the neighbor boy far more than he deserved to mow a dead lawn, pull the weeds out of the flower beds, and haul away the contents of the garage. Nothing was left in it but her garden spades and snow tires. She squirted the lighter fluid onto the mass of papers in the bin in a forceful stream, carefully set down the can, then threw in the match. Yellow flames shot up, along with a mournful tongue of black smoke that gradually dissipated into a cloud of ash. It snowed down upon her head, irritated her eyes, and stuck in her throat. She stood there for nearly half an hour feeding the flames.

By the time the gray morning had fully arrived, the house was sanitized and spotless, and she, though shaking with pain and fatigue and some muddy sour stew of emotions, took herself a bath with Calgon, washed her hair, and put on the new powder blue peignoir set she had ordered from the Sears catalog. She unplugged the oxygen one more time and, glancing at the *Danger, Flammable* sign pasted on the side, wheeled the tank out onto the porch, then came back inside, sat down on the couch, and reached under the cushion for her pack of Kool Menthols. She lit one and sucked at it hungrily as she thought about the one thing left. It was eating at her like Drano in a pipe. She looked over toward the desk and thought about the contents of the right bottom drawer as she smoked one cigarette after another, gasping as she worked her way through the hoarded pack. By the time the morning news was over and she'd taken the last drag of the last cigarette, she'd made up her mind.

She would leave it for her to find. She smiled a grim smile as she carried the full ashtray into the bathroom and flushed the contents down the toilet, then rinsed it out and dried it with a tissue. If Dorrie was so all fired determined to find something to blame her for, well, then, she would leave her something to find. Besides. She remembered on *Forensic Files* and *CSI* how the technicians went over the crime scenes with a fine-toothed comb. They always found some leavings. No matter how hard someone tried to cover his tracks and leave no trace. They sprayed their magic sprays, and suddenly there appeared a bloodstain. They used their special powder, and out popped a fingerprint. Well, so be it.

Noreen was breathing hard and wheezing as she brushed her teeth. She checked to see that her hair was combed and sprayed in place, put on a little lipstick, then retrieved her oxygen from the front porch. She finally collapsed on the sofa, covered up with her favorite afghan, and put the oxygen tube in her nose. She just sniffed when Dorrie came in and said good morning. Dorrie reappeared later and said she was going for a walk, but Noreen didn't answer.

She turned on the television and focused her attention there like a laser.

"I did the best I could," she said out loud, fiercely, as if someone had accused her of something. She *had* done the best she could, she told herself again, and she could almost see a door shutting firmly somewhere inside her, could almost hear a lock click tight. She had done the best she could, she repeated as she laid her head down and closed her eyes, the characters of the Lifetime channel's original movie droning on in the background. That was all that could be expected of a person in the end.

chapter 11

It was several days later when Dorrie found her mother lying still and cold in her bed. She went to Mr. Cooper's back door. He was drinking coffee at his kitchen table, reading his Bible, for it was not yet seven o'clock.

He opened the door and saw her standing there. "She's gone," he said, knowing without being told.

She nodded yes, unable to speak, and he took her hand like a little child and walked with her across the frosty lawn. They went together to Mama's room, and it was Mr. Cooper who took Mama's pulse, gently resting his dark fingers on Mama's neck, pressing gently and feeling nothing, then finally patting Mama's cool hand and leading Dorrie back to his small, warm kitchen, for she was very, very cold. She sat there and looked at the yellow and white flowers on the wallpaper while he brewed her a cup of coffee and made her scrambled eggs and toast. He prayed for her as he set the plate of steaming eggs before her. He rested his hand on her shoulder and said, "Lord Jesus, cover this child with your mercy and love and help her find her way home," which was a funny thing to say, since she was within spitting distance of the only home she had ever really known. But she had felt a strength flow into her after that, and whether it was the eggs and coffee or the love or something supernatural, she did not know. She didn't know what she believed about God and prayer, although you couldn't grow up next door to Mr. Cooper and not know about the Lord's plan of salvation. Besides, Mama had made her pray the prayer when she was five. But Mama had said over and over that Daddy was a sinner bound for hell, and if Mama was an example of a saint, then Dorrie was confused. But Dorrie believed in Mr. Cooper, and if Mr. Cooper's God was willing to help her, well, then, she would take it and say thank you. After she ate, Mr. Cooper walked back with her and helped her look through Mama's instructions, and they called the funeral home and Aunt Bobbie.

He stayed with her as the drivers came and took away Mama's earthly remains. Aunt Bobbie came over about noon, as soon as she could get away from work, and it was only then that he left her. Aunt Bobbie helped her look through Mama's things, and there were the suit and shoes and even the purse set out neatly, and Dorrie felt she ought to cry, but she didn't. Her tears seemed to have frozen up inside her. Aunt Bobbie didn't cry, either, but her face looked tired and careworn.

Mr. Cooper helped her arrange for the funeral, as Aunt Bobbie had to go back to work. She was a charge nurse at the nursing home and couldn't get time off except for the service. Dorrie found the folder Mama had put on top of the mantel, and inside was her will. It left everything to Dorrie. Dorrie wondered if Aunt Bobbie would be hurt. She didn't know how much of Mama's money would remain after all the bills were paid, but whatever there was, she would give some to Aunt Bobbie.

The funeral was on Thursday, and Dorrie wondered who, if anyone, would even take notice of Mama's death, much less attend the funeral. Mama hadn't darkened the door of the Methodist church for nearly twenty years, and she had few friends. But Mr. Cooper must have put the word out, because beginning Wednesday afternoon the covered dishes started arriving. One after another the people made their way to Dorrie's front porch, carrying casserole dishes full of potato salad and baked beans, hot pepper cabbage and deviled eggs, barbequed beef and fried chicken and salmon croquettes, pimiento cheese sandwiches and banana pudding, okra and tomatoes, and sweet-potato pie. They patted her cheeks with their dark hands and gave her pillowy hugs and prayed with her before they left, and she could feel the energy from those prayers bathing her and filling her.

They had the funeral at the Methodist church, for Mama would probably come back to life, dust off her suit, and walk dead across town if she were laid to rest in a colored church, as she would have called it. But as Dorrie had predicted, there were few white faces in attendance. Mr. Cooper and his friends came, and again they gathered around Dorrie and Aunt Bobbie and her children, covering them like a warm blanket on a cold day. Those good people moved through the hallowed halls of Asbury United Methodist as if they had built it, pouring the coffee and tea and rearranging the covered dishes, which they themselves had brought, sweeping and washing and drying afterward, turning out the lights, and delivering her back home with enough leftovers in plastic containers to feed her for a year.

"You're sure you'll be all right?" Mr. Cooper asked when the day was finally over, concern on his face.

"I'm sure," she said, nodding. She was so tired she could weep, but still she did not.

And so he had finally left her.

Feeling slightly dazed, she stood alone for the first time in her mother's house. She could see clearly now that that was what it was. Even though she had lived here all her life, now that her mother's force and personality was removed from it, there was little that was familiar or drew her.

She went to her room, looked at her pale face in the mirror. Her dark hair was drawn back, and her eyes had faint blue shadows beneath them. She changed into her nightgown and brushed her teeth and washed her face, looking at it again.

"*You're looking ragged,*" Mama had said to her that last night. "*You need a haircut. You ought to take better care of yourself, Dorrie.*" She felt something like a sword thrust when she realized those were her mother's last words to her. Her legacy. She thought briefly of all those childhood Bible classes, of the brother Esau who had never received the blessing.

She lay down on her bed, but she could not sleep. Finally she decided to write. She got out of bed and took down her journal. She found a blank page and lifted her pen. She hesitated, trying hard to think of something nice to write. You had to write nicely about the dead, didn't you? It wouldn't do to expose the flaws and viciousness of those who couldn't defend themselves. She searched her mind and finally came up with Christmas mornings.

> *Mama died today. I can hardly believe it.*
>
> *I am trying to think of something nice. Something good. I remember Christmas and that she always took down the Christmas tree on Christmas morning as soon as I finished opening my gifts. She seemed so happy bustling around that I forgot my disappointment at seeing all the pretty glitter and ornaments going away. I always got a book, a three-pack of underpants, a new pair of pajamas, and something she considered frivolous. One year it was a clock radio. I was nearly delirious with joy. Anyway, as soon as the gifts were opened, the paper went into the garbage sack, the vacuum and storage bins came out, and the tree came down while the turkey cooked. And ten minutes after Christmas dinner was consumed, the turkey carcass was simmering in the soup pot.*
>
> *She was an orderly person, my mother. She couldn't stand clutter, and she couldn't stand confusion. Life made sense when things happened the same way every time. She did the laundry on Monday, and if for some reason she couldn't, she did it Sunday night. Bathrooms Tuesday, floors on Wednesday, ironing on Thursday, shopping on*

Friday, baking on Saturday.

She was a beautiful woman. Tiny and shapely, she would have had a sort of grace about her if she hadn't moved so quickly. I'm not sure what color her hair was, since she had dyed it red as long as I can remember. She had warm skin with a slight golden cast, even in winter. Her eyes were startling blue, her face especially lovely with high cheekbones and a wide, pretty curved mouth when she smiled, but most often she wore a look of harried concentration, as if something, somewhere, wasn't quite right.

I am told I look something like her. I have the same cheekbones and mouth, but I have my father's coal dark hair and I'm told I have his disposition. At least that's what Mama said. She is gone now. It's hard to believe.

She sighed. She should look through Mama's things. Everything would be neat and orderly. Her mother had been preparing for this day all her life, living in perpetual fear that strangers going through her life would find it in disarray. Well. Only her daughter would be going through it, but she supposed she was a stranger, nonetheless. She should sort through the bills and pay for the funeral and figure out how much she would owe the doctor and the hospital for the final tests, but right now she was too tired. She should make an appointment and talk to a lawyer about settling the estate. And she supposed she ought to find Daddy and let him know.

Her room, usually small and stifling, suddenly seemed too big and empty. She went downstairs and wandered aimlessly through the house for a few minutes before she finally lay down on the sofa, turned on the television, pulled her mother's afghan around her shoulders, and fell into a restless sleep.

chapter 12

The nightmare came back. Dorrie was in a dark house, and a baby was crying. She knew it was important to get to the baby, and she felt a blind panic. Blind because she couldn't see. She wandered through the dark halls, feeling along the walls, stepping carefully in the dark, stumbling here and there against a piece of furniture. Sometimes the sound would get louder, and sometimes it would be so soft she could barely hear it. She would turn then and start going in the opposite direction, as if she were playing some cruel, tormented game of hot and cold. She never found the baby, of course. She woke up this time as she usually did, heart pounding, hands shaking. The television was still on. Some loud man was selling knives. She flicked it off, and the house was dark except for the blue glow from the screen, but after a minute that dissipated, too.

She got up and went back to her room, thinking how she could never get lost in this house because she knew every inch of it. And there was no baby here. She went into her room and turned back the covers and got into her bed. She tossed and turned for hours and finally dozed off when the sun was bright behind the shades. When she woke again, it was nearly eleven o'clock and dark. She felt a start of guilt and wondered why Mama hadn't come in here and goaded her out of bed with a sharp comment. Then she remembered. Mama wasn't going to ever say anything sharp to her again. Anything at all.

She felt a nudge of hunger, went downstairs, and opened the refrigerator. She ate some leftovers from the funeral, but after the first bite or two she was full. She thought about showering and getting dressed, but it seemed like too much effort. She went back to the couch and watched three movies in a row, then dozed off as the sun was coming up. When she woke the next time, it was four in the afternoon.

She got up and showered. She got dressed. She sat down at the kitchen table, and everywhere she looked, there was Mama. Mama in the orange placemats, and Dorrie could see Mama's hands as if they were there in front of her wiping them off, her pretty hands, small and quick. There was Mama at the sink, washing dishes with thorough efficiency. Everything was done with Mama's favorite colors and styles, and even though Mama had stripped the house clean of anything personal, she was still there in every stick of furniture and decoration.

Mr. Cooper came over and invited her to supper. She would have gone, but the truth was, she felt a little queasy. He gave her a worried look and said he'd be expecting her in a half hour. She agreed, though she really didn't feel like visiting. She took a Rolaids and lay down on the couch again.

She didn't know what was wrong with her. She felt witless and dull, as though she didn't have any connection at all anymore. She felt free-floating like one of those astronauts who drift off into space.

She could go back to work, but the thought made her feel so tired, she could barely move. She could take a trip, but she didn't have the energy. She realized with a jolt of ironic humor that she had finally gotten what she wanted. All her life, she had done one thing or another to get away from Mama or to spite Mama or to evade Mama. But the joke was on her, wasn't it? For one way or another, she had managed to organize her entire existence around one person. Defying her, running away from her, or coming back to take her place under that well-worn thumb until circumstances became unbearable and she ran away again. But no matter what, Mama had been the sun around which her universe had revolved. And now she was gone.

⊙

After a month they staged their little intervention. Dorrie was torn between amusement, irritation, and flat indifference when they showed up on her doorstep: Mr. Cooper with his Bible under his arm, kind concern on his face; Aunt Bobbie, looking weary and worn, still in her nurse's uniform; and Myra Jean from the Hasty Taste, peppy and smart with a new pink Capri pant outfit, freshly frosted hair, and a pan of cinnamon rolls balanced on one hip. Myra Jean firmly believed that all of life's difficulties could be eased with liberal helpings of the appropriate carbo-hydrates.

"May we come in?" Mr. Cooper asked with his customary courtliness.

"Of course," she said, stepping aside. "Make yourselves at home."

They came in. They made themselves at home. Myra Jean disappeared, and a few minutes later Dorrie smelled coffee.

Aunt Bobbie looked around, and Dorrie felt embarrassed following her gaze. She supposed she had let the place go. There were newspapers piled in the corner and dirty soup bowls and teacups here and there on the furniture. The table was covered with mail. Her pillow and blanket were rumpled on the couch, for that's where she'd been sleeping. The carpet needed to be vacuumed. She glanced down at herself, and the picture wasn't greatly improved. She had worn the same pair of sweatpants and T-shirt nearly every day for a week. Her hair needed to be washed.

Mr. Cooper moved a newspaper and sat down on the recliner. Aunt Bobbie found a spot on the couch. Dorrie picked up the blanket and pillow and tossed them in the corner and sat down. She turned off the television with the remote. Myra Jean came back in and flicked her gaze across the room, raising an eyebrow when it came to rest on Dorrie. "That whirring noise you hear is your mama," she said, "spinnin' in her grave."

Dorrie smiled. Mr. Cooper chuckled. Even Aunt Bobbie grinned. Myra Jean looked pleased with herself, returned to the kitchen, then came back with a tray of coffee cups, sugar, and nondairy coffee creamer, no doubt all she could find, since Dorrie hadn't bought milk in a month. The cinnamon rolls smelled wonderful, and when Myra Jean handed her the plate, Dorrie took it gratefully. She took a bite, surprised she could still enjoy the pleasure of the spicy sweetness and warm bread. The coffee was hot and good. As she ate, she discovered she was hungry. She sipped the coffee slowly and realized she hadn't been out of the house in weeks. She had just pulled the shades, pulled the blanket over her head, and lain on the couch.

"You look terrible," Myra Jean said, scraping the last little bit of icing from her saucer with her fork.

"I haven't been sleeping so good," Dorrie admitted. The dream was a constant companion, tormenting her every time she closed her eyes. She breathed out a deep sigh and set down her plate.

"Look here," Aunt Bobbie said, "this won't do."

Dorrie smiled. With Mama alive, Bobbie had been relegated to "yes, ma'am" like the rest of them. This was the most spunk she'd ever seen out of her aunt.

"Grief can swallow you up," Mr. Cooper said kindly. "I know. I've been there."

Dorrie felt a thrust of guilt. Was it grief she was feeling or just . . . what? Disorganization? "I can't seem to find my way," she said.

"Do you need some help?" Myra Jean asked. "'Cause I can *make* you a list of things to do."

Dorrie grinned again and Mr. Cooper, catching her eye, smiled back. "How can we help?" he asked.

Dorrie shrugged and shook her head, ashamed that she was still dry-eyed. She had not cried for her mother once.

"Well, I did something," Aunt Bobbie said. "I scheduled you two appointments." She reached into her purse and brought out two business cards and handed one to Dorrie. "This one's with your mama's lawyer. He's been calling me about getting you to schedule a time for him to dispose of your mama's estate. He's got the paper work all done, and he wants you to come and sign some things. The second one is with a counselor I know. She comes in and works with the old folks sometimes, but she's real nice and good to talk to no matter what your age. Her name's Sandra Lockwood. Here's her card." She handed her the other. "You're seeing the lawyer at two tomorrow and her on Wednesday at ten."

Dorrie took the cards, and to tell the truth she felt a little relieved. It had been so long since she had made a decision that wasn't in reaction to her mother that she'd forgotten how.

"And I've got an appointment scheduled for you, too," Myra Jean said, getting up and gathering up the plates and cups. "With Luann down at the Bob In. Your hair's looking terrible."

So that was how it happened that she got back on her feet again, so to speak. She went to see Mr. Ness, the attorney, and signed the things he had prepared. Although her mother's estate was modest, it would still take several months for things to be settled. She would have money but would have to wait for probate. She was surprised to find that the education account the adoptive parents had set up for her still had a substantial balance, but since it was in Mama's name, it, too, would have to go through probate. Mama had made some deposits, she realized, and she felt stirred up at the thought. A little angry, if the truth were told, for it was so like Mama to hide any reason for Dorrie to love and connect with her. Instead of enriched, she felt robbed.

She went to see Sandra Lockwood and talked to her twice a week for an hour for a month or so.

"You haven't formed many permanent attachments," she said. "Because deep down I don't think you believe you have what it takes to be worthy of deep, real love. You can't stop yourself from reaching for it, though, so what you do is break it at some point by finding fault with the circumstances or people in your life and telling yourself to move on."

"Uh-huh," Dorrie said, nodding and wondering if she had made a mistake to come. But the counselor did help her make a few decisions. For one, she decided to sell the house. Even though she had always thought of it as home, she realized now she had no desire to stay in Nashville. She would miss Mr. Cooper, but this was not her home. The second decision was even more momentous.

"Tell me about your name," Sandra asked her another time, so Dorrie told her the story of how Mama had changed it from what it had been to what it was now.

"Did you like that?" she asked.

"No. But I didn't have any choice in the matter."

"There were a lot of things you didn't have a choice in," Sandra observed quietly. "But that was then. This is now. It's a new day, Dorrie."

It was a new day. She repeated it to herself until she actually began to believe it. She went back to the lawyer and filled out the paper work to get her name back and got a court date.

She cleaned out the house and rented a storage unit for her few belongings. Aunt Bobbie would arrange for the house to be listed with a Realtor when the will was probated, and after the sale, Dorrie would give her aunt a generous share of the proceeds. Aunt Bobbie also agreed to have a garage sale for Mama's furniture. Dorrie didn't want any of it. Aunt Bobbie said there were a few things she would like. Dorrie told her to come and get them and began sorting through the little that remained of her mother's life.

Mama had already gotten rid of almost everything that was in any way personal. Odd, but totally in keeping with what she would have expected. Dorrie took down Mama's housecoat and carefully folded it, setting it down in the bottom of the Goodwill sack. She folded the few dresses that were left, two pantsuits, the jeans and jacket. She took the nightgown and peignoir set Mama had been so attached to and gently placed them on the pile. She went through the dresser, the hall closet, the bathroom medicine chest, the rest of the house, and she was amazed at how little there was that her mother had left behind.

Dorrie's old violin was on the bottom shelf of the guest room closet, and she was surprised Mama had never gotten rid of it. How odd. She picked it up and stroked the wood and even lifted it to her chin and played a scale. She had a little talent. She wondered again if she might have accomplished anything with it given the chance. She set it back down in the crushed velvet case and carefully set the bow inside the clips. She shut the case and after a moment added it to the pile for the storage unit instead of the Goodwill. *Who knows?* she thought. It was a new day. Anything was possible. Perhaps she would play it again someday.

She didn't go to the Bob In, in spite of Myra Jean's kind arrangements. She actually went to the Mall at Green Hills, an upscale sort of place that Mama studiously avoided. She took a look at herself in the plate-glass window as she walked in, and she had to agree with Myra Jean. She was a pathetic sight. She wore jeans today, and they were baggy, as she hadn't been eating much. She had on one of Mama's cotton blouses, which was also too big. She wore no makeup, and the bones on her face seemed too prominent. She had dark circles under her eyes, and her hair was a mess, hanging down over her face like a dark veil. She went over again what the counselor had said.

"It's not a sin to spend a little money on yourself. You don't have to take your pleasures and run away and hide with them. No one is going to take them away from you. God gives good gifts. Why don't you give yourself permission to enjoy them in His presence?"

The counselor talked about God quite a bit. Dorrie didn't mind. She actually liked it, although she still wasn't sure what she thought about it. She became thoughtful when she recalled the image that had come to mind when the counselor had delivered that particular nugget of wisdom. She had remembered a dog they had when Daddy lived with them—a mutt. That dog had the strangest habit of taking her food off behind the house where she would eat it with furtive glances and protective growls. Dorrie had been puzzled, but Daddy had explained. *"That dog was probably the runt of the litter,"* he said. *"She took her food off so no one would take it from her. Now that she's all by herself she still does it. Kind of sad, isn't it?"* he had commented, and Dorrie had agreed. Now she understood exactly how that dog had felt. She sighed and pulled open the heavy doors and stepped into the chilled mall.

She had her hair cut first. At a salon and spa, not at a beauty shop. "Scissors" was bare and clean with sparse lines and cool colors, metal and glass and the smell of almonds and cherries. They washed and kneaded her scalp and dried her hair with thick cotton towels. The stylist, a man named Jerome, snipped and clipped and razored with expert hands. He applied some hair color with a paintbrush, and when he blew her hair dry, it fell in sleek, plump curves around her face, burnished lights shimmering in the dark brown depths of her hair.

He handed her over to Candy, who oohed and aahed over her skin and bones. A funny thing, Dorrie decided, to praise someone for looking gaunt. She applied moisturizer and makeup and painted shadows above her eyes and covered up the ones beneath and made her lips a pouting pink.

Dorrie was hungry after all that prodding and pummeling, but she still had beauty to achieve. She went to Lord and Taylor and bought a pretty pink dress that swirled when she twirled and sandals to match. She bought two pairs of pants and loose, flowing peasant blouses in bright colors with a lace camisole and a wide circle skirt in pink and orange and flip-flops with jewels. She bought new undies and bras and a pearl necklace like the one her daddy had given her for Christmas when she was ten, lost by the time she was eleven, but she secretly suspected Mama had thrown it out. She had her nails and toenails done, bare pink with a tiny rim of white at the edge. She bought a tiny silver ring for her toe.

She was hungry. Interesting. She hadn't been hungry in weeks. She found the food court and bought a Happy Meal at McDonald's and sat by the carpeted play area and ate. She gave the toy to a little girl with sad eyes who did not thank her but grabbed it and ran away, and Dorrie thought again of that dog.

She put her bags in the trunk and then wandered to the toy store after that, killing time until three o'clock. It wasn't exactly a toy store. It was part nature, part discovery and book and education things and imagination, and she wandered the aisles, dreaming and pretending she was ten again.

She bought a box of sixty-four crayons, jacks and a rubber ball, a coloring book of pioneer children, a bag of seashells, their curved and pink insides hidden behind the protective walls of shell. She bought a bag full of pretty rocks, polished to a sheen, pink quartz crystal, black shiny malachite, green jade, fool's gold. She bought a china tea set with tiny blue flowers, and some books: *The Secret Garden, A Little Princess, Anne of Green Gables*. She bought a set of oil paints, a sketchbook, the first four volumes of *Nancy Drew*. She went back to the play area with the sacks of childhood, but the sad-eyed girl was gone. It was just as well. Somebody probably would have arrested her if she'd followed through on her impulse of making it Christmas in April. Besides, she had a feeling she had really bought them for herself. She kept her feelings of foolishness and guilt at her self-indulgence at bay by remembering that Mama was gone. There would be no one to look at her with incredulity and ask her if she'd lost her mind.

She stopped in the art supply store and bought a good set of watercolor pencils and a fine Rapidograph pen for her drawings. Mama would definitely not have approved of the amount of money she spent.

At three o'clock she got back in the car, drove through the busy streets, and parked outside the courthouse. Nashville was bustling with people who had important things to do, but she told herself her business, though humble, was important to her. She walked into the building and waited in a seat that felt like a church pew until her name was called.

chapter 13

"N ext matter before the court?"

"Item number 34017. Name change. Petitioner Dora Mae Gibson."

Dorrie stood up and wiped her hands nervously on her skirt. Why did she feel afraid? It wasn't as if she'd done anything wrong, but being here in the courthouse with its high vaulted ceilings and heavy dark woodwork made her feel small and unimportant. And she supposed Mama had something to do with it. The power of her mother's personality seemed to reach out and shame her, even from the grave.

Dorrie had paid the $120 filing fee and carefully filled out the forms. The judge looked down at them now. She was a thin woman with a pointed nose and pinkish white hair teased into a careful bubble, but her hair was so thin Dorrie could see the light shining through it. She looked down at Dorrie with a disapproving expression on her face, and Dorrie wondered if she and Mama were related.

"You're Dora Mae Gibson?" she asked suspiciously.

"Yes, ma'am, I am, Your Honor." Dorrie cleared her throat. It felt dry.

The judge frowned again, looked down at the papers, then back at Dorrie. "Dora Mae Gibson seems like a perfectly service-able name. What's wrong with it?"

Dorrie stared blankly. She hadn't expected to be challenged, and for a minute she teetered, leaning toward agreeing with the accusation. The part of her that was used to caving in to Mama wanted to say, *You're right, forget it,* and run from the piercing eyes. But suddenly a little spurt of starch straightened her backbone and raised her voice. "It's a *fine* name," she said, her voice growing stronger as she spoke. "And there's nothing whatever wrong with it. It just isn't *my* name." She felt a little better having gotten that out, but as usual, by the time the words landed back on her ear-drums, she regretted letting them escape. If the past was any pre-dictor of the future, there would be a payment required.

"I beg your pardon?"

Here it came. The judge frowned, and Dorrie almost expected to hear her mother's voice slice out and put her down where she belonged. She had a sudden vision of herself picking up litter by the side of the road.

"What I mean, Your Honor, is that Dora Mae Gibson isn't the name I was given at birth. The one on the form I filled out is the name I was given. But after my parents divorced, my mother changed it. She used my middle and her last. Sort of, anyway. And the point is, well, what I mean to say is, I just want it back. It's *mine*, after all. She had no right to take it away." Explaining made her angry, and it came out in her voice again, and she realized there was far too much anger bubbling up inside her for the present situation to justify.

"All right, all right." The judge held up her hand and glanced back at the courtroom full of other people waiting for a piece of her day. "Don't get your knickers knotted." She looked down at the paper again. "So this is the name you want? Your *real* name," she amended quickly as Dorrie opened her mouth to speak.

"Yes, ma'am." Dorrie could feel her face glowing and her pulse pounding in her ears.

"Are you changing your name to evade the law?"

"No, ma'am!" Dorrie shook her head vehemently.

She stared at Dorrie for a second or two. "So ordered," she said.

Dorrie wondered if she would pound the gavel or do something official, but all she did was sign the papers and hand them to her clerk.

She looked down at Dorrie again. "Congratulations, young woman. From this moment on you shall be known as *Miranda Isadora DeSpain*. It suits you," she said, and then for no reason at all, she smiled.

Dorrie took a shaky breath, then smiled back. Her knees felt a little weak. She took her copy of the name-change decree and walked out of the courtroom. She stood there on the sidewalk for a minute, looking around her in wonder.

Downtown Nashville was just as it had been when she walked in. The fancy restaurants were still serving lunch, the boutiques and galleries still displayed the same art, the cars still drove by.

Her heart thumped faster, and she went and sat down on the bench under the trees. She looked at the piece of paper and read her name, forming the words slowly. *Miranda Isadora DeSpain*. She took out the tiny mirror she kept in her purse and looked at her face. For the first time she thought it was possible she might be someone other than who she'd always thought. She saw burnished dark hair and mysterious eyes, and her lips parted in a secret smile.

A slight breeze ruffled her hair. She looked up and saw the wind trembling the new leaves of the maple above her. She shivered, whether from fear or anticipation she did not know. The only thing she knew was that she felt free and untethered for the first time in her life. She had the feeling of possibility. That anything might happen.

chapter 14

Miranda—she tried out her new/old name in her mind whenever she could. She had one final meeting with Sandra Lockwood. When they said good-bye she hugged her briefly and felt real sorrow, as if she had lost a true friend. She didn't fret for long, though, but came home and finished packing her suitcases. Tomorrow she would begin her adventure. She would set out for the Basque country. Tomorrow morning to New York, then on to Spain.

"You'll do fine," Sandra had said, waving her out the door. "Your life awaits."

And so it did, for the old life had finally ended. Her few belongings were packed in the Sentry Storage unit. The house was clean, ready to be sold. Aunt Bobbie had all the paper work she needed to put it up for sale. She had taken Mama's car, protesting all the while, but Miranda had insisted she take it, as well as the mahogany secretary from the living room and the harp chairs and end tables that matched them.

Miranda would sleep at Mr. Cooper's tonight, and he would drive her to the airport in the morning. She checked her suitcase for the tenth time, then took one more look around, glancing at all the scenes of her childhood, saying good-bye to Mama one last time. It wasn't the emotional time she had thought it would be. She was too tired and dry to cry.

The doorbell rang. She hoped it wasn't the Jehovah's Witnesses. She peeked out the upstairs window and startled when she saw Mama's car at the curb. Aunt Bobbie's car, she reminded herself and wondered why her aunt was here again. They had already said good-bye once, and it was nearly time for her aunt's shift to begin at the nursing home. Maybe she had forgotten to sign something her aunt would need to sell the house. She ran downstairs, opened the door, and it was indeed her aunt, dressed for work, standing on the welcome mat, looking sober.

"Hey, Aunt Bobbie," she said, standing back and motioning her in. "Did I forget to do something?"

"No," Aunt Bobbie said, stepping inside. "You didn't forget anything." Her lined face drooped a little more than usual. She looked worried and upset.

"What's wrong?" Miranda felt a little flutter of premonition.

"Maybe we should sit down," Aunt Bobbie said.

Miranda mutely gestured to the carpeted stairs. They sat. Aunt Bobbie twisted the handle of her purse. Miranda waited. "What's this about?" she finally asked.

"It's about the secretary," Aunt Bobbie said.

Miranda frowned and was truly dumfounded. "The desk?"

Aunt Bobbie nodded. Miranda grinned. "It doesn't fit where you wanted to put it? You want to bring it back? I'm sorry. All deals are final."

Aunt Bobbie wasn't smiling.

"There was something in it," she said. "Something taped up underneath the drawer."

Miranda stared at her. Where was she going with this? And if Aunt Bobbie hadn't looked so upset, Miranda would have made a joke. Did Mama have a secret life? Had she been selling crack or something? She shook her head in puzzlement, and a small smile played on her lips just at the thought. Aunt Bobbie reached into her purse and took out an envelope.

"I wasn't sure what I should do. I prayed on it and prayed on it, and I finally just decided you ought to have it. It just didn't seem right not to tell you. So here you are," she said, holding the envelope out.

Miranda took it from her and felt her smile fade. It was as if some part of her knew what it would be. She held it close to the light and could see that it was old and slightly yellowed. It was addressed to Noreen Gibson at 223 Eastmont Drive. This house. Postmarked December 14, 1996. She felt a chill run over her arms and up the back of her neck. There was no return address. Almost holding her breath she opened it up, and there was a photograph. She took it out. It was a baby, a year-old child. She knew this because on the back in black ball-point pen was written a simple phrase, *Twelve months old.*

She felt her pulse speed up, and her head became light. She forced herself to breathe normally and moved closer to the light. She couldn't tell if it was a girl or a boy, and she wondered if that was intentional. The child wore a red T-shirt and overalls. What little hair showed was dark. The eyes looked smudgy blue. Or maybe brown. It was hard to tell. The baby had pink cheeks and was smiling. Miranda felt something pierce her heart. She knew what this was. She knew *who* this was. She turned over the envelope and read the postmark more carefully. It was blurred, but she made it out. *Abingdon, Virginia.* She put the envelope over her heart as if to stop it from its wild beating.

"I hope I did the right thing," Aunt Bobbie said, looking worried now. "It just seemed like you never had a chance to decide what to do about that baby. You should at least be able to decide what to do with this. It's yours. It wasn't up to me to hide it from you."

"You did the right thing, Aunt Bobbie," Dorrie said, barely able to speak. "Thank you. Thank you so much."

Aunt Bobbie nodded. "I always felt bad about that situation," she said. "It just didn't seem right what your mama did to you, but I didn't think it was my place to interfere. Noreen always watched out for me. I figured I owed it to her."

Miranda barely heard her. She was staring at the picture. She looked up at her aunt, who had tears in her eyes, and she knew this was her chance to ask the question she'd always wanted to ask. "Do you know anything more about my baby, Aunt Bobbie?"

Aunt Bobbie shook her head. "Your mama didn't tell me, honey. She just said she'd made arrangements with somebody she trusted."

"That had to be a short list," Miranda said.

Aunt Bobbie nodded, then stood up. "I'm so sorry to leave you like this, but I have to go to work."

Miranda walked her to the door and hugged her, reassuring her she'd done the right thing. She watched her walk to the car, stop, and look back once. When she had driven away, Miranda went back to the stairs, sat down, and stared at that picture for a long time. Then she made up her mind.

She took out her cell phone and called the airline. It took her a half hour, but she canceled her ticket, leaving a credit with the airline. She had no idea where Abingdon was and had no map handy. She had her laptop but had canceled her Internet service, so she would just have to buy a map and drive. She would have to borrow or rent a car. And besides, she had no idea how or if she could find a nameless child even if she found the town.

She thought of a thousand reasons why she should just put that picture in the bottom of her suitcase and continue on with her plans, but she knew they were just thoughts, and she had no intention of acting on them. There were some times that you reasoned things out and decided what to do. Then there were other times when your brain just realized what your heart had already decided.

chapter 15

April in Abingdon was really quite lovely, even from this vantage point, Ruth Williams decided as she knelt in the dirt of last year's garden and turned the damp, red-clay soil. She wore a straw hat and overalls and knew she could have easily been mistaken for a scarecrow except for the extra padding she wore. She attacked the weeds with an old kitchen knife, but her mind was not on her garden.

She was not by temperament a worrier. Born in 1939, she had managed to live through the aftermath of the Great Depression, five wars, and widowhood. Even her childhood, happy though it was, had not been without trouble. In fact, she well remembered planting gardens just like this one, and not for the enjoyment of it. Their produce had fed the family. Before the Second World War came, her parents had lived on a large farm and grown acres of tobacco. After Dad joined up, Mama had tried to run the farm by herself but eventually lost it to the bank. Without a whisper of self-pity she had moved the family to a series of run-down rental houses in Richmond, where she found work in the can factory. Dad had died in the Pacific three years later. Ruth had no memories of him, but she well remembered how often they had moved, and she did not ever remember hearing her mother complain.

In fact, Ruth couldn't think of much to complain about, at least not from a child's perspective. She uprooted a dandelion and smiled as she remembered her childhood. Their home had been a cheerful place. Mama had never been one to sit down and cry when there was something that could be done, and Ruth supposed she was like her in that respect. Which was why she was weeding the garden today instead of sitting inside worrying, even though her family was in disarray and there was nothing she could do to fix it. She wished there were. She wished desperately this was the kind of situation that determination and energy could remedy. Those words reminded her again of her mother. After saving money for years, Mama had finally been able to buy their own place. She could still see the determined expression on her mother's face as she had stood in the doorway and surveyed the dingy little house.

"Well, the first thing to be done is to clean it up," Mama had said in her matter-of-fact way, and she'd set all of them to sweeping and scrubbing and washing, which had put the doldrums right out of them. Ruth tried to recall how many washtubs of brown water she had slung out that back door the first day or so in that house. Twenty perhaps. Thirty. It had taken time and patience, but within a year Mama had painted the walls a clean white, sewn her own curtains on her treadle sewing machine for the now spotless windows, made rag rugs for the kitchen floor, and planted a rosebush by the front porch. They had made do with what they had, and it had been plenty.

Mama had given them separate garden plots because agreeing about what to plant and where to plant it would have been impossible. Dorothy was still bossy, Ruth thought, expertly dislodging a hogweed with a flick of her knife blade. And Shirley was just as bad. She chuckled briefly, thinking what they would say about her. She and her sisters had put their younger brother, Walter, to work collecting manure, which they used for fertilizer.

It had been one decision they had all agreed on. She grinned, thinking of his outrage.

She tried to remember if there had been darkness over their spirits in those days. If there had been, she couldn't remember it. And if her mother had worried, she had hidden it well from her children. Ruth herself had been worried at one time. When she was twelve, Minnie Harper had told her the Koreans were going to fly right over Richmond and drop bombs on them just like the Japanese had done to Pearl Harbor. She remembered confiding those fears to her sister Dorothy who, being the ninny tattletale she was at that time, had passed them directly on to Mother. To tell the truth, she had been a little bit relieved to have her secret fears brought out into the light.

"Not likely to happen, Ruth," Mama had said the next day, bringing the matter up as she stirred a pot of beans for their supper and waited for the golden cornbread to turn brown on top. *"There's enough real trouble in the world without inventing more. Where's the quilt square you were sewing? Get your scissors out. That seam is crooked."* And that had been that.

Even growing up without a father hadn't crushed their spirits. Ruth could see the difference now between that and this circumstance of theirs. They still knew that God was on His throne. Good was good and evil was evil, and if Dad had died doing his part to stand against Hitler and Mussolini and Hirohito, then they would be proud he had spent his life well. Now it seemed the lines weren't so clearly drawn. Things had gotten confusing.

She remembered her mother, could see every line of her face as clearly as if she stood before her now. She remembered suppertime with the table covered with steaming food, the bounty of the jewel-toned mason jars gleaming proudly from the kitchen shelves, and for a moment she wished sharply she could be back in her mother's kitchen again. Oh, how she longed to lay her head on her mother's shoulder and feel her strong hand patting and smoothing her hair. She closed her eyes and could see the red-and-white gingham curtains and the checkered tablecloth.

She could feel the warmth of the woodstove and hear the hiss of the kettle. But there was no mother for her now. She *was* the mother.

She sighed and felt the burden settle on her back again. She had seen the world go from party lines to cell phones, from street-cars to moon landings. She had buried her own husband. Yes, she supposed she had seen her share of changes and dealt with her share of adversity. But this? This was tearing her very heart out.

She wiped her eyes furiously with the back of her hand, the only clean part she could find, then leaned back against her heels and dug in the pocket of her overalls for a rumpled, smudged index card. It was her prayer list, warped with her tears and frayed from being carried in her purse or pocket these past four months. Not that she needed it. She set it before her more to remind herself of the promises she'd scrawled along the bottom than the names upon it. The people who had occupied most of her thoughts and her prayers still stood on center stage, herself a sometimes anxious, sometimes faith-filled audience. There would be David lying broken in his bed with sweet Sarah beside him, Eden buzzing around the edges like a frenzied little bee, and Joseph, dear Joseph, marching back and forth, turning, marching again, peering sternly out over the wings, alert for danger. She felt a familiar downward pull of grief and loss but quickly snapped the cable with the shears of faith. She had gone back and forth between those two states so often and so quickly during the past year that she felt herself to be on a kind of emotional spin cycle. She read the words she had inscribed on the card. *For I am persuaded beyond doubt that neither death nor life, nor angels nor principalities, nor things impending and threatening nor things to come, nor powers, nor height nor depth, nor anything else in all creation will be able to separate us from the love of God which is in Christ Jesus our Lord.*

She believed it. She did. She sighed, tucked the card away, and dug back into the dirt with determination.

She finished the row and stood up and surveyed things. There were four rows of corn, two each of peas, green beans and pole beans, parsnips, turnips, carrots, broccoli, cauliflower, lettuce, lots of cucumbers, some to eat and some to pickle, a row of water-melons, a row of pumpkins for fall, and a small plastic-covered greenhouse for the tomatoes. She turned and surveyed the flower gardens. They were a little messy, but she loved them anyway. They were in the style of an English cottage garden, with plants growing very close together like beautiful women with shoulders brushing and their children jostling at their feet.

The moss between the flagstones was coming along nicely, and the path twisted and curled past the little nooks she had cre-ated, each separated by vines creeping up a section of fence or a weeping tree. There were huge lilacs ready to bloom and dangling wisteria, azaleas, and laurels that had already flamed and gone out. That's the way it was with all living things, she realized. You had to seize their beauty while it was there. It didn't last forever.

Joseph had helped her fashion a raised bed surrounded by a wall made of river rock. The pink and white and purple foxgloves stood sprightly among a sea of purple and white phlox. Peeping impatiens and green swords of hosta nestled beneath the huge trees—oaks and maples planted by her husband's grandmother. This had been his home, and she liked to think of him growing up here. It gave her happiness and reminded her of their life together. She gazed off for a moment, then remembered that she could be grateful for many things now. She had her sons and her granddaughter. Her bed-and-breakfast had been busy, and that was a saving grace. It always made her feel better to be doing something. Anything.

Which made it even harder with David's injury. There was nothing she could do. Not for him. Not for Sarah. Even helping Eden had turned out to be more of an exercise in ingenuity than direct intervention.

Her granddaughter had wanted to go stay in Minneapolis to be with David and Sarah for these last months, but that idea had been vetoed. *"You could help best by taking Eden,"* Sarah had told her, and she had been willing, of course. Still, it was hard to know her son was suffering miles away. But she couldn't leave Joseph to cope with her granddaughter alone, although he did admirably. She just wished she could fix them all. She sniffed and wiped her eyes on the sleeve of her shirt.

Well, at least they would all be here soon. Sarah said they would be coming to stay here with her for a while. It had seemed good in the ideal, but now that the real was upon her she wondered if she would be able to see her son so broken and not give in to despair. She would just deal with it. She had to. That was all there was to it. One good thing had come of the whole horrible situation. Her sons would be in the same place at the same time, and perhaps there would be the possibility of reconciliation.

She picked up her knife and stretched out her sore muscles. She was getting old. Too old for this kind of thing, she supposed, though she could not envision herself sitting on the porch. She checked her watch again. She wasn't sure about the system Joseph had devised for keeping track of Eden, but at least there had been no more disappearing acts since they'd started it. She shook her head, feeling weak just remembering how panicked she'd been the first time Eden had simply not come home after school. She'd called Joseph, and he'd had the entire police force out looking for her. She'd been discovered calmly sitting in the rectory of St. James, playing hearts with Pastor Hector the first time, and the second time she'd been in the public library, hunkered over an encyclopedia, making cryptic notes. Ruth sighed, suddenly tired.

Even as a little child Eden had liked to run off without telling anyone where she was going. A frightening and dangerous pastime. The adults in her world had passed the point of amusement with the habit and moved on to aggravation, but it didn't seem to matter in the least to Eden. She would simply disappear, and the hunt would be on. Her parents would call, cajole, and finally threaten, but to no avail. She would be gone somewhere on one of her mysterious errands and would come back when and if she wanted to, and always with a faintly satisfied air. Even as a toddler, she would sling an old Easter basket over her arm and visit the downhill neighbor without permission. She couldn't be held down. One could only hope to keep her safe.

It always seemed slightly irrational to Ruth that David and Sarah punished Eden for running off by making her stay alone. Somehow Ruth had the idea that Eden's wanderlust was a message of some kind, if only they could understand it. *Ask her what she's looking for,* she wanted to plead, but they only gave her a "time out"—the fashionable discipline these days. It seemed to make much better sense to put Eden in the midst of things—have her bake cookies with her mother or help her father clean the garage, to involve her in the life of the home so she wouldn't feel the need to go looking for companionship elsewhere. But David and Sarah felt they knew best, so off to her room she would go, apparently unconcerned but with that busy look in her eye, as if she were already making plans for her next escapade.

Ruth dusted off her hands, picked up her phone, and punched a number on the speed dial. After one ring Joseph answered. "Lieutenant Williams."

"My goodness, you sound so businesslike."

"Hi, Ma."

"Hello, dear. Will you be here for dinner?"

Pause. "Sure. I'll come for dinner."

"You'll bring Eden."

"I'll round her up."

"Have you heard from her yet?"

"Not yet. She should be reaching the first checkpoint in . . . twenty minutes."

"Call me if there's a problem."

"Will do."

Ruth hung up and put the phone in her pocket, and greatly relieved that Joseph was here and willing to take charge of his light-footed niece, she went inside to start supper.

chapter 16

There were sure ways of knowing when spring had arrived in southwestern Virginia, Joseph reflected. Catkins covered the willows and the ash trees, and tulip poplars were full of buds. Under the trees, snowdrops and skunk cabbage gave way to trillium and Solomon's seal. The warm-weather birds returned, and the first people got lost in the woods—this year it was a group of tourists in search of ramps, the wild leeks that grew in patches on the forest floor and were so prized by local people. Joseph had taken a search and rescue team in three nights ago. Although the tourists were frightened and cold, they had been easily found, having left tracks as plain as handwritten directions. But the real sign of spring—the one that never varied from year to year, that arrived on or about the first of April and departed with the first frost of winter—wasn't in the woods or on the lake or in the air. This migration came up Highway 25 from Murphy Village in North Augusta, South Carolina, whereupon the flock split, each one fanning out into the countryside to ply their shiftless trades or sell their worthless wares—in short, to see what poor bumpkins could be fleeced. The true arrival of spring came with the first Irish Travelers.

Their names were few—all Murphys or Gormans, Toogoods, Rileys, Sherlocks, or Carrolls. The men seemed to all be Pats or Mikes, Jimmys or Petes. They carried many sets of false identification and an assortment of license plates from Alabama, Tennessee, Arkansas, and Texas that could be shuffled and switched at will. Some drove commercial trucks and would offer to sell an inexperienced business owner a load of machine parts or tools at rock-bottom prices, always offering an explanation that only the hardest of hearts could resist. *"The man who ordered these died,"* or *"I have to unload these quickly. I just got word my wife has had an accident, and I don't have money to get home."* The tools, so shiny and new, fell apart at first use. The phone number on the bills of lading was disconnected. They would offer to seal your driveway, repair your roof, trim your trees, exterminate your pests, and either do nothing and charge you top prices or steal you blind on departing. Or all of the above. They preyed on the elderly, on people who trusted strangers. Joseph hated them and had made it his mission to keep his town free of them. He thought of them as vermin that should be poisoned or trapped. They were predators. They didn't belong here.

He stood now with Henry in Ernest Norwood's living room and burned with anger. The old man's white hair stood on end from running his trembling hands through it. The shaking of his head could be either from dismay or from palsy. *Who could steal from someone so helpless?* Joseph wondered again and wished for twenty minutes alone with the perpetrators. Since Norwood's farm was outside the county line and in Henry's territory, he was asking the questions, leaving Joseph to fume in silence. Unfortunately, the description Mr. Norwood provided could fit seven out of ten men—medium height and build with dark complexion. He drove a white utility van. Of course, he hadn't thought to note the license plate number.

"He seemed like a nice fella," Ernest said, ducking his head in shame. Joseph could imagine how he felt. Useless, stupid, not even a competent human being, much less the vigorous man he used to be. Mr. Norwood had been a deacon in the church when Joseph was a boy, and he remembered seeing him drive his tractor down the road every day as he rode the school bus home. Mr. Norwood grew tobacco and tied the finest fishing flies around. Joseph had one in his own tackle box, as a matter of fact. He had been strong, hardworking, and kind. It wasn't right that he should be victimized this way.

"He said he had some paving materials left over and if I let him seal my driveway, he'd give me half off. It wasn't until this morning that I noticed my bankbook was gone."

"The sealant was probably water or just plain oil," Henry said. "Have you called the bank?"

Ernest nodded. He wiped his mouth and shook his head. "I was too late. He cleaned out my account with a check he cashed in Beckley with false identification." So he had driven across the state line to West Virginia, where no one knew Ernest Norwood from Adam. "They said I might get my money back, but they'll have to look into it."

"Don't feel bad, Mr. Norwood," Joseph said. "These people are slick. They make it their business to know how to get people to trust them. We'll get your money back for you. Never mind the bank." Henry gave him a warning look, which he ignored. If he had to pay it out of his own pocket, he would.

Mr. Norwood shuffled back to his chair, and Henry and Joseph left.

"Don't you think you'd better just cool your engine there, sonny?" Henry asked him as soon as they were out of earshot. "You look like you're about to explode. Besides, you shouldn't make promises you can't keep."

"I'll keep it."

Henry gave him an appraising look and said nothing more.

"So where are you going to start?" Joseph asked.

"With the bank in West Virginia, I suppose. Get a description and a copy of the ID. Do a records search. Put out an APB on the car. Keep my eyes open and put out the word that people should keep their doors locked and not trust anyone." He looked as disgusted as Joseph felt.

Joseph drove back to the office feeling anger, but underneath it was something deeper, a grief of sorts that he felt every time a crime happened, even though this one was not technically on his watch. It was a disruption, a tear in the fabric of their world, a blot on a white garment, a snake in the garden. He tightened his jaw and felt the grief turn to something uglier. There should be no mercy for people like that. And when he found whoever was responsible, he would show none.

He had a wry twist of humor, thinking that he pitied the next person who crossed his path while committing any infraction of the law. He would have to mind himself or they would become the target for all of his pent-up frustration and powerlessness. He had no sooner formed the thought than a huge silver Cadillac pulled out in front of him, causing him to stand on the brakes to avoid a collision. The driver never even saw him. Shaking his head in disgust, Joseph flipped on the lights and gave the siren a whoop. After a few more seconds the big Caddy awkwardly pulled over to the shoulder.

"Well, for crying out loud!" Miranda said to nobody in particular. "Of all the luck!" She obediently pulled over to the side of the road, trying not to drive Mr. Cooper's late wife's Cadillac into the ditch, then shook her head and gathered her thoughts, all the while glancing in the rearview mirror. A very big, very tall man was unfolding himself from what she now realized was an unmarked police car, and he didn't look any too happy. He covered the distance to her in a few long strides and in seconds was leaning down into her window. Looming over it, more accurately. He had sand-colored hair, greenish gold eyes, and a nice enough face except for the fact that it looked like it never smiled. She pasted on a happy grin herself and tried to look suitably apologetic. He was having none of it.

"You pulled out in front of me back there," he accused her.

"If I hadn't slammed on the brakes, I would have hit you."

She didn't like being scolded, though heaven knows she had taken enough of it in her life. She felt her back tense up. "I apologize," she said stiffly, her chin going into the air in spite of herself. She thought about mounting a defense of some kind but decided the least said, the better. The truth was, she had been so busy thinking about her mission here and wondering where to start that she hadn't even seen him.

"May I please see your driver's license?" he asked with the exaggerated politeness that policemen always have before they write you a ticket.

"Certainly, you may." She dug around in her purse and found her wallet, then dug around some more until she remembered she had pulled out her driver's license the last time she'd used her charge card and had put it in her change purse. "It's right here," she said, smiling encouragingly at him. "I just forgot where I put it."

He glared at her and took it from her hand. He studied it, then glanced at her, studied it some more, gave her another look, turned it over and inspected it front and back, then put it on his clipboard. It was always bad when they brought the clipboard.

"May I see your registration and proof of insurance please?"

Uh-oh. She kept her dismay to herself, though, and gave him another smile. "Well, of course you may." She opened the glove compartment and dug around. She finally found the registration and handed it over, but the last proof of insurance she could find was dated 1998.

He read the registration, then looked down at her with a frown. "This vehicle is registered to William Cooper of Nashville, Tennessee."

"He's a friend of mine," she explained. "He loaned me the car."

The policeman frowned again, then went back to his car. He stayed gone for ten minutes or so, then came back and handed her the registration.

"So you found out it wasn't stolen?" All right, some of the sweetness may have been wearing a bit thin by then.

He didn't answer her. He was busy writing. He tore off the ticket and handed it through the open window. *Failure to yield right of way. Failure to provide proof of insurance.*

"Since you're just passing through, I'd appreciate it if you would proceed to the city hall and pay this fine right now. And you'll have to schedule a court date."

"A court date! What for?"

"Failure to yield doesn't have a preset fine. It can be a misdemeanor or an infraction. The judge will decide."

She opened her mouth to speak but didn't get a word out before he continued.

"Go down to the next intersection, turn right, then make another right and park in the visitors spot in front of the town hall right by the statue. I'll follow you just to make sure you don't get lost."

She shook her head in disbelief and started to protest, but on seeing his suspicious expression, she thought better of it. She didn't know why she had ever thought him attractive. "Suit yourself," she said smartly and rolled up the window. No need to be overly polite anymore. She did not look at him, just stared straight ahead. After a minute he went back to his car. She started up the Cadillac and drove very, very slowly—well, maybe even more slowly than she should have. She plodded along at about ten miles per hour. Another whoop of the siren nearly made her jump out of her skin.

"Do you want another ticket for obstructing traffic?" His voice came echoing over the loudspeaker, turning heads and drawing stares and not a few smiles.

"What traffic?" she hollered back, but thankfully he couldn't hear her. She drove at twenty-five the rest of the way, then parked in front of the city hall. He pulled in behind her car so she couldn't back out. Well, of all the nerve. She gathered up her purse and ticket, along with what remained of her dignity, and walked up the stairs. She could almost hear her mama scolding her. *You walk around with your nose in the air, all high and mighty, and somebody'll bring you down a peg or two.* She stepped inside the swinging door, and it was only then that she looked back. He was watching her, and he gave her a little salute with two fingers. Well, of all the cheek. Her face grew hot with anger. Of all the things in the world she couldn't stand, arrogant men were at the top of the list, and arrogant policemen were even worse, she now knew. She thought about going down there right now and telling him what she thought, but on second thought, she didn't want to spend the night in jail. With a longsuffering sigh, she turned toward the desk and followed the signs to schedule her court date.

chapter 17

Her dealings with the criminal justice system finished for the time being, Miranda came out of the courthouse and looked around furtively before climbing into the Cadillac, ready to proceed with her search. The only problem was, she had no idea where to begin. She drove up and down the quaint streets for a while, a little nervously, expecting the whoop of a siren to blare out at any second.

She left the town center and entered the outskirts, happy to put a little more distance between her and the police head-quarters. On each side of the highway were green pastures and fields and rolling hills. A green-and-yellow John Deere tractor went slowly by in the opposite direction. She shook her head, marveling at the irony of it all. Middle of nowhere, Virginia! That's where she had ended up. She had wandered all over crea-tion in her footloose days, and now she realized she had been looking for her child in every little face she saw. But it was plain to see that she needn't have been wandering to Minnesota and Maine and New York and Los Angeles. The only clue had pointed here all along. This was where she should have been looking, just two hours' drive away from her home.

Abingdon, Virginia. It hadn't been hard to find. She had bought a travel atlas and located it easily. It was about twenty miles northwest of Bristol in southwestern Virginia, within a stone's throw of Tennessee, Kentucky, and West Virginia. She supposed it wasn't a random choice that Mama had picked the adoptive parents from here. She and Aunt Bobbie had grown up somewhere close by. Were there relatives still living near here? She supposed the answers to the questions had died with Mama. They were things she never talked about.

She knew they had left West Virginia and gone to Nashville and had nothing to do with their people after that. They didn't speak of them, either. Whenever she brought it up, Aunt Bobbie just gave her a weary look, and Mama's tight lips became even tighter. Miranda looked down at the envelope again, then out the window. Mama had thought of her home when she had dispatched her grandchild. But whether that was an act of love or revenge remained to be seen.

She sighed again. All her life she had imagined her child living somewhere exotic like New York City or Los Angeles. Taking violin lessons and ballet dancing and going to concerts and vacations on Martha's Vineyard. She consoled herself with the fact that maybe her baby's family had moved to somewhere a little more exotic. But then she remembered that this address was the only link she had to her baby. If they had moved, she would probably never find them. For crying out loud, she would probably never find them anyhow, but here she was, driving up and down streets, craning her neck out the window, as if she had good sense.

She tried to think of what to do next. She would see an attorney. She didn't really think Virginia law would be much different from Tennessee's, but she would find out at least. After that she had no idea. Maybe she could just stand outside the school and see if anyone looked familiar. Maybe she could ask around about who had adopted children. She shook her head in frustration. They would think she was a kidnapper or worse. She heaved a great sigh and knew it was ridiculous, her coming here. It would serve no purpose, but actually, now that she thought about it, it would. When she followed this lead to its bitter end and found out nothing more than she'd known at the beginning, at least then she would be done. She would be finished looking for this child once and for all, and she would go on with her life.

She fished the picture out of the envelope and brought it up to eye level. She stared at it again. What a beautiful child. It was a girl, she was sure. She was almost certain. She brought her finger to her lips, kissed it, then gently touched the tiny cheek on the photograph, and she knew the truth of the matter. She would never forget. She might go on with her life, but she would never forget.

She drove a little longer and found herself at the entrance to the highway leading out of town. She stopped at the intersection, idling her engine. She felt sad and hungry and tired. She didn't know what she'd been thinking to come here. It was hopeless. She would never find that child. It was a human impossibility. She very nearly turned Mr. Cooper's car toward 81 South and Tennessee.

But oddly enough, she remembered two things that kept her from doing so. The first were Mr. Cooper's parting words to her yesterday. *"With God, all things are possible,"* he'd said, giving her a gentle smile good-bye. And the other came to her suddenly with the detail and emotion of having happened just this afternoon rather than eleven years ago. She was fifteen again, frightened and in pain, and feeling as though some vital part of her had been ripped away and she was left bleeding. And then the door to her room had opened, and there was the kind nurse handing her that sweet bundle. She closed her eyes now and smelled the baby's skin, felt the tender cheek against hers, and heard the funny little squeaks that babies make. She remembered drinking them in, then feeling a hand on her head and hearing the tired, kind nurse pray for God to bring her and her baby back together again someday. She felt a shiver, a chill, as if she'd brushed up against something that was not of this world.

A car honked tentatively behind her, bringing her back to the present quickly. Miranda opened her eyes. She went on through the intersection and pulled to the shoulder, hunted around in her purse, and finally found a McDonald's napkin, which she used to blow her nose and wipe her eyes. She nodded decisively, made a U-turn, still looking over her shoulder for Wyatt Earp, then drove back toward town, to where this winding two-lane road with pastures and fields on either side became the bustling streets of Abingdon. She checked into the Super 8.

Across the street was a Shoney's. She bought a burger and fries and coffee and, after eating, felt a little calmer, although still not very hopeful. She went back to the hotel room, took the Abingdon telephone directory, the *Welcome to Abingdon* binder the hotel provided, and her notebook, then went outside and sat down in the grass at the crest of a hill and watched the bluish purple evening creep up from the valley while she wrote down anything that seemed helpful. Finally, when she had gooseflesh on her arms and her rear end was damp, she went into her room, took a hot shower, put on her pajamas, and looked at her list.

It was pitiful.

"How to Find an Eleven-Year-Old Child," she'd titled it.

"Without knowing their name, sex, address, interests, or history," she muttered to herself. The only thing she knew was the date of birth—December 14, 1995.

She read what she'd written.

Eleven-year-olds:
Go to school
Play on sports teams
Join Boy Scouts, Girl Scouts, Camp Fire Girls
Go to the pediatrician
Go to Sunday school
Go to the dentist

Possibilities:
Hire attorney
Hire private investigator

It seemed pretty hopeless now that she looked at it on paper. She had little hope for the last two options. She'd heard people had found success with professional searchers, but they usually had something to go on. A name, a parent's name, an address. Something. She knew nothing. Not even the sex. All she knew was the date of birth. She set the notebook on top of her open suitcase, got into bed, turned out the light, and lay staring at the ceiling.

"Dear God," she said out loud. Her voice sounded lonely, like an echo over a deep, dark canyon. "If you're there, would you help me find my baby?" Nothing happened for a minute or two. She was listening hard, and she realized she really expected to hear something. And it was the oddest thing, but after a minute the feeling sort of came over her that she was exactly where she was supposed to be. It wasn't anything scary or sensational, just a quiet sort of peace. She didn't know any more than she had a few minutes ago, but the dark hotel room now felt like a holy place. She had done right to come here, she realized, and it may have been the first time in her life she'd had that assurance about one of her decisions. It was definitely the first time she felt one of her prayers had been answered. She let out her breath in a long, relieved sigh and rolled over to sleep. She didn't know how, and she didn't know when or who, but she knew that if she stayed here, somehow she would find what she was seeking.

chapter 18

The next morning Miranda rose, showered, dressed in a businesslike but uninspired pair of blue pants and a white blouse, and walked to Shoney's again. After a muffin and a cup of coffee, she returned to her room and began phoning the attorneys in town. She found, to her chagrin, that no one could see her before the next afternoon. She told herself another day wouldn't matter and booked another night at the Super 8.

There was no sense getting herself completely worked up about the quest to find her child, she told herself. What she should do was lower her expectations. She would look for her child, but she wouldn't lose her mind over it. Anyway, that baby had been lost to her for eleven years now. She didn't suppose what she did in the next month or two was of the utmost importance. She would take things a day at a time. Meanwhile, she would treat Abingdon, Virginia, as just another stop in the milk run that was her life. She would behave here as she had in Washington, D.C., New York City, Bozeman, Santa Fe, Minneapolis, and Seattle. So, first of all, she needed to get a job.

She got into Mr. Cooper's Cadillac and headed toward town, keeping a wary eye out for law enforcement. The day was fine, the sun already gently shining. Abingdon seemed bustling with pent-up springtime energy. Her mood picked up in response, and she felt a sense of optimism. She passed a nursery and garden center, a huge lot filled with trees and flowering bushes and pots of colorful blossoms. They were doing a booming business, as was the feed and grain store and the John Deere outlet nearby, if the cars in the lots were any indication. She stopped and asked both places if they were hiring and took applications, though neither one had openings at the moment.

She bought a newspaper at the first Stop and Go, then quickly scanned the want ads. There was a job opening at a retirement home and another one at a grocery store. But first she would follow her heart. She headed toward the elementary school.

It looked different with the children present. Something about it seemed alive and vital today, instead of quiet and dead, as it had the day before. An American flag was flapping in the breeze, the metal clip clanging cheerfully against the flagpole like a tinny bell. The school was new and low slung with lots of windows. As she came closer, she could see inside some of the classrooms. A group of upper elementary-age students were staring toward the front of the room looking bored. One boy sitting near the window watched her, and she smiled at him. She passed a first- or second-grade class that had the children's artwork taped to the windows. They were vibrant scenes in primary colors with neckless people and strange perspectives. She grinned. She liked kids. She had missed being around them. However, she was disappointed when she made her inquiries.

"I'm sorry, we're not doing any more hiring this year," the principal told her. "We just filled our last position in the lunchroom, and unless you're a certified teacher who can substitute, I don't have anything else available. And even in that case, there wouldn't be time left in the school year to process your security clearance."

Miranda thanked her and left. She didn't bother to leave her résumé. She wouldn't be here in the fall.

She went to the high school and middle school, but there was only one opening between them, again for a certified position. The same problems with the security clearance and fingerprints existed there. She'd come too late to work at any of the schools. Having access to student records could have been invaluable. Frustrated, she sighed.

She stopped by the nursing home next. A tall, thin woman with curly gray hair and an awkward manner looked over Miranda's application and said they were looking for someone with training and experience to work as a physical therapy aide.

"I'm a fast learner," Miranda said hopefully.

"Sorry," the woman said, shaking her head.

Disheartened, Miranda went to the grocery store, where she filled out another application but was told she would be called.

By then it was dinnertime. She stopped at a Hardee's and had a hamburger—she was really going to have to start eating something besides hamburgers—then took her coffee back outside and sat under a tree while she drank it. Would she have been discouraged if this were Kankakee or Pittsburgh? No, this was just the first day. She almost never got a job on the first day, but she almost always had one by the end of the first week.

She watched television in her hotel room, then spent the next morning filling out applications everywhere else she could think of: two banks, a gas station, the Barter Theatre—a local historic attraction—a pet store, an art gallery, the Dixie pottery store, a hairdresser, three boutiques, two restaurants. She stopped in plenty of time to find the attorney's office, which was near the downtown area.

She passed bookstores, art galleries, antique shops, a few fancy clothing boutiques and jewelry stores, a wine shop, a quilt shop, and a sporting goods store that advertised guided hikes on the Virginia Creeper trail, part of the Appalachian Trail, which apparently passed near here. After a few more minutes of looking, she found the attorney's office, parked the car behind the building where it wouldn't attract unwanted attention in the form of a hot-dog-small-town policeman who had too much time on his hands, and went inside. She filled out a few generic forms and, after fifteen minutes or so, was ushered into the inner sanctum.

C. Dwight Judson looked every bit the part of the gentrified country lawyer. He was portly and well dressed with a florid complexion and dark hair dramatically streaked with gray. His office consisted of wall-to-wall mahogany bookshelves, a huge mahogany desk, and oriental carpets on the hardwood floors. Miranda didn't feel an instinctive affinity, but she suspended judgment. She didn't need to be his new best friend; she just needed some advice.

"Please, sit down," he invited, rising from his chair with courtly graciousness.

She sat.

"May I offer you coffee or tea?"

"No thank you," she said.

"Well, then, how may I help you today?" he asked in his genteel accent.

She plunged off the high dive without a preliminary toe dip. "I had a baby eleven years ago and gave it up for adoption. I want to find it," she said.

To his credit, C. Dwight didn't bat an eye. "Don't know the sex?"

She shook her head. "I was a child and drugged. They were quick."

"What state?"

"Tennessee."

"Know anything at all about the adoptive parents?"

She reached into her purse and brought out the envelope. He took it from her, looked carefully at the postmark, then took the photograph out and held it up to the light. "Not much to go on," he said, handing it back. His expression was sober.

"No." She felt hope sag.

"Well, let's see what we know," he said briskly, taking a yellow legal tablet out of his top drawer.

Hope bobbed up again.

He asked her a series of rapid-fire questions, and she answered them the best she could. Who was the father? Who had been her legal guardian at the time of birth? What hospital? What date? Who was the physician?

"Were you given any non-identifying information about the adoptive family?"

"No," she said.

"Did you sign a relinquishment of parental rights?"

"Probably," she admitted. "There were a bunch of legal papers my mother made me sign."

"Do you know what she did with your copies afterward?"

"She's dead," she said bluntly. "And I assume she destroyed them. It would be like her to do that. I've looked through all her effects, including her safety deposit box. This is all there was," she said, nodding toward the picture she now clutched in her hand.

"Do you have your copy of the original birth certificate?" he asked.

She shook her head. "If she had it, I never saw it."

C. Dwight shook his head, then leaned back in his chair, making his ample middle even more rotund. "Let me give you a little lesson. The short version of Adoption 101."

She nodded and listened carefully.

"When a child is born whose birth parents have decided to arrange for adoption, an original birth certificate is issued in the state of birth with the names of the birth parents, the time of birth, the weight, sex of the child, and so on. The birth parents are entitled to that certificate, no matter what comes later."

Her pulse fluttered a little, thinking of the things she could learn from just one document.

"At the time of the adoption hearing, before which appropriate notice has been served to the birth parents, the attorney, or whoever is handling the adoption, presents the judge in the state of the child's birth with a release of parental rights signed by both birth parents. At that time the judge severs the birth parents' rights."

It sounded very final, and her stomach gave a lurch.

"Meanwhile, the adoptive parents' attorney presents the court with a petition of adoption. The judge evaluates whether they would make suitable parents, and if everything is in order, he usually grants it. At that time, a second birth certificate is issued, called the amended birth certificate. It has the child's name, sex, weight, place, time, and date of birth just like the original, but instead of the birth parents' names, the adoptive mother and father are named as the child's parents."

"That's just wrong," Miranda burst out. "That's a lie. On a *legal* paper."

C. Dwight tipped his head philosophically. "That's the meaning of adoption," he said gently. "Adopted children become indistinguishable from birth children in every sense of the word that matters."

She sniffed back tears and cleared her throat. And she felt for all the world as if she'd just been robbed. "So the child might not even know he or she is adopted."

"I suppose not," he allowed, "though most of the people who know about such things highly discourage that kind of secrecy any longer. Bad for everybody when it comes out," he said. "And it always does."

She sat in silence.

"Anyhow," he said, "that's the long and the short of it. The amended birth certificate is the one the adoptee uses all his or her life to register for school, get a passport, get married, whatever. The original birth certificate is sealed along with the adoption records, but you should have received a copy. You were entitled to it."

She noticed his use of the past tense. "So there's nothing I can do now?"

"Actually, you should be seeing a Tennessee lawyer, since

Tennessee was the state of the birth and the adoption. But it really doesn't matter."

"Since there's no hope."

C. Dwight looked genuinely sorry. "There is no provision in the law for allowing any identifying information of a minor child to the birth mother or of the birth mother to a minor child. And there won't be any in the original birth certificate, even if you could obtain a copy. But the state of Tennessee just passed a law that allows adopted children to petition for those records to become unsealed after they turn twenty-one."

"That's a long time from now," she said. "My child is only eleven." She thought for a minute. "I'm over twenty-one, though. Can I look at the records and contact the adoptive parents? Maybe through an intermediary?"

He shook his head. "Unfortunately, it all depends on the age of the adoptee, not the birth mother. And I'm also afraid you may never be given any more information than is on the original birth certificate. I'm sorry," he said again. "You can register with the Tennessee Department of Human Services," he said. "When your child turns twenty-one, he or she can contact them and, with your consent on file, will be given your identifying information."

"That seems like a long time from now." She was trying not to cry.

They sat in silence for a minute.

"I can call a friend of mine who practices in Tennessee. We can request a court order to get you a copy of the original birth certificate."

"What are the chances?"

He shrugged. "Usually there needs to be a compelling reason."

"So there's nothing else you can suggest?" she asked, her voice sounding pitiful and small in his large room.

He folded his hands, leaned back again, and stared at the ceiling, obviously thinking. "You could hire an investigator," he said. "But I have to tell you, it's a long shot."

Miranda shook her head. "I want to keep a low profile," she said. "Besides, an investigator wouldn't have anything more to go on than I do."

"I think you're probably right."

She blinked and cleared her throat. "What do I owe you?" she asked, reaching for her purse.

C. Dwight held up his hand. "You don't owe me a thing," he said. "I'm only sorry I can't do more to help you."

Miranda nodded and stood. "Thank you," she said. They shook hands and she left.

The day was still fine. The birds were still singing, but it might as well have been raining. She left the car where it was and started walking. She found herself at an intersection with a huge church on each corner. She went toward the closest one, St. James Methodist, and sat down on the white marble steps. The sun shone on her, and the warm steps gave her a momentary feeling of comfort. She took out the picture and looked at it again.

This was her baby. She had looked at the image so many times in the last few days that she had memorized that face. Dark eyes, though it was hard to see whether they were blue or brown, dark hair that was short and curly, a round smooth face, pink cheeks. And most importantly, the baby was smiling and looked well fed and happy. That's what mattered, she told herself again. That her baby had a good home.

"I thought I saw someone out here."

Startled, Miranda turned to see a man coming through the double doors of the church. He was probably sixty-five or so and looked Hispanic. He was fit and lean, had closely cropped, graying hair and wore a goatee, a friendly smile, jeans, and a T-shirt. "I'm Hector Ruiz," he said, sticking out his hand. "I work here."

"Miranda DeSpain," she said, rising to shake his hand. "I hope it's all right for me to be here."

"Sit, sit," he urged her. "This is a great spot to enjoy the sunshine. In fact, do you mind if I join you for a moment?"

"Be my guest," she said smiling. He nodded and smiled, too,

then sat down. She put the picture back in the envelope and slipped it into her purse. "What do you do here?" she asked.

"I'm the pastor," he said, "but I run the food bank today. And for a second, just glancing at the top of your head, I thought you were someone else." He glanced at his watch. "It's a little early for her, though." He smiled. He had a nice, gentle smile, and Miranda liked him instinctively.

She returned his smile.

"You new around these parts?" he asked.

She nodded. "I'm from Nashville originally, but I've been sort of roaming around the country for the last six or seven years."

"Doing what, if you don't mind my asking?"

"Little of this. Little of that." She glanced toward him. His eyes were interested, but he seemed to sense she didn't want to divulge much.

"What brings you here?" he asked.

She swallowed. She was going to have to answer that question eventually, but she hadn't planned on doing so quite so soon. She looked toward the kind face, the warm eyes, and she couldn't bring herself to lie to him. "I don't think I should say."

He tipped his head to the side a little. "That's fair enough. Although you never know—if you share your burdens, someone might be able to help you."

She frowned. It was certainly a point, and he had put his finger on her exact dilemma. She needed information, but she had to keep a secret. It seemed like the two were mutually exclusive goals. She could take a chance and trust someone, and suddenly she saw in her mind a rickety rope bridge spanning a razor-sharp chasm. This fellow, Pastor Hector, with the warm eyes and friendly smile whom she did not know from Adam, was out in the middle, beckoning her to follow him. What was she? Insane? She shook her head slightly. He nodded his.

"You're absolutely right," he said, even though she had not spoken. "You have no reason to trust me."

And she supposed it was what her mother had called her

contrary nature, but having him say that made her want to argue with him that she should. Was she crazy? She gave an ironic little chuckle. "I'm a real piece of work," she said, shaking her head. She wished she could root out that part of her that was like her mother, so mistrustful and doubting. She hated it.

"You certainly are," he said, and she startled back to the present.

"You're His *poema*," he said, "His masterpiece, His magnum opus."

Before she could question who the "he" was or argue, the pastor rose up and brushed off his jeans.

"Alas, I must go," he said, extending his hand.

She smiled again. He reminded her of some Spanish noble, some chivalrous Don Quixote who would tilt at windmills in her defense.

"It was a pleasure to meet you, Miranda DeSpain. I hope our paths cross again soon."

She shook his hand again, nodded and smiled, and watched his back disappearing into the church. She almost followed him in, but she was struck with the foolishness of that course of action. She had things to find out, and the answers most certainly did not lie inside those doors.

Miranda spent the rest of the week on a futile search for jobs, getting more and more discouraged with each day that went by. By Sunday afternoon she was so lonely she called Aunt Bobbie. Her aunt was friendly, but her conversation was sparse. Miranda had the feeling Aunt Bobbie regretted giving her the picture, or at least regretted opening a sensitive subject. Her aunt listened while Miranda described her talk with the attorney and disavowed any knowledge of an original birth certificate.

"I gave you all I found," she said wearily. "But there is something else I should tell you."

Her voice sounded as if she dreaded the prospect, and Miranda wondered how many more surprises there could be.

"Your daddy called looking for you," she said.

When Miranda heard it, her heart dropped like a stone. "When?" she asked, and she heard a child's forlorn wail come out of her mouth.

"Just after you left," Aunt Bobbie said.

"Why didn't you call me?" she demanded, all attempt at civility abandoned. She felt angry, tired of having things kept from her by well-meaning people.

"I should have," Aunt Bobbie said, "but he didn't leave a number or say where he was. I thought it would just upset you. And I was right," she added, a tiny bit of reproach in her voice.

"Did he say anything?" Desperation was in her voice now and she felt once more the bitter irony. She had missed out on her own chance for reunion with her flesh-and-blood father while chasing after her phantom child.

"Just that he was wondering how you were and that he got concerned when your mama's phone was disconnected. He was real sorry to hear of her passing. Said he would have sent flowers if he had known."

Miranda took a deep breath and sighed it out. "All right." There was nothing to be done for it now. She knew well enough that Daddy wasn't someone you found. When he was ready, he found you. She would have to make peace with the fact that she had missed a chance and hope she lived to see another one.

She said good-bye to her aunt, regretting that she'd made the call. She slept poorly, and on Monday morning she was back to the point of discouraged desperation. She wanted to continue on with her quest, but she was completely stumped as to what to do next. Or where to even begin to look for her child. What she needed was someone in the know. A go-to person. Someone whose finger was on the pulse of the whole town of Abingdon.

chapter 19

E den coasted down Green Spring Road on the new red Schwinn bicycle Uncle Joseph had bought for her and thought about what she might have been doing after school if it weren't for him. She shuddered and made her Brussels-sprouts face. Mom had sent Grandma a list of the stuff she did at home: ballet lessons—*boring*, swimming lessons—*okay, but how many more things could she learn now that she could do the crawl, the butterfly, and the backstroke, and she couldn't take lifesaving until she was sixteen?* There were flute lessons—*more boring*, gymboree—*gag me with a spoon*, art lessons—*kind of interesting. At least there she had learned how to draw things she wanted to remember*, creative writing—*she had to admit that wasn't so bad.* And, of course, violin—*barf, barf, barf.* But the whole deal was that Mom just wanted to keep her busy because she didn't want her around. She knew this because she'd been listening one night when Mom was telling Dad how tired she was and how she really needed some time to herself, and she was thinking of finding another after-school program. Eden's throat felt tight just thinking about it. Mom hadn't wanted her in Minneapolis with her and Dad, either. Her eyes stung as she thought about why she'd spent the last four months here at

157

Grandma's. But one good thing, she reminded herself, the big gulps of cool breeze blowing away the tears, was that Uncle Joseph had talked to Grandma, so now she didn't have to do anything except violin, and she could quit that when school was out. And another good thing—the best thing ever—was that he had given her the radio. She could turn it to the same frequency as the police and listen to all the calls. And if she should come upon a crime? She could call it in herself.

She put her feet up on the bike frame and held her arms out from her sides as she soared down the hill. No hands, no feet. She put her hands back on the handlebars but kept her feet propped up, admiring her new red tennis shoes. The jeans were new, too, but they would be comfortable in a few more washings. Mom had sent her two dresses and three sets of matching pants and sweaters, but Eden had begged Grandma to let her wear jeans. Grandma said no at first, that Mom had told her what she should wear, but then Uncle Joseph had another talk with her, and afterward Eden was allowed to wear whatever she wanted. Today she was wearing her favorite outfit: jeans, tennis shoes, and a red-and-white print blouse with horses on it, the gold locket Dad had given her, and her friendship bracelet from Riley Thompson. The horse shirt was her favorite. Uncle Joseph had sent it to her last Christmas. He'd also given her the watch she wore—a genuine Smith & Wesson police watch for clandestine assaults. It was all black, and it lit up for night vision. It had a Velcro band that covered it over. The book that came with it said it was ideal for jumping, water ops, and rappelling. And then, of course, there was her brand-new Kenwood mobile radio. She patted her belt with satisfaction. It was just like the one Uncle Joseph and the other officers wore on their belts.

The only thing left that she wanted was a shoulder holster. In fact, she had found one up in the storage room at the police station beside the old file boxes and office supplies. She had it in her desk down at the station and she planned to ask Uncle Joseph today if she could have it. She didn't know what she would put in it yet, but she would find something.

Eden shook her head slightly and felt the cool breeze stream through her hair. She put her feet back down on the pedals and braked to a stop outside St. James. She hopped off her bike and left it under the big tree in the yard, then took the radio off her belt and pressed the button to send.

"Wolf Mountain One, come in. This is Wolf Mountain Two. Over."

Scratchy static, then Uncle Joseph's voice replied, "Wolf Mountain Two, this is Wolf Mountain One. What is your location? Over."

"I'm located at the corner of Main and Elm," she said, sitting down on the warm marble of the church steps.

"Roger that, Wolf Mountain Two. Tell Pastor Hector I said hello. Talk to you at your next checkpoint. Over."

"Copy that, Wolf Mountain One. Ten-four. Over and out." She put the walkie-talkie back on her belt, then stood up and went inside the church.

It was old in here. Really old. It even smelled old. She peered into the sanctuary, and it was deserted. The ceilings looked about a hundred feet high, and there were all kinds of stained-glass windows. The sun was shining in, and it looked all peaceful and cool, but she wasn't staying here today. She went out and around the corner to the back of the building where Pastor Hector was running the food bank.

She looked around and it took her a second to find him. He was kneeling on the floor, stacking bags of rice that someone had donated. People were always giving things to Pastor Hector. The back of his car was full of boxes of canned food and bags of clothes. She practiced describing him the way people were described on the Wanted posters she filed for Uncle Joseph. *Approximately five-feet-ten-inches tall, medium build, partially bald with short gray hair and beard, dark eyebrows. Last seen wearing jeans and a red T-shirt. If you have seen this man, please contact the Abingdon Police Department or the Washington County Sheriff.*

"Well, well," he said, getting up and dusting off his knees. "I was hoping you'd come along and spare my back. How are you today, Ms. Williams?" He always called her Ms. Williams.

"Fine." She took his place on the floor and stacked the rest of the bags, then pulled the other box toward her. It was filled with pinto beans and dried black-eyed peas. She made neat stacks of both while Pastor Hector plugged in the coffeepot and made them each a cup of coffee. She finished stocking the dry spaghetti and unpacked a box of canned food from the warehouse store. Two people came in, and Pastor Hector gave them sacks. They took some food and some clothes and some diapers. *Man approximately five-feet-six-inches tall, one hundred fifty pounds, dark hair and eyes, goatee. Tattoo of coiled snake on right forearm. Woman five-feet-four, approximately two hundred pounds, blond hair, blue eyes.*

"Coffee's ready," he said as the couple exited the building. "Or do you need to do something, er, official?"

She gave the man and woman one last glance and frowned, then shook her head. "No. I guess not." She followed him to the table in the corner. He moved aside a box of canned tuna and brought another chair from the storage room. She took a sip of her coffee. "Aah," she said, just like Uncle Joseph did when he sipped his coffee.

"Did I get it the way you like it? I put three spoons of sugar and three spoons of Coffee-Mate."

"It's just right," she said and took another sip, then frowned. "This isn't decaf, is it?"

"Oh, heavens no." He shook his head. "I wouldn't dream of insulting you with anything less than full-bodied Colombian."

She frowned. He was teasing her. Everyone always teased her.

They sipped companionably for a minute or two; then she took out her notebook.

"Anything happening I should know about?" He nodded toward the pages filled with entries she had made after yesterday's rounds.

She read over them quickly. "Well, somebody poked a hole

in Clyde Turner's hot air balloon."

"The one he uses to give rides to tourists, or the one that used to be the World War II weather balloon?"

"The tourist one. While he was at church on Sunday morning. They started the hole with a knife and then tore it."

Pastor Hector shook his head. "You don't say."

Eden nodded. "He thinks Harvey Winthrop did it."

"Harvey! Why on earth would he do that?"

"Because, you know, he does the horse and carriage rides, and people usually don't have enough money for that and a balloon ride, too."

Pastor Hector was nodding. That was one thing Eden liked about him. She hardly ever had to explain things. He caught on quick.

"I see. Of course. His motive would be to hobble the competition, so to speak."

Eden wasn't exactly sure what that meant, but she was pretty sure Pastor Hector had the right idea, so she nodded back.

"I'm checkin' Harvey Winthrop's alibi. Says he was at church."

Pastor Hector lifted up his eyebrow and shook his head. "He's a Baptist," he said. "I wouldn't know."

She wrote that down.

"What else have you got in there?"

She looked down again. "Well, Robert Jacobs was arrested for public drunkenness. He was outside the Wash-O-Matic, howlin' like a wolf, and when Cletus Turner tried to get him to stop, he bit him. He's in the jail this very minute, unless somebody posted bail for him since I left for school this morning."

Pastor Hector didn't say anything to that, just raised his eyebrows again and took another sip of coffee. "Intriguing."

She checked her list again. Flipped back a page, then forward. "That's about all since yesterday. Except Elna at the Hasty Taste has to have surgery on her back. Busted disk."

Now Pastor Hector took out his notebook and pen. He made

a note. "Thank you for the information," he said. "I'll call on her. She's one of my parishioners."

"Scheduled for next Tuesday. She's going to the hospital in Bristol, 'cause that's where her daughter lives. She'll be off work for three months."

"Umm." He shook his head in sympathy.

"I guess that's about it," she said. "Have you got any information for me?"

He cleared his throat and leaned forward. "I did hear something."

She took out her pen that changed colors and used green ink. Pastor Hector was green, Father Leonard at the Catholics was black, Pastor Annenberg over at the Presbyterians was red, and Father Stallworth over at the Episcopals would have been blue, but he never told her anything. She had tried to be friendly a time or two, but he had just looked at her with his buggy old wrinkly eyes and asked could he *help* her with something, so she had made friends with Roy the groundskeeper instead. Roy gave her a tip now and then and so did Sue, the secretary. "Okay," she said, "I'm ready."

"It's probably not the kind of thing you're looking for, but you know Frank Applegate up on White Mountain Road?"

Eden nodded.

"Well, his youngest daughter just went off to college at Sweetbrier."

Eden looked at Pastor Hector, then down at her pad. She made a few scribbles just so she wouldn't hurt his feelings.

"Okeydokey," she said.

He cleared his throat. "I mention it because the daughter— Susannah is her name, I believe—has a horse that she had to leave at home, of course. I don't know much about such things, but Frank was mentioning that he was in a bind. Horse needs exercising, but he and his wife are too old. Anyway, I just thought you might want to know."

Eden's brain was ticking along. Now she could definitely see some possibilities. "Applegate?" She wrote it down in capital letters and put an exclamation point after the name.

"That's right. Frank Applegate. White Mountain Road. Big white house with a rail fence. I imagine your uncle knows how to reach him."

Her uncle. She checked her watch. "Gotta go. Thanks for the coffee. And the information."

"My pleasure, as always." He held his hand out to her, palm up. She slapped it, then hooked her fingers into his. "Friends forever," he said.

"Friends forever," she repeated. She took the stairs two at a time and made her second call-in from St. James's.

"Over and out," Uncle Joseph said, and she was good for another half hour.

Not much was going on at the Catholics. Father Leonard was answering the phones today because the secretary, Maude Lucy, was out with a sick baby, so he was in a bad mood and she didn't stay long. He was like that. Really grouchy some days and really nice others. She made a note about Maude Lucy's baby and then went on to the Episcopals. She hit the jackpot because Father Stallworth wasn't there, but the Ladies' Circle was meeting, so she just sat under a window near the kitchen and found out that the pastor at the Soda Springs Baptist Church had gotten replaced and Bernadette Jacobs was leaving her husband. Eden flipped back to the note she'd made about Robert Jacobs and the public drunkenness and howling at the moon and reckoned he was still in the jail unless he'd talked his mother into posting bail. But it was a known fact she didn't have two nickels to rub together. She noted a few more things, then got on her bike again. She still had to stop at the post office and the Hasty Taste and show Floyd at the bus station the new Wanted posters to see if any drifters had come through town. And she was supposed to be at work at the PD by four. There was a stack of Wanted posters and arrest reports to file. But instead, she turned her bike around and headed in the opposite direction. Toward White Mountain Road and the big white house with the rail fence and the horse that needed exercise.

She made good time and was nearly there when she glanced at her watch. It was nearly time for a check-in, and it wouldn't do to have Uncle Joseph ask where she was. She wasn't supposed to go anywhere that wasn't on the approved list. She pedaled faster.

She didn't see the tree branch until she'd hit it, and by then she was on her way over the handlebars. She took note that she was flying through the air, but the next thing she knew she was on her face in the middle of the road, and there was gravel on her cheek and in her palms and she couldn't breathe or even cry. She heard feet scrambling and a shout. Then somebody helped her sit up, and a boy with blue eyes and freckles like hers and the reddest hair she'd ever seen was kneeling beside her looking real worried.

chapter 20

"You just about broke your neck," he said.

Eden felt like her insides were being sucked out. Finally she gave a cough and pulled in a good breath or two. Ordinarily she would have cried, but not with this boy reared back on his haunches, watching her.

She leaned over again and concentrated on taking some breaths, ignoring the tears that were backing up in her eyes and dripping down her nose. The boy picked up her bike and walked it to the side of the road.

He came back and held out his hand. She shook her head and leaned over again. She hoped she wasn't going to throw up right here in the middle of the road. In front of that boy.

"You better get yourself up before a car comes by and runs you flat," he said and held out his hand again.

She ignored his hand. She gasped again two or three times, then started wiggling things to see if anything was broken. After a minute or two she stood up without his help and brushed the gravel out of her hands. She would not cry. She would not cry. She would not cry.

"You're bleeding pretty good on your face." He looked and

sounded as if this was something he admired.

She raised her hand and felt the sticky blood on the side of her cheek. She felt a moment of panic. Grandma would have a fit, and then no matter what Uncle Joseph said, she would be sitting at home every day after school watching stupid after-school specials and baking cookies.

"Stupid stick!" she exploded and sent it flying with a kick. "Stupid, stupid, stupid stick!" She kicked it again and spit on it.

He looked even more admiring.

"I can't go home looking like this," she said, probably sounding as desperate as she felt.

He looked thoughtful for a minute and chewed the inside of his lip. "You could come to our place and wash up. I guess my dad wouldn't mind."

Eden thought about it. She knew it was against the rules. She should never go off with strangers. But the boy didn't mean to harm her, or he would have already done it. And besides, there was a lot at stake here. She checked her watch. It was still on and still ticking. She patted her radio. Still all right. Her notebook was lying by the ditch. She picked it up and brushed it off. Her bike had a few scratches on it, but nothing was bent or broken. There was a little tear in the elbow of her horse shirt, but other than that things were okay. But they wouldn't be okay for long if Grandma found out about this.

"All right," she said briefly. "Where's it at?"

"Follow me," he said and took off through the woods.

Eden gave a glance at her bike and at the winding trail through the trees.

The boy stopped walking after a few paces and looked back to see why she wasn't following. "Hide it over here," he said, taking the bike from her and expertly rolling it behind a thicket of blackberry vines.

She wondered for a minute if this was all a trick. Maybe he was working in cahoots with somebody. He threw the stick into the road, and when the victim came along and fell, one of them offered help while the other one stole the bike. She looked around suspiciously, but there was only a slight breeze ruffling the new leaves of the trees and fluffing the tall grasses. A drop of blood fell from her face onto her arm, reminding her of her problem.

"All right," she said, but she might as well have saved her breath because he was already headed down the path. She trotted to keep up, and after a minute he turned around and waited for her.

They walked along together for a minute.

"Where's your house?" she asked.

"Over yonder in the hollow. And it ain't a house. It's a trailer."

"You mean a mobile home?" Grandma said not to call trailers *trailers* because sometimes people were sensitive about it.

"No. I mean a trailer." They pulled into a clearing, and she saw what he meant. There, parked under a bunch of trees was a silver trailer hooked up to a new dark green Dodge truck. Somebody had set up a campsite with the fire going and a coffeepot perking on the grate, two lawn chairs on either side, a welcome mat under the fold-down stairs. The door to the trailer was open, and coming from inside Eden could hear country music and somebody singing. Not very good at it.

"That's my dad," the boy said.

"I don't even know who you are," Eden accused.

"Well, I don't know you, neither," he shot back.

Eden was about to let fly with something else, but just then the father came to the doorway and down the steps. She gave him the once-over.

White male, dark brown hair mixed with gray, approximately six feet tall, medium build, no markings or tattoos, blue work pants, a white cotton shirt.

He looked a little startled and stared at her for a minute, then spoke. "Well, well, well," he said, giving her a friendly smile. "Whom have we here? A damsel in distress?"

"I'm Eden," she said, ignoring the part about the damsel in distress. "Eden Williams."

"Pleased to meet you, Eden Williams," the man said. "My name is Johnny," and he sort of bent over a little bit like a bow.

"Pleased to meet you," she said, still giving him the eye.

The boy didn't say anything. His father gave him a little shove. "Don't stand there like a lout, boy. Show some manners. Tell the young lady your name."

The boy didn't bow. In fact, he looked down at the ground and started drawing in the dirt with the toe of his shoe. "Name's Grady," he said.

She could barely hear him, he mumbled so.

"Grady Adair."

chapter 21

J oseph frowned and checked his watch. He'd been back at the station for nearly an hour since taking the report with Henry. Eden had missed one check-in and was due for another one in just a few minutes.

He walked down to the dispatcher's office. Loni was on the phone.

"Did my niece call in?" he half mouthed, half whispered.

Loni shook her head no without breaking her concentration.

Joseph went back out into the foyer and looked out the glass doors. He could call his mother, but that would only alarm her. He supposed he would have to go and find Eden. She was probably over at the post office memorizing the Wanted posters or at the bus station asking Floyd if any of the Ten Most Wanted had come through. He had to smile thinking about Eden. She was a scrapper, all right. Well, he would go find her and take her home. Besides, the fresh air would clear his head. He had spent the better part of an hour reading last year's police reports about Traveler scams, and his blood pressure was rising by the minute.

He went back up to his office and told his assistant where he was going, then stepped out onto the broad steps of the building, took in a deep breath, and looked around. It was a beautiful day. The trees were covered with new half-furled leaves, the air was moist and cool, the grass green and tender, the sun shining. He looked up toward the mountains and felt the springtime eagerness to be up on the trail. Maybe he could find some time this weekend. It had been too long of a winter, and his muscles ached to be stretched and moving once again.

He immediately thought of his brother and felt a stab of grief and remorse. David would never have the privilege of climbing a hill or running a race again. Joseph felt guilty for his fitness. And for his silence and distance.

It was mid-April, and he had not been to see his brother since the accident had first occurred. He had called often, of course, and passed messages to David through Sarah. There had been a few awkward telephone conversations between his brother and him. Lots of halting starts and trailing middles and abrupt endings and too long silences in between. He supposed ten years of enmity could not be mended with a few condolence calls.

He should have gone in person again. He should go even now, and he felt shame that he would not do so. But he could not imagine standing over his brother and talking about trivialities, and the conversation they had always needed to have would never take place now. For how could you accuse someone in David's situation? How could he add to David's troubles by a confrontation? So Joseph shut his mouth firmly and clenched his jaw. His brother would come here to recuperate. He would be pleasant and kind, and then David would go back to Fairfax, and he would go back to his life.

His thoughts made him irritable and anxious, and it was in this state that he went to find Eden, his discomfort at her radio silence growing into something slightly more, although it would certainly not be the first time she had gone absent without leave. He tried to call her again.

"Wolf Mountain Two, this is Wolf Mountain One. Come in." Nothing but static. She must have her radio turned off.

"Wolf Mountain Two, this is Wolf Mountain One. Are you there?"

More nothing.

He drove through town and parked outside St. James. He went in the side door. Hector would be running the food bank today. Sure enough, he was there. He was making entries in a ledger book. He looked up with a pleasant expression that changed to quizzical when he saw Joseph's face. "Uh-oh," he said. "How late is she?"

"She's missed two check-ins," Joseph said briefly.

Hector shook his head and glanced toward the clock. "She left here about an hour ago. I assumed she was headed for St. John's."

"I'll check there next," Joseph said.

Pastor Hector chuckled. "She's a corker, that one."

The comment brought a smile to Joseph, albeit a grudging one. "That she is."

"She's probably found a story she needs to track down or a crime in progress."

"That's what I'm afraid of," Joseph said wryly. "She's a good kid, but she scares me sometimes. She'll follow her imagination anywhere, and I'm afraid someday it'll lead her into trouble."

"I know what you mean," Hector said, his face becoming serious. "By the way,"—Joseph tensed, for he knew what was coming—"how's David?"

"About the same," he answered. "Some good days. Some bad."

Hector nodded soberly and said nothing more as Joseph walked out.

No one was around at St. John's. The office was dark, the door locked, Father Stallworth apparently having closed up shop and gone home and the Ladies' Circle having adjourned. Joseph drove slowly past the Catholic and the Presbyterian churches. He didn't see Eden's bike. He was just about to call his mother when his cell phone rang. He flipped it open and saw *St. James Methodist Church* on the caller ID.

"Did you find her yet?" Hector's voice, not exactly worried but concerned.

"Not yet." His own clipped and abrupt.

"I thought of one more thing. I told her about Susannah Applegate going to college and that horse of hers needing exercise. I wouldn't be surprised if she headed over that way. Sorry," Hector said. "I should have cleared it with you first."

"No problem," Joseph answered. "Thanks for the lead. I'll check it out." He turned the car away from town and headed out toward White Mountain Road. He picked up his radio and tried one more time to reach her, though his anxiety was all but gone now that he had a pretty good idea of where she had gone. He had no doubt he would find her standing at the edge of Frank Applegate's horse pasture, pining after Susannah's horse. Well, every girl needed a horse, didn't she? He spent the next few minutes wondering what Ma would say about a Thoroughbred grazing in the backyard of the B and B.

He drove to the Applegate farm but saw no sign of his niece. He went up the graveled driveway and spoke briefly to Mrs. Applegate, who had been home all afternoon and hadn't seen anyone come or go. He thanked her and left, now truly worried.

"Wolf Mountain Two, this is Wolf Mountain One. Come in." Still nothing.

He called his mother and worried her, then tried calling Eden on the radio one more time, driving slowly down the road. He was thinking about what to do next when he saw the flash of red behind a thicket of blackberry vines in the field over to his right. His heart began thumping, and his blood roared in his ears. He stopped the car, slung it into park, and ran across the field.

It was the Schwinn he had bought her. He squatted and, without touching anything, saw the scrapes on the paint. He stood up and felt himself slide into another mode. His emotions were packed away to be dealt with later. For now he turned and began scanning the scene. He didn't say *crime scene* yet, even to himself.

He began searching with his eyes in that state of exaggerated calm. Tracking and finding someone was just like any puzzle. You began by examining all the pieces. He swept his eyes around the fallen bicycle in a three-hundred-sixty-degree arc. Humans and animals left evidence of their presence. There was a partial footprint, but the heel was too wide to be Eden's, and the sole had the waffled appearance of a hiking boot, not the crisscross of Eden's new tennis shoes. He saw her bright eyes and quick smile the day he'd bought them for her and had to press his emotions down again.

He followed the boot tracks back to the roadside and saw that whoever it was had made a round trip to the blackberry thicket where he had dumped the bike and come back here to the roadside. He knelt down, and there were Eden's prints in the soft dirt on the shoulder of the road, clearly indented from the new soles. Both sets headed across the field from here toward the woods. The tall grass was bent down, and some of the brush had been disturbed, showing the pale undersides of the leaves. There was a broken twig beside the larger boot print. He saw something. He stopped, squinted, and, hoping he was wrong, bent low to examine a dry leaf by the side of the trail. He touched it gently, and the droplet was still a bit liquid. It was blood, and it had been shed recently. His pulse pounded harder. He wanted to go crashing into the woods, but first he would behave rationally.

He picked up his radio to call for backup and search and rescue, but before he could press send, Eden's voice, as clear as if she were beside him, came through. "Wolf Mountain One, this is Wolf Mountain Two. Come in."

"Eden! Where are you?" he demanded, all playacting put aside, relief quickly becoming fury.

And then he saw her at the edge of the woods, looking at him with trepidation. "I'm right here," she said, then lowered the radio to her side.

"What happened? I was worried sick," he shouted as he covered the ground between them. "I was just about ready to bring in the dogs. What happened to your face? Are you all right? Who was with you?" he demanded, remembering the waffled hiking boots. And somewhere in the midst of all that, he noticed her glancing back behind her and then turning her face toward him, the trepidation now replaced with a look of barely veiled defiance. He had seen a look like that recently and thought of the woman he had followed into town at ten miles per hour. Repentance was obviously not on either of their minds.

"Well?" he demanded. "Are you going to answer me?"

She stared down at his boots. "I fell off my bike."

He saw the scrapes on her face, neatly washed with some kind of lotion applied, the tear in the sleeve of her shirt. The collar and shoulder of her shirt had wet spots and pinkish stains where she had obviously tried to wash off blood. He picked up her hands, and both were scraped but also washed clean. There was a dirty smudge on the side of her jeans.

"You just fell?"

"There was a stick in the road."

"Then what?"

Her small mouth thinned as she pressed it shut.

"Where did you go?" he asked. "Who did you go with?"

"Nowhere." The chin jutted forward. "Nobody." The jaw clamped shut.

So that's how it was going to be.

"Come on." He walked her to the blackberry thicket, where she retrieved her bike, then marched her back to his car, where he had to remind himself that she was not a suspect in a crime. She was a kid who'd missed a curfew and told a lie. "Hop in," he said, holding open the front door. "I'll put your bike in the trunk."

She climbed in. He popped the trunk and set the bike in beside his shotgun and accident kit. They drove home in silence. His mother was standing on the porch and greeted Eden with a hailstorm of remonstrances and consolations the moment he stopped the car.

He wasn't in the mood to answer questions, so he just unloaded the bike, then held up a hand in good-bye. He looked in the rearview mirror and saw his mother holding Eden's hand in an iron grip.

He didn't go back to the office, though. Not yet. Instead, he drove slowly back the way he'd come and parked the car in the same spot he had a few moments before. He followed the tracks again, only this time he went past the blackberry thicket to the edge of the woods. Here he could clearly see two sets of prints heading in and two out. Until right here. Then there was another set going back in alone. Whoever Mr. or Miss Hiking Boot was, he or she had walked this far back with Eden, then turned back. Those solitary tracks were wider spaced with deep heel marks and scrapes by the toe as the foot left the ground. He'd been running away, back into the woods.

Joseph followed the tracks for about a quarter of a mile. They turned at the edge of the woods, and he was in another field. The land belonged to Amos Schwartz, he thought, but he didn't think Amos, a simple Amish farmer, would have been renting out camping spots. He saw tire tracks of a truck and trailer, drag marks and crushed grass from where camp had been broken down. But he didn't need to be a tracker to know someone had been here. There was a circle where the grass had been scraped away and a fire laid. Dirt had been thrown over it, but the logs were still smoking.

He drove the long way around to Amos's place and saw Amos himself plowing his far pasture with a mule. Joseph waved and walked to meet him.

"Hello, Lieutenant Williams." Amos took off his hat and wiped the sweat from his forehead with the sleeve of his shirt. Like most Amishmen, he wore a beard but no mustache. "What brings you here?"

"Your land up there?" Joseph asked, gesturing toward the hilltop.

Amos nodded in the affirmative.

"Anyone camping?"

"Not to my knowledge," Amos answered. "Is there trouble?"

"I don't know," Joseph said. "Somebody's been there, but they're gone now."

Amos tilted his head, considering. "Maybe Travelers," he said, speaking aloud Joseph's own thoughts.

"Maybe," Joseph answered. He thanked Amos and walked back to his car. The whole matter was strange and came too close on the heels of the Traveler scam for his comfort. The woman he had ticketed came to his mind. The name on the registration had been Cooper. It was Irish, wasn't it? True, he was more familiar with the standard Traveler surnames, but not all of them were Sherlocks and Gormans. Plus, the driver's license had a different name and was new, showing no wear at all, just as you might expect if she'd pulled it out of a box of different possible identities. She hadn't looked like a con woman, but then again, that was the point, wasn't it? If they looked like criminals, no one would trust them. Besides, he had heard some of the Travelers were recruiting their women to run their scams. He ran it all over in his mind and drove back into town, keeping an eye out for the silver Cadillac.

chapter 22

Sarah watched her husband struggle with the simple act of moving from his bed to his power wheelchair and asked herself the question that had been on her mind and she knew was on David's mind, as well, whether he spoke it or not. *Will he walk again?*

The spinal cord had not been severed. David had sensation—translation, pain—in his legs, but the muscle and nerve damage had been severe. Now that it was less probable that David would die, the question of whether he would walk again was the dragon curled in the center of the room, fixing her with its beady stare, threatening to finish off fragile hope with a flick of its tail.

Everything felt overwhelming, the future a scarred patchwork of fears and anxieties. First she had feared he would die. Now she feared everything else.

She was afraid about money. The insurance companies were haggling, and there was no income. She, who had never even paid the bills, had taken out a home equity loan on the house and used it to make the payments, but that plate wouldn't keep spinning forever.

She was afraid about Eden. She felt guilt every time she spoke to her daughter. In fact, in these weeks of aloneness—for she was alone even with David—she had relived each one of the mistakes she had made with her daughter. She worried that Eden was irreparably scarred by them. She began to believe there was a reason she had not been entrusted with a child.

She was afraid for the future. She could barely manage her life as it was now, getting up in the small apartment the hospital had rented to her, making herself toast and coffee, then walking over to be at David's room by seven when the doctors made their rounds. Then another day of treatments and therapies would begin, and the agonizingly slow recovery continued. It had been four months almost to the day since David had his accident. They had warned her to expect six to nine months of hospitalization.

Watching him struggle made her afraid. And that was, perhaps, the deepest fear of all. From the time she'd first met him, it had felt as if he was the missing half of her heart. She was whole with him. It seemed so wrong that he should be helpless. He was the helper of the helpless, was he not? He was the one who made sense of life, who kept her sane. Without that help she was just as broken as he was. The doctors and nurses had begun strongly encouraging her to take over some of David's care. She tried, but she hated touching his wounds, and he seemed to hate it, as well.

She pretended to look out the window, watching sidelong as David struggled to make the eighteen-inch journey along the transfer board from the bed to the chair. His knuckles were white as he gripped the triangular trapeze bar and swung himself over. He dropped the bar and had to stop midway in an uncomfortable position. His face grimaced in pain, and Sarah moved to help him, earning a frown and a dismissive gesture from the physical therapy aide.

"Come on. You can do it." The aide stood with hands at his side while David sweated and strained.

Sarah felt a flush of shame as she turned and left the room.

One of the nurses had spoken sharply to her yesterday. "This is his battle," the woman had said to her, taking her aside out in the hall. "You can't do it for him, but he needs your support. His future depends on becoming independent. He needs your encouragement. Your pity isn't going to help him." Sarah had blinked back tears and nodded meekly.

She looked out the double-glazed windows to the hospital grounds. It was an unseasonably warm day, and although the grass was still winter brown, there were people outside without coats and jackets. Someone was delivering flowers. A woman shepherded three children into a van. She watched, amazed that the lives of people below could go on so normally in the shadow of this place of tears and wounds.

She thought of Eden, as she did many times each day, and felt the usual piercing guilt. After David's accident, she had felt as if they'd all been treading water in a rough sea, the wreckage of the boats all around them. She'd seen Eden hanging on to a piece of drifting wood and David with his head underwater. She had chosen her husband and stowed her daughter in what she hoped was a safe place. Perhaps she had made a mistake, since she didn't seem to be doing either of them much good.

She thought of her mother-in-law. Oh, how she wished Ruth were here. There was something about the older woman's sound common sense that Sarah longed for. Leaning her head on that willing shoulder and resting for a moment would be pure bliss. In fact, they had discussed Ruth's coming here to stay and having Eden come with her, but Sarah knew how Eden was, and now Ruth was finding out, too. The thought of Eden running unsupervised through Minneapolis gave Sarah a shudder. Better for her to be in Abingdon, where it was safe. Where Joseph would keep her safe as he had promised. She thought of Joseph briefly and still felt the guilt of that betrayal. He was a good man, but he had expected her to be more than she was. He had been unwilling to see her in her weakness. And when she had shown it, he had not been able to forgive it.

Sarah called Eden every day and talked briefly to her and then put David on the telephone. Eden seemed a little flat, a little angry, and answered questions with monosyllables, rarely volunteering any information. Ruth always assured her that Eden was fine and seemed happy most of the time. She would have to leave it at that. Sarah took a few deep breaths and walked back into David's room. He had successfully completed his transfer and was sitting in his power chair, his untouched lunch tray on the table before him. She forced a smile and approached him.

"You made it," she said cheerily, and he turned an equally false face to her. His smile didn't quite reach his eyes.

"I'm getting there. I'll be racing around in no time."

She smiled back, then they lapsed into silence.

"When did Warren say to expect him?" David asked.

"He said his plane would get in around two, and he would come straight from the airport."

David nodded and Sarah could see the tension on his face. Although David's agent had assured him the visit was purely friendly, she knew David felt the pressure of his unfinished manuscript. There was only one chapter left, but now, who could even think about stringing words together when the body was so broken? Besides, she thought of the message of the book: God could heal a wounded heart. It was a book he needed to read right now rather than write.

But then there was the small matter of the advance, already spent, the due date long past, the publication date fast approaching. There had been no pressure from the publisher. Just a gentle question. Will you write again? Or should we remove the book from the schedule? She didn't know what he had answered and hadn't the heart to ask.

"Do you want your computer?" she asked, her voice hesitant.

"No, I don't want it," he said, his tone almost distracted. "Not today."

It was then that the thought came. It was pointed and aimed right at her heart. She thought of another question, different from the one that normally tormented her. And she knew that this one had to do with the fate of her husband's heart rather than his legs.

She knew it was the one she ought to be asking. Not will he walk. Instead, she wondered if he would ever laugh again. It had been that laugh that had drawn her to him. It was so full of life and joy, so full of his heart thrown out upon the world. He hadn't laughed in months. But even this she could not control.

chapter 23

Dispirited, Eden picked up her backpack and slung it over her shoulder. She usually threw her books into her bag, hurried out the door as soon as the bell rang, and was waiting on the bus while most of the other kids were still hanging around. But today she couldn't think of a single reason to hurry. Or yesterday. Or the day before. She wouldn't be getting off at the police department and finding her bike chained to the rack, waiting for her. Her two-way radio wasn't stashed in the bottom of her book bag. Uncle Joseph had taken both of them away. She was on restriction.

"Behavior has consequences, Eden," Grandma had said, patting her on the back, but something about her voice made Eden think Grandma felt just as bad as she did.

"You play, you pay" was all Uncle Joseph said, but he didn't look happy either when he told her she was restricted. *"You're on house arrest until Friday,"* he said.

So there was no reason to hurry home today. She would just shuffle down to the bus and get off on Main Street, where Grandma would be waiting for her. They would walk home together, and Grandma would have to stop at Aunt Vi's, who really wasn't her aunt but acted like one, and the two old ladies would have coffee and cookies, and Eden would have milk and cookies because Grandma thought she was too young to drink coffee. And who knew what was happening without her to keep tabs on things? Why, just anybody might be sneaking into town, and Floyd at the bus station wouldn't know who to watch out for, and now she didn't have Elna to keep her posted about things going on in the Hasty Taste because she'd gone to her daughter's in Bristol to have her surgery. Pastor Hector had been having to run the food bank all by himself, and her notebook was totally empty, and she didn't even feel like writing any more detective stories. It just wasn't fair.

And she totally knew that if she had just told the truth about Grady Adair, she probably wouldn't be in trouble. But something about the panicky look in his eyes when he'd seen Uncle Joseph drive up and asked if he was a policeman had made her shut her mouth tight, and even though they'd asked her about it again, *"Where did you go? Who did you go with?"* she had just said, *"Nowhere"* and *"Nobody,"* and they had said, *"Fine, go to your room."* So that's where she'd been. *Forever.* Staring at the walls and at all the dumb old toys that she didn't want to play with anymore. With nothing to do but homework. She wasn't even allowed to go to the library to use the Internet, so who knew how much e-mail she was missing?

At least at Aunt Vi's she was allowed to watch the television, only she always had it on a stupid kid's show when Eden came in. Eden waited until she and Grandma were busy talking, and then she changed it to *Guiding Light*. It was pretty interesting, actually. Yesterday a girl named Tammy brought this guy named Jonathan to this guy named Coop's party. But Coop turns out to be really mad about it—the party. Anyway, this lady named Ava likes him and is kissing him, but this woman named Lizzie butts in. Then Lizzie pushes Ava into an elevator and locks her inside, but later on in the party Ava escapes and pushes Lizzie's face into the birthday cake. That's when Grandma came in and turned it off. Eden decided to watch again today and find out what happened after that.

The bus finally started, the door closed, and they drove into town. She got off. Grandma was waiting for her, as she'd expected. "Hello, sweetheart! How was your day?"

"Fine."

They started walking. "Do you have much homework?"

"No."

"Would you like me to carry your backpack?"

"No thank you."

"You know, Eden, I was wondering, are there any of the children you'd like to have over next week to play after school? I'd be happy to have them."

"Oh. Um. I don't think so. Thanks."

Grandma patted her on the back, and Eden forced herself to give her a little smile. She kind of felt bad, because she could tell Grandma felt bad. Grandma was always asking her if she'd made any friends yet and if she wanted to have anybody over. Everybody was pretty nice at school, and she knew everybody's name and was sort of friends with this girl named Hayley. They sat together at lunch and everything, but she didn't think she'd invite her home. It just felt too hard to explain everything. Whenever she told people about Dad, they either asked her all kinds of questions she didn't know the answers to, or they looked at her really sad, like they felt sorry for her, and she didn't like that, either. She didn't like to cry, and that always made her feel like she was going to cry. So she just made her rounds after school and wrote in her notebook and stuff, and that was pretty fun. Until now. She would just be glad when it was tomorrow and she could get back to her normal life.

Grandma started talking, telling her all about Plumb Alley Day that was coming up at the end of May and how she was going to be running the dunk tank and Mr. Purvis, the fifth grade teacher, was going to be dunked. That was kind of interesting, but in a boring kind of way. Pretty soon they were at Aunt Vi's.

She was waiting for them on her porch, wearing a red bandana around her hair, old jeans, and a blue shirt that was too big for her, and her clothes had paint all over them. She was an artist, but mostly she just painted pictures of birds and flowers and sheep and stuff like that. Nothing really interesting. Today Aunt Carol Jean was there, too. She wasn't really her aunt, either, but actually it was sort of like having three grandmas. Aunt Carol Jean was short and had blond hair that was white at the roots. She was wearing a pink sweatshirt that said *When Life Hands You Scraps, Make Quilts.* There was a bird sitting on a clothesline with quilts hanging down from it. Aunt Carol Jean was always asking Eden if she wanted to learn to quilt, and she always said, *"No thank you,"* but she was getting pretty bored. Maybe she would try it next time she got on restriction.

"Hello, lovey," Aunt Vi said, and Aunt Carol Jean had to give her a hug, but after a few minutes she escaped to the den with her cookies and milk. Aunt Vi had Mr. Rogers on the television. *Oh, barf.* She was way too old to be watching Mr. Rogers. She was almost twelve. Well, she supposed she could watch for a minute. She sighed and leaned back on the couch. She glanced out the window, but no one was coming up the flagstone walkway. No one would see her watching a kid's show. She leaned back and took a bite of cookie. They were oatmeal, and even though chocolate chip were her favorite, these were pretty good.

The music started. The door opened. Mr. Rogers came in with his umbrella, and though he said, "Hello, neighbor," and looked the same as he had when she was little, Eden could tell right away something was wrong. She frowned. It was raining in the neighborhood. She felt a little bit mad. It wasn't supposed to rain on Mr. Rogers. And there was more stuff wrong, too. In the Neighborhood of Make Believe, Prince Tuesday was afraid his parents were going to get a divorce because they were arguing. Mr. Rogers started explaining that every time parents quarreled, it didn't mean they would get a divorce, but it made her so mad she flipped the station over to *Guiding Light* again.

But it was too late. It had started her thinking, so she couldn't help but keep on thinking, even though the lady named Ava and the lady named Lizzie were fighting again today. She wondered if Dad and Mom would get a divorce now that he was hurt and couldn't walk. They would be coming here in a couple of weeks or months. Nobody would tell her when or what was going on. She was worried about that, too. There were too many things to think about.

And things not to tell.

There were secrets. Stuff she wasn't supposed to know, or ask.

She knew a secret, but she wasn't allowed to talk about it to Grandma or Uncle Joseph. And she thought there was some secret that Uncle Joseph and Grandma knew that they weren't supposed to talk about to her. She didn't know what that one was. But she knew there was something, because Uncle Joseph didn't ever want to talk to her dad or her mom, and Grandma would get upset with him, and then they would start talking, and when they saw her, they would get quiet all of a sudden and put on these really fakey smiles. She didn't know what was going on there, but she would probably find out someday when she had time to ask around. Maybe Vi or Carol Jean would tell her.

The one she wasn't supposed to tell Uncle Joseph or Grandma was that she was adopted. *"Grandma knows,"* Mom had said, *"but it's best just not to talk to either one of them about it. Okay?"* Dad had just looked really sad and said, *"Sarah, is that kind of secrecy necessary?"* Then Mom started getting upset and started to cry, and Dad said, *"Okay, fine, whatever. I just don't think Eden should be carrying that kind of burden,"* and then Mom had said why didn't she go out and play. She had tried to hear the rest from the hall, but they'd gone upstairs to their bedroom and shut the door. So she had never told. She didn't really want to anyway. She didn't like to talk about being adopted. She didn't really know what she thought about it, either. At first she had thought everybody was adopted. Then she understood that was wrong. After that Mom made a really big deal about always saying she was special. How they had picked her out. But at the same time, she was always complaining to Dad how tired she was and how much trouble it was taking care of her. And she wondered why her real mom hadn't wanted her. All the other kids' real moms had kept them. What was wrong with her? She hated it in school when they had to draw their family tree. Mom would tell her whose names to put where, but Eden knew it wasn't real. That wasn't her real family.

She wanted to know who her real mom and dad were, and once she had asked Dad because at least he didn't cry, but he said they didn't really know much about the man and the woman, just that they weren't able to take care of her, so they'd given her to Mom and Dad. And then he'd said, *"Maybe you'd better not ask your mom because . . . you know."* Anyway, he looked sort of sad, so Eden hadn't asked any more. But Dad said maybe someday the time would be right to find out more, and she would know when the time was. Lately Eden had been wondering if now was the time.

She hadn't let herself say it, even to herself, but now the thought just popped up and wouldn't go away. Maybe she could find out who her real mom was. She had started wondering ever since she'd gone to the hospital to see Dad and they'd sent her back here.

That's when she'd figured out they were probably sorry they'd adopted her in the first place.

Ever since then she'd been thinking about her mother more. Her real mother, not Mom. She had thought about her before but not as much. She had even written her a letter, but she didn't know where to send it. She felt bad when she thought about Dad and Mom up there in Minnesota, but then she got kind of mad when she remembered how Mom hadn't wanted her there, so she decided she'd keep the dad she had, but it might be a good idea to get a back-up mom.

After all, her real mom might be anybody. That was the only good thing about it. About not knowing. Her mom might be rich or famous. Her mom might be somebody like a soldier or a general or a spy who knew kickboxing like that girl on the show on TV that Grandma wouldn't let her watch.

Her real mom wouldn't be thin and blond like Mom was. She would have dark hair like Eden and do fun stuff and not sit around and worry all the time. Maybe her real mom was just sort of pretty and kind of looked like her, and maybe she would look at Eden and say someday she might look okay, too. And her real mom would like her and want to be around her. She wouldn't send her away, and she wouldn't sign her up for a bunch of dumb classes just so she wouldn't have her around.

Eden looked around Aunt Vi's den and sighed. Probably her real mom, her birth mother, Mom and Dad called her, was none of those things in real life. IRL. She was probably just a normal person who hadn't wanted her.

She missed Dad. He liked her. He liked to be around her, and she never made him tired. But he was sick, and who knew if he would ever get well. She'd been reading the Bible Dad had given her for her tenth birthday. He used to always buy her a special present on her birthday and take her out to dinner, just the two of them. She blinked and sniffed and remembered. The page edges were gold, and he had written inside *To Eden, my delight*. Dad said that was what her name meant. Delight. And that's why they had named her that.

She got up and went into the hall. Grandma and her friends were still in the kitchen talking. She went out onto the porch and sat down and was just watching a green snake slide under Aunt Vi's big bush when she looked up, and there was Grady Adair, riding an old rusted bike. He rode right up to Aunt Vi's gate and stopped.

"Where you been at?" he asked, looking like he didn't care.

She looked back over her shoulder. Nobody inside was paying any attention to her. She walked over toward the gate. "In my room mostly. You got me in trouble, and I'm on restriction."

"How'd I get you into trouble?" He frowned and looked mad.

"'Cause you acted so lame and ran away when my uncle came, and then I was afraid I'd get you in trouble, so I didn't tell where I was, and so then I got on restriction."

"Oh." He lowered his eyes and went back to kicking the ground, even while he balanced on the seat of the bicycle.

Eden thought about asking him what he'd done that he had to run off like that, but she was going to run the plates on his dad's truck as soon as she got back to work. She'd made a note in her notebook. If he was a criminal, he'd probably only lie anyhow.

"So when do you get off?" he asked, finally looking back up at her.

"Tomorrow."

"Huh." He grunted like he couldn't care less.

Then why'd you ask? she almost said, but instead she just shook her head. "I gotta go back inside, or they'll come looking for me."

"Well," he said, like he was doing her a big favor or something, "maybe tomorrow we could ride our bikes or something."

"After school?"

"I don't go to school."

"You're s'posed to."

"Well, I don't."

"Is that why you run away from the police?"

"Do you want to ride bikes or not?" His blue eyes got squinty, and he glared at her.

"I got things to do."

"Like what?"

"I've got to take the new Wanted posters to the bus station and show them around. I've got to find out who took Elna's place at the Hasty Taste. I've got to go see Pastor Hector and find out what's happening, and there's a horse I might need to ride."

He squinted up his eyes again. "Maybe I could help you."

"I don't see how you could be much help." But then Grady

Adair lowered his eyes again and looked ashamed, and Eden was ashamed she'd said that.

"Well, I guess you could come along," she said.

He lifted his chin and acted like he didn't care, but she could tell he was happy.

"I'll meet you where we were before."

"We ain't there no more."

"Where are you?"

"I'm not supposed to tell."

She gave him a look. "Are we friends or aren't we?" she said, a frown heavy on her face.

He sighed and paused. "Over by that fellow Miller's pond."

"I know that old place. My dad used to take me fishing there."

"Don't come there. My pa will get mad if I told you."

"Well, where then?"

"You just go on. I'll find you." And then he hopped on his bike and rode off.

Eden watched him go, wondering if he might know some things after all.

After supper Uncle Joseph let her off restriction. "Here's the deal," he said. "From now on you come straight home after school and do your homework."

"Straight home!" She felt panicky. She knew how that worked. Once she got home, she would never get out. Grandma would find things for her to do, and pretty soon it would be dinnertime, and then she would have to help with the dishes, and then Dad and Mom would call, and there would be no time left to do her rounds or make her calls. "Why?"

Uncle Joseph gave her a Duh! look. Grandma shook her head a little bit and looked sad.

Eden felt kind of bad that Grandma's feelings might be hurt, but she couldn't stand the thought of being cooped up here every day.

An idea came out of desperation. "What if I go straight to the library? I could check in with Miss Branch and do my homework there, and you could ask her, and she could rat me out if I mess around or leave or anything. I could stay an hour or even longer," she vowed. "Please? Please?" She totally couldn't stand it if Uncle Joseph said no. He was staring at her face, and all of a sudden he just smiled, and she breathed out a sigh of relief. "Oh, thank you, thank you, thank you." She got up and started clearing off the table.

"Well, for pity's sake," Grandma said to Uncle Joseph. "I had no idea it was such a trial being here with me."

"Oh, come on now, Ma, you know it's nothing personal," he said.

Eden had a flash of remorse, but it left pretty quickly. By the time she had finished scraping the plates and loading the dishwasher, in fact.

chapter 24

By Friday Miranda had been in Abingdon for nearly two weeks, and she was beginning to think the quest for a job was as impossible as that for her child. Around two she called it quits and went to the library. She had come here to find someone. Perhaps she was wasting her time looking for employment. She spent the rest of the afternoon on the Internet and in the stacks, searching on "finding people" and surrounded by every book she could find on the topic, including: *You Can Find Anybody! Public Records Online, Get the Facts on Anyone* and *Check It Out! A Top Investigator Shows You How to Find Out Practically Anything About Anybody.*

She Googled every combination of words she could think of that had anything to do with searching or finding, skip trace, and private investigation. It was all very interesting, but so far there was nothing that could help you find someone you didn't know the first thing about. Almost every book assumed you were starting your search with a full name, social security number, or at least a handful of facts about habits and history. She had nothing. No name, occupation, address, social security number. She had nothing. Nothing, and suddenly the impossibility of the whole thing hit her. She needed a psychic, not a detective.

She went outside for a breath of air and wondered again why she was here. If doors were supposed to open and she was in the right place, someone had forgotten to send the memo ahead of her.

A few kids walked past her and entered the library. They were dragging backpacks and laughing. A few more followed. The elementary school must have just gotten out. They kept coming for a few minutes in a pretty steady stream. Ten or twelve. Tall and short and in between. Cute and homely, fat and thin, boys and girls, and suddenly the hopelessness of it all overwhelmed her. Why, in just this library right this minute there were too many possibilities to guess at. In the elementary school alone were probably a hundred or so children the right age, and she hadn't even considered private school kids or home-schooled kids in the town. Or the ones that had moved away. She stared, letting her eyes go out of focus, and realized it was time she made peace with the empty aching socket that went right down to her bones. She would never find that child.

She went back inside and started stacking her books. She sniffed and wiped at her eyes. Two girls sitting at the table opposite her stared and looked at her curiously. It seemed like all she did now was cry. The two girls said something to each other and giggled, then turned their attention toward the door. A younger girl came in and looked for a seat. She saw the one across from Miranda. Her table was the only one with no kids. The girl looked around for a minute, then came toward her and spoke.

"Is it okay if I sit here?"

"Sure," Miranda said. "I'm going to be leaving in a few minutes, and you can have it to yourself."

The girl flumped down and hoisted her backpack onto the table.

"*Neighhhh!*" One of the girls at the other table made horse noises. Miranda looked up with a frown. They were giggling and pointing at the girl who had just sat down, and Miranda saw why.

The smaller girl was wearing a shirt with horse heads all over it. She didn't react to the taunting; instead, she unzipped her back-pack, took out a notebook, and began writing furiously. They neighed again. She glanced toward them with scorn, as if they were the ones who had suddenly grown three heads.

"Whatever," said the blonde, probably a future cheerleader.

The girl with the horse shirt turned around toward the Bar-bies and made an L in front of her forehead, then swiveled back around and went back to her writing.

Miranda grinned. She took a closer look at the upstart. She was a short, compact girl, probably about ten or eleven. She had freckles on her face and dark hair that was a little wild. Her eyes were slate blue. Miranda started looking for something familiar in the face or mannerisms, knowing she was being ridiculous but playing her game anyway. The girl had neat, compact hands, and the ends of her fingernails tipped slightly up, just like her own. And a million other people's, she supposed. She searched the face and didn't see much resemblance to herself. She tried to remem-ber Danny Loomis. He'd had freckles. That was something. His eyes had been blue, hadn't they? She couldn't remember. She shook her head, and the hopelessness came over her again. She was being silly. She took out a tissue and blew her nose.

The girl looked up. "You all right?" she asked.

"Me?"

The girl nodded.

Miranda felt touched and almost teared up again. Instead she nodded vigorously. "Yeah. I'm all right. Thanks."

The girl cocked an eyebrow, as if she didn't quite believe her, but went back to her notebook.

"Are you all right?" Miranda asked the girl.

"Who, me?" She looked surprised.

Miranda grinned. She nodded. "They were pretty snotty."

"Oh." She shrugged. "That's just the popular girls." As if nothing else could realistically be expected.

Smart kid. She'd do all right in junior high.

"You from around here?" the girl asked her, and Miranda shook her head.

"Me neither," she said. "I'm staying with my grandma."

Miranda felt a disappointing lurch. She supposed she had been hoping, and she asked herself if she would ever be able to talk to a strange child without calculating his or her age and wondering.

"Have you ever lived here?" Miranda asked, knowing she was being stupid, but she felt compelled to know.

"Nope."

"Has your grandmother always lived here?" The last hope, and she knew she was being ridiculous. She wondered if she would feel compelled to cross-examine every eleven-year-old in Abingdon.

"Nope," the girl said. "She used to live somewhere else. She moved to town about"—her eyes cast upward in thought—"ten years ago." She paused and gave Miranda an evaluating look. "You ask a lot of questions."

Miranda blushed. If she wasn't careful Joe Policeman would come after her again. "Sorry," she said, "but how else is a person supposed to find out things?"

The girl seemed to consider this for a moment, then nodded, as if it made sense to her.

Obviously, it was her turn to offer some information. "My name's Miranda," she said.

"Mine's Eden."

"Eden. That's a pretty name."

She shrugged. "I guess."

"What grade are you in?"

"Fifth."

"Do you like it?"

Eden shrugged. "It's better than my old school," she said. "We had to wear uniforms there."

Miranda made a face. "I've never been big on uniforms. It seems like deciding what to wear is a pretty basic part of being a person, if you know what I mean."

"I know exactly what you mean," the girl said and gave a satisfied little nod, as if Miranda had validated something important. It seemed to inspire a disclosure. "This is my favorite shirt," she said, leaning forward confidentially. She had a look of modest pride.

Miranda looked it over. It was a fifties vintage print but probably new. It had been freshly washed and ironed stiff, but she could see a tiny tear just below the elbow that had been carefully mended.

"It's a great shirt." She admired it without reservation. "It would be my favorite, too."

"I tore it, but it's okay now."

"You can barely tell," Miranda agreed. "Did you sew it up yourself?"

Eden shook her head. "Grandma," she said.

Miranda nodded but noticed she hadn't said Mom had mended it, as she'd expected. She wondered what circumstances had brought the girl here, but she wasn't going to ask.

"My mom and dad are at a hospital up in Minnesota. My dad got in a car wreck."

"Oh. I'm sorry."

"He got hurt pretty bad."

"How bad?"

"He might be in a wheelchair."

Miranda blew out her breath and felt a swell of pity. "That must be really hard for him. For all of you."

Eden blinked. "But he's going to be all right."

"Oh, sure. Sure."

Eden seemed to have reached her tolerance for conversation. She opened up her backpack and took out a two-way radio. "I'll be right back," she said. "Would you watch my stuff so those losers don't mess with it?"

"Be happy to," Miranda said and shot a stern look over at the snotty girls just in case they were thinking about it. Eden disappeared for a few minutes and then returned. Miranda got a glimpse of the radio as she put it in her backpack. It looked authentic and expensive. She wondered why Grandma didn't just buy Eden a cell phone.

"That's a pretty cool radio," she said.

Eden nodded and didn't say more. She took out a pencil and started doing math problems. She erased. Chewed the pencil, Twirled the part of her bangs that didn't lie straight. Scribbled something down on the worksheet and erased again. Miranda smiled, then went back to the book she was perusing on how to find anyone anywhere. They both worked in silence for fifteen minutes or so.

"You looking for somebody?" Eden's voice startled her out of her concentration. Apparently she was switching subjects. She shut her math book and took the social studies book out of her backpack.

Miranda nodded.

"Who?"

Her heart sank at being asked that question straight out, even by a child. And almost without thought, she answered, picking a name out of the blue, and it was only after she'd spoken it that she realized how right it was that she start her search with her mother. Wasn't Noreen the key to the entire mystery? She realized then that if she understood Noreen, perhaps then, and only then, would she have a clue as to what her mother had done with her baby. Once she understood the why, perhaps the what would be the logical next step.

"I'm researching my mom's life," she said. "She just died, and I realized I didn't really know much about her."

Eden nodded soberly. "Maybe I could help you," she offered. "I could look your mom up on the computer at my uncle's office."

Miranda smiled. That was cute. And sweet. "Thanks," she said. "If my leads dry up, I might take you up on that."

Eden nodded again, then went back to her homework. She scribbled and chewed for another fifteen minutes or so, then shut her books with a decisive thunk. She reloaded her backpack, stood up, and slung it over her shoulder. "Well," she said, "I gotta go. I've got things to do."

Miranda smiled. She wondered what kind of errands Eden's day included. She would bet they were interesting and a lot more fun than what the two girls at the table across from them would be doing. She could tell from their brief meeting that Eden had personality and spunk. "It was nice to meet you, Eden," she said. "Maybe we'll run across each other again."

"Nice to meet you, too," she answered.

Miranda returned the reference item to the desk and crossed the room to reshelve the other books. She glanced outside the window and saw Eden at the bike rack. She unlocked her bike, got on, and sailed down the street, pedaling furiously for a minute before balancing with her arms. Miranda smiled as she disappeared from sight. What a character. She hoped they did meet again.

chapter 25

D avid felt ground down, broken, and above all else, weary. He knew it was time to go home, but somehow he couldn't muster up the strength. The thought of going to his mother's was bad enough; the thought of going back to Fairfax with his wife and daughter seemed completely beyond him. He was just so tired. Ironic, for someone who hadn't moved for the last six months.

Sarah looked at him hopefully. She was wanting something from him, and it seemed that exact dynamic summed up the history of their relationship.

I don't know what to do with Eden, David. Please tell me.

I don't know what to do with my life, David. Could you tell me?

I don't want to marry your brother, David. Could you help me?

Was he angry? he asked himself brutally. The answer came back a weary no. He wasn't angry. He was—and there it was again. He was tired.

"What shall I tell her?" Sarah spoke now, her hand on the telephone, which she would pick up in a few seconds and use to call their daughter.

Whatever you like, he wanted to say. He did not, of course. He did what he always did. He turned patient eyes on his wife and loved her. All of her, including the hesitation and doubt, but for just a moment he had doubts of his own. Had he really been helping her all these years by making decisions for her? She had let him. No, had urged him. There had been only one decision about which she had stood firm. They must not tell Joseph about Eden. He wondered now why he had let her have her way in this, when it would have been within his power to dissuade her.

But there was still this decision to make now. He sighed. Of course it was obvious what Sarah should tell her. Eden could not come here. They both knew that. Their days were confined to the hospital, and Eden was a girl who needed to roam free. It would be like corralling a wild pony in the basement. But he also knew why Sarah asked him. If he said the words, then it was not her fault. She could avoid the guilt of making a choice.

"Tell her she needs to be patient for a little while longer," he said. "Tell her I love her. I want to be with her. I just need a little more time to recover."

He looked down at his emaciated body, his useless legs. He tried to remember what they had looked like before, but it was as if this broken body was the only one he had ever known. This was who he was now. Wholeness was something that existed only in his dreams.

"Could you tell her?" Sarah's voice, hesitant, tentative.

He nodded. Sarah passed the phone to him. He dialed.

Eden answered. She was expecting their call tonight, the same time it always came. But tonight she sounded more eager than usual.

"Hi, Dad!"

"Hi, baby. How are you tonight?"

"Good. Uncle Joseph let me off restriction today. And there's some people that are gonna let me ride their daughter's horse if it's okay with you."

"What do Grandma and Uncle Joseph say?"

"Grandma says I need to wear a helmet. Uncle Joseph said I

shouldn't have asked Grandma. Next time ask him first."

David smiled. It felt odd to do so. "Uncle Joseph is right," he said. It had always given him quiet joy that his brother loved his child. It was a gesture, however small, a thin thread of hope across a wide chasm.

"When are you coming to get me, Dad?"

He sighed. He silently prayed. "Not quite yet, Eden."

"I thought you were coming in a week or two."

"No. I'm afraid not, sweetheart."

She was silent.

"When?"

"Maybe by the end of the summer."

"Why-y?" A slight, quiet wail. Not a petulant whine, but a genuine cry of grief.

What should he say? That he needed two more surgeries to close wounds in his abdomen and graft skin over them? That he was still learning to move himself from his bed to his chair? That he needed to learn to change his own ostomy bags? To move around town in his power chair? To drive a car and ride an elevator? To do the things a normal three-year-old could do?

"I'm not quite well yet, Eden. There were a lot of things broken and hurt."

She was silent now, probably remembering the horrific sight of him, and he wondered if it had been right to bring her here, yet he couldn't judge his brother's decision. Joseph loved her. He had done what he thought best for her.

"Can I come there, then?"

There it was, the question Sarah couldn't bear, and it skidded into his own heart and tore open another wound as it hit.

"Oh, baby, I wish you could."

"Why can't I?" He could hear tears in her voice now.

"There's nothing to do here, Eden. You'd be cooped up in the hospital room all day long every day."

"I could help you. Please!"

"No, honey. I'm sorry. I wish you could."

A clunk. Silence. After a moment his mother's voice came on the line. "Hello, sweetheart."

"Hi, Mom. I'm afraid we've upset Eden."

"I heard some of her end, David." Her voice was low.

"I'm so sorry. I wish things were different." He took a deep breath.

"You mustn't worry about this now, David," his mother said in her calm way. "Of course she can't come there. You just concentrate on getting well. She's doing fine here. Really. She's very happy."

"Thanks, Mom."

"I love you, David."

"I love you, too."

He hung up the phone.

Sarah was chewing on her fingernails. "How did she take it?"

The weariness returned. "About like you'd expect."

Silence. Tears. Then the doubt he expected. A hesitant question. "Do you think we did the right thing?"

He could have gotten angry if he'd had the energy. "Yes."

He turned his eyes toward the television and turned on the sound. After a moment Sarah left the room.

Eden went into the closet of her room. She always used to hide here when she was a little girl. She went there today because she didn't want Grandma to hear her cry. She wasn't sure why, but having Mom and Dad not want her would seem even worse if Grandma felt all sorry for her. And Grandma would tell her, *Oh, they love you, Eden, they really want you,* but they didn't. And Eden knew it. Grandma probably knew it, too. They were probably sorry they'd adopted her. She grabbed the extra quilt from the shelf, threw it on the floor, and piled herself onto it. And cried.

She cried for quite a while. When she heard Grandma open

the bedroom door and walk toward the door of the closet, she quit crying and held her breath. She tried to be quiet, but finally she let out her breath and took another one in, but it was *uh-uh-uh-uh* sounding, and then she kind of coughed and cried again. She heard the doorknob turn and held her breath again; then she heard Grandma walk away and the bedroom door close softly. So she let her breath out and cried some more, and finally she was too tired to cry. She felt like a party balloon she found one time behind the couch, all wrinkly and saggy. She just rested her head on the blanket and wished she had Wallace Lovelace, a stuffed sock monkey she used to have. But she thought he was up in Grandma's attic. Grandma had made him, and even though Eden knew she was too old for stuffed animals, she wished she had something to hug, but she didn't, so she opened her eyes and looked into the dark, and she could see colors against the black. Little blots of pink and green and purple, and when she looked down, she could see a thin line of light at the bottom of the door.

She thought about Dad. And it bothered her that she could barely remember his face. She tried to remember something about him, and she saw his hands teaching her how to drive. She was sitting on his lap and looking out and aiming the little circle on the hood of Grandpa's big car for the middle of the dirt road. Dad's hands were resting lightly on top of hers, but she was driving, and she could feel the car moving wherever she turned it. Then he had taken away his hands, and she had almost gone into the ditch, but she had called out, *"Dad!!"* and he had laughed and put his hands back over hers and made a tiny little move of the wheel, and things had been all right. She had driven all the way to the highway, and then Dad turned the car around, and she drove all the way back. Grandma had smiled and shaken her head; Mom had shaken her head and hadn't smiled. But Dad had just winked at Eden, and they had gone driving every day of their visit, and on the last day Dad hadn't put his hands over hers at all. She had done it all herself, and she had said, *"What about the pedals?"* and he said, *"Maybe next year when your legs get longer."*

She thought about Dad's face, and she could see it perfectly now. He had lots of lines on his face, but they were happy lines and made him look kind, and when he smiled they creased into a smile, too. Dad said the lines came from too many years in the sun, and then Mom started talking about skin cancer. But Dad winked at Eden and said, *"Sarah, you worry too much."* He had brown eyes, and his hair was longer than Uncle Joseph's. It brushed his shoulders. Suddenly she wanted very much to see a picture of her dad. She knew there were some downstairs in the photo albums, but then Grandma would see her and would try to get her to play cribbage, and she didn't want to talk to anybody right now. She knew there were some pictures upstairs in Grandma's attic. And she thought Wallace Lovelace was up there, too. She stood up and wiped her eyes and nose on the sleeve of her shirt. Not her favorite horse shirt, because she would never wipe her nose on that, but just a shirt that she wore today because her horse shirt was in the wash.

She stood up and pulled the rope that brought the attic ladder down. She was really glad the ladder was in her closet. The stairs came down and she climbed onto them. They were a little rickety, but it was okay. She thought for a minute, then came back down and opened the door and found her backpack and took out her flashlight, then went into the closet again and closed the door behind her. Somehow she didn't think Grandma would like it if she went up into the attic. She climbed up the stairs, and when she got to the top she turned on the flashlight. Everything was just the way she remembered it from when she had come up here last Christmas to help Grandma put away the Christmas decorations. She had wanted to look around then, but Grandma had said, *"Let's go make some cookies, Eden,"* so she had come down. And then Grandma said, *"There's nothing up there that's fun. Just a bunch of old papers and things,"* but Eden knew there were some pictures, because she'd seen a photo album in a box in the corner when she was putting away the Christmas lights. That's where she headed now.

She looked around slowly. There were piles of things, and it wasn't very neat. There were model airplanes that Grandma said had belonged to Uncle Joseph hanging from the ceiling in the corner. There were two big boxes of baseball cards, and Grandma said that someday she could bring them down and see if they were worth any money. There were skates and skateboards and baseball bats and gloves and a hockey mask and Uncle Joseph's baseball trophies. And his football trophies and his basketball trophies. One time she had asked Dad why he didn't have any trophies, and he had just laughed and said Uncle Joseph had gotten all of the talent in the family, but then he looked sort of sad like he always did whenever she asked about Uncle Joseph, so she hadn't asked anything else.

She sat down on the floor in front of the box she was looking for. There was a big pile of school papers on top. They were her dad's, and she read his name, David Williams, written in printing on some and in cursive on others. They always had checks or happy faces or stars or As on them. She set them aside and pushed past a bunch of report cards, and finally she found what she was looking for underneath a bunch of old bank papers and stuff.

She knew the pictures were there because she had seen Grandma putting them away, carrying them up from downstairs when she had come to stay. Grandma had tucked a whole photo album up here, and when Eden asked what it was, Grandma had just said some old pictures of the family.

She reached down now and took out the album and flipped it open, expecting to see her dad, but instead, there was her mom. She sighed. Mom was so pretty. Eden would never look like Mom. Mom had long, silky blond hair, not curly and stupid like hers. And her skin was so smooth and golden, not freckled like Eden's. She looked at the next picture and there was Mom again. With Uncle Joseph.

She frowned. Mom and Uncle Joseph were hugging each other. The next one was bad, too. Mom was standing beside Uncle Joseph, and she was wearing a pink dress and had a flower on her wrist and Uncle Joseph was wearing a suit. But that wasn't the worst of it. Their arms were around each other, and Mom's head was up against Uncle Joseph's chest. Eden looked at their faces, and they both were smiling really happy-like, and she felt a little sick to her stomach. She glanced through the rest of the album. They were all of Mom and Uncle Joseph. She put the album back in the box and started down the stairs. She was sorry she'd come up here. At the last minute she remembered Wallace Lovelace, but she didn't want to take any more time to find him.

She climbed down and shoved the ladder back up into the attic. Then she just went and climbed into bed and pulled the covers up over her head, but inside she felt lonely and scared. It felt like there was a big wind blowing, and the house was going to fall down. And nobody could help her, because who could she trust? After a few minutes she got hot under the covers, so she went to the window and opened it up and looked outside. The air was cool and it was dark, but she could still see because there was a bright moon, and the branches of the big tree still brushed the window. She wished she had someone to talk to, but she couldn't think of anybody. Suddenly she remembered someone, so very quietly she went back to the bed and plumped up the covers, so it would look like someone was in there, and found an old doll with brown hair and made it so the edge of its curls stuck out from the edge of the bedspread. She repacked her backpack, went to the window, and climbed out onto the tree branch. It wasn't quite big enough to hold her, and it swooped down a little at first, but then she was able to climb down onto a thicker one below it, and she kept moving to lower branches until she could drop to the ground.

She pressed the button on her night ops watch, and the light came on. Eight o'clock. Not too late to go visiting. Quietly she took her bike from the garage, and in a few minutes she was pedaling down Greer Creek Road, heading for the Millers' pond.

chapter 26

E den rode through town, then into the dark countryside and
felt a little scared. She hadn't quite realized how dark it
would be out here. There were no streetlights, of course, but she
had the little searchlight on the front of her bike. She trained it
on the road in front of her, but she still had to concentrate to
keep from running into the ditch. A few cars swerved over to give
her room as they passed her, and one person honked. She hoped
nobody told Uncle Joseph. He had ways of finding out everything. She felt cold and angry when she thought of Uncle Joseph
and Mom. Why did everyone lie to her? She was relieved when
she came to the turnoff for the Millers' place. It was gravel, and
she had to pay attention so she didn't slide. She couldn't do that
and think about the other thing, too.

The road wound around for a while before it arrived at the
pond. She couldn't see the pond from here, just a cow pasture on
one side and woods on the other. She didn't see any cows. There
were a few dark shapes that she supposed might have been cows.
Or something else. She looked quickly to the other side, but it
looked dark and scary in the thicket of trees, and she was beginning to wonder if she should have come. She passed the Millers'

house. It was dark and closed up. She happened to know for a fact that they had gone to Phoenix to see their son and wouldn't be back until the first of June. She got a funny feeling then. She didn't really know Grady or his father, and for just a second she thought about turning around and going back to Grandma's.

But as she came around the corner, she saw the trailer parked by the side of the pond. The front door was open, and golden light spilled out of the windows. Someone had made a fire on the ground in front of the trailer, and Grady and his dad were sitting there in folding chairs.

She got off her bike and set it down, then walked the rest of the way down to the trailer.

"Well, well, well," Grady's dad said. "It's the lovely Miss Eden. To what do we owe this honor?"

"I just thought I'd come and see where y'all lived."

Grady eyed her with puzzlement. Mr. Adair just smiled and then stood up and said, "Please, sit down," and went inside to get another folding chair.

"What's the matter with you?" Grady asked when his father had gone inside the trailer.

"What do you mean, what's the matter with me?"

"You look like you been crying. Your eyes is all swollen up, and your nose is red."

Eden sniffed her nose and cleared her throat. "Nothing's wrong with me. I just felt like taking a ride. That's all."

Grady's dad came back just then and unfolded the chair and sat down. "Eden, could I offer you some refreshment? A Coca-Cola or 7-Up perhaps?"

"I wouldn't turn down a Coca-Cola," she said with dignity. She was a little parched from all that crying and from the long ride.

"I'll be right back with it." He went inside again and brought her back a can of Coke, and she popped the top and drank some. It felt good going down, and the sweetness made her feel a little better.

"So Grady here tells me you're not from around these parts. That you live with your grandmother."

"That's right," she said and took another drink and tried not to slurp or drink so fast that she'd burp.

"Where do you hail from originally?"

"Fairfax," she said. "Up by Washington, D.C."

"I'm familiar with it," he said with a nod. "A beautiful place. My current business seldom brings me that far north, but I have enjoyed it in my youth."

Mr. Adair was funny. Different, but she liked him. "What kind of business are you in?" she asked and took another sip.

Grady ducked his head. Mr. Adair smiled. "I'm in the people business, Eden. Sometimes I sell goods, sometimes services, but what it all boils down to is people. That's what I always say."

Eden thought that didn't really answer her question, and she was getting ready to ask another when Grady reminded her why she'd come. "When's your folks coming?" he asked. "I thought you was going home soon."

"Were, son, were," Mr. Adair said with a gentle smile.

"Yes, sir." Grady ducked his head again.

"They're not coming," she said. The words came out dull and flat, and her tone made Mr. Adair and Grady both look at her. This time Eden ducked her head. She dug her tennis shoe around in the dirt and made some scuffs.

"Not ever?" Grady asked.

She shrugged. "My dad said he needed some more time to get well."

"Your father isn't well?" Mr. Adair asked.

Eden shook her head. "He got in a car accident. My mom's with him in Minnesota. I've been here since Christmas."

"Umm." Mr. Adair shook his head sympathetically.

"My mom left," Grady said, looking down at his shoes and then flicking his eyes up at her.

Mr. Adair said nothing. She glanced at him to see if he was angry with Grady, but he just looked sort of sad. And older. The fire cracked and popped, and a little meteor of sparks showered up and rained down, dissolving into darkness again. Eden didn't say anything, either, but she felt a little better somehow. Grady and Mr. Adair both knew how it felt to have somebody not want you around. She felt comforted.

They sat there in silence for a few minutes with the fire popping. Then Grady said, "Why don't we roast some marshmallows," and he went inside to get them. Mr. Adair helped her find some sticks, and he sharpened the ends with his pocketknife. Grady came back with the bag, and they speared them onto the sticks and roasted them. Eden ate the brown outside first, liking the way it crunched and then collapsed. Then she licked the soft middle, and finally she ate the very center.

They were spearing another marshmallow each when Eden heard a car coming down the gravel road toward them. She tensed, wondering if Uncle Joseph or Grandma had found her. She glanced toward Grady and his dad, and oddly enough, they were both looking worried, too. Mr. Adair stood up, but when the white van came around the corner, he relaxed. She looked at Grady's face, and it lost the pinched, scared look.

"That's my dad's business partner," he said. "Mikey."

"Don't bore our guest with things she's not interested in, son," Mr. Adair said.

Eden almost said she was interested and wished she had her notebook to prove it, but she remembered she'd left it at Grandma's on her bedside table.

The man named Mikey parked the van and got out. *White male, midthirties, approximately five-feet-ten-inches tall, stocky build with light brown hair and a mustache.* He looked over toward Eden and Grady and started to say something, but Mr. Adair had gotten up to meet him, which was too bad, because it meant Eden couldn't hear what they were saying. They stood a little ways away. Mikey started talking first. Mr. Adair nodded a few times, but he didn't look very happy. Mikey handed him an envelope, and Mr. Adair took it. Mr. Adair said something, then shook his head. Mikey smiled sort of like the mean girls at school did, and then pointed over toward her and Grady. Mr. Adair looked mad and said something else. Mr. Adair turned around and walked away then, and Mikey smiled again and got into the van. "I'll see you tomorrow, Johnny," he hollered out and waved at her and Grady. Eden sniffed and turned away. She didn't like him. She didn't know why, she just didn't, and just on a hunch she looked back and made a note of the license plate. She was running it over in her mind to memorize it when Mr. Adair sat down again. He looked sad, so Eden thought she'd better leave.

She checked the time on her night ops watch. She had tried not to think about Grandma and Uncle Joseph, but she knew she couldn't put it off forever.

"I'd better go home now," she said.

Mr. Adair was still frowning, but he stopped and looked at her when she spoke. "I'll drive you," he said. "You can put your bike in the back of the truck."

But Eden shook her head so hard her hair got in her eyes and stuck to the marshmallow around her mouth. "No," she said. "I'll be fine."

Mr. Adair looked at her for a minute, then nodded. "Grady, get your bike and see Eden home."

Grady nodded and flew to his bike. The two of them walked to the end of the graveled road; then Grady went first and she went after.

Miranda stayed in the library until it closed at nine. After she had named the object of her search to her new acquaintance, Eden, she wondered why she had been so slow to think of the obvious. To understand what Noreen had done with her child and why, she needed to understand Noreen. The key wasn't in trying to guess at some random spot in the universe and go there to find her baby. The only way Noreen's decision would make sense would be when Miranda understood the one who had made it.

Her mother's life held the clues that would lead to the baby. Miranda just knew it. The only hint she had was what Aunt Bobbie had said. Mama had put the baby with someone she trusted. To know who she trusted, Miranda would need to understand her wounds. When she knew the wounds, she would understand the medicine needed. When she knew who had administered it, then she would know the truth. She marveled. She shook her head at the direction her search was leading. Back over ground she had been told to ignore, into caves she had been warned away from. She had to admit she had been perfectly happy to leave them unexplored. But now she knew that the only way out was to go further in. All this time she'd been looking for her baby. She should have been searching for her mother.

She pulled out another stack of reference books, and the research was much simpler now that she had a definite person to search for. She could see very quickly that it would begin by getting her mother's vital records. Birth certificate, death certificate, marriage license. She tried to remember. Where had they been when they married? Mother had come from either Virginia or West Virginia. She wasn't sure which. An Internet search revealed that the Virginia and West Virginia Departments of Vital Statistics would provide her with copies of all the documents for a fee. However, she didn't know everything she needed to fill out the application. A phone call to Aunt Bobbie was in order. Perhaps now that Mama was gone and Aunt Bobbie had given her the baby's picture, details of their early life would be a little more forthcoming.

She stood up and stretched, returned the books to the shelves, and left the library just as the staff were turning out the lights. The night was cool and cloudless, the moon full. It was beautiful. She could hear crickets and frogs, and a gentle breeze shushed the trees. She got in Mr. Cooper's car and rolled down the window, letting the cool air blow on her face as she drove. She headed toward the motel, and after a moment she passed two kids on bikes coming toward her on a side road. One of them was Eden. Behind her was a boy.

"Hey, Eden," she called.

"Oh, hi," Eden answered, as casually as if she rode her bike on dark roads every day of the week.

"What are you guys doing out here?"

The boy looked alarmed, Eden more inconvenienced.

"She's okay," Eden said to the boy, turning halfway around. The boy still looked unconvinced.

Miranda had to smile. He was a beanpole, and although it was dark, she could tell he had red hair and freckles. He reminded her of Opie on *Andy Griffith*.

"What arc you two doing out here so late?" she repeated.

"He was just riding me home," Eden said, and it was not lost on Miranda that she hadn't answered the question.

"Get in and I'll drive you," she said.

Eden looked back at the boy and shrugged. "Okay," she said.

Miranda put the car in park and got out to open the trunk. She looked up and the boy had disappeared. "Wow, that was quick," she said.

"He's like that," Eden said matter-of-factly. "A little bit shy."

They got the bike situated, Eden got in and buckled her belt, and Miranda was just pulling out onto the road again when she saw flashing lights behind her. "Oh no," she said. "It couldn't be!"

But it was. The same unmarked cop car that had pulled her over a few weeks ago was behind her now.

Eden looked just as alarmed as she felt. In fact, she ducked down as if she expected a hail of bullets.

"This jerk of a cop has been harassing me ever since I got to town." Just as the words left Miranda's mouth, the lights went on, quickly followed by a whoop of the siren.

She exhaled noisily and pulled over to the side of the road.

"Can you get out and talk to him?" Eden asked.

Miranda frowned and was just getting ready to ask why Eden

didn't want to encounter the police when a shadow loomed in front of the window. His face peered in again. His expression began as incredulous and quickly sobered into grim, barely disguised anger.

"Get out of the car, Eden."

"What next? Are you going to tell her to keep her hands where you can see them?" Miranda burst out. "She's a kid, for crying out loud, not a perp. And I'm not kidnapping her. I'm giving her a ride home."

The policeman gave Miranda a withering glare. "Do what I said," he told Eden.

She started to open the door, but Miranda stopped her, putting a hand on her arm.

"Hold on just a minute," she said. "Who do you think you are? You don't have any right to tell this child to get out of my car."

"I don't have to explain myself to you," he said, and the glare became deeper.

"I think you do," she said. "You're forcibly taking this child, and she doesn't want to go with you."

"It's okay," Eden said, looking dismayed at the turn of events.

"No. It's not okay." Miranda turned toward the policeman again. "I'm a private citizen doing nothing unlawful."

"Except transporting a minor, who is away from home without permission, and, I suspect, driving without insurance. May I see your driver's license and proof of insurance?"

Miranda shook her head and fumed. "I'm being harassed," she said. "And I still want an explanation."

"Eden!" His voice was raised. "Step out of the car right now."

She opened the door and got out. "I'm sorry, Uncle Joseph," she said.

Miranda closed her eyes. *Uncle Joseph.* Well, that was great. Just great.

"Your driver's license and insurance card?" he repeated.

She handed him her license and waited while he wrote out

another ticket. City Hall was closed, so at least she wouldn't have him following her back to town.

She signed the ticket and threw her copy on the seat beside her.

"Miranda, can I get my bike?" Eden asked in a small voice.

"Sure," she said and got out and opened the trunk.

Policeman Joseph grabbed it and had it stowed in the back of his car before she could move to do it herself. Eden got into the passenger side of the unmarked car looking unhappy. Uncle Joseph followed Miranda back as she got back into Mr. Cooper's Caddy.

"What are you doing here?" he asked quietly. His eyes were cold, his expression grim.

She gave him what she hoped was an equally cold glare. "That's none of your business."

He eyed her, and she wondered if he would arrest her on the spot. He seemed to be thinking the same thing. "I need to get her home. Her grandmother is worried sick. Otherwise I'd arrest you."

"On what charge?" Her tone was outraged, her voice raised. Eden looked very unhappy.

"Aiding in the delinquency of a minor, for starters."

"Oh, that's absolutely ridiculous, and you know it. I saw her and a boy riding in the dark and offered to drive her home. That's all. You can ask at the library. I've been there—alone—all evening."

He lost the know-it-all look and glanced back at Eden. When he looked back at Miranda, his expression still wasn't friendly, but at least she didn't think she'd be tossed into the pokey tonight.

"If I find you driving that car again without insurance, I'll have it impounded."

Miranda didn't answer. Her tongue was feeling raw and tooth-marked. She started the car.

He stood there watching her as she drove away, then turned away toward his own car. She drove back to the motel muttering and shaking her head and feeling sorry for poor Eden.

chapter 27

Ruth waited by the window, watching for Joseph and Eden to return. Joseph had still been at the office when she had called him, a state of affairs for which she usually scolded him, but tonight she was grateful. He had come straight over. She hadn't had time to tell him why Eden had been so upset. As soon as he understood that she had run off again, he had become furious in that tight-lipped, controlled way he had. "I'll find her," he had said. Ruth had no doubt he would.

She had been waiting no more than twenty-five minutes or so when he returned. She could see Eden's outline in the passenger seat, and she said a quick prayer of thanks. No one spoke when they came in. Eden gave her a guilty look and then ran up the stairs. Joseph shook his head.

"I don't understand what's come over her," he said. "She was doing fine. She likes her adventures, but there was nothing like this."

"I'm afraid I understand," Ruth said, and she watched his face harden even more as she explained about the telephone call from David and Sarah.

"I think she feels abandoned," Ruth said.

"Anyone would." A tightening of his jaw was the only sign of emotion.

"Well, what would you do?" she challenged, suddenly tired of the tug-of-war between these warring factions of her family. "David is lying helpless in a hospital bed. If it's all *we* can do to keep up with her, how do you expect him to manage?"

"It's not him I'm expecting something from," Joseph said.

Ruth closed her eyes and prayed for patience and wisdom. *When will you give up this bitterness?* she wanted to fling at him. *When will you forgive?* She said nothing. Just took another deep breath, prayed silently, and faced the situation before her now. "We need to decide what to do about Eden's behavior tonight," she said as calmly as she could.

Now his face did soften. He sat down in the chair and ran his hands through his hair. He looked tired.

"Have you had any supper?" she asked.

He looked surprised, then shook his head. "No. I guess not."

"Come with me," she invited, and he followed her into the kitchen and sat down at the small table while she worked. She put on a pot of coffee and brought out her old cast-iron skillet. She quickly chopped up an onion and cubed three potatoes, seasoning them and browning them in the skillet. She rummaged around in the refrigerator and found a green pepper and some ham to chop up and add to the pan. When it was all sautéed, she added three eggs, threw a handful of grated cheese on top, and served her son a steaming plateful, along with toast and a cup of coffee, then put the kettle on to make herself some tea.

Joseph tucked into his food. Ruth went upstairs to see if Eden was hungry, but she was already asleep, lying fully dressed on top of the bedspread. Besides, from the sticky residue around her mouth, Ruth judged that wherever she'd been, they'd served refreshments. She pulled the quilt up over Eden's shoulders, shut the door quietly, and went back downstairs.

Joseph was finishing up his meal and looking a bit more cheerful when she returned to the kitchen, and her water was boiling. She made herself a cup of her friend Vi's own organically grown calming tea with chamomile and passionflower. She sipped and prayed quietly, and between the Lord and the medicinal herbs and the plate of hobo hash and cup of good, strong coffee, both she and Joseph were calmer when they faced each other over Joseph's empty plate.

"Thank you," he said, leaning back and sighing in satisfaction. "I don't think I've had anything to eat since this morning and nothing that good since the last meal you cooked for me."

Ruth thought about lecturing him but smiled instead. "You know you're welcome, son." She sipped and he sipped, and after a moment he spoke, rubbing his hand over his mouth and chin before he did so. She had heard that meant something in body language, but she couldn't remember what. She felt like pulling out her hair, a less subtle cue.

"So tell me again about Eden's conversation with David," he said quietly.

She shrugged. "I don't think there's much more to tell," she said. "I wasn't listening in, but from her side of the conversation I gathered David told her they aren't coming back this month, as they'd first thought."

Joseph was silent then, as was she. Probably both of them were realizing that coping with trauma and rehabilitation would be made even more difficult by Eden, the brave and the free. She smiled. Joseph did, as well.

"She is a handful," he said.

Ruth nodded.

"Okay." Joseph nodded.

Ruth was again amazed at his strength. How many times had she seen him do this? Face some trouble or trial, and after a brief surge of emotion, set it aside and begin to "work the problem," as he would say.

"I guess we need to decide how to handle this episode."

"Where was she?" Ruth asked.

Joseph's face creased into worry. "She was in the car with a woman I've seen around. She said Eden was riding her bike with a boy, and she offered her a lift."

"A boy?"

He nodded.

"You don't suppose she's . . ."

He dismissed the thought with a shake of his head. "Nah. Probably just a buddy. I don't see any of the signs of anything more. But it worries me. If it's the same friend as last time, they were playing up on Amos Schwartz's land, and it looked like they weren't the only ones. Somebody was squatting up there—camping out—and I wonder if it was Travelers. It worries me that she and her friend were so close to people who might have been up to no good. Knowing Eden, she was doing surveillance or some such."

Ruth felt her usual dismay at Joseph's suspicions. She supposed it was his job, but she wished he could be a little more trusting.

"Besides," he said, "I don't know any of the players."

Ruth agreed. "However, I'm a little glad she has some sort of friend, at least. But I'd like to meet him. He must live within riding distance," she said, and smiled at Eden's resourcefulness in spite of her concern.

"I know. But this woman bothers me. I have a feeling she's mixed up in something."

"Why?"

"She drives without insurance," he said, barely suppressing a smile. "And she's got a mouth on her."

"Sounds like a lot of people around here," Ruth said dryly and took another sip of her tea.

"Actually, I don't know why I don't trust her. JDFR, I guess."

Ruth smiled. *Just Doesn't Feel Right* was Joseph's name for times when his instincts warned him of something his brain didn't see. She had taught both boys about it growing up, calling it the "uh-oh feeling." *"Always listen to the uh-oh feeling,"* she'd said. *"You don't need to figure out why. When you feel it, just get away as quickly as you can. You can understand later."* She nodded at Joseph soberly. If his gut was telling him there was more to the situation than appeared obvious, he was probably right.

"I'm looking into her," he said. "I'm going to run her through the system tomorrow and see if she has a record."

"And I'll see if I can find out more about this boy," Ruth said. "But in the meantime, what do you think? Another restriction? And how long this time?"

Joseph paused and rubbed his mouth again.

She was going to have to look up that body language thing.

Finally he shook his head. "You're always talking about the healing power of grace," he said with a wry smile. "Let's try it out."

Ruth felt a rush of peace, as if her small ship of emotions had been righted. "That sounds good," she said. "But I'll talk to her about her choices first."

"So will I," Joseph said.

He got up, carried his plate to the sink, and patted her clumsily on the shoulder. She laid her small hand over his large one, and it felt as if their strength merged. Perhaps they would make it through this time after all.

Miranda left the car at the motel the next morning, walked the short way into town, and paid for last night's ticket. She wasn't exactly sure what "Uncle Joseph" would do if she didn't, but she didn't think she wanted to find out. She seethed with resentment and on an impulse walked a few blocks farther down Main Street to the police department. There was a glass-fronted reception desk whose attendant was conveniently on the phone. Miranda walked past her, rode the elevator up, then walked surreptitiously up and down the hallways, glancing into doorways.

Aha. There he was. The sign on the door said *Investigative Division Supervisor, Joseph Williams.* So why was he giving her traffic tickets and harassing her? Weren't there criminals to catch? She stood at an angle beyond his line of vision and peeked in. He was at his desk already. Wearing a light blue shirt, the sleeves of which he had already rolled up to the elbow and a tie that he had already loosened. Tough day and it was only nine o'clock. He was at his computer and deep in thought, jabbing at the keyboard now and then, and rubbing his hand over his mouth. She watched for a few seconds more, then crept away, feeling slightly foolish.

She rode the elevator down and went outside. It was a beautiful day. She walked for a while and saw the Methodist church where she had rested the day before. The marble steps were still there and inviting. She went to them, sat down, dumped out the contents of her purse, and counted her money. It wasn't a pretty picture. Eventually she would be all right, after the will was probated and the house sold, but she had used the rest of Mama's checking account to pay off bills and had given Aunt Bobbie the contents of Mama's savings account to use in getting the house fixed up and ready to sell. There were several not so minor repairs that needed to be done. She had come to Abingdon with what was to have been spending money for her trip. She wondered how much longer she would be able to stay without a job.

She walked to the library and read the want ads, copied the information from a few, and was just thinking of whether to call Mr. Cooper and arrange for some insurance or risk driving without it when the school kids came in. She checked her watch. It was only noon. They must have had early dismissal for some reason.

The mean girls came in and sat down in their customary places. She looked for the red-haired boy but didn't see him. She looked around for Eden, and sure enough, here she came, carrying her backpack and wearing a green T-shirt today. The horse shirt must be in the wash. Miranda was somewhat surprised to see her. She had expected the wings to be clipped if Uncle Joseph's reaction was any indication.

Eden came over and set her backpack on the table. "Hey," she said, ducking her head.

Maybe she was embarrassed. Well, she wasn't alone. Miranda had her own reasons to feel foolish.

"I guess we both got in trouble last night, didn't we?" Miranda asked with a rueful smile.

Eden looked up, met her gaze, and nodded. "I didn't get on restriction, though," she said, amazement in her voice.

"Really?" Miranda asked. "I have to say that surprises me. Your uncle looked pretty mad."

"I know. But Grandma talked to me this morning and said when I ran away it made them afraid and sad, but they were going to give me grace this time."

Miranda felt a little startled. They were going to give her grace. "That's nice," she said quietly.

Eden nodded, but there was something in her expression that was still troubled. A jut of the chin and darkening of the eyes that was something between anger and hurt. Neither one of them seemed to have anything else to say, so Eden went to work on her homework. Miranda returned to her want ads and lists. After fifteen minutes or so, Eden switched subjects, did her social studies, then pulled out a red notebook and began scribbling furiously. Miranda smiled. Whatever she was writing had her full concentration.

Eden Williams, girl reporter, tapped away at the keyboard! There were only twenty minutes left until deadline, and she wasn't going to let the murder of her editor stop the paper from coming out with the story! She had found out who had shot Malcolm Hendricks as he sat alone in his office late last week working on the final version of the Daily Mirror*! It was Edwin LaCross, the rude society*

editor, but first she had needed to eliminate Duke Smith,
the sportswriter who was angry at Malcolm for demoting
him, and Malcolm's long-lost son who hated his dad for
not leaving him a gob of money!

She, Eden Williams, girl reporter, had followed each
suspect until she had overheard Edwin talking on his cell
phone and booking his ticket to . . . (find out later)

Eden stopped writing for a minute and looked across the
library. She remembered when she had written this part of her
story. Mom had kept bugging her. *"Eden, open the door! I know*
you're in there!" She had just torn up a Kleenex and stuffed it in
her ears. She had pretended that she really was Eden Williams,
girl reporter, and she had five minutes until deadline.

Anyway, she, Eden Williams, had gone through his gar-
bage and found the gloves with the gunpowder on them!!
She, Eden Williams, had notified handsome police detec-
tive Cal Dakota, who right this minute was decoding the
message she had e-mailed him and would arrive to rescue
her!! And she, Eden Williams, would publish the story
that would bring justice to poor dead Malcolm!!

"Eden Elizabeth Williams!" Mom had hollered. *"Open the door*
this instant. You know you're supposed to be off the computer by nine-
thirty."

"Just a minute!" she hollered back. *"It's almost finished."*

"What's almost finished?" Mom sounded all wigged out, as
usual. *"You'd better not be watching those grisly detective shows."*
She wrote as fast as she could. She was almost done.

She, Eden Williams, girl reporter, heard footsteps
behind her. She quickly ran the spell-check on her article
and pasted it into the front page. Then, as her finger
aimed at the Enter key, she heard a sound!!!

"Hold it right there!" The silky voice of Edwin La-Cross gave a shiver up her spine!!!

"All right, young lady!" Mom had hollered. *"You leave me no choice."* Then she'd heard the sound of a nail file being scratched around the doorknob. It had taken Mom about three more minutes to get in, giving her time to finish her story.

Eden, the reporter, punched down the Enter key, and just as Edwin LaCross made a dive for her computer, Cal Dakota tackled him!! The gun flew across the room!!!
"You rescued me!!!" Eden cried while running to-ward Cal.
Eden hugged Cal, and they kissed.
The paper ran the story the next day, and the owner liked it so much he made Eden the new editor!!! She and Cal got married!!!
The End

"What are you writing there?" Mom had wanted to know.
"Nothing," she said.
As usual, Mom had been mad. *"Get to bed, Eden. I'm too tired for your games tonight."*
She had gone to bed thinking that Mom was always too tired for her games.
Eden shook her head now and went back to her story. She didn't want to think about Mom today. The problem was, she was temporarily stumped for a new adventure of Eden Williams, girl reporter. But that never really stopped her for long. The secret was, you just started writing, and sooner or later something was bound to happen. She read the beginning of the story again and decided to start part two with Cal Dakota getting kidnapped by terrorists, who would firebomb the newspaper building, and Eden Williams, the girl reporter, would have to rescue him.
She felt a little guilty, but she had to admit she was kind of

glad Mom wasn't here. At least not right here right now. If Mom read that she was making up a story about terrorists and fire-bombs, she would get all worried and probably make her go talk to Mrs. Jones again, or whoever the Mrs. Jones was here. In Fairfax the school counselor was Mrs. Jones, and Eden had already had to go and talk to her once. It was after she tried to see if alcohol would catch on fire. It did, but it didn't burn very well. It was too watery. She had tried lighting it by pouring it in the bathroom sink and throwing in a few matches. Mom had freaked out and called 9-1-1. Then after they'd left she'd gotten all worried and asked her if something was bothering her. Eden had tried to tell her that Eden Williams, girl reporter, was going to have to make a bomb out of what was in the medicine cabinet of her house, so she, Eden Williams, the writer, had to see if alcohol would burn, but when she said *bomb* Mom had gone berserk and searched her room and read all her stories and made her go and talk to Mrs. Jones, since Dad was going to be out of town for a week.

Miranda sighed. Eden looked up. Miranda turned the page of the newspaper. She didn't look very happy.

"What are you looking for?" Eden asked.

"A place to stay," Miranda said. "And a job." She looked pretty discouraged.

"Where are you staying now?" Eden asked.

"Super 8, but I can't afford that forever. I need a job, and I need to buy some insurance, too. I don't think your uncle is going to be understanding if I get another ticket."

"Maybe he'll give you grace, too."

Miranda gave her a funny look, then said, "Yeah. Maybe."

Eden got an idea! She turned to the front of her notebook, temporarily leaving Cal Dakota and Eden Williams, girl reporter. She leafed through the pages. Well, duh! She knew how to solve every one of Miranda's problems. "Come with me," she said.

"Why? Where are we going?"

"Do you know how to be a waitress?" Eden asked her.

225

"In my sleep."

"Come on, then," Eden said.

Miranda set down the paper, picked up her notebook and pen, and followed her.

chapter 28

S o you can work the day shift starting tomorrow?" the man named Wally asked Miranda. He was tall and thin with a worried face. His apron was spotlessly clean and his canvas shoes freshly washed, an unusual thing for a fry cook.

"Absolutely," she said. She looked around. The restaurant was cozy and clean. Booths were red leather, tabletops were silver-starred Formica, the floor old polished wood. It was real and vintage. Again she was reminded of Mayberry.

"I can pay you minimum plus a dollar and, of course, there's tips."

"Sounds fine," she said, putting out of her mind that she would never be able to afford rent and groceries and insurance on that. "Do you need references?"

He shook his head. "It's just short-term." The worried look deepened. "You understand that, right?"

"I understand." She gave him a reassuring smile. Hopefully her business here would be finished before the lately departed Elna returned from her back surgery.

"And if Eden will vouch for you, that's good enough for me," Wally added.

Just don't ask Eden's uncle, Miranda thought. "Thank you," she said.

Eden looked as pleased as the proverbial cat with feathers sticking out of the corners of its mouth. "Okay," she said. "Now for a place to stay."

By now Miranda had gained a healthy respect for Eden's prowess as a Life Coach. She followed on foot, and Eden rode her bike slowly along the tree-shaded streets until they were near the police department. Not an auspicious location. Eden pulled up in front of a redbrick building that looked like a cross between a church without a steeple and a miniature town hall. *Stone's Mortuary,* the sign said. Miranda hesitated.

"Come on," Eden urged. "Trust me. You'll like it."

Miranda trusted her. She followed her inside after Eden carefully chained her bike to the porch railing. It was dim and cool in here. The floors were polished hardwood, the interior plaster walls had curved archways and mahogany trim. It was a beautiful old building, and from what she could see it was decorated with antique furniture—probably original to the building—and huge potted palms. She glimpsed into one side room separated from the hallway by French doors. She could see a casket and the velvet ropes that would guide the viewers past. She was too busy gawking to notice when a man appeared, moving soundlessly through the hallway.

"Hey, Mr. Cornwell," Eden said.

His face broke into a warm smile, immediately shattering Miranda's stereotype of the typical mortician.

"Hey there, gal. I haven't seen you around in a few days."

"I've been busy," she said. "But I'm here today on business." Not a trace of a smile.

Mr. Cornwell immediately sobered himself. "Please, come into my office," he said, so they followed him down the hall into a small modern suite of rooms, obviously added later as an addition to the back of the building. They went in and took the chairs he offered.

Miranda was wondering where this was all going to lead. Perhaps the man had a house he rented.

"You still looking for a custodian?" Eden asked.

"Why yes, I am," he said.

"Well, then, here's your woman," Eden said, leaning back in her chair with a look of pleased modesty, as if she were extremely proud of her performance.

Mr. Cornwell turned interested eyes toward Miranda. "Have you done any custodial work before?"

She remembered her job at the dog clippers. She had been responsible for the cleanup. And she'd also worked as a hotel maid in Minneapolis. "Sort of," she said and told him of her experience.

"I can't pay you anything," he said. "I offer free lodging in return for the work. That usually puts off applicants."

"It doesn't discourage me," she said. "How much custodial work is involved?"

"Vacuuming all the viewing rooms and the hallway, and cleaning bathrooms every day there's a viewing or funeral. Cleaning the kitchen and dusting the offices once a week. I think there's about six to eight hours of work a week. If you're interested, I'll show you the apartment."

"I'm interested," she said.

They went up a staircase, and Mr. Cornwell unlocked the door to a small apartment directly over the office suite. There was a kitchen and a living area, a small bedroom and a bath. It was sunny and clean and furnished with spare basics. "It's perfect," she said. "But I have to be honest with you. I don't know how long I'll be here."

Mr. Cornwell shrugged. "This job has been open for some time. As long as you leave things as good or better than you found them, no harm done."

They agreed. She filled out another application, and they left.

She looked at Eden with something like awe. "How do you know all this stuff?"

Eden gave her a wise look. "Always keep your eyes and ears open. You never know when something you find out might come in handy. Last week I heard Mr. Cornwell tell Wally that the student who'd been caretaker graduated last year and he couldn't find anybody to replace him, that kids nowadays were spoiled and all. I wrote it down in my notebook. Except for the spoiled part. Now, for your transportation." She hopped on her bike again, and Miranda followed her on foot.

They meandered through town, finally stopping on a shaded back street not far from the library. Eden pulled her bike up to a huge, charming Victorian house on a tree-shaded lot. The house was two stories, maybe two and a half with the gabled top floor. It had hexagonal turrets on one side and long, graceful casement windows with lace curtains that were gently blowing in the breeze. There was a wraparound porch with window boxes beneath the ground-floor windows spilling over with trailing ivy and pops of red geraniums. The walkway and front flower beds were a mass of delphiniums, nasturtiums, peonies, and bachelor's buttons, and the latticed archway in the picket fence was covered with sweet peas and clematis and climbing roses on the other side. A sign by the front gate said *Travelers' Rest Bed and Breakfast*.

"Oh!" Miranda exclaimed. It looked like a doll house, a picture in a lovely book.

"This is my grandma's house," Eden said, opening the gate. "Come on in."

She felt a little hesitant.

"It's okay," Eden said. "She's real nice."

Miranda followed her to the porch.

"Come on in. I need to ask her something."

"I'll wait here."

Eden shrugged and banged through the gingerbread-cornered white screen door.

"Grandma!" she called.

"In here," a voice answered.

"Can my friend borrow that bike in the shed?"

"Of course, honey. I think the tires are flat, though."

Miranda grinned at Eden's solution to her transportation problem. Why not? The exercise would do her good. For longer trips she would work out something else.

The voice got closer; then someone Miranda assumed was Eden's grandmother stepped out onto the porch. She was a tall, gracious woman of ample proportions with a pouf of silver hair that still showed streaks of blond. Her eyes were warm brown, and there was a sprinkling of freckles on her arms, face, and neck. She had a kind face and wore an expression of interest. She had on burnt-orange pants and a wild geometric print blouse of gold, green, and rich sable brown. Her shoes were gold metallic flats with gemstones. She wore a gold bracelet, two long necklaces, one of which, upon close examination, proved to be a watch and the other a cross, and gold bangle earrings. When she spoke, Miranda was reminded of slow, sweet things: honey and taffy and hot fudge.

"I'm Ruth," she said, holding out her hand, which was warm and soft. "Ruth Williams. Welcome."

"Thank you," she answered, suddenly shy.

"Won't you come in and have something to drink?"

"She made a cake last night," Eden volunteered.

Miranda hesitated for just a moment, but Eden was obviously anxious, and Ruth seemed to sincerely welcome her. "Thank you," Miranda said, "I'd be grateful."

She followed them into the house, which was as delightful inside as it was out. The living room had a red-and-white checked sofa and lots of trailing ivy plants. There was furniture of golden oak, a braided rug of gold and cream and red and green, and lots of sunshine and lace. There was a quilt over the back of the couch in the same colors and another one in the dining room on the table, mostly covered by a sewing machine on one end and stacks of papers on the other.

"I'm writing my column," Ruth said. "Once a month I write 'Simple Pleasures' for the *Blue Ridge Journal*."

"That sounds nice," Miranda said. "What's this column on?"

Ruth smiled. "This month I'm writing about springhouses. How my grandmother used to keep her milk and cheese and butter cold by building a little box over the creek or spring. I write about these things so that children can know and remember when all of us are gone."

"I don't like to think about that."

"I know," Ruth said gently. "But the Lord takes us all when our time is done. And times change with the people."

They went into the kitchen, where Eden was already taking down cake plates and getting out the knife. The cake proved to be of the Bundt variety and was studded with nuts.

"You're not allergic to black walnuts, are you?" Ruth asked.

"No, ma'am," Miranda answered.

"This is my brown sugar pound cake with black walnuts," Ruth said. "I was raised up near Richmond, and there were three black walnut trees at the edge of our property. Every year it was my job to gather the nuts and hull and shell them. What a chore!" she said, putting coffee on to brew without seeming to exert any effort or break the thread of her conversation at all. "Are you from around here?" she asked.

"Tennessee," Miranda answered. "Nashville."

"Well, you're not very far from home," Ruth said. "What brings you to Abingdon?"

She was going to have to answer that question more often now that she was becoming a temporary resident rather than simply passing through. For now, though, she fell back on her usual explanation for why she was in Kankakee or New Orleans or Philadelphia or New York. "I just like to travel around," she said. "I'd like to see as much of the world as I can before I die."

Ruth smiled. "That must be an interesting life," she said. "You must have met lots of different people. Think of the stories you could write."

Miranda nodded and smiled.

"Miranda's gonna work at the Hasty Taste," Eden volunteered. "She taking Elna's place."

"Well, what a blessing for Wally," Ruth said. "I know he was worried about how he was going to manage. Do you have a place to stay, dear?"

Miranda grinned and nodded toward Eden. "That was thanks to Eden, too. I'm going to be the custodian at the mortuary."

"Is that right?" Ruth beamed. "Well, welcome to our town."

There was a clatter on the porch, and the screen door opened and twanged shut. Heavy footsteps clumped on the wood floor of the hall. Uncle Joseph's bulk filled up the doorway. He looked like a storm cloud about to rain, and Miranda felt a perverse satisfaction as she leaned back in her chair and took a bite of cake.

"Joseph, I'd like you to meet—"

"We've met," he answered curtly.

His mother gave him the eye, which he ignored. "What's my old bike doing out on the porch?"

"Oh, is that yours?" Ruth asked, eyes wide. "I wasn't sure which of you boys had left it here, unused and rusting all these years."

Miranda suppressed a smile and felt a healthy respect. She was in the presence of a master.

"Miranda's gonna use it, so she doesn't have to buy insurance," Eden contributed.

At that Miranda's cheeks flamed, and Joseph got a chance to look superior. "Oh, is that a fact?"

"If that's all right with you," Eden added, and Ruth and Eden looked toward him with expectant faces. Miranda pointed hers toward her shoes.

"Sure," he mumbled, "I guess," then turned to leave.

"Won't you have some cake, darling?"

He mumbled something else, and then Miranda heard the screen door shut and his boots clumping back across the porch and down the stairs.

"What's wrong with Uncle Joseph?" Eden asked. "He's grouchy."

"He works too hard," Ruth said with a shake of her head. "Don't pay him any mind. Now, where were we?"

By the end of the day, Miranda's immediate problems had all been solved, thanks to Eden. She had taken Joseph's bike to the gas station and had the tires patched and filled and some oil applied to its various joints and gears. It rode like a dream when she was finished, and she felt young and carefree with the wind ruffling her hair. She rode to the hardware store and purchased a lock for it, and drove Mr. Cooper's car only once as she checked out of the Super 8. She actually walked to the police department and spied on Joseph Williams again before she did so, hoping he would stay put until it was parked again, this time behind the mortuary. She was in luck.

She moved it with no incidents; however, she did phone Mr. Cooper and, after a brief update on her activities, arranged to have the Cadillac added to his insurance. She wrote out a check for an amount that should cover a few months' worth of premiums and dropped it in the mail, then unpacked her suitcases. When she was finished, she took a small satchel she'd brought with her and rode to the grocery store, bought eggs and bread and peanut butter and coffee, and rode back home. By nightfall she had arranged her things in the bedroom, eaten supper and cleaned up, and had even set out clothes for work in the morning. There was no television, which was fine. She walked outside and sat down in front of the funeral home and enjoyed the dusk. She would have to think of something nice to do for Eden to thank her for all her help.

As the sun set she came back inside, showered, and got ready for bed. When she set the alarm on her cell phone for 5:00 A.M., she realized with chagrin that she had completely forgotten to call

Aunt Bobbie. She checked her watch. It was only nine-thirty. She took a chance and dialed her aunt's number. She answered on the third ring.

She sounded tired, as usual, but this time she seemed more interested in Miranda's progress. "How's the search coming?" she asked.

"Pretty well," Miranda answered. "I don't really have any leads on the baby yet, but I've gotten myself established here. And made a few new friends," she added, thinking of Eden's bright face and Ruth's kind one.

"That's good," Aunt Bobbie said.

Miranda imagined how silly this must seem to her, someone with real-life responsibilities who probably didn't have time to go digging around in the past. "Aunt Bobbie, I just wondered if you could tell me a few things."

"All right," her aunt answered, but her voice sounded wary.

Miranda sighed. There was a wall that shut down over her and Mama whenever she tried to get any information on their past history. "Where exactly did you and Mama grow up?"

Hesitation. "Why do you want to know that?"

"Just a hunch. Might not pan out."

"It was near Thurmond. In West Virginia," Aunt Bobbie said. "But I don't see how that can help you."

"Where were Mama and Daddy married?" she asked, ignoring the discouraging attitude.

"At a justice of the peace in Nashville," Aunt Bobbie said, a little more easily.

"Do you know exactly where Daddy was from?" she asked Aunt Bobbie.

"No, I don't. I just remember it was somewhere south of us— maybe Georgia or Florida."

That was a pretty wide territory. Miranda didn't say so, though, just thanked her for the information. "And you don't have any ideas about the connection to Abingdon?"

"No," Aunt Bobbie said. "Honey, I've got to go. I've got to

get my uniform in the dryer. I'm working graveyard tonight."

"Thank you, Aunt Bobbie," she said, and after hearing her aunt's tired good-night, she hung up the phone.

What had happened to those girls? she wondered. What had made them want to never say the name of their home again, to never see their people? What had made Mama so brittle and angry and dangerous and Aunt Bobbie such a worn shell of a person?

She wrote in her journal for a while, of her questions and frustrations, then made a few pages of collage. She tore up a magazine and put in pictures of locks and keys and drew a heart with a chain and padlock.

She felt sad for the both of them as she pondered it, but she also felt a thrust of anger. She was tired of secrets. She was going to get to the bottom of a few. She was going to find things out.

chapter 29

J oseph stayed late at the office. He took the copies of the traffic tickets he had issued to Miranda DeSpain and ran the
information through the National Crime Information Center
database. She had no criminal history or outstanding warrants
anywhere. He Googled her just on a whim and found a tantaliz-
ing bit of information. The Spokane, Washington, *Spokesman
Review* reported that in 2001 a marriage license had been issued
to a Charles E. Porter and Miranda M. DeSpain, both of Coeur
d'Alene. He checked the ticket he had issued. Miranda's middle
initial was I, not M. He ran his hand over his face. He needed a
shave. He got up and went to the window. He should go home,
but there was really no reason, now that he thought about it. Flick
had been staying at his mom's ever since Eden had come. There
was no one waiting for him, not even a dog. He chuckled silently
to himself for his pathetic thoughts.

He looked down on the street below. The storefronts and
streetlights were decorated with hanging baskets of spring flowers,
the trees in full leaf. Tourists came to Abingdon because of its
history and because of its character. It had the feeling of a place
apart, where life was protected or at least partially shielded from

the harsh realities of the world. People lived here and loved this place because it was safe. There was goodness here. He felt a fierce protectiveness toward it, and he realized he would do whatever was necessary to keep it that way. A little thought nagged him then that bad things happened in Abingdon the same as everywhere else. Evil found its way in through people's hearts, not through holes in fences.

He set the thought aside, then went back to his desk and pulled out the county sheriff's reports on the crimes of the Irish Travelers. They had been a busy bunch. Mr. Norwood had been the first casualty with the asphalt sealant scam. Then there had been a gas station owner out on Highway 58. They had sold him a box of worthless tools. A Mrs. Frederick Mueller had paid them to prune her fruit orchard. They had indiscriminately chopped away at half the trees, then told her she had bud moths and they would have to spray, but they needed another three hundred dollars to buy the supplies. She gave it to them, and they were never seen again. The county extension agent had looked things over after they left. There were no bud moths, and the trees that had been "pruned" would need years to recover before they bore fruit again.

There were two others who had been taken in by a roofing scam. They hired the Traveler crew to replace their barn roof at bargain prices, paid half down, and after one day of work, the crew disappeared with the money. All in the county, Henry's jurisdiction, but it rankled him just the same. Joseph set down the papers with frustration. The Travelers were like insects, like a plague of locusts. They got into things and spoiled them. They didn't make anything good in the world, just took and thieved and blighted everything they touched.

He thought again of Miranda DeSpain and wondered if he was wrong about her association with them. His mother thought so. She had called him to come to supper and then over meat loaf and mashed potatoes proceeded to tell him that she thought Miranda was a "sweet girl" and that Joseph should try to get to know her. Well, he fully intended to do that. For he knew she was up to something, even though he couldn't say what. Most people would tell you why they were here. They were tourists sight-seeing, they were relatives of someone who lived here, they were passing through on their way to somewhere else, or they intended to move here and settle down. Miranda DeSpain was none of those. He wondered if the reason for her secrecy was that she was a point person and lookout for the Travelers. Maybe she spied the easy marks and directed the crews accordingly. She seemed trust-worthy and likeable, and it did seem to run counter to reason to chum up the law enforcement's family if you were planning something illegal. But what better way to catch people off guard? He had a very strong feeling that when the Travelers were gone, Miranda DeSpain would be, also.

chapter 30

Miranda arrived at the Hasty Taste Café at 5:30 A.M., met Venita, Wally's wife, who would also be working the day shift, put on her apron, made four pots of coffee, and drank a cup herself before Wally unlocked the doors at 5:55. It was technically five minutes until opening time, but already three or four regulars were waiting outside to come in. They eyed her curiously as they entered and headed for what she assumed were seats that had been theirs from before the foundation of the world. Two old-timers went and sat in the corner booth. One was wearing a John Deere cap and the other bib overalls. She grabbed a coffeepot and went to take their orders, not bothering with menus. This type always knew what they wanted.

"I'll have my usual," the first one said, then laughed delightedly because she obviously didn't know what it was.

She smiled like a good sport. "Lukewarm milk toast and a side of Brussels sprouts," she called out to Wally, getting a blank look from him but big guffaws from the two old men.

"She got you good, Roy," the John Deere cap told the other.

"I guess she did," Roy allowed, then ordered biscuits and gravy. She made a point of remembering, so tomorrow she could beat him to it.

The place filled up quickly, and between herself and Venita, they kept the orders up to date, the coffee cups filled, and the food delivered while it was still steaming.

"You're doing real good, honey," Venita told her, beaming.

"Thank you," Miranda said and supposed it was good to be competent at something.

It would have been a fine beginning to the day if the next jingle of the door hadn't brought in Lieutenant Williams. He came with an older man wearing the uniform of the Washington County Sheriff's department. In fact, according to Venita's whispered bio, he was Henry Wilkes, *the* Washington County Sheriff. Miranda played dumb so she could hear what Venita had to say about Joseph Williams. "He was a war hero, you know," she said. "And before that he played football in high school. Handsome thing, isn't he? Was engaged to a real pretty gal, but she up and married his brother." She shook her head in sympathy.

"How long ago was that?" Miranda asked Venita.

"Oh, it was eleven or twelve years ago, I think. Joseph went off and joined the marines right after she left him. They say she was pregnant with his brother's baby. Ain't that just the livin' end?"

"Does he have more than one brother?" she asked.

"No, just the one," Venita said. "And they don't speak. I know it just about tore their mama's heart out. She's a *real* sweet woman. Teaches Bible classes over at the Methodist church. Salt of the earth."

Interesting. Miranda mused on that thumbnail sketch of Joseph's family history, and a few things made sense. Why Eden's father might be loath to bring his wife and come to Abingdon, and why Joseph Williams seemed to be permanently out of sorts. Still, she thought, shaking her head, twelve years was a long time to carry a grudge. But, then again, that was a deep betrayal coming from a brother and the woman you loved. Two relationships with deep, tender roots. She suddenly felt a real sympathy for all of the players in the little drama. She could feel for Joseph, even though he had a sour disposition. She felt for the ex-fiancée, now the sister-in-law. She herself knew how a foolish decision could have a life-changing impact and how it felt to live with the consequences in the cold light of day. She wondered if Eden's mother had regretted her indiscretion and the circumstances of her daughter's birth. She supposed, given all the facts, she might even feel sorry for the brother, although right now he was looking like the villain in the story. She felt a stirring of pity for the whole family, and especially for Ruth, who must even now feel torn between her sons.

But the one she did not have to stretch to feel compassion for at all was Eden, for she was obviously the child who'd been conceived in all that confusion. She mused on it for a minute more and had an even greater appreciation for Eden's grounded charm and Joseph's obvious love for her. Perhaps she had misjudged him. Anyone who could love his brother and ex-fiancée's child in spite of their betrayal must have something deep and genuine somewhere inside.

Venita saw her look of concentration and must have taken it for romantic interest. "They usually eat here every day," she said. "And they always sit at your table. And you know, Joseph is still single. He's the nicest man, and he hasn't ever been married."

"Is that right?" she said noncommittally.

Venita nodded, gave her an encouraging look, than went to deliver an order.

Miranda took a deep breath and headed for the law-enforcement booth.

Joseph seemed about as glad to see her as she'd been initially to see him. "You're taking Elna's place?" he asked with one of his sun-blocking frowns.

"Yes, I am," she answered pleasantly. "Temporarily, of course."

"I'm Henry Wilkes," the sheriff said, giving Joseph a puzzled glance and extending his hand.

"Miranda DeSpain," she answered, shaking it.

"You've met Detective Williams?"

"I have." She gave what she hoped was a gracious smile and clicked her pen open.

Joseph was still frowning. She felt herself bristle. She stowed it. "What can I get you gentlemen?" she asked, the smile beginning to feel stiff.

The sheriff seemed baffled at the undercurrents. "Uh, I'll have oatmeal with whole-wheat toast and a side order of peaches," he said.

She nodded and turned to Joseph, who was staring at her in a way that made her uncomfortable. "And you, sir?"

He said nothing for a beat or two, then handed her the menu, still unopened. "I'll have two eggs over easy, bacon, crisp, and a short stack."

"Anything to drink?"

"Coffee." He turned over his cup. She filled it expertly.

"Coffee for you, sir?"

"Decaf, please," the other man said with a sigh.

"I'll be right back with it."

They were talking intently when she approached the table but were suddenly quiet when she arrived. She didn't chat, just filled up the sheriff's cup with decaf, refilled Joseph's regular, and went about her business. She served their food without mishap, filled their coffee cups twice more, then set the bill on the table. The sheriff left first, and Joseph came to the register to pay. She rang him up but still felt awkward and ill at ease as he stared at her intently.

"Here's your change," she said.

"For you," he answered.

Which embarrassed her even more. It was a very generous tip. She couldn't very well give it back, but she felt awkward, just the same. "Thank you," she said and put it in her pocket.

He tipped his head chivalrously. "You gave excellent service."

"Thank you," she repeated. She wished he would leave.

He did not. Instead, he helped himself to a toothpick and went back to staring. "How's the bike riding?" he asked.

She flushed, her face and neck hot. "Just fine. Thank you for the loan."

"My pleasure," he answered.

A smile crept at the corner of his mouth, and she couldn't tell if he was mocking her or just thawing slightly. She felt herself becoming even more defensive and hot. He dismissed her before she could think of what to say.

"You have a good day," he said with another tip of his head.

She watched him leave, her initial embarrassment now replaced by annoyance. There was something about him that just brushed her hair backward, as her father used to say. She wondered if she had the same effect on him.

chapter 31

E den woke up on Friday morning and lay in bed for a minute. She looked around the bedroom. It had been her bedroom at Grandma's since she was a tiny baby. It still had all the
toys from then, and even though she hardly ever played with
them anymore, this morning she looked around and remembered.

She liked this room. The ceilings were low and made an
upside down V over her head. Aunt Vi had come over a few
summers ago and had painted the ceiling blue with puffy white
clouds, and she had painted the walls with interesting things, too.
One wall was dark blue with all the planets and stars on it. Eden
used to pretend she was on a space ship, that she was exploring
the galaxy and her bed was a starship like the starship *Enterprise*,
only she was the captain.

Another wall was all princes and princesses and knights and
ladies, and off in the distance was a castle with flags flying from it.
She used to pretend that she was like Joan of Arc, a lady, but with
her own set of armor and stuff. The third wall was her favorite. It
was her Annie Oakley wall. She loved Annie Oakley. Annie Oakley was about the best woman that ever was. She had read a book
about her, and so Aunt Vi had painted Buffalo Bill's Traveling

Wild West Show on that wall. There was a buffalo and an Indian chief and cowboys, and Aunt Vi had even painted Annie Oakley herself, wearing her boots and her hat and her dress with her sharpshooter gun. Annie Oakley never missed. She always hit what she was aiming for. Thinking about Annie Oakley made Eden feel brave, and she jumped out of bed and got dressed. Her horse shirt was clean, so she put it on. It was going to be a good day. She could just tell.

She went into the bathroom and washed her face and brushed her teeth and brushed her hair. She found her shoes and socks and put them on and jammed her books and her radio into her backpack, and then she found her night ops watch and put it on. She checked the time. It was only 6:45. There was time to go to the Hasty Taste before school. She pulled down the attic stairs and quickly performed her task.

She went downstairs and ate her scrambled egg and toast while Grandma drank her coffee and worked the crossword puzzle. Today was Friday and Grandma's friends Aunt Vi and Carol Jean were coming over to pray, but Grandma had already made the brown sugar pound cake, so there wasn't much to do. Usually Grandma was busy getting ready on Friday mornings, and usually Eden took her time with her chores, but today when she was done eating, she unloaded the clean dishes from the dishwasher as fast as she could, fixed Flick's breakfast and petted him real quick, then watered all the plants on the front porch. She went back into the kitchen and put her dirty dishes into the dishwasher and kissed Grandma good-bye.

"My, but you're in a hurry this morning," Grandma said.

"I've got things to do," she said and left before Grandma could ask her any questions. She got on her bike and rode down the hill into town. She loved the way she felt on her bike with the wind in her hair and her hands out at her sides. She wished Dad could see her, but when she thought of Dad she felt sad and not just because of his being hurt and all. She felt sad because of what she'd seen in the attic. Something inside her twisted and felt all torn up when she saw that picture of Mom hugging Uncle Joseph. She felt guilty herself, like she'd done something wrong. She wasn't sure what to do about it. She had taken one of the pictures this morning, and it sat inside her backpack now. She could almost feel it in there, burning hot through the canvas.

She felt heavy about it, but then, all of a sudden, she felt something happy light on her, like when Jenny Sanders's parakeet had flown around and then landed on her shoulder. She had stood very still and just barely turned her head and looked at that little bird, afraid if she moved or made a sound, she would frighten it away. And right now, thinking about Dad and Mom and Uncle Joseph, she felt that way again. Like something very good just came and lit on the sore place in the middle of her chest and told her it was going to be all right. She thought it was Jesus. She was pretty sure it was.

"Was that you?" she asked Him out loud. She knew He was listening. Dad had said so. She talked to Jesus sometimes the way Dad had told her. *"Don't worry about calling it praying,"* he'd said. *"Just talk to Him. He hears when His children talk to Him, Eden,"* he had said. *"Just like I hear and love it when you talk to me."*

God didn't answer back out loud, but she was pretty sure if He did, He would say, *Yeah, that was me. Couldn't you tell?*

"God, I don't know what the deal is with that picture," she said, and even though her heart still hurt, she felt a little bit better. "Would you figure it out?" she asked. "And while you're at it, would you help my dad to get better and make my mom like me?" She felt hollow inside when she prayed that part. "Or else help me to find my real mom if she would like me, but if not, then forget it."

She was at the Hasty Taste. She braked to a stop and chained up her bike. Uncle Joseph said if he saw her bike unlocked again, he would impound it and make her pay to get it back. Then Grandma said, *"Oh, Joseph, do you really think someone's going to steal it in downtown Abingdon?"* And Uncle Joseph said, *"Ma, the whole world isn't Abingdon,"* and that reminded her of one more thing to pray about. "And, Jesus, would you please make Uncle Joseph not be so grouchy, like he was yesterday," she said. "Amen."

She went into the Hasty Taste and looked around. She quickly realized Uncle Joseph and Uncle Henry had left already.

"Hey there, Eden!" Miranda came out from the kitchen. She looked pretty today. "Your uncle has already left."

"I didn't come to see him," she said, and before Miranda could ask her who she had come to see, Pastor Hector came in.

"Well, well, you're up and about early today, Ms. Williams," he said.

"I came to see you," she said.

"Well, what an honor. Come sit down. Could I treat you to some breakfast or perhaps a cup of coffee?"

"Coffee would be fine," Eden answered, and she followed Pastor Hector to a booth and sat down. It was cool because Miranda came and filled up her coffee cup without even acting like it was any big deal and didn't even tell her she shouldn't drink coffee. And Pastor Hector knew Miranda.

"How are you doing?" he asked Miranda. "I see you've decided to stay with us for a while."

"Yes, thanks to Eden," she said, and Eden felt a little shy when Pastor Hector looked at her with a smile.

"That doesn't surprise me at all," he said. "Eden is always watching out for the people she cares about. She's like her uncle that way."

She picked at her fingernail, and after a minute Miranda took Pastor Hector's order.

"Would you like something to eat?" she asked Eden.

Eden said, "No thank you," and opened four little containers of cream and poured them into her coffee, then stirred in five little packs of sugar. When she was done and it tasted right, she looked up at Pastor Hector. "I was wondering if I could talk to you about something," she said.

He looked at her seriously and nodded. That's what she liked about him. He didn't treat her like she was lame or something just because she was a kid.

"Sure," he said. "Anything."

She took the picture she had taken from the attic and set it in front of him. He looked down at it, then back up at her, then reached into his pocket and put on his glasses and looked at it again. When he was finished looking, he nodded and handed it back to her. She put it in her backpack so she wouldn't have to look at it.

Eden thought he might say something, but he didn't. He just looked at her but really quiet and calm, and all of a sudden that little bird came back, and she felt quiet and calm, too.

"I didn't know about that," she said.

Pastor Hector looked real serious. "You like to know about things, don't you?"

She nodded. She waited again, but he just looked at her. So she finally asked a question. "Did you know about this?"

He nodded. "Yes," he said. "I knew."

"How come no one told me?"

He was quiet for a minute; then he said, "I can't answer that, Eden. I can only tell you why I didn't tell you."

"Oh. Well, why didn't you tell me?"

"Because it wasn't mine to tell."

"Whose was it, then?" she asked, but she knew the answer.

"Your mother's. Your uncle Joseph's. But I will tell you one thing."

"What?"

"This happened before your mother married your father."

She felt a lot of the tight things come off of her then. "A long time ago?"

Pastor Hector nodded. "Yes. It happened before you were even born."

She thought about before she was born, and in her mind she saw the outer-space wall in her room. Why, before she was born was so long ago and far away that it was almost like it hadn't happened at all.

"Does that help?" he asked.

She nodded, and all of a sudden she liked Pastor Hector so much she thought she would cry. So she frowned and took a sip of her coffee. He reached over the table and held his palm out in front of her. She slapped it, and then they hooked their fingers together in the special handshake Pastor Hector had taught her. "Friends for life," he said.

"Friends for life," she repeated, and she was feeling lots better by the time she finished her coffee and rode her bike to school.

School seemed to take forever. Finally the last bell rang, and Eden hurried outside. It was a good day. The sun was still shining and it was warm. Pretty soon it would be too hot for long sleeves. She would have to ask Grandma to make her a horse shirt with short sleeves. Thank goodness she was done with her library restriction. Today she could do her rounds. She would be back to her normal routine on Monday, and she could do her homework after supper. Nobody had been doing her work, and there was a lot of stuff to catch up on. She crunched on the extra apple Grandma had put in her backpack, rode the bus into town, unchained her bike, then got on and rode down the hill, the wind cooling her head.

She made her first stop, parking her bike in front of the Hasty Taste and chaining it to the pump that had a bunch of flowers around it and water trickling out of it. Elna always fussed at her for doing it, but this time she was careful not to mash any of the flowers, and besides, Elna wasn't here.

The bell on the door jingled when she went in. She always liked that bell. It made her feel happy. Miranda was standing by the cash register with her sweater and purse.

"Hey, gal," she said. "I was just getting ready to call it a day.

I'm beat. This getting up at five o'clock routine is something I'm going to have to get used to. But I love the job," she said, and she looked like she meant it. Her eyes were shiny, and she was smiling like she was happy.

"Do you like your apartment?" Eden asked.

"I love it, love it, love it," Miranda said. "Thank you. In fact, as soon as I get my first paycheck, I'm going to buy one of those little grills, and you can come over for hot dogs."

"Okay," Eden said, "but before you go, I need to ask you something."

"Shoot," Miranda said.

She waited while Eden set down her backpack and got out her notebook, and she didn't even laugh or smile like some grown-ups did when she wrote things down. "Okay," Eden said, "I need to know if there's any news you've heard today."

"Hmm. What kind of news?"

"You know. Just anything that might come in handy."

"Let's see." She looked up at the ceiling and then smiled. "I know. I heard Fred Ingalls tell Wally that his dog had puppies."

"That bluetick hound?"

"That's the one." Miranda nodded.

"How many?"

"Five," she said, "and only one of them is promised. Henry Wilkes is taking it."

"Good," Eden said, writing it all down. "Anything else."

"Um, yeah. Amos Schultz's wife went into labor in the middle of the night, and since they don't have a car, Amos had to ride his horse over to the firehouse, and a volunteer fireman came and was driving her to the hospital, but he ended up delivering the baby on the way."

Now, that was news! She wrote it down, putting in a bunch of exclamation points. "Who was the fireman?"

Miranda made a face. "Sorry," she said. "I didn't get that."

"That's all right," she said. "I'll find out. Was it a boy or a girl?"

"Oh! Ah, I don't know that, either." Miranda gave her an apologetic look. "I didn't do such a good job of gathering information, did I?"

"You did all right," she said. "It takes a while before you get the hang of it."

"Well, I'll keep working at it. Maybe I'll do better next time."

Eden was tired of writing things down then, so Miranda got her a chocolate doughnut and milk and said good-bye, and Eden felt happy again watching her walk across the street. She liked Miranda a lot. She suddenly had a great idea. She wrote it down in her notebook in capital letters and added a few exclamation points.

MIRANDA AND UNCLE JOSEPH SHOULD GET MARRIED!!!

But then she remembered that they didn't really like each other, so she scratched it out.

She took her doughnut to the table in front of the window. She ate all the icing first, then took tiny little bites and a drink of milk in between each one. When she was finished, she carried her plate back to the kitchen and left.

Next she went across the street to the post office.

"Hey, Eden, where you been?" Mr. Poncey gave her a big smile and handed her a stack of Wanted posters.

"It's a long story," she said, not really feeling like going into the details right now. She thanked him and took the Wanted posters to the copy machine in the back room, where she made copies for her files and then punched holes in the new ones and took them out into the lobby and put them in the binder that was attached to the bulletin board. That way people could leaf through them while they were waiting in line and maybe catch somebody. Bad guys had to eat and go to the Laundromat just like everybody else, didn't they? Well, then, some regular people might just catch one of them.

"Bye, Mr. Poncey," she said.

"Good-bye, Eden. Thanks. See you Monday."

She waved good-bye, then went across the street to the bus station. Mrs. Joyce was working today instead of Floyd, and she was waiting on somebody now. *White female approximately five-feet-six-inches tall, gray curly hair, wearing a white pantsuit and carrying a green-and-white pocketbook. No visible markings or tattoos.* The lady finished at the counter and then went and sat down next to the door with one suitcase. Eden happened to know that the only bus leaving this afternoon was for Bluefield, West Virginia, with a final destination of Charleston.

"I'm done now, sugar," Mrs. Joyce said. "Come on over and show me the pictures."

So Eden took the new Wanted posters to the counter, and Mrs. Joyce put on her glasses. She leafed past the one of Usama bin Laden. There was a twenty-five-million-dollar reward for him, but Eden had already shown him around and nobody'd seen him, and Mrs. Joyce said there wasn't much chance he would come through Abingdon. But you never knew. She went through the others, even though Mrs. Joyce had already seen them, and then one by one she looked and shook her head. She took a minute when she came to the man who had too many wives.

"He sort of takes after that fellow that bought the butcher shop over at Damascus, but I guess not. I believe that new fellow has blond hair, and this fellow has brown."

"He might dye his hair," Eden said.

Mrs. Joyce shook her head. "I don't think it's him."

But Eden wrote a note on the back anyway. She would show it to Uncle Joseph.

"I still don't think you ought to be reading all this stuff, child."

"I don't read the small print." Uncle Joseph had said to just read the heading at the top and look at the pictures. She asked him why and he'd said, *"Sometimes things get too heavy to carry, Eden. Let the bigger people carry this stuff for you until you're old enough."* She had disobeyed him at first. She read about a man who killed his wife and his two children and set their house on fire, and she hadn't been able to forget about it for a long time.

So after that she just read the top line like Uncle Joseph said.

"See you later," she called to Mrs. Joyce. And she set out for the police station.

Uncle Joseph wasn't there. Her desk was in the room across from his office where they kept the copy machine, and it was covered with papers to file, so she sat down and went to work. Officer Prentiss was the one she was supposed to go to if she needed help anyway, but mostly she helped him. He was kind of old and didn't know how to get on the Internet or type things, so she had shown him how to do that and how to Google things.

First off she separated all the papers into three piles: arrest reports, Wanted posters, and new warrants. Then she put them all into alphabetical order. She took a few minutes to look them over after that. There was an arrest report on Rachel Adkins for passing bad checks. Didn't know her. Another one for Donald Christopher Barnes for contempt of court. Didn't know him, either. There was another one for David Harklewood Jr. for trespassing at Wal-Mart after being forbidden to do so. She thought there were some Harklewoods who went to the Catholic church, which reminded her she hadn't checked in with any of her contacts there in nearly a week. She would have to do it on Monday. She glanced at the new Wanted posters and warrants, then started filing. When she was done, she marked her time on the card and set it on Uncle Joseph's desk. He paid her every Saturday morning. Three dollars for every hour she worked, and so far she had saved a hundred and fifty dollars. She didn't know what she was going to do with it yet, but it would be something good. She was thinking about buying a Buck knife, but Grandma had said no, and Uncle Joseph had shaken his head and said, *When are you going to learn? Ask me first.* So she had to wait awhile now.

She was just unchaining her bike to ride home when somebody stepped out of the alley beside the building.

"Hey," Grady Adair said.

"What are you doing, jumping out at me like that?" she demanded. "You almost scared me to death."

"I didn't jump out at you. And it's not my fault if you're scared."

"It's an *expression*, Grady. That's all. Where you been, anyway? I went out to Millers' pond, and you were gone. Don't you even believe in saying good-bye to a person?"

He didn't bother to answer that, just gave her a disgusted look. "I ain't been around because we had to move again, and now we're clean over at Damascus, and my daddy said I can't just wander around town."

"Well, what if you were visiting somebody?"

"Well, that would probably be okay."

"Well, then, why don't you come over tomorrow and visit me. Bring your bike, and I'll show you someplace cool."

"I'll ask."

"Meet me in the park where the creek is tomorrow morning," she said.

"Do you need to ask your grandma?"

"I'm sure it's okay," she said.

"All right," Grady said, but he had a look on his face that Eden thought she recognized. It was the look of somebody who doesn't believe a good thing is real. It was a look that expected to be disappointed. Well, she would just have to make sure things worked out, that was all.

chapter 32

W hy not?" Eden was trying to watch her tone like Grandma said, but it was hard. She had the day all planned, and Grady would be in the park waiting for her, but Grandma was saying she couldn't have him over without a grown-up to supervise, and she couldn't do it because she was teaching a quilting class today.

"I'll call Uncle Joseph," she said.

Grandma shook her head. "Your uncle is busy today, dear. He has a search and rescue meeting. They're starting a new training class."

"He didn't tell me!"

"You have to be sixteen, Eden. You know that."

She decided she'd better not pitch a fit about that. "Well, can't he come over, Grandma? Please? I was going to take him to the campground. We'll be careful." But Grandma was shaking her head, and when she got that look on her face, Eden knew it was useless to argue. She turned around and left, maybe stomping her feet just a little.

"Eden Elizabeth, where are you going?"

"I'm going to tell Grady," she said, kicking the kickstand on her bike so hard she bruised her ankle.

"Well, you see to it that you come right back."

She pressed her lips together tightly. She could hear Grandma's footsteps.

"I didn't hear you." Grandma was standing at the door. "And I know you're going to answer politely because you know how it would grieve me to have to restrict you again."

The prospect of staying inside for another week was too horrible to think about. Plus, the truth was she didn't want to upset Grandma. "Yes, ma'am," she said.

"You'll come home when you've found Grady, and then you can come with me to the quilt shop."

"Yes, ma'am." She got on her bike and rode away before Grandma could decide to make her stay. She was so upset her cheeks were hot, and it took all the way to town before she began to cool off. Now Grady would go away disappointed and sad, and she was disappointed and sad, too. She hated to admit it, but he was the only friend she had. She tried not to think about it, just like she tried not to think about Mom and Dad not wanting her, but she had that same tight feeling in her throat, and her chest hurt. She saw Grady waiting for her, and it was then that she thought of a plan and immediately felt better. Duh! She knew who they could get to supervise them. Hadn't Miranda said just yesterday that she wished there was something nice she could do for her?

"We got a problem," she said, pulling her bike to a stop, and she was a little surprised because Grady actually looked afraid. The color went out of his face so that his freckles stood out.

"What is it?" he asked.

"You look plumb scared," she said.

"I ain't neither."

"Are so. I can tell by looking that you're scared as can be."

"Well, what is it that's the problem?" he asked, getting mad now, which Eden thought was better than being scared, anyhow.

"The problem is my grandma won't let me hang out with

you today unless a grown-up is around to make sure we don't get ourselves killed or something."

"Oh." He looked relieved.

"What'd you think it was?"

"Nothing."

She decided not to argue, even though it was obvious he wasn't telling her the whole truth. "What's your dad doing today? Maybe we could go to your house."

"He's working," Grady said, and he looked kind of sad about it.

"That's okay," she said, "because I've got another idea. Follow me."

"Why do I always have to follow you?" he complained.

"Because I'm the one with the idea. Do you have an idea? 'Cause if you get an idea, then I'll follow you. But as long as I'm the one getting the ideas, you'll have to follow me." She shook her head. She was surprised that a person with good sense couldn't figure that out.

Grady grumbled, but she looked back once, slyly, so he couldn't tell she cared, and she could see he was behind her. She rode down Main Street for blocks and blocks to the funeral home. She began chaining her bike.

"What are we coming here for?" Grady asked. "This is a funeral home."

Grady must think she was a total ignoramus. She thought about saying something smart, but she remembered how scared he'd looked just a few minutes ago. "Somebody lives upstairs," she said.

"Who?" Grady asked.

"Somebody who owes me a favor," Eden answered, because she had read it in a detective story.

It was Saturday, one of her days off, and Miranda had slept soundly after making sure the viewing rooms were vacuumed and the bathrooms clean last night. At first she had worried that it would give her the creeps working and even sleeping in such close proximity to those no longer living. But it hadn't bothered her at all. There was a peaceful atmosphere in the little apartment and even in the funeral home itself. She had gotten up and dressed and was sipping her second cup of coffee now, watching the birds fly around the beautifully landscaped grounds.

There was a birdbath back there nestled in a tangled, exuberant garden of forget-me-nots and lilies. Some chickadees and sparrows were splashing and scolding one another. She sighed and realized she hadn't done much about her search for her mother's family. She went and got the file she had made. She had inquired about getting a copy of her mother's birth and marriage certificates and realized she would have to call Aunt Bobbie again. Well, there was no time like the present.

She picked up the telephone and dialed. She got the machine. "Hey, Aunt Bobbie," she said. "Could you give me a call?" Better not to say what she wanted. A better chance her aunt would call her back if she didn't expect another grilling.

She hung up the telephone and was just thinking about what she would do today when she heard footsteps on the stairs and a knock at the door. She got up and could hear stage whispers and muted voices arguing. She smiled.

"Do you think she'll do it?" a boy's voice asked.

"I think so, but be quiet or she'll hear us."

She opened the door and smiled. It was Eden, of course, and with her the same red-haired, freckle-faced boy she had seen riding away the night she had given Eden the ride home.

"Hello!" she greeted them. "Come in, come in."

They came in. At least Eden did, then turned and took the boy's hand and pulled him over the threshold.

"Miranda, this is my friend, Grady."

"Pleased to meet you, Grady."

"Yes, ma'am," he said. His cheeks were red under the freckles, and Miranda wondered if it was because of meeting an adult or because Eden had called him her friend.

Eden didn't waste any time getting to the point.

"Miranda, we need your help."

She looked so earnest that Miranda had to stifle a smile. Eden would be very hurt if she thought she was the object of amusement. "Sure," she said. "Name it."

"We were going to ride out to a campground on the trail today, but my grandma said I can't go without a grown-up."

"Oh." She considered. She didn't really have plans today, and she had wanted to explore the Virginia Creeper Trail for as long as she'd been in town. "What about your uncle?" she asked.

"He's busy," Eden said. "He's teaching a search and rescue class."

Miranda nodded and counted it as an advantage that he wouldn't be popping in. "How far is it to the campground?"

"Just a couple of miles." Her conscience must have gotten the better of her. "Actually six or so," she amended, "but hardly any of it's uphill."

Miranda smiled. "Well, sure," she said, "I guess I could go."

"Oh, thank you, thank you, thank you!" Eden said. "Can I use your phone?"

Miranda handed her the cell and was about to show her how to use it when Eden flipped it open and dialed. Really, what had she been thinking? She listened to Eden's side of the conversation with her grandmother and had to get on and assure Ruth that she was indeed willing to accompany the kids on their trip.

"What exactly is it we're going to see?" she asked Ruth.

"It's a Bible camp my husband and I used to run, and I still own. It's about seven or eight miles out of town just off the trail. Nobody uses it now, but Eden loves it there. I would be happy to take them, but I'm teaching a class today. Thank you for going with them."

"You're welcome," Miranda said. "I'm glad to do it."

"Come for supper when you're done," Ruth invited.

Miranda accepted after deciding it would be too rude to inquire if Joseph would be there before giving her answer.

"Okay," she said after hanging up, "let me go put on my shoes, and we'll be off. Do you need to call anyone, Grady?" she asked.

His face flushed crimson again, and he shook his head. "No, ma'am," he said.

She got out bread and peanut butter and jelly, and they made six sandwiches and split them up so each carried two. She got her bicycle, they stopped at the Neighborhood Grocery and bought six bottles of water, six apples, and three candy bars, divided those up for easy carrying, and they were off. Eden led the way.

"I've been wanting to try this," Miranda said. "It looks so beautiful." It was green and peaceful, and she understood the path followed an old railroad track. "Where, exactly, is the campground?" she asked Eden.

"You go just past the River Knobs, and then it's after the river trestle but before the lake trestle."

"Well, I'm glad you know where we're going."

"I do. Don't you worry."

Grady seemed a little bewildered. He pulled out a sandwich and took a bite.

Miranda decided to just enjoy the scenery. And the company. Not that they were alone. There were lots of families and people out enjoying the day. Apparently this was a very popular way to spend a vacation. They quickly left Abingdon behind, and then it was all peace and greenery for a while. For a mountainous region, it was pretty flat. The riding was easy. She supposed it made sense, considering they were following what had been a railroad track.

"My uncle Joseph does search and rescue in the woods and along the trail," Eden said.

"This trail?" Miranda looked in vain for someplace people might get lost. All she saw was a cow pasture.

"The Appalachian Trail," Eden said kindly, and Miranda realized there was a lot she didn't know about this region.

They rode companionably, passing walkers and twice pulling aside to let people on horseback pass them. Eden looked after them longingly. "There used to be horses at the camp," she said, "and paddleboats and fishing and canoes. Grandma and Aunt Vi worked in the kitchen and cooked, and Pastor Hector and Grandpa were the teachers."

"Did you ever live there?" she asked.

"No. They closed it when I was a baby. But I think about what it was like," she said.

Miranda could hear the longing in her voice. Eleven was young to have left paradise behind. She wondered what the future would hold for Eden with her family fractured, as well as her father. She put it aside. *She is not your child,* she told herself. *She is not your child.*

They were coming up to Watauga Station and decided to stop and eat lunch. There was a grove of trees off to the side, so they set down their bikes and started in on their food. They decided to eat one sandwich and one apple and half the candy bar, saving the rest for later. Except for Grady, who said he was too hungry to wait and ate both of his sandwiches. After resting for a few minutes, they continued on.

Finally they went over the curved trestle Eden had spoken of. It was built over green rolling hills and kept the path level. They followed it, and when they could see the concrete buttresses and the pretty blue waters of Lake Holston itself, Eden pointed off the trail to a narrow dirt road, hardly more than a path, leading down the hillside.

They walked their bikes down to the campground. The road curved once, twice, and then the view opened up. They were at the crest of a hill, and beautiful green grass folded down into more hills and hollows toward the blue water of the lake. There was a big log building, a barnlike structure, a smaller house beside it, and then several tiny cabins tucked into the woods.

"The big one is the lodge. The smaller one is where Grandma and Grandpa used to live. The barn thingie is the chapel, and all the little cabins are for campers. There's seven of them, and then there's the teepees."

"Teepees?"

Eden nodded. "They're really just tents with wooden floors, but they're fun to sleep in." She sighed. "Grandma and Uncle Joseph bring me here sometimes."

They passed under a signpost. "Camp Berachah," Miranda read. "I wonder what that means?"

"It means 'valley of blessing,'" Eden said. "It's from the Bible."

Miranda stood still and was quiet. It was a little foolish, perhaps, but she felt something prick her then, and she remembered the pastor she had spoken with so many months ago. She couldn't remember his name, but she remembered his kind face and his warm eyes and how he told her that Jesus would help her and bring life into her heart if she would let Him, but He was a gentleman and would never force her to do anything she didn't want to do. She felt that same feeling here as she had felt that night. A warmth, but mixed with longing and a desire to move closer. To what? To whom? She shook her head to clear her mind. Eden and Grady were both looking at her strangely. She put on a smile, and this time she led the way toward the big wooden chapel.

She tried the door and felt a pang of disappointment when it was locked. She should have known better. After a moment of jingling and digging in her backpack, Eden handed her the keys. She unlocked the double doors, and they swung open easily, as if inviting them in. They stepped inside. The air was dusty and close but smelled good, a mixture of woodsmoke and dry warmth, and Miranda could almost see the rows of wriggling, warm children sitting here, scratching mosquito bites and shifting bare legs on the polished wooden benches. She could imagine Pastor Hector teaching them, and an older man who looked like Joseph but with a kinder, gentler face teaching them how to row and fish and swim, then blowing a whistle for them to line up for supper. She shook her head, for it was almost as if the presence of the children who had been through here was still strong. It was a foolish thought. Perhaps it was another Presence she felt. She felt a longing even deeper than the one she had felt before, and to her dismay tears were pressing at her eyes.

"Let's go look at the lodge," Eden said.

"You go on. I'll be right behind you," she said, and after they took off running she had a moment to wipe her eyes on her shirttail.

She followed them to the lodge. Eden unlocked and swung open the door, and they all stepped inside. It was beautiful. The exterior walls were all of log and chinking, and the logs were a rich golden color. There were long trestle tables of the same golden wood in rows, with benches on each side. In the center was a huge fireplace, the chimney made of rounded river rock, the inside blackened from fires Miranda could still smell lingering in the air. The floor was tongue and groove. In the back she could see the doorway to the kitchen and the pass-through where she could imagine Ruth setting out bowls and platters of steaming food. There were plaques on the wall in various places with Bible verses:

Trust in the Lord with all your heart and lean not to your own understanding. In all your ways acknowledge him, and he will make your paths straight.

Whoever drinks the water I give him will never thirst. Indeed, the water I give him will become in him a spring of water welling up to eternal life.

We have received the spirit of adoption, the spirit of sonship, in the bliss of which we cry, Abba, Father.

She was shaken again, and she wondered why this place, so long abandoned, had the power to move her. It was as if there were something still living here. If she hadn't felt the sweetness of it, she might have said it was haunted. But there was no ghost here. Just a deep sense of calm and peace.

They went back outside and then over to the house. Eden

unlocked it. It was unfurnished. A beautiful home but in need of some repairs. They inspected one cabin, which was standard camp with four sets of bunks and a bathroom, and a teepee, which was a wall tent. The particular one they looked at was sagging, its pole having been knocked askew in the last windstorm. It looked as if a family of squirrels had built a nest in the corner.

After that she let the children run wild, and she walked down to the lake. The water was calm. She walked to the edge and splashed some on her hand. It was cold and refreshing. She wished she'd brought her suit, although the air was a little too cool for swimming. It was just the beginning of May. In another month it would be perfect. Eden and Grady returned. They continued their exploration, visiting the swimming area, the horseshoe pits, and the craft area, and Eden pointed out the shed that had once been the snack shop and trading post, and the ramshackle remains of the horse barn.

"This was quite a spread," Miranda said in admiration. "I'm surprised your grandmother doesn't sell it."

"She said she couldn't," Eden said. "I think she always wanted my dad to run it, or Uncle Joseph."

Miranda didn't say anything, since neither subject seemed safe. They wandered and talked, and after they had eaten the other half of their lunches and made sure all the buildings were locked again, they walked back up the road toward their bikes and the trail. At the top of the hill, Eden turned and looked back down, and so did Miranda and Grady. She could have been mistaken, but it was as if none of them wanted to go.

"Good-bye," yelled Eden, and then Grady joined in and so did Miranda, and their voices echoed down the lake. Miranda smiled and thought she would try to remember this minute. This day, because she was happy and the children were happy and what did it matter if they were hers or not? She was with them, and there was this moment, and she would have it for always.

Ruth had supper waiting for them when they returned, and they were famished. The children took their plates into the family room to watch some television show. She and Ruth chatted easily through dinner. Miranda liked her. She was interesting and had a sharp sense of humor. After finishing her pork chops, creamed corn, mashed potatoes, and salad, Miranda stayed a little longer but excused herself before Ruth brought out the Key lime pie.

"I absolutely cannot fit another bite," she said. "And I do have to get back and make a telephone call before it gets too late."

"You come again, Miranda," Ruth invited. "And thank you so much for going with the children today."

"It was my pleasure," she said. "I loved being there. Something about it was sweet and refreshing."

Ruth smiled. "You must feel free to go there whenever you want."

Miranda felt that she had been given a great gift. She would like to go there again, perhaps by herself, but of course that would depend on how long she stayed around these parts.

chapter 33

G rady, shouldn't you call your father?" Ruth asked after Miranda had gone and the dishes were done. Grady looked guilty, which told her the answer to her question.

"Here," she said, handing him the telephone. He dialed, and she couldn't help but hear his end of the conversation.

"Hi, Dad, it's me, Grady."

Pause.

"Just around."

Pause and a buzzing from the phone.

"Uh. No, sir." Pause. "Yes, sir."

More buzzing.

"I'm at Eden's house. We ate supper here."

Pause.

"Yes, sir. Her grandmother's at home."

Pause.

"Yes, sir." Then the phone was handed to her. "My dad wants to talk to you."

Ruth smiled and took the telephone. "Hello, Mr. Adair," she said.

"Ma'am, I apologize for my son's behavior. I didn't know he

was going to impose on your hospitality like this."

"Why, it was no problem, Mr. Adair, and I apologize, as well. If I had known you wanted him home sooner, I would never have allowed him to stay."

"If you'll be so kind as to tell me where you live, I'll come and fetch him."

Ruth gave directions, finished cleaning the kitchen, and had a pot of coffee on by the time Mr. Adair arrived.

She went to the door and greeted him. He was a tall, lanky man, six feet or so. He was suntanned and had dark hair salted with gray. His face looked weathered and careworn, but he had a very pleasant smile. He was holding his hat in his hands. She opened the door and invited him in.

"How do you do, ma'am. My name is Johnny Adair."

"I'm pleased to meet you," she said. "Won't you come in and have a piece of pie and some coffee? The children were just having their dessert."

His eyes lit up. "You're tempting me."

"It's Key lime. Homemade."

He shook his head. "I haven't had a piece of homemade Key lime pie since my mama passed away."

"Well, come in, then. Please."

She led him through the family room into the kitchen. They passed Grady and Eden, who were eating ice cream and watching television. Grady looked up guiltily, but his father just ruffled his hair going by.

"I'll call next time, Dad."

"I know you will, son," Johnny said.

"Please, sit down," Ruth said. "I hope you don't mind eating in the kitchen."

"Not at all, ma'am."

She had a thought. "Have you had your supper yet?"

"I'll get something on the way home."

"Heavens no, you won't," she said in dismay. "I told my son the other day, I throw away enough to feed another person. I've got some beautiful pork chops and mashed potatoes and creamed corn that are just going to go to waste. Won't you have some? You'll enjoy your dessert more after you've eaten a good meal."

He gave a mild protest, but she knew she had him. She fixed him a plate and sipped her coffee while he ate, exclaiming and groaning over her cooking. In between bites, he asked her questions, and she found herself telling him her life story. How she grew up in Richmond, how her father died, and how she taught school and then married her husband, how he had taken the job as police chief in the town here, and how they had bought the campground and run it until her husband was diagnosed with cancer, and how her two best friends and her son helped her for a few years, but she had finally given up.

"I know I should sell it," she said, "but somehow I can't bear to part with it."

"It's part of your life," he said simply.

"You're right," she said, feeling warmth at being understood.

"It would be wonderful if it could return to its former glory," he said.

"I'm afraid that's not going to happen. Barring an act of God." She didn't want to speak of David and Joseph.

They chatted a bit more. Mr. Adair had his pie, then he regretfully said he had to leave. He called Grady, carried his plate to the sink, and thanked her for the supper.

"I haven't eaten like that in longer than I can remember," he said. "Thank you."

"You are more than welcome," Ruth said.

Grady and Eden appeared.

"Son, we have taken up enough of these good people's time."

More protests, but Johnny Adair was firm. "I like to be rested on the Lord's day," he said. "I'm not in the ministry any longer, but old habits die hard."

"You were a minister?" Ruth asked.

"Not exactly, ma'am. I was a musician. I provided the music for Ernest Grayson's Traveling Crusades."

"Well, imagine that," Ruth said, and she looked at Johnny Adair with different eyes. They told each other good-night, and Ruth watched them leave. As she came inside she felt a twinge of apprehension. About Joseph and what he would say. She could almost hear his voice. *You let someone you don't know in the house? You fed him dinner? How do you know he's not a con man? How do you know he's not out to fleece you? You shouldn't be so trusting,* and so on and so on. Joseph couldn't understand, she realized. He had forgotten how to trust many years ago.

"Eden," she said hesitantly.

Eden looked up, eyes wide, face innocent.

"I'm not sure your uncle Joseph would approve of letting Mr. Adair come to supper. Why don't you let me tell him about it," she said.

"Sure," Eden agreed. "Can I ride my bike until it gets dark?"

"Ride your bike!" she exclaimed. "That's all you've done all day! Aren't you tired?"

"No, I'm not tired," Eden protested.

"Well, I think it's time for you to take your bath," she said. "We've got church in the morning." And in the fuss and confusion that followed, the business of telling Joseph conveniently faded from her mind.

chapter 34

The Hasty Taste was closed on Sunday, so Miranda decided today was the day she would get the answers she needed from Aunt Bobbie. After a quick breakfast, she took a walk for a mile or two up the trail and back, rehearsing all the while what she would say to her aunt. Back in her little apartment, she made the call. She asked for what she wanted and didn't back down, even though her aunt was again reluctant.

"This is my life, Aunt Bobbie," she said. "I have a right to know, and you're the only one who can tell me." So there was a little of Noreen's grit in her, after all. Or at least some of Noreen's bullying, for Aunt Bobbie provided her with the information she wanted in a tone of resignation. Miranda felt a little guilty when she ended the call, knowing that she had intimidated and harassed her aunt into helping her, but she was on an important quest. And she did have a right to know. Everyone had a right to know their roots, no matter how unpleasant an experience it was for the guardians of the secrets.

She didn't waste any time mulling over what she'd been told. She went on the Internet to West Virginia's Web site and followed the link to VitalChek, the company that would expedite official documents for a thirty-dollar charge. She paid the fee with her debit card and requested her mother's birth certificate and then went to the Tennessee Web site and did the same for her mother's marriage license. They would arrive in two or three days. In the meantime she went over what her aunt had told her. The information was scant but interesting.

"We were born in Thurmond," Aunt Bobbie had said. "And I don't think there's much there anymore. Since the coal gave out, the railroads stopped coming. Then there were no jobs and everybody left."

"Are any of our relatives still there?"

"I don't know," Aunt Bobbie said, and then she said something that shocked Miranda. "And if you find out there are, I don't want to know. I don't want to know anything about it. Nothing, do you understand?" Her voice quavered with emotion.

Miranda had ended the call soberly and wondered if she had been wrong to force her aunt to talk.

Well, there was no undoing it, she realized. The only thing to do now was to push ahead.

She got a pen and determined to write down everything she knew, smiling when she thought of Eden and her notebook. She was proving to be just as obsessive. She had bought a three-ring binder at the discount store and currently had sections for her mother, herself, and one labeled Baby. She turned to the mother section and started writing down what Aunt Bobbie had told her. Noreen Louise Gibson had been born to Beck Maddux and Lois Mae Gibson, and that was the first thing that struck her like a dash of cold water. Noreen's mother and father had not been married, and suddenly a lot of things became clearer. Why her mother was so ashamed when she found out her daughter was fifteen and pregnant. She had lived through that shame herself, in a time when illegitimate children were whispered about. Miranda wondered if things would have been different if she had known this instead of its being a deeply buried secret. If perhaps she and her mother would have been able to talk about it instead of shout.

Noreen had been born at home. A doctor had delivered her, but Aunt Bobbie had long since forgotten his name, so there would be no medical records.

The information Aunt Bobbie had provided about the wedding was a little clearer. She gave Miranda the date and told her they had been married in Nashville, Tennessee, at the county courthouse by a judge.

Miranda stared at the wall and thought about what she had learned from just the bare facts Aunt Bobbie had told her. It reminded her of those shows she saw from time to time on television where an artist begins a picture with a few odd, random strokes on a canvas. He shades and colors, and still there is no sense to it. A few more lines and shadows and the eye barely makes out a shape. Then, sometimes suddenly and sometimes slowly, the brain begins to "see" some sense in what was purely random before. And then, once you know what you are looking at, the delicate details are filled in. Before, she had had only a few broad, nonsensical lines, random pieces that fit into no discernible whole. Now, with the new information she had a vague outline of a story. A history barely glimpsed through a thick fog. But with any luck, and with a FedEx delivery and perhaps a trip across the state line to West Virginia, she would learn more and eventually have a whole picture. She realized she had been deprived of the secrets of her birth and background as surely as her own child had been.

She got up, stretched, then returned to the computer, determined to see it through. She searched for Thurmond, West Virginia, and learned more than she wanted to. She sat back when she was finished and stared into space. She wondered that she'd ever had the audacity to think she knew her mother. How could you know someone until you knew where they'd been? Until you knew the places and the people who had shaped them?

Thurmond, she learned, was in the rugged coal country of southern West Virginia. The New River ran through town, leading to the joke about the town's reputation. "How is Thurmond different from hell?" it went. "A river runs through Thurmond."

She felt a chill as she read it, for even though the facts were colorful and might be amusing to some, she had a picture of two little girls who had somehow been so traumatized by their past that they would not even speak the name of the place that had spawned them.

Thurmond had been a coal and railroad town at the turn of the century. It was a lawless, brutal place, giving birth to another saying: "There's no Sunday west of Clifton Forge and no God west of Hinton." The sins of the place were nothing new, she saw as she continued reading. Gambling, prostitution, and alcohol served as a backdrop to the soul-numbing business of coal mining and the darkness of lives lived underground. She read, she looked at photographs. When she signed off, she shook her head to clear it. The day outside looked wonderfully bright and cheerful compared to what she had just seen. She felt she needed to feel the sun on her head, if for no other reason than to remind her that she was here now, that only her mind had traveled to that place. She went outside, walked through town, then onto the trail, drinking in the sweetness of the air. She wondered what she had opened up. She had a feeling she was close to the answers. The only question now was whether she really wanted to know them.

Joseph went to church with his mother and Eden, ate dinner with them, then left, pleading work as an excuse but still feeling guilty. He knew Eden was a handful for his mom, but apparently a friend of his niece's was coming over for the afternoon, so she would have someone to play with. Besides, there were things he needed to do. And the sooner the better. He had already been regaled with stories about Miranda taking Eden and her new friend on a trip to the camp yesterday. He felt a sense of urgency about finding out the background of Miss DeSpain. She was worming her way into his family's lives, and better to nip things in the bud if she was up to no good.

He reviewed what he already knew as he walked to his office. She had no outstanding warrants and no criminal history. But that didn't preclude civil lawsuits. He thought about where to start looking, for there was no central database for those. He had to know a county. The car was registered in Nashville. He would start there. She might have evaded jail but still caused enough ire to prompt a lawsuit or two. He unlocked the door and climbed the stairs to his office. He made his notes quickly, scribbling on a yellow legal pad.

Call Nashville—check out pending civil cases
Check credit report
Check driving record
*Ask Wally and Ed Cornwell what she put on employment
    applications for former jobs*

He sighed in frustration. All of these except one would have to wait for tomorrow. He phoned Wally and asked for a copy of her employment application.

"Is she up to something?" Wally asked.

"If she is, I'll let you know."

Wally's deep-rooted lack of curiosity took over then, and he said he would have it for him in the morning. Joseph stared around the office for a few minutes, then decided to take a walk. He headed for the woods to clear his mind. He would walk a mile or two up the trail.

He was by no means alone in his intentions. It was busy for this early in the season. He walked briskly until he was past the commotion of the other hikers, then slowed his pace and breathed. He was unusually involved emotionally in this whole case of the Irish Travelers, he knew. And he had to admit that Ms. Miranda DeSpain had gotten under his skin. Why? he wondered. It was possible he was wrong about the whole thing. It could be sheer coincidence that she appeared the same time as the plague of crime. She might actually be telling the truth, that she just enjoyed living in different locales for six or seven months at a time and Abingdon was the current in a lifetime of temporary stops. After all, she had gotten a job and found a place to live.

He looked up the trail toward the giant sycamore. It was so huge a man could stand inside the hollow made by the roots. He and David had loved playing in it as boys, and he thought of his brother with pain. He would go back to his mother's in time to call him tonight. It was the right thing to do. He stared and walked and thought, and for a moment he doubted his eyes, but after he stared a minute longer he realized Miranda DeSpain herself was headed toward him, coming down the trail.

She saw him and smiled, raised her hand in a tentative wave. He nodded but didn't wave back, and part of him felt angry at himself for being such a curmudgeon. What if she was just a nice girl who couldn't make up her mind what she wanted to be when she grew up? But what if his instincts were right and she was a trickster, another untrustworthy woman who was nestling her way into his family's lives and hearts, another part of him answered back. It had happened before, and he thought of the past with pain. By the time they approached each other he was angry again. At Sarah. At himself. At Miranda DeSpain.

"Hello, Lieutenant Williams." She smiled at him, and he had to admit she was very pretty in a fresh, clean way. Her dark hair swung around her shoulders, her eyes were bright and interested, her cheeks pink with health and exercise. Today she wore a T-shirt and denim shorts. Noticing all that made him feel even more annoyed. He glanced at her feet, which, he tried not to notice, were at the bottom of shapely legs. She was wearing hiking boots. He frowned, remembering the prints near the scene of the mysterious trailer.

"Hello, Ms. DeSpain," he answered coolly. "What's the matter? You get tired of pedaling, or did the bike get a flat tire?"

She gave him another smile, and he suddenly felt ashamed of

himself. He seemed to bounce between acting like a suspicious parent and an obnoxious child.

"Actually, I arranged for some car insurance," she said. "When I get the paper work, I'll bring it by your office so you know you don't have to keep pulling me over."

For some reason her transparency annoyed him. "Do you expect me to congratulate you for obeying the law like you should have done in the first place?"

Her smile disappeared and was replaced by a look that was somewhere between irritation and regret. "I don't expect anything," she said.

He was a little embarrassed. He tried a lighter tone. "What prompted the change of heart?" he asked.

"Summer's coming," she said back with a tight smile. "It'll be hard riding up and down all these hills."

"So you're planning on being here come summertime."

"You sound less than pleased at the prospect."

"It's immaterial to me either way. As long as you obey the law, you're welcome here. If you don't, I assure you, I'll find out." Well, then. There it was. Out for both of them to see.

The smile went away. Her eyes registered hurt, then anger. "Look," she said, "I don't know what your problem is, but I would like you to stop harassing me."

"Harassing you? Exactly how have I harassed you?"

She apparently ran through the facts in her mind and couldn't come up with an answer that held together. "What is it, exactly, that you find so threatening about me?" she asked. "What have I done to make you so hostile?"

He thought about defending himself. Once again he was thrown off balance. And he knew what the problem was. He didn't have his facts. If he knew the facts, he could answer that question. He wished heartily that it was Monday or that at least he hadn't encountered Miranda again until he had the results of tomorrow's inquiries.

"Why are you here?" he asked.

"I told you. I travel around."

"And I don't believe you."

"Well, I'm sorry, but it's the truth."

"But is it the whole truth?" he asked, and an expression flashed across her face so quickly he barely saw it before it was gone. Bingo. He had struck pay dirt. The expression he had seen was guilt and a hint of something else. Fear?

"I don't have to tell you anything," she said quietly.

This time it was he who felt a flash of some emotion travel through him like a bolt, because as he watched, her face closed. The friendliness and childlike trust just disappeared and was replaced by a mirror that showed him the same cold suspicion he had shown her.

She walked around him and then away without looking back.

He stood and watched her until the trail curved. He continued walking, but it was without the peace the place usually brought him. His thoughts darted like a fretful bird. If Miranda DeSpain was a criminal, he had just put her on her guard. And if she was not, he had a feeling he had made a grave mistake.

chapter 35

B y morning, Joseph had gotten over his remorse. He was all detective again, and after a brief breakfast at the Hasty Taste, during which he and Miranda DeSpain coldly ignored each other and Henry looked bewildered, he was back at his office, a copy of her Hasty Taste employment application in his hand, ready to find the facts. He scanned it briefly. She had listed only one job, at the Sip and Bite diner in Nashville, Tennessee. Under dates of employment, she had put that she'd begun working there in 1996 and worked until two months ago with the notation "off and on" appearing at the bottom of the page. Sounded like she'd left plenty of room for wiggling.

He called the Sip and Bite. The phone rang six or seven times before it was answered. The woman's voice sounded breathless, and in the background he could hear the clatter of dishes and the chatter of voices and the strains of "Jesus, Take the Wheel."

"I'm looking for some information on one of your former employees," he said. "Miranda DeSpain."

"Who?"

"Miranda DeSpain," he repeated.

"Just a minute," the voice said; then the phone was set down with a clunk. He waited. The song played and ended. "When I Get Where I'm Going" started up.

"This is Myra Jean." Her voice was smoky, her accent twangy.

"Are you the manager?"

"Manager, owner, you name it. Now, how can I help you? I happen to be a little bit busy here."

"Sorry," he said. "I'm looking for some information regarding one of your former employees, Miranda DeSpain."

"Who wants to know?"

"My name's Joseph Williams. Lieutenant Joseph Williams with the Abingdon, Virginia, police."

A pause. "Why are you wantin' to know about Miranda?"

"So you know her?"

"Of course I know her. I've known her since she was born. I knew her mama. I knew her daddy. I know her aunt, and I went to her high school graduation. Listen here, what are you getting at? Because she may have been *confused* a time or two, but that girl has never done a *thing* against the law. *Besides,*" she said, her voice tightening with suspicion, "how do I know you are who you say you are? What are you up to, anyway?"

"I'm not up to anything. It's routine," he said.

"She applied for a job there or something?"

"Something like that," he said. Then quickly before she could come back with another question, he asked his. "So you know her? She really worked for you? She is who she says she is?"

"Of course she is. She's a good worker, and you're darned lucky to have her, and by the way, I don't exactly *appreciate* what you're *insinuatin'*. I've a good mind to take down your *badge number* and call your *superiors.*"

"I'm very sorry," he said. "I had no intention of showing any disrespect to Miss DeSpain."

She sniffed. "Well, here's a *tip* for you, *Lieutenant.* The next time you want to get information, try keeping a civil tongue in your head. It'll get you a lot further than that smart-alecky routine you're using now." With that she hung up the phone.

Thus chastised, he performed the credit check—Ms. DeSpain had no outstanding loans and no credit history. Odd, but some people liked to pay cash.

He checked her driving record. No tickets or accidents in the last six months.

He called the Davidson County, Tennessee, District Court office and asked about any pending lawsuits with Miranda DeSpain named as defendant. There were none. He repeated the process with Superior Court. There were none.

He called Ed Cornwell at the funeral home.

"Oh yeah," Ed said. "Seems like a real nice girl. She's done a good job so far. Why are you interested?"

By then he was beginning to get the sinking feeling that his unerring instincts just might have erred in this case. "Purely a formality, Ed."

"Well, let's just see. She listed a prior address in Nashville, and a next of kin as Roberta Thompson, also in Nashville. Says it's her aunt. Put down references of Myra Jean Mayfield in Nashville at the Sip and Bite Restaurant and a Mr. William Cooper."

Cooper. That was the name on the car registration.

"Thank you, Ed."

"No problem."

Joseph hung up the telephone and performed one last check, just so he could lay the matter to rest. He retrieved the telephone number for William Cooper at the address on the registration. It was listed in the Nashville telephone book. He dialed. The phone rang three times and then was answered by a pleasant-sounding man. Joseph identified himself thoroughly, only this time he had a more logical reason to call. He explained that he was curious about the car registration, and he carefully watched his tone.

"You know, I thought of the insurance lapse after she left. I'm so sorry it got her into trouble. We've corrected it now. She sent me the money, and I've added the car to my policy."

"So she has your permission to use the car?"

"For as long as she needs it," he said.

"Have you known Miss DeSpain long?" he asked.

"I've known her since she was a baby. Her daddy brought her over and introduced her to me the day she came home from the hospital."

They chatted a little more, and their conversation confirmed what Myra Jean at the diner had said but added a few details. Miss DeSpain had come home from her wanderings to take care of her mother, who had recently died of cancer. Joseph felt more and more like a heel.

"So she does have a pattern of traveling around?"

Mr. Cooper chuckled. "Oh yes, but I know she'll get it out of her system someday. She's a good girl with a beautiful heart. She'll settle down when the right time comes. Tell her I said hello, won't you?"

"Thank you for your help," he said quickly. He had no intention of telling Miranda DeSpain he had been calling her neighbors.

He shook his head and wondered where his instincts had led him astray. Then the last nail was pounded into his coffin. Henry called.

"Well," he said without preamble, "the Travelers struck again. Yesterday a bunch sold and installed heat pumps for two folks out by Glade Spring. Had some worthless parts encased in a Trane exterior. The pumps worked for about three hours, then started to fall apart. The crooks took them for five grand each. When the customers called and reported the problems, of course the phone was disconnected, and the address given was bogus."

"So when did the money change hands?" Joseph asked.

"Yesterday afternoon."

About the time he'd been sparring with Miranda on the Creeper Trail. He sighed. An apology was looming large in his future. He hated apologizing.

"But we did find something interesting," Henry continued.

"What was that?" Joseph asked, the sinking feeling increasing.

"A local resident returned early from vacation and found a

trespasser camping on his property. Of course, by the time we got there he was gone, but this time we got a physical description of the vehicle, the trailer, and the man."

"So what's the description?" he asked, training his mind back on business.

"The man was around fifty, medium height and build, gray/black hair, weathered face. No distinguishing marks. This time he went by the name of Jimmy Stewart."

"A comedian."

"Yeah. The trailer was a new Jayco. The truck was a late model Dodge Ram. Dark green or black."

"I don't suppose they got the plate number?"

"No."

"Well, this is definitely a start," Joseph said. "And nobody who dealt with the guy mentioned a woman?"

Henry was silent for a minute. "Oh. I get it now," he said "That's what's going on between you and the new waitress. Why did you think she was in on it?"

Now that he'd had every one of his reasons blown out of the water, he had no intention of reciting his humiliation aloud. "Because I'm a suspicious, distrustful jerk who thinks if a pretty girl is nice, she must have an agenda."

Henry chuckled. "Don't be so hard on yourself. Maybe she's as forgiving as she is beautiful. And who knows, maybe she'd even be interested in a rusty-hearted fool like you."

Joseph sighed. He thanked Henry and hung up. He tapped his pencil on the desk, making staccato vibrations, then got up abruptly and picked up his keys. Like his pop used to say, *"If you've got to swallow a frog, it's best not to look at it too long."*

chapter 36

Miranda finished work by one-thirty, did her cleanup, restocked her supplies, and was out of the Hasty Taste by two o'clock. She had printed out directions last night, filled her tank full of gas, and packed a small cooler containing sandwiches, fruit, and bottled water. She had worn Capris and tennis shoes to work, so there was no need to change. She glanced at the sky and wondered if she should go back to the apartment for a jacket. It was overcast and cool today, and rain was forecast. She decided not to bother. She hopped in the car and headed for Highway 81 east to Wytheville, where she would get on Highway 77 north, which would take her into West Virginia and on up pretty close to Thurmond. At least to the end of the highway, where she would pick up the tangled thread of roads she must follow to reach the abandoned coal town. She felt a little apprehensive but also excited. This was a mystery she had needed to understand for a long time. And who knew? Perhaps there would be some clues here. She had a feeling of festivity and holiday.

She had searched MapQuest with the only Thurmond address she could come up with, a river rafting outfitter. Apparently the two thousand census had listed eight inhabitants. It would take approximately two and a half hours to drive there, according to the directions. She set out, enjoying the scenery.

The southwest of Virginia was lovely, especially in the spring, in spite of the gray day. The land was a series of undulating green waves, the fields turned and newly planted, the trees lovely in their lace of tender new leaves. The dogwoods were blooming, along with redbud, and the pink and white blossoms dotted the hillsides, peeking shyly from beneath the larger trees. Behind them the Blue Ridge Mountains, soft blue mounds, stood silent guard.

She pulled off the road and ate her lunch. The traffic picked up. She went through the Big Walker Mountain Tunnel near Wytheville, then through the longer East River Mountain Tunnel that went on for just over a mile. It was odd, knowing she was under the mountain. She felt a sense of oppression in spite of the yellow tiles and bright lights, and oddly, emerging from the tunnel on the other side in West Virginia, it didn't abate but grew in intensity the farther into the state she went.

It was still lovely country, with a fierce and rugged beauty. But as she passed Beckley and left the interstate for smaller local roads, her uneasiness grew. The mountains rose up on either side of her, jagged and sharp. They blocked out the sun, what little there was, and the woods beneath them looked wild and lonely and cruel. These were the kind of woods of evil enchantments and fairy tales, of witches and lost children.

It began to rain and darkness fell. She turned off the highway and drove through small pockets of houses perched between the riverbank and the mountain. The roads were very narrow and winding. The buildings were put so close together it reminded her of beach property. The town, such as it was, was divided on both sides of the river with the railroad tracks running along the banks. She imagined what it might be like to live here. Everything felt tight and cramped and heavy and dark. She rolled the window down and took a few deep breaths. She thought of her mother. Had she lived somewhere near here?

She came to the New River and looked down warily as she crossed the bridge. The tree-covered mountains rose up beneath her. The muddy river made a lazy S with the black starkness of train tracks beside it, a coal tipple and a black trestle going across the narrow part. So here was Thurmond. She drove between a few buildings and parked the car, got out, and looked around. There was not much to see. The Internet had told the truth. It was a ghost town. The only things left were various industrial-looking structures she presumed had to do with coal or the railroad, which seemed to be the only two industries the town had ever had. There was a brick bank building, abandoned. A line of other brick buildings, presumably the famous saloon and rooming house, were now hollow shells. She walked to the trestle and peered down at the churning muddy river. She didn't know if some trains still ran, so she decided not to walk across. There were a few more dilapidated buildings made of brick and stone, all covered with weeds. In the field beside the tracks was the rusted hulk of a car with kudzu trailing out of its broken windows.

The train depot had been turned into a visitor center. She walked toward it and went inside. This, at least, was a little comforting. A pleasant woman in her fifties greeted her. She could smell coffee brewing. The air-conditioning in here made her shiver. She looked at the antique furnishings and followed the self-guided tour. She learned that in its heyday Thurmond had boasted a hotel, a meat-packing plant, a drugstore, a bank, a department store, and several restaurants and boardinghouses. Twice as much commerce had come through Thurmond as through Richmond, Virginia, and Cincinnati, Ohio, put together. Fourteen passenger trains had passed each day. But then the thirties came, and with them the Depression. It had hit Thurmond hard. Things recovered during World War II, but by the seventies, when diesel locomotives came into wide use, Thurmond officially died.

She wondered where the people had lived and where they had gone. She looked through the books, but nothing really addressed that question. In the end she purchased a book about the New River Gorge, another about Dry Creek, a New River mining community, and one about a naturalist's view of the area. She paid, rubbing her arms while the woman bagged her purchases.

"Have you lived here long?" Miranda asked, with what she hoped was a nonthreatening smile.

"I live in Oak Hill," the woman said. "Back down the road a ways."

"I believe my mother was from around here."

She looked at Miranda, interested. "Is that right?"

Miranda nodded. "Would you know anyone who might have grown up here and is still around?"

She shook her head sympathetically. "I really couldn't tell you. I grew up near Charleston. I could ask Frank for you, though. He works Tuesdays and Thursdays. He's the real expert on the area. He's an old-timer, and I believe he's from these parts."

"I would appreciate it." Miranda wrote down her name and telephone number, then jotted theirs for herself.

She got into the car and drove slowly back toward Virginia. At one point she started down one of the little roads that led off what passed for the main thoroughfare in search of a house or two, but her way was soon blocked by brush. She backed her way to the highway, then turned back the way she'd come. She passed through two small towns. She thought briefly about stopping, but there was really no town center to either one, just a railroad station, a post office, and a few small houses dotted around the ever present railroad tracks. Besides, what would she do? Walk up to someone's door and say, *Excuse me, did you know Noreen Gibson?*

She drove to the main highway, got on, and barreled south. And for a moment she felt closer to her mother than she ever had in her life. For in this moment, there was nothing she wanted more than to get away from this place. As far and as fast as she could.

It was nearly eight o'clock by the time she arrived back in Abingdon. The sun was just setting. On impulse, she drove past the funeral home and stopped at the small park near the head of the Creeper Trail. She parked the car and got out, locking it, but leaving the cooler and her purse for now. She walked to the little creek, just needing to be in a serene place. The golden light was dappling through the trees, shading and sunning her. She felt peaceful for the first time since she had left this afternoon. She sat. down by the edge of water. It ran cheerfully past her, and little by little, her tension began to melt.

She heard someone approaching and reluctantly turned to look. Joseph Williams was walking toward her through the park.

She sighed and moved to stand up. She was probably breaking some law.

"Wait," he said.

She turned to face him, wondering what she had done this time to earn his ire. "Look," she said. "I'm sure I'm not supposed to be sitting here, so why don't I just make it easy on both of us and go home?"

"No. You're fine. Really."

His face looked different. Less hostile?

"Please, sit back down," he said.

She closed her eyes with weariness. "I've had a really tough day," she said. "I don't have the energy to fight." When she opened them, she saw that he was holding up two brown bottles. She read the label. *Uncle Bob's Homemade Sarsaparilla Soda.*

"Actually, I've been looking for you. When I saw you drive in, I followed you. Will you join me?" He raised the bottle, then uncapped it and held it out to her. It was cold and sweating.

"Thank you," she said. She took a sip. It tasted tangy and refreshing. "Where did you get these?"

"Over at the market," he said. "Jerry mostly sells them to rich tourists. Usually I drink Mountain Dew, but I wanted to impress you."

"Is this Abingdon's version of taking a lady out for a drink?"

"Pretty much. Afterward we could go see the tractor pull if you want." He smiled and they both sat down.

"You seem . . . happy today," she said.

"What you really mean to say is that I seem less of a jerk than all the other times we've met."

"Well, yes, I suppose you could put it that way."

He took another drink of his soda, then turned to face her. "I messed up. I was wrong about you. I was sure you were part of a bunch of scam artists who travel around here each spring, but I realize now that I was wrong."

She watched his earnest face, and several competing emotions rose up. Anger, curiosity, amusement. The sarsaparilla was cold, the music of the creek soothing, and to tell the truth, a familiar face, even his, seemed like heaven after the stark oppression of her journey. Amusement won by a hair. She smiled and shook her head. "I don't think I'm smart enough to scam anybody. I barely get by."

"I doubt that."

"You don't know me," she said with a rueful smile, and she heard a little bitterness in her voice. Would he think her honest and right and good if he did know her?

"Anyway, I apologize. I was wrong and I acted rudely."

She looked at him curiously. His face was stern, as if he were scolding himself, and she realized then that Joseph Williams was probably as harsh with himself as he had been with her. "It's okay," she said quietly. "Everyone makes mistakes."

He looked at her with mild surprise, and then his eyes warmed. He really became a different person when the hard mask was removed.

"I guess Henry was right about you," he said.

"Oh, and what did Henry say?"

"That you would probably forgive me," he answered.

But she had a feeling now he was the one not telling the whole truth.

chapter 37

Abingdon was not like any other place Miranda had lived. In other cities—Seattle, Minneapolis, New York, Pittsburgh, San Jose—business marched along on Sunday. Oh, the banks might be closed and the mail not delivered, but stores were open, the streets were busy, and people were out and about. Even in Nashville, the very epicenter of the Bible Belt, there was activity on Sundays. In their neighborhood the bars opened at noon, and the regulars arrived soon after, but here in Abingdon, things were different. In downtown Abingdon the bar was closed. The shops were closed. In Abingdon on Sunday morning people went to church.

The Hasty Taste was closed, so Miranda decided to take another walk down the trail, and as she passed through town she saw the steady parade of people going into their various houses of worship. She felt a little out of step. She wondered if she might like to go to church again. Maybe someday, she decided. She walked down the middle of Main Street, past the four big churches on their respective corners.

She read the reader boards outside each one and glanced surreptitiously at the people entering. At the Episcopal church, people had formed an orderly line and were filing in. They were generally a well-dressed crowd, though she did see an occasional pair of jeans or khaki pants. The Catholic Mass must have already started. The doors were closed, and no one was going in late. She read the name. Shepherd of the Hills. She liked it very much. She liked thinking about God like that—a kind and trustworthy Shepherd.

Abingdon Presbyterian must be beginning, as well. The congregation was flowing in from the parking lot. A few greeted her. And lastly, there was St. James Methodist, where she had rested and where she had met the kind Pastor Hector. The reader board held a sentiment in plastic letters behind glass. *Come to me*, it said, *all you who are weary and burdened, and I will give you rest*, and Miranda remembered the Scripture plaques at the campground that had seemed like words of life to her.

It sounded good, she realized. Perhaps for the first time since going to the church service in Minneapolis, she was tempted to go in. The prospect of rest and living water, succor and shade for the traveler, seemed cool and inviting. The service was ready to start, perhaps had already started. She hesitated, was ready to turn away, and just like magic Eden came running across the lawn from the parking lot, clutching something in her hand. She waved madly at Miranda, and Miranda smiled and waved back. Today Eden was wearing a pair of khaki-colored Capris, a red T-shirt, and some flip-flops, probably as close to dressed up as she got. "I forgot my Bible in the car. I was thinking about you. And here you are! It's like it was *meant to be*! You are coming to church, aren't you?" She looked so excited and hopeful Miranda almost weakened.

"No," she said, shaking her head. "I was just heading toward the trail."

"Oh, come on! Pastor Hector would really like it. You could sit by me."

Ruth appeared at the door and came toward Eden. "Oh, Miranda," she said warmly, "are you coming in?" She looked pleased and excited, as well, and for just a second Miranda thought of herself as a weary, thirsty traveler being invited in to drink cool water and rest. *Why would you resist?* she wondered. *Why would you not follow them into a place of peace and comfort?*

"I'm not dressed for church," she protested, throwing her last card on the table and hoping it was a winner.

"Nonsense," Ruth said. "Whatever you're wearing is church attire. Isn't that right, Eden?"

Eden nodded quickly, and seeing she was defeated, Miranda followed them inside, wincing as she looked down at her jeans and cotton shirt. Ruth shepherded her to the aisle along the right wall, then stood aside and pointed for her to go in. She did so, stepping over people and excusing herself, watching her feet until she came to an empty section of pew. Relieved, she sat down, then looked to her left to see she was sitting beside Mr. Thundercloud himself. She chided herself. She wondered if he would still be a kinder, gentler Joseph. She would find out, for Eden slid in beside her, sealing her fate.

"Look who's here!" Eden leaned across her and whispered to her uncle excitedly.

He lifted his eyebrows and nodded slightly. "I see," he said.

Miranda pointed her face straight ahead and tried to concentrate on the service.

Eden handed her a bulletin. On the front was a pen-and-ink drawing of the church. She opened it up, saw the order of service, and noted the theme of every song, verse, and of the sermon, then sat stunned as she read the greeting under the date. It was Mother's Day.

How had she forgotten this? It was the second worst day of the year for her after her baby's birthday. She had known it was coming, of course. The ads in the paper had been all about Mother's Day presents and such. But with her new job and her new apartment and driving to West Virginia and looking for her baby, she had forgotten all about it. And now it ambushed her. She'd had no time to prepare. She felt sick to her stomach. She felt lightheaded. She told herself to get a grip. Eden was staring at her. She looked up and Joseph was staring at her, too, with an expression of concern rather than the suspicion she normally expected from him.

"Are you all right?" he asked. "You're as white as a sheet."

"I'm feeling a little dizzy," she said. "I'll be all right in a minute."

Someone stepped up to the pulpit, welcomed them, and made the announcements. The organ played the prelude; the pastor read the invocation. They sang a hymn, and by the time they'd recited the Apostles' Creed, which she read along in the hymnal, she was able to breathe.

They sat back down. She glanced at Eden, who was looking at her worriedly. She focused on the words in front of her as they did a responsive prayer for Mother's Day: *"For our mothers who have given us life and love . . ."*

"We pray to the Lord."

"For mothers who have lost a child through death, that their faith may give them hope, and their family and friends support and console them . . ."

She thought of her mother taking her baby away from her and giving it to someone else, someone more deserving. She thought maybe that was sort of like a death.

The congregation answered, "We pray to the Lord."

"For women, though without children of their own, who like mothers have nurtured and cared for us . . ."

She thought of the woman who had mothered her baby and hoped she was kind and good.

"We pray to the Lord."

"For mothers who have been unable to be a source of strength, who have not responded to their children and have not sustained their families . . ." the pastor said.

And she felt as if she could take a deep breath after that, that at least someone acknowledged that there were other mothers like that, who wounded instead of healed. Then she noticed Eden's rigid posture and blank stare, and suddenly Miranda realized how selfish she'd been. *Think of what poor Eden is going through,* she told herself. Eden had already intimated that she felt her mother didn't want her with them in Minneapolis. Being eleven and having to cope with what felt like rejection, not to mention her father's injury, was an incredible load to carry.

She held her hand out toward Eden, and their eyes met. They exchanged a glance that only two people who have known that pain could share, and quietly Eden slipped her hand into Miranda's. The reading concluded.

"Loving God, you said you love us as a mother loves the child she has borne, and that even though we might forget you, you would never forget us. For you have engraved us on the palms of your hands . . ."

"We pray to the Lord."

"Amen."

She looked down at Eden's hand in her own for a moment. It was small and fit inside hers as if it had been made to go there. The nails were clean, but there was a Band-Aid and a scar on the thumb. It was warm and sun-browned, and for a moment Miranda let herself pretend that Eden was her child, that they were a mother and daughter in church on Mother's Day. It was a sweet fantasy. The pastor's voice brought her out of it. She gave Eden a smile, her hand a final squeeze, and let it go. Eden smiled back, and Miranda felt as if they had been shipmates together on a rough patch of sea.

There were more hymns and prayers, and finally Pastor Hector got up and preached a sermon, but she barely heard any of it. And finally, it was over.

People stood milling about. She would have loved to have ducked out, but there were ten people between her and the far aisle, and Joseph was on the other side. Eden was deep in discussion with her grandmother. That left her and Joseph.

He turned toward her. "How are you this morning?" he asked.

She felt a sense of relief, maybe because of the tension, and she was afraid for a minute that she might burst into hysterical laughter. She smiled instead. "Fine, thank you. And you?"

"Very well." He cleared his throat. "It's another beautiful day," he observed, glancing at the sun streaming in the windows.

"Yes. It looks like it will be." She smiled. He nodded. They seemed to have run out of weather conversation. Thankfully, they were saved again by Eden. "Miranda, can you come for dinner?"

"Oh no, Eden, thank you."

"It was my idea," Ruth said, leaning over to speak to her. "Please come. It will make the day more special for me. We're going home to change, and then we're going out to the camp-ground. Hector is coming and a few other friends. We're going to barbeque and play softball. Please join us."

It sounded like fun. And suddenly going back to the little apartment to sit by herself and wonder about her baby all day did not. She glanced toward Joseph. He lifted his head from his feet to meet her eyes. "Come," he said. "I would like it if you did." And for no good reason she blushed. Eden grinned delightedly.

"Well," Miranda said. "Yes, then. Thank you."

They filed out, and she was very aware that Joseph was behind her. At the door a young boy was standing with a box full of carnations. "For the mothers," he said. Ruth took one and thanked him profusely. Eden passed. And then it was her turn. "Are you a mother?" the boy asked her, and it was her imagina-tion, she knew, but for a beat it seemed as if the whole world stopped to hear her answer.

"I don't have any children," she murmured, and whether it was technically the truth or not, she knew she didn't deserve a flower.

chapter 38

The weather was trying to do its part to make up for her gloomy trip into West Virginia. Miranda went with Eden, Joseph, and Ruth back to Ruth's house and helped them pack up lunch. Ruth changed into jeans, a short-sleeved chambray blouse, and tennis shoes. Miranda could picture her running a camp full of screaming kids. Joseph came in, now dressed in jeans and an Abingdon Police baseball team T-shirt. He carried a canvas sack full of balls and gloves and bats. Eden was now wearing denim shorts.

"They're better for grass stains," Ruth pointed out.

Grady showed up at some point and was introduced to Joseph. Grady seemed intimidated, but Miranda could understand that. Joseph could be an intimidating figure.

"Unbend a little," Ruth chided her son. "He's shy."

Joseph gave her a longsuffering look.

Miranda watched. She felt lucky just to be here, but if she spoke out of turn, they might suddenly look at her and realize they had made a mistake to invite her.

"Eden," Ruth said. "Do you want to call your mom now?"

"No. I'll call her later. When we get home." The little face closed.

Ruth nodded. "Did you bring some extra clothes or swim trunks, Grady?" Ruth asked.

"Yes, ma'am," he said.

"I'm sorry your father couldn't come."

"Yes, ma'am. He had to work."

Miranda wondered what had happened to Grady's mother and realized again that she was not alone in her sorrow or in the brokenness of her family.

Finally the food was packed into Ruth's car, and baseball equipment, towels, swimsuits, and Flick were loaded in the back of Joseph's truck. Miranda rode with Ruth. Joseph took the children. Ruth drove expertly through town and down winding roads, then turned onto the little dirt road, now familiar to Miranda. Ruth's expression grew sentimental as she pulled the car to a stop in the graveled lot at the top of the hill. Joseph and the children pulled in behind them. Grady and Eden erupted out of the truck and went running down to the lake with Flick leading the way, a blur of black and white. Joseph unloaded the truck, but Ruth just sat still and looked out at the cabins and lake.

Miranda waited quietly. She tried to imagine what it would feel like to have a place where you felt you belonged and then to lose it. After a moment Ruth turned her face to Miranda's and gave her a smile. "We'd better get out. The hordes will be here soon, and they'll be hungry."

Pastor Hector arrived. Ruth's friend Vi and her husband, Henry, the sheriff, arrived and another friend of theirs named Carol Jean. Miranda liked the two women immediately. Father Leonard, the Catholic priest, arrived with five youngsters—foster children from the group home he ran, Ruth explained, and Miranda's pulse began racing. A group home for foster children. Why, any one of them could be her child. She tried to assimilate the fact that this could be the answer to her quest. That she had just come here and her child had been delivered to her. On Mother's Day. But a foster home?

She wondered if her mother could have been so cold. To not

even try to place her child with an adoptive family but send him or her off to a group home. Would she have done that? Could she have been so cruel? Or perhaps the adoption had fallen through, unbeknownst to her mother?

She became aware that Ruth and Vi and Carol Jean were staring at her.

"How long has the group home been here?" she asked, her voice unsteady.

The three women frowned and tried to think. "Oh, it's been twenty or thirty years, I think," Ruth answered. "New crops of children all the time, of course."

"New crops?"

"Yes," Carol Jean answered. "Some get placed for adoption. Some grow up and leave. Some move to other facilities when they hit teen years."

"Do they go to the public school?"

"I believe they take them over to St. Anne's School in Bristol." Ruth gave Miranda a curious look. Vi did, as well.

Miranda barely noticed. Her mind was frozen, and she was almost mute. She stared at the children and tried to make out their faces. What if her child had somehow ended up there?

"Excuse me for a moment," she said to the women and walked down to the water to get a closer look.

She stood close but not among them. She looked them over. There were three boys and two girls. One boy was tall and gangly, an adolescent, African-American, and obviously older than eleven. One was very small and thin and was a possibility, though he looked too young. The other was about the right age, and she searched him to see if he looked familiar in any way. Nondescript brown hair, average face. She saw nothing that made her think he might be hers. She scrutinized the girls. One was seven or eight, obviously too young. The other looked the right age, but both were African-American. She stared at the small boy and the average one. One of them could be hers.

Eden came over, obviously happy. "Want to come swimming, Miranda?"

I don't care about swimming, she wanted to say. *Go find out that boy's birthday for me,* she wanted to demand, *and that one's, also.* Of course, she said nothing of the kind. "Maybe later," she smiled. "I'd better get back and help." And with one last look at the children, she climbed back up the hill.

She forced herself to calm down. She made a plan. She would find out the two boys' birth dates. She would look for a way, and the way would present itself. But even if she had to resort to walking up to them and asking, she would not leave here until she had done it. Having decided, she felt a little better, and she knew she must come back to the here and now.

Other cars arrived, and soon there were more women and men and everywhere children. She remembered that Ruth had vaguely referred to "a few friends" and smiled. Ruth seemed to collect people the same way others collected stamps or coins.

"The lodge is open if anyone needs a bathroom or kitchen supplies or a fridge," Ruth hollered. Hector, Henry, Joseph, and Father Leonard went inside and then emerged after a few minutes, carrying out long tables, which Ruth and Miranda covered with white sheets. Then they began setting out the food.

There were salads of all kinds and cut-up fruit, chips, squeeze bottles of condiments, and plates with pickles and lettuce and tomatoes. There were baked beans and creamed corn, mounds of fried chicken and pimiento-and-cheese sandwiches. There were coolers full of soda and ice and jars full of iced tea. The dessert table was filled with cakes and pies and fruit cobblers, some decadent-looking dessert bars with coconut and chocolate, and someone had a hand-cranked ice cream freezer going under the trees.

Joseph had appeared with an oil drum barbeque grill as big as Ruth's car, which he fired up immediately. He and Henry began mixing up barbeque sauce from an assortment of bottles. Soon there were hot dogs, hamburgers, and chicken sizzling on the grill.

The children laughed and screeched down by the water. Miranda smiled at the sound of splashing and the sight of the bare arms and legs. The men laughed and joked and drank sodas and grilled the food. The women bustled and worked and smiled and talked, and there were two babies, plump and drooly, and over it all, the sound of laughter and the warm sun on her head. She helped and then just watched, drinking it in like something her soul had thirsted for, and suddenly she remembered a plaque in the dining hall. What had it said? She had memorized it that day and could say it by heart. *Whoever drinks the water I give him will never thirst. Indeed, the water I give him will become in him a spring of water welling up to eternal life.*

She engaged in conversation with several of the women, wishing she had better answers to give their kind questions. She realized she was a woman without a history. She had never stayed put long enough to make one. Hers was a patched-together life, and she wondered if it would always be this way.

They prayed. They ate. And ate some more. The children screamed and splashed and ran around. Looking puffy and comical in their orange life vests, they took paddle boats out onto the lake. Joseph organized a softball game. Miranda got two hits and then struck out on Father Leonard's fastball.

She rested after the game and chatted with the priest as they watched the children play. He was probably in his late sixties with a shock of unruly white hair and dark eyebrows. Her pulse sped up again as she realized this was her chance.

"How old are most of the children in your home, Father?" she asked.

"They range from eight to fourteen right now," he said.

Not the answer she wanted. "The two younger boys," she said. "They're awfully cute."

"Um-hmm." A noncommittal answer.

"How old are they?" she asked.

He gave her a curious stare. "Mark is eleven. Joshua is nine."

She nodded and they sat in silence. She debated whether or not she should ask another question. "Do you have any foster children whose parents gave them up for adoption?" she finally asked.

"All of them," he answered, giving her a blank look.

"No, I mean, has there ever been a child who had an adopted family lined up, and then for some reason it fell through?"

He frowned. "Why do you ask?"

"Just curious," she said, trying for a shrug.

"Yes," he said. "There's one." He nodded toward the mob. "Something was wrong with him, and the adoptive parents backed out. They wanted a perfect child," he said.

"What was the matter?"

"A genetic defect," he said. "A blood disorder. He bounced around a few times and finally landed with us. He's been here six years now."

"Wouldn't he be returned to the birth parent in a case like that?"

Father Leonard gave her a searching look. "They're not merchandise, you know. They're children. They're nonreturnable."

She felt shamed and stung by his rebuke, but she could hardly bear the thought of her child suffering apart from her, unwanted and tossed aside. Not once but twice. Three times. "Which boy was it?" she asked.

"Are you shopping, Miss DeSpain?" His tone was incredulous.

She turned to face him, unwilling to back down. He gazed back, meeting her eyes, face still as stone. Obviously, he was not going to talk.

"Is he all right now?" she finally asked quietly.

Father Leonard paused, then nodded, a little more kindly. "He's all right."

She gave a quick return nod, and an awkward pause stretched out, which she feared would be followed by questions. "I'd better go see if I can help clean up," she said. The day didn't look pleasant and bright any longer. The sooner she was out of here the better. Perhaps she would walk home by herself.

"Look, I'm sorry I spoke sharply," Father Leonard said. "It's a tender subject for me."

"It's a tender subject for me, too," she said, her voice tight, then turned away and stood quickly. She was afraid she would cry.

Joseph appeared and stood between them, looking from one to the other. "Am I interrupting something?" he asked.

"No," Miranda said, "I was just going to help clean up."

"And I was going to go back for another burger," Father Leonard said, rising. "Fine job, my boy." The priest moved off toward the food. She turned to follow.

"Wait," Joseph said, and he caught her wrist gently.

She stopped and faced him. She was surprised, for he looked a little vulnerable, an expression she hadn't seen on him.

"Would you like to take a walk up the trail?" he asked.

She hesitated, wondering if it was an ambush. He seemed to read her thoughts.

"No agenda or ulterior motive," he said, making an X over his chest. "Other than a few minutes of what I hope will be pleasant conversation on a beautiful day."

"I'm upset," she finally admitted. She sniffed away her tears, but she could feel the red splotches beginning on her neck. She always broke out with them when she became angry or cried.

"I can see that." His voice was kind. "I'm a detective, you know." A quirky smile. "Come take a walk," he said. "I'll do the talking, and you can regroup. After fifteen minutes I guarantee your troubles will seem like nothing compared to your boredom."

She smiled in spite of herself. Another minute's pause. "Okay," she said. "I'll take a walk."

They walked. He talked, as promised. She breathed deeply and reeled in her stinging heart.

"This trail is thirty-four miles long," he said. "It follows an abandoned railroad and is named after the train, the Virginia

Creeper, which is about what it had to do to climb up the mountains. But this part is flat and perfect for walking."

She could feel her pulse slow, her face cool. He continued in a quiet voice, deliberately distracting her, she suspected, giving her time to gather herself together.

"My great-grandmother and great-grandfather on my pop's side used to live over there on Whitetop Mountain," he said, pointing east, "not far from where I live now. For years up on the mountain there was no railroad and barely any roads. There were pockets of people up there like them who might as well have lived in another time. They built log houses and plowed with mules and doctored themselves with plants and roots. Those are my people," he said.

She saw who he was for the first time and realized he could not be really known in any place but here. Some people belonged to their settings.

"Anyway, the trail runs from Abingdon down to the Carolina border and intersects with the Appalachian Trail near here. We get bird watchers, fishermen, naturalists, and historians. The rock around here is almost all limestone. Underground streams eat it away and make sinkholes and caverns. You never know what's under your feet."

She smiled. He smiled back. He was really quite handsome when he smiled. He had an almost perfectly symmetrical face, a straight nose. His mouth was relaxed into a smile today instead of the grim line she had first seen. His forehead was unlined, and his green eyes gentle.

"What kind of tree is this?" she asked, pointing toward the huge mammoth with the opening as big as a man in the roots.

"It's a giant sycamore," he said. "They like their feet to be wet. Look for them near streams. The first settlers slept inside them while they were clearing the land for their cabins. I've heard the woods were so thick they couldn't grow grains. They ate turkey breast and called it bread."

She tried to imagine the woods so dark and deep and didn't

have to strain her imagination. "I went to West Virginia the day we had sarsaparilla by the creek," she said.

"Oh?"

She nodded. "I was looking for my mother's people. She was from Thurmond."

"Where the only difference between it and hell is the river," Joseph said.

She nodded and barely suppressed a shudder. "It's true," she said. "There's a darkness there. I could feel it."

He didn't ridicule her, just looked at her wisely. "I know what you mean," he said. "I can feel it, too, in different places. I don't feel it here, though," he said. "I suppose that's why I stayed on when I probably should have left. To try to do everything I can to keep the darkness out."

"I'm glad you did," she said, and then felt a little embarrassed, but he didn't seem to read more into the comment than he should have. They walked on peaceably, and he pointed out more trees and birds. He told her there were bears that sometimes wandered onto the trail, and bobcats. He showed her his favorite fishing stream but said to find the best spot he followed it deep into the woods.

"Was it fun growing up at the camp?" she asked.

He smiled. "It was a boy's paradise. My brother and I had forts in the woods, and BB guns. We swam in the lake and fished and rowed. We hunted in the woods. There were always kids to play with. School was the only insult."

She smiled. "I can imagine. It seems like a wonderful place to live."

"You should have met my dad," he said. "He was a great man."

"How long ago did he die?"

"About thirteen years ago," he said.

"I wish I could have met him, too."

They had reached the bridge over the confluence of the two branches of the Holston River. "I suppose we should turn back," he said. "They'll be wondering where we went."

They watched the muddy water of the Middle Fork merge with the clear water of the South. "The Middle Fork drains farmland," Joseph explained. "Lots of dirt and sludge. The South drains the mountains where it's too rocky to farm, so it's clear."

She wished she, too, had a history. A place. Somewhere she knew she belonged, whose features she knew. "I envy you," she said.

"Why on earth do you envy me?" He looked genuinely surprised.

"Because you know where you belong."

He gave her an inscrutable look. "I suppose."

They turned and walked back. "Thank you," she said after they'd traveled awhile. He didn't ask what for, and she was glad.

"You're welcome," he said. "Do you feel like talking about what upset you?"

She was tempted. Genuinely tempted. She desperately needed an ally. Someone she could trust, but she didn't know if he fit that description. Would she ever know? she wondered. "Maybe someday," she said, and he nodded, seeming content for now with that answer.

As they walked back toward the campground, Miranda was aware of many sets of eyes on them.

Apparently Joseph was, as well. "It's a small town," he said. "I'm afraid they'll all be talking tomorrow."

"Let them talk," she said easily and continued walking beside him.

The party was breaking up. Miranda waited for a chance to talk to the two boys, but she had none. In fact, they were dressed and loading back into Father Leonard's van. She felt a sinking feeling as they did so. Fortunately, Lieutenant Joseph was busy moving tables and loading up equipment, so she didn't have to contend with his probing eyes.

She helped Ruth pack up, and just as they were ready to leave, both Henry and Joseph got calls on their cell phones within minutes of each other. They both conversed in monosyllables, and right before her eyes, the kind, relaxed Joseph became the suspicious detective again. He closed his phone with a snap just seconds before Henry did, and arrangements were quickly made for Ruth and her and the children to be transported back to town without Joseph's truck.

"I've got to go, sweetie," Henry said to Vi. "The Travelers have struck again."

"Who are they?" Miranda asked Ruth, who was shaking her head in dismay.

"They're thieves and criminals," Joseph answered grimly, and as he and Henry headed for their cars, Miranda caught sight of Grady. He had gone pale beneath his freckles, and he looked as if he might cry.

chapter 39

Miranda recovered her optimism as she slept, and when she awoke on Monday morning she was hopeful and bold. How hard, after all, could it be to find out the birth date of one eleven-year-old boy? She served breakfast, looking up in anticipation whenever the bell jingled but had to admit she was a little disappointed when Henry Wilkes came in alone for his oatmeal and peaches. The other side of the booth stayed empty. She glanced at it when she was taking Henry's order and flushed when she noticed him noticing. He smiled knowingly when she served him. She left his booth in a flustered hurry. After he left, she looked at the empty booth and wondered for a fleeting minute if the walk yesterday had just been a mirage. "Everything's not always about you," she muttered to herself; then she centered her mind on her job and stayed busy.

Pastor Hector came in around eight, and she served him breakfast. On an impulse she asked Venita if she could take a short break, and upon getting permission, she stopped at Hector's booth. "May I ask you a question?" she asked.

"Of course. Please, sit down." He put aside the book he was reading. *The Story of Christianity* by Justo Gonzalez.

"Interesting reading," she said as she slid into the booth.

"Indeed. Gonzales was one of my seminary professors. Also a compatriot. We are both native Cubans. Now Americans. He's first generation. I'm second."

Miranda looked at Pastor Hector with interest. You never knew a person's story, she realized, unless you asked.

"Your parents came from Cuba?"

He nodded. "They escaped on a leaky boat, but once their feet touched American soil they were safe."

"Like the cities of refuge in the Bible. Places where, no matter who you'd been before, you had a new chance."

He looked at her, interested. "Exactly."

"My neighbor used to tell me about them," she said. "He was a Christian, too."

She expected he would ask her if she was one then, and try to talk her into becoming one, but he just looked at her with that interested smile and something else in his eyes. It was as if he liked whom he was looking at, whether she believed the same things he did or not, and she felt a warm surge of acceptance.

"I was wondering about something," she said, heading the conversation back to her mission.

"Shoot."

"I would like to find out a little bit about one of the children at the group home. Do you have any ideas how I could do that?"

He was silent for a minute. "I assume the obvious answer has already been ruled out."

She nodded. "I put his dander up the other day."

Pastor Hector laughed. "That's not hard to do."

She waited. He seemed to be considering. "Your best friend here in Abingdon is probably the person who knows the most about what's going on. She prides herself on being well informed." His grin told her immediately whom he meant.

She laughed and nodded. Of course. She should just ask Eden. "I'll talk to her after school." She thanked him, stood up, and went back to work, and it wasn't until he had left that she realized he had never asked her why she wanted to know. Odd, now that she thought about it.

Joseph had skipped breakfast at the Hasty Taste and arrived at work early on Monday morning, then proceeded to stew in frustration. Yesterday's scam involved two more heat pump sales, this time in his jurisdiction. He had already spent too much time berating himself for going to the picnic while the Travelers invaded his territory. Now he was going to work the problem. He had spent hours yesterday afternoon visiting every trailer lot and campground, talking to managers and residents in search of the mysterious Ram truck and Jayco trailer. They were elusive, to say the least. According to his inquiries, those driving RVs were families or sportsmen. No one had aroused suspicion of any kind. He had even driven around any spots on private land that he thought might be inviting to someone wanting to lay low. He had turned up nothing.

His interviews with the crime victims had yielded some interesting facts, though. There was a group of these scam artists, not just one or two. Not exactly a surprise. One man had done the initial selling in both cases. He had been tall, gray-haired, and described by both victims—who happened to be women—as "charming." The actual work, however, had been done by two-men crews, separate ones, according to the descriptions given. In all cases the con men had driven white vans.

One homeowner had become suspicious during the installation and had gotten the plate number of the van. But that, too, was a dead end. The plate turned out to have been stolen from a car in Alabama six months ago. Joseph was heartily sick of these fellows' activities.

He decided to take the offensive. He knocked at the chief's office door and was admitted. Ray Craddock was probably Joseph's own age but more of a bureaucrat than a policeman. He

had been hired from outside the department, an upstart from the
D.C. area. Part of the town manager's idea to bring in new blood.
The chief listened attentively to Joseph, then gave him leave to do
whatever he thought best. Joseph proposed a town meeting to
inform the residents of Abingdon of the threat, as well as a press
release to the news media. A joint operation with the Washington
County Sheriff's Department.

"All right," Chief Craddock said, "as long as we get credit for
the idea."

"Why don't you take credit personally, Chief?" Joseph suggested. "You can talk about it when you speak to the reporters."

"Good idea, Williams. I like the way you think."

Joseph suppressed a smile. He had found early on that the two
of them could have a smooth working relationship if he did the
police work and left the posturing and cameras to the chief. Both
of them seemed perfectly satisfied with the arrangement. "Great,"
he said. "I'll get the meeting arranged."

An hour later the high school gym had been reserved, the
press release composed, and the town meeting set for Thursday
night. Chief Craddock would conduct it, but Joseph and Henry
would be on hand to answer questions. He stopped by the chief's
office to tell him about the arrangements and to give him a copy
of the release.

"This won't do," the chief said, shaking his head as he read
what Joseph had written. "You need to be more careful how you
phrase things. I don't want any lawsuits."

"What do you mean, sir?" Joseph asked, confused.

"You can't call them Irish Travelers," he said.

"Well, what should I call them?" Joseph asked, trying not to
show his ire.

"Call them . . . ah . . . itinerant self-employed vendors and
craftspeople who may be of Western European descent and sometimes misrepresent their products or abilities. And say something
about this by no means indicating that all such people belonging
to the Western European–American community are criminals."

Joseph kept his eyes from rolling by sheer force of will. "Then why have the meeting at all, sir?" he asked.

"Because if we don't, it will look bad." Craddock looked at him as if he were a simpleminded child.

Joseph took his leave and left his boss rewriting the press release. Well, he had done all he could on that for now. Besides, he was hungry. He decided to go to the Hasty Taste and get an early lunch. His step quickened and he brightened at the thought, although he didn't examine the feelings too deeply.

⟨ᘓ⟩

"Oh, hello, Mr. Adair, please come in." Ruth held the door open. Johnny Adair again had his hat in his hands.

"I'm sorry to bother you, ma'am."

"Why, it's no bother at all. Come in, come in."

Mr. Adair stooped and picked up a bushel basket at his feet. It was full of the prettiest peaches Ruth had ever seen.

"I know it's not much, but I just wanted to say thank you for how kind you've been to my boy."

"Oh, my goodness! Why, you shouldn't have. You know we enjoy having Grady. Come into the house, please."

He stepped inside. "Just tell me where you want these, and I'll set them down."

"In the kitchen, please, Mr. Adair. Oh my! They're going to make some lovely pies. And just in time for the church supper."

"These are June Blush peaches from South Carolina," he said, following her into the kitchen. "They have seventeen to eighteen percent sugar content. Once you taste one of these, you've tasted a peach."

"Let's cut one up now, shall we?" Ruth asked, anxious to sample.

He grinned. "You're a woman after my own heart."

She smiled and turned to find her paring knife. "Where's Grady?" she asked.

"I left him back at the trailer," he said. "I don't want him wearing out his welcome."

Ruth's outrage was sincere. "Oh, Mr. Adair, you mustn't feel that way. Honestly . . ." She went to the hallway and checked to make sure Eden wasn't home from school yet. "We're just so glad Eden has a friend," she said confidentially. "And Grady is such a wonderful boy. You'd be doing us both a favor if you let him come every day."

He looked hesitant. She would give him a minute to let the thought grow on him. She took one of the peaches, peeled and sliced it, and brought it to the table on a saucer. They each had a slice. Ruth closed her eyes. "Oh, this is heavenly."

"I told you."

She smiled, suddenly liking Mr. Adair very much. "Would you like a cup of coffee? I was just ready to take a break from my sewing, and I'd love the company."

He hesitated a minute, then apparently decided to accept her hospitality. "Yes, I would. I tell you, Mrs. Williams, sometimes this old life gets the best of me." He set his hat on the extra chair and suddenly looked older and more tired than he had the other day.

She put the coffee on, then sat down across from him. "Are you hungry?"

He shook his head. "I had lunch not long ago. Let's both of us just rest."

She nodded and let herself relax. He was pleasant company, Mr. Adair. He reminded her of someone she'd known. And liked. Funny how those things worked. She had seen it go the other way, too. She'd taken a dislike to someone because they reminded her of a mean teacher or a boy who'd snubbed her.

"Please, call me Ruth," she said in a sudden burst of warmth.

"I'd like that," he said. "And you call me Johnny."

The coffee brewed. She poured them each a cup. They sipped appreciatively. She cut up another peach. "These are going to be wonderful in a cobbler."

"They'll need very little sugar, Ruth. They're just as sweet as they can be all by themselves. But it's not just sugar that makes a good peach," Johnny continued, seriously intense. "It's the right balance of sugar and acidity. And you have to leave them on the tree until they're ready to drop. And by then, they're too ripe to ship. So to get a good peach you almost have to be there when it falls into your hand and then eat it on the spot." He smiled and his face creased into lines. "There are a lot of things like that in life, aren't there?"

"Yes. There are," she said, smiling, thinking of moments of joy that she'd let pass because she thought there would be an inexhaustible supply.

They each kept the company of their own thoughts for a moment. Then she spoke. "How has life gotten the best of you, Johnny?"

He sighed and shook his head. "It's this chasing around on the road. It's about to wear me out. A day here. Two days there. And the work I do is not . . . fulfilling. Sometimes I would just like to be able to stop. To settle down and rest." And the look he gave her was pure weariness.

"Why don't you, then?"

He shook his head. "I can't. I've got debts to pay. And I have to take care of Grady."

"What kind of work is it that you do, exactly, Johnny?"

He paused. "A little of this. A little of that. Sales. Home improvement. Appliance installation and repair. I travel around with the work. When there's a boom in one area, I stay until it's bust. Then I go somewhere else."

Ruth got up and reached for the coffeepot. She topped off each of their cups and chose her words very carefully. "It's a shame Grady didn't get here in time to enroll in school. Eden would have loved having him in her class."

He looked up with genuine regret in his eyes. "I know he needs to be in school. I feel bad about that. I really do. It's a bad life for him, moving around, but he was worse off with his mama." His mouth shut tight after that, signaling he had said all he was going to say. Ruth respected him for that. The woman was Grady's mother, no matter what she'd done.

"How can I help, Johnny?"

"You've helped already."

"I meant what I said about Grady. We'd love to have him every day."

He smiled, the corners of his eyes crinkling. "I know you meant it, Ruth. I can tell you're not one to say one thing and mean another. But the truth is, I'm not sure if we'll be around here much longer."

"Why not? There's plenty of work, isn't there?"

He nodded. "But the place I was parking the camper—well, I had to move it. And to be honest with you, I just can't find a place that suits me."

"I know it." She shook her head and clicked her tongue in disapproval. "It's absolutely immoral what Earl and Jim charge the tourists in the summer." She wished there was something she could do. Suddenly the answer dawned on her, and it was so elegant, so absolutely right, that she could barely keep from shouting. "Why, you can stay at my campground!" she said triumphantly.

Johnny gave her a blank look.

"Come on," she said, glancing at her watch. "We've got time to run out there."

He appeared bewildered but followed her and allowed her to drive him, since she knew the way. They pulled into the graveled lot at the hillside and stopped. "The RV sites are across that hollow behind those trees. You can't see them well from here. It's all grown up since we ran it."

"This place is yours?"

"Every inch of it," she said. "We bought this back when land was cheap and built it all ourselves. My husband and I ran this place for thirty years. Those were the sweetest times," she said, and once again she thought of those moments of joy.

He got out of the car, and she followed suit. He walked around for a few minutes looking into windows, stepping on sagging floorboards, shaking timbers, getting down on one knee and looking underneath the lodge at the foundation. He brushed off his jeans and his hands and rejoined her at the car; then they both swept their eyes across the placid lake, the green rolling grass. The wind gently brushed the leaves of the trees, and the peace that she always felt at this place descended on her.

"What do you think?" she asked.

"I think it's beautiful. And I would love to stay here."

She felt as pleased as if he had given her a gift.

"But only on one condition."

"What's that?"

"That I do some projects around here. Like shoring up that porch. Replacing those joists under there. Reglazing the windows. And it looks like the chapel could use a new roof."

Ruth felt herself getting excited. She didn't know why. There was absolutely no sense in repairing this place. There was no way she could run it herself, and neither of her sons was interested. Yet she had the feeling that this was a divinely orchestrated meeting. She had the feeling it was something that was meant to be. She was so excited she could barely contain herself. "I insist on paying you," she said.

"No, ma'am." Johnny was shaking his head. "Uh-uh."

"I can't let you do all that work for nothing."

"It's not for nothing. I'm using your land."

"Then let me keep Grady every day while you work. School's out. He and Eden will have a wonderful time together. It would be helping me. Honestly."

He hesitated. Then he nodded. "All right. I'd appreciate that. I hate for him to be alone all the time."

Ruth beamed. "And I insist on paying for the materials for the repairs."

"I still feel like I'm getting the best of things." He smiled sheepishly.

"I'm happy if you're happy," Ruth said, beaming. She felt a sweet joy at the thought of the old place hearing the sounds of joy and laughter again. And Mr. Adair looked happy, too. She could see in his eyes a look of deep satisfaction.

chapter 40

The week passed quickly for Miranda. Eden did indeed prove to be a miracle worker in the matter of the group home. Miranda had solicited her help, saying that she intended to do something for the children when their birthdays came. Not a lie, because she went to the local pizza parlor/amusement hall and purchased gift certificates for five pizza parties including game tokens. It cost a bit but was money well spent. She gave the five envelopes to Eden, saying she would like a name and birth date for each one.

"Shall I pay you to do the job?" she asked Eden, but Eden only looked insulted.

"I may need help from you someday," she said. "That's how it works with these things."

Miranda accepted her judgment and grinned as Eden rode away, today's Wanted posters tucked into the basket of her bike. She was a corker, that one. She wondered what the latest developments were with David and Sarah but didn't ask.

On Tuesday, while awaiting Eden's detective work, Miranda called Mr. Galton at the Thurmond Visitor Center. He was in and proved to be a very nice man. He sounded older, in his seventies, perhaps. It was refreshing to be able to tell the truth.

"I'm wanting to find out about my mother's life," she said. "I know she and my aunt came from Thurmond but left in the late sixties."

"Do you know their maiden name or whereabouts they lived?"

"My grandmother's name was Lois Gibson, and my grand-father's was Beck Maddux. I think they were from somewhere near Thurmond. I don't know any more than that."

"There were some Madduxes who lived up above Piney Ridge," he said. "And I might know somebody who can help you. She's old, though, and doesn't hear so well. She can't use the telephone much."

Miranda sighed. "I can come there again."

Arrangements were made. Frank graciously volunteered to meet her on his day off—this Saturday. He would personally take her to the resource person who lived deep in the woods. She suppressed a chill at the prospect of entering those dark woods again. She firmly took herself in hand. Answers were what she had come for, and if answers lay in the dark forest, then that's where she would go.

Her mother's documents arrived the next day, and she opened them eagerly. They didn't really tell her much she didn't already know, though.

She didn't see much of Lieutenant Joseph. He was busy arranging for the town meeting. There had been so much media coverage that Miranda didn't see how anyone in the small town could fail to be informed of the threat with the Irish Travelers by now. However, Abingdon was also a tourist destination in the summer, and many decent folks came through town with their campers and fifth wheels and RVs, especially when the various festivals came around. Earl and Jim's was full of vehicles, which kept Eden extremely busy making notes of all the license plates. For all the bad PR the Travelers were getting, Abingdon folks seemed friendly and trusting, certain that all the bad people were in the next county over from their own.

Miranda attended the town meeting with everyone else and was duly warned. She actually thought Joseph and Henry did an excellent job of outlining the different scams and giving people guidelines of what to watch for. After the meeting she looked his way, but he was busy at the front of the auditorium answering questions. Miranda left the meeting and was leaving to walk home when Eden appeared on her bike. She waved a manila envelope. "I got what you wanted," she said with a big grin.

"I can't believe how quickly you got all this. How did you do it?"

"Easy," she said. "Maude Lucy, the secretary at the church, was there and I just asked her. She wrote it all down and said you were real nice to think of the children."

Miranda felt a little twist of guilt, which she ignored because she was going to make it true. She took the envelope and thanked Eden, who grinned again and took off on her bike. She hurried home to her small apartment, went inside, and turned on the light. Her hands shook as she opened the clasp on the manila envelope and slid out the smaller ones. She read through the names and birth dates.

Rhonda Hatch   *July 8, 1994*
Letitia Hoyt   *December 2, 1999*
Jason Lester   *April 19, 1998*
Evan Montgomery   *February 2, 1996*
Darnell Smith   *June 10, 1991*

She put them aside with a sigh. None was her child. She had known that, though, hadn't she? Tomorrow she would ask Eden to return the envelopes to the secretary with a request to deliver one to each child on his or her birthday. From an anonymous donor.

She was set back a little by that dead end, but by Saturday morning she felt refreshed, and she steeled herself for the return to West Virginia. She packed another lunch and decided to make a quick stop at the farmers' market in the ball park across the street before leaving. It was in full swing, and she needed a few things. Besides, the day shouldn't be totally without cheer, should it? She walked slowly through the booths. There were farm fresh eggs, local honey, fruits and vegetables, baked goods, and crafts. She bought eggs, a sack of peaches, a jar of honey, and a Ziploc bag of homemade peanut butter cookies and was ready to leave when she heard a familiar voice behind her.

"Try the strawberries," he said. "They're perfect right now."

She turned with a smile. "Hello, Joseph," she said without thinking, then blushed. She usually called him Lieutenant Williams.

He smiled in return. "Hello, Miranda. Where are you off to?"

"You can tell?"

"You have a very determined expression on your face. And besides, I saw you loading up your car."

"I'm trying to keep up my spirits. I'm going back to West Virginia today."

"I thought you'd had enough."

She shrugged. "I've been given the name of someone who might have known my mother's people. The gentleman from the visitor center is going to take me to the woman's house."

He frowned and got a concerned look on his face. "You're going off with someone you don't know into the back roads of West Virginia?"

She grinned. "I don't think there are very many seventy-year-old serial killers who volunteer at the Thurmond Visitor Center."

He didn't smile. The frown didn't budge. "Even so, I don't think it's wise for you to go driving around those mountain roads alone."

"I've got my cell phone," she reassured him. "And Mr. Cooper's car is in pretty good shape."

He continued to frown, then glanced at his watch. "If you can give me another half hour, I'll take you myself."

She was speechless. She hadn't been expecting that, but

suddenly the prospect of having solid, dependable, protective Joseph sitting beside her as she drove into the dark woods seemed very appealing. "Thank you," she said. "I would like that very much."

The frown disappeared. "I'll go back to my office and take care of a few things. Shall I meet you at your place?"

She nodded. "I'll put the eggs away and make a few more sandwiches."

He smiled. She turned away before she could embarrass herself any further.

Miranda made three more sandwiches, added the peaches and cookies and a few more bottles of water, and was ready and waiting when Joseph knocked on the door.

"Let's take my truck," he suggested. "It'll take the curves better, and it looks like rain."

She glanced up at what had been a sunny sky. Sure enough, a bank of dark clouds was gathering along the western horizon.

"You'll get no argument from me," she said.

He took the cooler and put it in the back of the truck and then opened the door for her. After a few more minutes they were driving slowly through downtown Abingdon, then headed for the interstate.

"What's Eden doing today?" she asked.

"I believe she and Grady have plans. Something about going down to the campground and making traps for crooks. Ma's going with them," he said, "so it should be all right."

Miranda smiled. "I like Eden. A lot."

Joseph nodded. "I do, too. She's a lot for one person to manage, though. She's kind of like a border collie. You've got to give them work to do or they dig up the garden and chew on the hose."

Miranda laughed. "That sounds like the voice of experience."

"With both the dogs and the child." He smiled and they drove in companionable silence for a few miles.

"Have you ever lived away from here?" she asked.

"I went away to Ferrum, Virginia, to go to college."

"What did you study?"

"This," he said. "Criminal Justice. I knew I wanted to be a cop from the time I was a kid. My dad was police chief."

"I'm surprised you didn't take over his job."

Joseph shook his head. "Not for me."

"Have you been anywhere else?" she asked.

"I did a hitch in the marines," he said. "Went to Haiti and Somalia. I like it better here."

Miranda tried to recall what she knew about those conflicts. "I'm sure," she said.

His face looked sober. "It was an awful mess," he said. "After my tour of duty I came back home. I suppose you know the parts of the story I've left out."

She felt a little embarrassed. "As you said before, it's a small town."

"Your turn now," he said. "Tell me about yourself."

She did, leaving out some facts of her own—only one important fact, *the* important fact—and as she wove a tale around it, she wondered why she didn't tell him. Why she didn't tell anyone. Shame, perhaps? Yes. That was it. She was ashamed, not so much of having gotten pregnant but of having lost her baby. It felt for all the world as if she'd been horribly careless, had just mislaid him or her, set the baby down somewhere and then walked away. Maybe after she found the child, she would be able to admit having had it to begin with.

"So your father left when you were eleven. Have you seen him since?"

"I went after him twice," she said. "Found him once. The first time."

"But nothing after that?"

She shook her head and thought about telling him that he had called looking for her, but that would just lead to questions about why she was here. Besides, she had missed the call, and who knew when or if he would call again. She supposed it just wasn't meant to be. "I wouldn't have any idea where to look for him, even if I took a notion to. My mother died earlier this spring. Cancer. So I came here."

"Why here?" he asked, and he didn't look accusing, simply curious.

"My mother had a connection in Abingdon," she said. "I don't know who it was, and I'd like to find out."

"Hmm." He looked intrigued. "What led you to the conclusion she was connected to someone here?"

"A postmark on a letter."

He turned to look at her. "That's it?"

"It was an important letter." She closed her mouth. She had already said too much, and she sincerely hoped he didn't ask her any more questions because then she would have to tell him she wasn't going to answer them, and it would spoil their nice day.

He didn't ask, though, just continued driving. "Tell me some of the places you've been," he said.

She warmed to the subject, telling him about all the places she'd visited and the ridiculous jobs she'd had, about clipping a prize-winning poodle and it turning out like a rat and her having to leave town because the owner threatened to sue, about her job at the school and dressing up like Pippi Longstocking when she was crossing guard, about doing pest inspections for Mice B Gone Exterminators and the reproductive habits of rodents. They ate the sandwiches and laughed and talked so much that she was surprised when they turned off the highway and climbed the winding road to Thurmond.

Joseph got out first and looked around the abandoned town. He could see why it had spooked Miranda last time. There was a rushing sound that turned out to be the New River passing through the gorge. Misnamed, for it was actually one of the oldest rivers in the world, second only to the Nile. The town itself was at the bottom of the gorge, and the steep rock rose high above his head. It did feel oppressive and ominous. A light rain had begun falling, and all around was gravel and slick wet black tracks and coal tipples and water towers and old abandoned locomotives. The town looked as if soot had been ground down into it, as if everything would be forever coated with a gray shadow that no rains could wash away. As usual in West Virginia, the town, or what was left of it, was a narrow strip situated between the mountain, the railroad tracks, and the river.

Joseph followed Miranda into the visitor center. As she had said, an old man was there to meet her. Joseph realized his concern had been groundless. The man was probably seventy or so, tall but stooped. He had white hair and a gallant manner.

"I'm pleased to meet you both," Frank Galton said upon being introduced. After a few pleasantries, he gave them the specifics of their destination. "The person we're going to see is Ada Tallert. She was the schoolteacher in Thurmond at the one-room schoolhouse. After that closed down, the children took the bus to Oak Hill. Anyway, she's the only one who's still around who might have known your mother. Most everybody's died or left," he said.

Joseph wondered why Mr. Galton had stayed around Thurmond but didn't ask. A person's home was their home, no matter how bleak it seemed to outsiders. He felt a sense of apprehension for what Miranda might find, though. He didn't analyze the protective feelings he had for her, but he was glad he had come along. The rain went from light to pelting.

"I'll drive my own car, introduce you, and then be gone," Mr. Galton said.

Miranda thanked him. They climbed back into the truck and began the slow crawl up the sheer mountain above them. The rain poured harder. Miranda began to shiver. Joseph turned on the heater. She reached for her jacket.

"I'm awfully glad you're here," she said.

"Me too."

They followed Mr. Galton's small car up the winding road,

taking dogleg turns that would be challenging in the dark. After a half hour or so, they turned off on a small graveled road and pulled to a stop in front of a wood-frame house. The porch was cluttered with children's toys and a refrigerator box that looked as if it doubled as a playhouse. There was a bike someone had left out in the rain.

"Mrs. Tallert lives here with her granddaughter," Mr. Galton said. He knocked on the door, and a young woman answered. She was barely five feet tall with short blond hair and a friendly smile. Mr. Galton introduced them and excused himself.

"Y'all come on in," the woman said, opening the door wide. Two small girls wearing pajamas sat on the sofa drinking juice out of boxes. Their faces were covered with scabs and spots. "I hope y'all have had the chicken pox."

They both assured her they had. She led the way to a bedroom in the back where a woman Joseph presumed was Ada Tallert sat prim and straight in a recliner watching a preacher on the television.

"Some people here to see you, Grandma," the young woman shouted.

"Well, lower your voice, Francie. I'm not completely deaf, you know." She turned her sharp-boned face toward the two of them and graced them with a smile. "Come in and sit down. Will you have some refreshment?"

"I can make y'all some coffee," Francie volunteered.

"I would love a cup of coffee," Miranda said with a grateful smile, and Joseph added his own thanks.

"Grandma, you want something?" she shouted again.

"No, thank you, darling," Mrs. Tallert answered in a normal tone of voice and gave her head a little shake. The granddaughter left the room. Mrs. Tallert turned her steady gaze on the two of them.

"Sit down," she invited them.

Joseph found a folding chair and set it up for Miranda. He sat down on the foot of the bed.

Miranda chatted with Mrs. Tallert for a minute or two. Miranda was really very good at drawing people out, he noticed. The old woman was telling about her daughter, who had died recently, about the early days of the school, about her husband, who had been the yardmaster of the railroad. The granddaughter came in and handed them each a mug of coffee. They both refused cream and sugar, and she left, closing the door after her.

The conversation lagged for a moment as they sipped. Mrs. Tallert took in a deep breath and let it out slowly. She pulled the wrap she wore around her shoulders a little tighter. "So," she said, her expression becoming sober, her voice almost grieved. "I hear you want to know about what Wolf Maddux did to his girls."

And even though he was drinking hot coffee and the kerosene heater at his feet breathed out warm air, Joseph felt the hairs on his neck stand on end.

chapter 41

The room was absolutely silent except for the pelting of the rain on the window as she began to speak.

"It was back in the forties when I first met him. He was a little boy. His real name was Beck. Beck Maddux. Now that I think on it, he wasn't an especially evil child. He just had a, well, I don't know, like a blank spot where most of us know right from wrong. He could've been a handsome child if it weren't for those eyes. He was towheaded, just real white blond hair on him, so white it looked like cotton. But those eyes were the palest blue and just like a piece of glass, but there wasn't anything behind them. It was like looking into a doll's eyes. There was no life back of them.

"His home was bad, but so was some others that turned out preachers and good men. I guess it's just no telling what makes one do one way and another do another. I was schoolteacher down at Thurmond in those days. I boarded with the Anse Holt family. They were decent people, because my daddy came himself and saw to it before he would leave me. But I had the school there at Thurmond and would teach there five days a week, and on the weekends my daddy would drive over from Hinton and carry me home.

"That boy, Beck, was a smart child. He knew how to read and could do his sums, but he wouldn't work for nothing. Just stared out the window most of the time. I sent a note home to his parents telling them he wasn't doing his work, and his daddy came and met me after school. He said he was sorry, and then right in front of my eyes he pulled off his belt and whipped that child bloody. I hollered for him to stop, and cried and took on, but he didn't even change expression. He was just like a machine. *Whomp, whomp, whomp, whomp.* And the strangest thing was, I looked down at Beck, and he wasn't changing expression either. That child's face was frozen into a mask, and from that day on no matter what Beck did, I never told his parents. Maybe I should have, but I didn't.

"I saw him do some things that frightened me, just chilled me down to my bones. I saw him take a dog once . . ." She paused and looked at their faces, then shook her head. "Well, eventually he grew up and went to work in the mines. His daddy died of the black lung, and for a while it looked like Beck might be going to turn out all right. I guess he didn't have much energy left for fighting and fussing after a day below ground. I saw him one day down at the company store, and he spoke to me real sweet. He said 'Miss White'—that was my name before I married—he said, 'Miss White, you was one of the only people in my life that's been good to me, and I want you to know I appreciate it.' I cried about that." She was crying now, and Joseph saw Miranda reach for her hand.

"I asked myself for years after that, what could I have done? What could I have done different to help him, and I never can see what it might have been. Anyway, he went on and I got married to a supervisor down at the railroad, and we had a nice house and had four children. Buried one, but raised three, and every now and then I'd see Beck. He didn't live in town but up in the hills in the same house he'd grown up in. It's dark up there. Real dark, soul dark, if you know what I mean." She shook her head.

"Anyway, after I'd been married a year or so, Beck went off

to the army. They sent him to Korea. He stayed gone a few years and then come back, and everybody said he'd been dishonorably discharged. They said he'd killed another soldier, but they weren't able to prove it. He went on back up to the hills, but he didn't go back to work in the mine. The coal had just about give out by then, anyway. I heard he ran liquor up there, but I don't know. After a time he took a shine to one of the miners' girls. Her name was Lois. Lois Gibson. She was a pretty thing, now. She had blond hair, too, and pink cheeks and the sweetest smile. She wasn't one of my students. Her daddy hired on after I'd quit teaching. You know, people used to move around the camps a lot. One seam would give out, and they'd go to another.

"Well, Beck took on about Lois, and it seemed like she was in love with him, too. Her daddy wouldn't have it, though. Put his foot down one night and met Beck with the shotgun. Beck said, 'Lois, you come out here. I don't want to shoot your daddy.' And Mr. Gibson said, 'Stay where you are, Lois. You go off with him, and I guarantee you'll wish I'd have killed you both this night.'

"Well, you know what happened. That night Beck went on home, but in the morning when her daddy went into the children's room, Lois was gone. They ran off to Beckley. Stayed gone six months or so working a mine over in Mingo County, and when they came back, she was expecting a baby.

"They went back up in the hills and hardly anybody ever saw Lois after that. Her daddy went after her, and he didn't come back, and even the law was afraid of Beck by then. They started calling him Wolf, because he had a way of knowing a person's weak spot and hurting them there and because of the way he'd get somebody off alone and hurt them.

"He and Lois had three daughters. The first one, Rebecca, drowned when she was ten. That's what they said, anyway. The second was named Noreen, and the least one was Roberta. They called her Bobbie."

Miranda looked stunned. Her eyes were glassy. "Noreen," she

repeated. "Noreen was my mother." Mrs. Tallert looked shocked at first, then as Joseph watched, her face softened into sadness. After a moment she took up her story again.

"That winter Lois took influenza and died, and it was just Beck and the two little girls up in the woods. All of Lois's people had left by then. After Beck shot her daddy they'd moved to Arkansas, where they had some people. Those two little children were all alone. And that's when I knew I had to do something. My husband didn't want me to, but you know, sometimes there's things a person feels *called* to do. So the preacher's wife and I went up there together, with our husbands waiting in the car. The preacher was praying and Jimmy, my husband, had his twelve-gauge aimed out the window. But we went on up to the door, and I called out, 'Beck, it's Miss White, your teacher.' He came to the door himself after a little bit, and I wouldn't have recognized him if it weren't for that hair and those eyes. He'd just sort of withered away from the inside. It's hard to tell it.

"He spoke to me just as nice as you please, and I asked if I could come in, and he said it was a mess right now, that he couldn't make those girls do a thing. And I said, 'Beck, that's what I come to talk to you about. I want you to let those girls come down and go to school. The bus will pick them up down at the road in the morning and let them off in the afternoon. You ought to do it, Beck,' I said. 'It's the right thing.' And he said, 'You know, that's something I always did appreciate about you, Miss White. You never did act like you knew what I was like.'

"I'll never forget him saying that, but the next day the girls were there at the school. Ragged and pitiful, but they were there.

"There were some good years then, I think. Beck started letting the girls come down and go to church on Sundays. They even got to go off on trips with the young people a time or two. The only time they'd ever been out of West Virginia or even Thurmond, for that matter. The minister's wife hired Noreen and Roberta to work for her twice a week, cleaning house and taking care of her children. It was a way to give them money, you see, without hurting anybody's pride. Things went on that way for a while.

"I believe Noreen finished seventh grade. She was such a smart girl, your mama. Just as smart as a whip, and Bobbie was, too. But one day Noreen came in with a big whelp on her face, and I asked her what was wrong, and she said she'd been taking care of her sister. After that she came in with marks and bruises nearly every week. My husband and the preacher talked to the sheriff and to the mine boss, but everybody was afraid of Wolf, and back then things were different. The women were like the man's property, and he could do whatever he pleased with them.

"Well, finally one day Noreen told the preacher's wife that she was going to have a child. The preacher's wife said, 'Come away and live down here with us,' because we all knew whose child it was. But Noreen said she couldn't leave her little sister, because if she left he would just start in on her. 'Bring her, too,' the preacher's wife said—Helen was her name—but Noreen said, 'Now, Mrs. Webb, you know he'd just as soon kill us as let us go.'

"So Helen carried Noreen to see the doctor, and she was expecting, sure enough. She didn't come to school anymore after that, but the preacher's wife and I would take her things from time to time. Eggs and milk and some vegetables, when we had them. The baby was born, but it was too little and didn't live long. It was a boy and had white hair just like Wolf's.

"Shame, shame, shame. That's all she was after that. She would hold her head up real fierce, but it was shame that had her down deep. The preacher and his wife tried to help her, but something had turned hard down deep in her soul. I tried to talk to her, too, but it didn't do any good. She started slipping off from home and going down to Thurmond to the saloon there, and after a while she took up with a fellow passing through. He was a handsome thing. Name of Tommy something. Something Spanish."

"DeSpain," Miranda said, her voice hardly more than a whisper.

"That's it." Mrs. Tallert smiled gently. "Well, Tommy took a shine to Noreen and started waiting for her every night, and one night she didn't come to the saloon. Everybody warned him, but he said he wasn't afraid of some old hillbilly with a shotgun, and he drove his truck right up the mountain and parked it in front of the house.

"Some of the men followed him up there. I don't know if they meant to help or just watch the show. I believe the Lord had His hand on them that day, because Wolf had taken sick and was a–laying in the bed, or I'm sure he would have shot that young fellow. Some say one of the girls put something in his food, but I don't know about that. Anyway, Tommy went in there and saw the bruises on Noreen's face, and they said that little Bobbie was crying and begging him not to kill her daddy. They said that was the only thing that saved Beck. Said Tommy DeSpain had his pistol out and was ready to shoot him. But in the end, he just took those two girls with the clothes on their backs and left.

"I never saw them again. Neither did Helen, far as I know. She's gone now, too. She had the sugar diabetes real bad.

"Anyway, that's the story of Wolf. He died right after those girls left. He was walking across the trestle down there by town one night, drunk, and he fell and killed himself. I reckon he fell, anyway," she said.

The silence filled the room again. Joseph looked down. At some point he had reached for Miranda's hand, and their fingers were now laced tightly together.

chapter 42

Miranda was stunned. She was beyond tears. She sat in the silence after Mrs. Tallert finished telling the story. After a moment the old woman spoke again.

"I could draw you a map if you want to go up there where Lois and Rebecca and the baby are buried. Beck's cabin was just down the hollow from there. It burned down a few years back, but you can still see the chimney."

Miranda recoiled but forced herself to not run away from the pain this time. She felt as if she had to be a witness to what had happened to her mother. She nodded mutely. Joseph looked concerned. Mrs. Tallert gave him simple directions, and he nodded and thanked her.

Miranda had come with other questions, but they had been buried under this avalanche of evil. Right now she could not think. She thanked Mrs. Tallert and stood up but was surprised when the old lady held up a warning finger.

"I've got three things to say to you, child, before you leave."

What more could there be? Miranda steeled herself, nodded, and sat back down.

"You can't hear a story like that and stay right in your mind unless you know these things," she said. "So listen to me."

Miranda recognized the faint shadow of the schoolmarm at the Thurmond school.

"The first is, there's none righteous. Not one. Every one of us could have been a Beck Maddux if it weren't for the grace of God. Some might look better on the outside, but every one of us follows in Adam's footsteps one way or another."

Miranda nodded mutely.

"The second is, Ezekiel eighteen says God doesn't hold the child responsible for the sins of the parents. Or the grandparents.

"And the last thing is this. Jesus was kin to the prostitute, Rahab. He pardoned the thief on the cross, and what does Paul say about the murderers and adulterers and thieves? He says, 'Such were some of you, but you were washed.' Don't take on about this," she warned, giving Miranda a look that was both stern and compassionate. "When you see those graves, remember . . . that's your history, not your future."

She stood up and walked them to the door with much trembling and shuffling. Her granddaughter fussed, but she insisted, standing on the porch until they walked away.

They got into the car, and Joseph backed out to the main road. He stopped, then turned and faced her. "Do you really want to go up to the cabin?" he asked.

Miranda looked out the window. It was getting dark. Maybe she could come back another time, and suddenly she wanted to leave, to be out of here. But it was odd, for it was just as if someone kind and strong took her hand then, someone bigger than Joseph, and told her she should look, and she knew it would be all right. She nodded. "I do," she said.

He didn't argue but shifted, executed a quick turn, and headed up the winding road. They drove for another ten or fifteen minutes; then he turned in where Mrs. Tallert had told him. The road ended shortly afterward. They got out, and after a moment Miranda saw the chimney. It was red brick, now burned black and covered with kudzu. It was dark up here, the trees dripping rain. She walked around the ruins but got no feelings at all other than sadness this time. After a moment she and Joseph walked a ways uphill and found the three graves. They were marked with piles of stones, one large, two small. Miranda stared for a minute, and suddenly her mother's bitterness seemed amazing in its smallness. What was not understandable was how she had been able to function at all. How she had given herself to a man—to any man. How she had managed to keep a child fed and clothed. Suddenly she was remembering the presents under the tree instead of the speed with which the decorations had been put away. She had an overwhelming sense of gratitude to her mother, who had certainly given more than she'd received.

Miranda cried then for her mother and was sorry for her own hatefulness. Joseph took her hand again, and they stood there until she felt finished.

The drive home was silent. When they pulled up in front of the funeral home, Joseph unloaded the cooler and walked her upstairs to the door of the apartment.

"Thank you," she said, her voice sounding small to her ears. "I can't imagine what it would have been like without you."

His face was serious. "You're welcome. I was glad to do it."

She didn't want to be alone, but she couldn't talk, either. Finally she said good-night. He gave her hand a final squeeze and, after a last searching look, left her.

She closed the door, then went to the little window and stared out, not seeing anything but the past. Remembering and understanding. So much made sense now. About her mother and her aunt. Even about her father, who must have realized Noreen's heart could not receive him.

But something bothered her, too. Was this where she had gotten the distance, the emotional coldness that allowed her to leave without good-byes? That made her shut people out before they became indispensable? Had Beck passed that on to her? She did not want to be like Beck. She did not want his blood in her veins. She tried to remember what Mrs. Tallert had said. It had been comforting, but it eluded her now. She wished she had some proof, something real before her eyes that would remind her that goodness could come out of her, that she wasn't doomed or too far gone to redeem.

There came a tapping on the door. She drew her eyes back from the gaping stare and focused them. She shook her head and went to answer it.

"Who's there?" she asked.

"It's Eden," a voice answered.

Miranda opened the door and looked down. It was Eden, all right. She was wearing shorts and flip-flops, scratching one leg with the other foot. In her hands she carried her two-way radio, a grocery sack, and her sleeping bag and pillow. On her back was her pack. Miranda stared, puzzled.

"Uncle Joseph brought me. He said you could use some company, and Grandma said it was all right. She sent over some dinner and some brownies. I brought my scrapbook and my stories," she hurried on. "I'm working on a new plot about Annie Oakley and some train robbers. Grady helped start it today, but you could help finish. If you want to. I mean, if you want me to stay. Uncle Joseph is waiting in case you'd rather I didn't."

And suddenly there was no sweeter sight than the freckled face surrounded by thick brown cowlicks. She threw open the door. "Of course I want you," she said. "Come in."

Eden grinned, then turned and looked down over her shoulder. She made an okay sign with her thumb and forefinger.

Miranda followed her eyes. Joseph sat there in the truck, lights on, watching. She smiled and held up a hand in thanks. He nodded and drove away, and as Eden stepped inside, Miranda closed the door behind her.

chapter 43

Ruth couldn't interest Joseph in Sunday dinner. He went to work directly after church, hot on the trail of the Irish Travelers. There had been another sighting of them yesterday evening, but he'd been gone somewhere. Somewhere with Miranda, according to Eden and Grady, who had been spying on them at the farmers' market. Ruth usually disliked for him to miss Sunday dinner, but she had to admit she wasn't entirely disappointed he would be occupied today. It would give her an opportunity to talk to Johnny Adair about the campground. She felt a slight twinge of guilt for keeping the project a secret from Joseph, not to mention her trusting Johnny Adair at all. But she knew what Joseph would say, and she felt that in this case he was entirely wrong. Ruth could look into a person's eyes and tell if they were honest or not. And when she looked into Mr. Adair's eyes, she saw who he was, who he could become.

She phoned him after church and made arrangements to meet him at the camp at suppertime.

"Then allow me to introduce you to my barbeque skills," he said. "I've got some ribs that will be wonderful on the grill."

The plans were made. Grady showed up on his bike a little

later, and he and Eden went off and did whatever Eden did with her stacks of Wanted posters and her notebook. Ruth was less worried about her granddaughter now that Grady was along. He seemed to have a calming influence, or perhaps it was just harder for Eden to follow every impulse when she had to at least take the time to instruct Grady on what she had in mind. Those two were well suited to each other, she thought, and she gave a secret smile and an inward prayer of thanks. It was almost as if it had been planned.

In fact, it seemed that way about a lot of things in their lives right now. Even though she knew Miranda did not share her faith, Ruth had the feeling that God was at work. She could see it in Miranda's face as they sat together in church, and Eden had told her that Miranda had been talking with Pastor Hector. And Joseph seemed to be mellowing. In fact, she thought those two were good for each other now that the initial sparks had flown. Time would tell.

David and Sarah were the faith test right now. There was always at least one thing in her life about which Ruth must simply believe. Whenever she thought of David and Sarah, she prayed and she trusted. That was all she could do, but she told herself it was enough.

She passed the afternoon baking a cake and quilting, a rare opportunity for her these last months. She finished piecing the Mariner's Compass and sewed on the sashing and borders and pinned it together with the batting and backing. Now it was ready to quilt. She would take it upstairs and begin that process tomorrow.

By suppertime Eden and Grady were cleaned up somewhat and loaded into the car, along with a sack of sweet corn Ruth had gotten at the farmers' market and the chocolate cake she had made that afternoon. They drove to the camp. The children immediately ran off yelling, and Ruth looked around in wonder.

The porch on the lodge had been replaced, as had the roof supports. The lawn had been mowed; the fragrance of the freshly cut grass was as sweet as perfume. The old roof had been taken off the chapel and new plywood nailed down. She looked closer and saw that the windows in both buildings had been reglazed. Then she saw Johnny walking up the hill toward her.

"I'm wanting to start the new roof next, and then I need to see about jacking up the foundation of the lodge and shoring up the floor joists," he said as he approached.

"I can't believe all you've accomplished," Ruth said, her eyes tearing up. "This is more than I ever imagined." She sat down on the porch steps and looked out over the lake, and she was seeing the crowds of children whose lives had been changed here. "This has been a holy place," she murmured.

Johnny looked sober. "I can feel that as I work here," he said.

Then Ruth knew as clearly as she'd ever known anything in her life that this was what God wanted. For this place to be restored. She had a picture in her mind of new crowds of children jostling and shouting in the lake, sitting in the chapel, and clattering in the dining hall. She knew it no matter what her son might say. And she had a clear feeling that Johnny Adair was to be an integral part of the plan.

"I want you to finish fixing this place up, Johnny," she said, looking directly into his face.

He gave her an uncomfortable look. "Ruth, the work I've done so far I could do alone, and it's been fairly inexpensive. To do more will involve other people and more money."

"I want to do it," she repeated. "I've got a lot of equity in my house and in this land. I'll take out a line of credit to pay for it."

He looked doubtful. "And then what?"

"You could stay here," she said. "Between your construction skills and my experience, we could run it. And you and I would be in ministry again. Doing something of eternal value."

She expected him to withdraw from her wild suggestion, but he did not. His face grew wistful and he looked out over the lake as if he, too, were seeing crowds of children and another kind of life for himself.

"That sounds sweet," he said. "Like a sweet dream."

"It doesn't have to be a dream. It can be reality."

He sighed, then turned to her with a glint in his eye. "Well, then, you're going to need bigger work done than porches and windows. You'll need wiring, plumbing, foundation work. I can get some of my friends to do it at cut rates, but I'll need to be your designated contractor."

"Fine," she said.

"You're sure you want to do this?" he said.

She thought of her money, sitting in the bank, buried instead of doing what it was intended to do. "Yes," she said. "I'm sure."

"I'll arrange for the subcontractors, then," he said, "and get the papers drawn up."

She took out her checkbook. "How much have you spent here?"

"No," he said. "I absolutely refuse."

They quibbled back and forth for a while. She finally wrote him a check for five hundred dollars, which he said was too much.

"Use it to buy new materials for the new projects, then. Now, I'm hungry. Let's get those ribs going."

"They're browning even as we speak," he said.

"I brought some things to go along," she said. "Some corn and a cake."

"Why does that not surprise me?" He smiled.

They ate. They chatted. After the delicious supper, Johnny made a fire in the fire pit, and the children roasted marshmallows. He disappeared inside the camper and returned with a violin case.

"Oh, you're going to play for us," Ruth exclaimed, delighted. Even Grady and Eden stopped their antics long enough to listen.

He took out the violin and adjusted the strings, rosined the bow, then lifted it to his chin and played. He began with "Turkey in the Straw." He was a magnificent violinist—"fiddle player," he corrected her when she complimented him. He followed with the "Orange Blossom Special," making all the train noises with the fiddle, to their delight. He quieted them with "Amazing Grace" and finished with "Turn Your Eyes Upon Jesus," the last notes quivering with emotion.

Ruth was silent afterward. The children went to steal a few more minutes of play.

"You know Him, don't you?" Ruth asked quietly.

Johnny gave a twisted smile. "We used to be on speaking terms. I'm not sure anymore."

"He'll never walk away from *you*," Ruth said.

"I know that," he said.

"May I pray for you?" she asked quietly.

Johnny looked surprised, then troubled.

"It's all right if you'd rather not," she said.

"No. I'd like to pray with you," Johnny said.

Ruth closed her eyes and cleared her mind of the distractions of the day. "Thank you, Father," she said softly, "for my brother Johnny. Thank you for his life. For his quiet faithfulness. Thank you for his loving heart and his desire to see your will accomplished for himself and his son and for the others that you will touch through him. I pray that your mighty hand would rest upon him." She hesitated, waiting for more, but that was all. "Amen," she said.

She looked up, but instead of the peaceful expression she'd expected to see on his face, she was surprised to find him looking even more troubled than before. It would seem her words had not comforted him at all.

chapter 44

By the middle of the next week Miranda had recovered somewhat from the trip to West Virginia. The emotional impact had been so great that she had needed a few days before she could begin to sort out the information the visit had garnered. There was really only one lead that might help her in her quest to know who her mother would have trusted with the baby. On Wednesday during her break she called Mrs. Tallert and asked for the name of the minister who had pastored the church at Thurmond where Noreen and Bobbie had gone.

"It was a Baptist church," Mrs. Tallert said. "Pastor's name was . . . let me think . . . yes, it was Webb."

On her lunch hour she went to the library and found that there were hundreds of Webbs in West Virginia. She called the West Virginia Convention of Southern Baptists and got lucky when the woman she spoke to gave her the pastor's full name and the location of his last church assignment. Harold Webb had last pastored Calvary Hill Baptist Church in Mingo County.

She had returned to work and could barely stand it until her afternoon break. She stood now on the sidewalk with her cell phone outside the Hasty Taste, the hot, humid summer enveloping her, and felt a chill as the secretary of that church said yes, she knew Pastor Webb and yes, she knew where he was.

"He's living in the Baptist rest home in Bluefield," she said. "He's in poor health, but his mind is good."

Miranda's hands were shaking as she hung up the phone and went back inside the Hasty Taste to finish her shift.

"You look like you seen a ghost," Venita said when she went inside.

"Not yet, but I'm getting close," she answered cryptically and made plans to travel back to West Virginia as soon as her shift was through.

Miranda left for Bluefield at two o'clock. She didn't bother to change clothes, just got into the car and left after hastily printing out MapQuest directions on the library computer. She felt vaguely guilty not inviting Joseph along or at least telling him where she was going, but he would be at work. Besides, this really was her quest. Joseph wouldn't always be around to hold her hand. And this, she reminded herself, was the reason she had come. Not to meet Joseph. Not to play with Eden. Not to pretend that Ruth was her mother to or serve pancakes and eggs at the Hasty Taste. She had come to find her baby, and this was the next step.

The trip to Bluefield was uneventful and without the dark drama of the other two trips. The town was just on the West Virginia/Virginia border, not far and deep in the woods. She drove for an hour and a half, then followed the MapQuest directions to the rest home. It was a nice brick building, sprawled on a good-sized lot with well-manicured grounds. She parked the car and went in, signed the guest book, then asked for Reverend Webb. The receptionist gave her the room number, and she walked down the corridors as directed.

The floors were clean and polished, the doors decorated with flowered wreaths, but there was still a faint institutional air. It wasn't a *home,* no matter how hard they tried to make it seem like one. Still, it was nicer than most. She stopped at the door to 1015, peeked inside, and tapped on the door.

An old white-haired man was dozing in a chair, the television on in front of him. It was a private room and obviously filled with quite a few of his own furnishings.

She went in and spoke softly. There was no answer from Reverend Webb but another deep breath.

An aide came in just then, a sweet-faced woman who looked at her merrily. "Honey, when he's sleeping, a train whistle won't wake him." She took his arm and gave him a gentle shake. "Reverend Webb, there's somebody here to see you."

He roused and, after a minute of reorientation, his eyes fell on her.

"I'm Miranda DeSpain, Reverend Webb," she said. She spoke at a normal volume and was pleased when he seemed to hear her well.

"Pleased to meet you," he said. "Are you from the business office?"

"No, sir," she answered. "I don't work here."

He nodded but looked confused. She explained her visit. "Mrs. Ada Tallert gave me your name and said you might be able to help me with something."

"My," he said, looking surprised, "that's a name I haven't heard in years. Ada Tallert. Sit down," he invited. "How is Ada?"

"I think she's well," Miranda answered, perching on the edge of his bed. "She was living with her granddaughter. I went by to see her last weekend."

Reverend Webb gazed past her head, and she knew he was moving through scenes from the past.

"What's your name again?" he asked.

"Miranda. Miranda DeSpain."

"And what's your connection with Ada Tallert?"

"I was looking for information about my mother," Miranda said. "She lived in Thurmond, and I understand she attended your church."

"That was a long time ago," he said. "But I'll try to help you if I can."

She nodded and took a deep breath. "Her name was Noreen Gibson."

The pastor brought his eyes from the distance and focused them on her. He nodded sadly. "One of Beck Maddux's girls."

"That's right," she said, and a shiver passed over her like a dark cloud.

"Now that you tell me, I can see it," he said. "You're the image of her except for the dark hair. She had blond hair. Not white like Beck's but lighter than yours."

Another fact she had never known. Her mother's hair had been dyed red for as long as she could remember. Now that she knew more about Mama's life, she wondered if her mother had dyed her hair so she would have no visible reminders of her father. She smiled at Reverend Webb. "I've been told that I favor her," she said.

He rubbed his hand over his cheek. "You do." He looked carefully at her face, then shook his head. "That was a sad business," he said. "All around."

She took in a deep breath and let it out. "Reverend Webb, about ten or eleven years ago, did my mother contact you or your wife?"

He frowned, and she waited, not breathing. He shook his head. "My wife died fifteen years ago, and I haven't heard from or seen Noreen since the day she ran off with that young man."

Miranda felt hope sink down then. Like a great slab of iron let go in her chest, it sank down to her stomach and settled on the bottom.

"My mother had an important decision to make about the time I mentioned," she finally managed to get out. "All we know is that she turned to someone she said she trusted. If it wasn't you, do you know who that person might have been?" she asked.

Reverend Webb's head shook, whether from palsy or intention, she couldn't tell. "I don't believe there was anyone who cared two figs for those girls save Ada Tallert and the folks in the church. Certainly not their daddy, may God have mercy on his soul."

"How many were in your church?" she asked. "Do you suppose I could find the membership records?"

He shook his head. "Church burned down, but everybody's gone now, anyway. Moved away or died. I wouldn't know how to find any of them. I don't expect your mama would have been able to, either."

"You can't think of anyone she trusted besides Mrs. Tallert and your wife?"

He shook his head again. "They were forsaken by man, those girls. But loved by God."

Miranda's eyes filled with tears. For her mother and Aunt Bobbie. For her baby. For herself.

"Have I helped you?" he asked, the cloudiness returning to his eyes. "I want to if I can."

"You've helped," she said. "You told me the truth. Thank you."

"Let me pray for you before you leave," Reverend Webb said.

She bowed her head. He put his shaky hand on top of it and prayed over her in formal King James English. A jumble of words that her mind could barely take in, but she felt the warm pressure of his hand. "Amen," he finally said, and she raised her head.

She wiped her eyes and blew her nose and drove back to Abingdon in a fog, staring straight ahead but seeing the door to her hopes close slowly and finally. This, she knew, was the end of the trail. Every other avenue had fizzled out. This had been the last hope, and now it was gone. She would have to find a way to put this all behind her, but that would be very hard if she continued living here, knowing she was so close but not able to reach what she longed for. Perhaps the time had arrived, she thought. Perhaps it was time to start thinking about leaving.

Yet, she did not leave. She stayed, a sweet inertia taking hold of her like a deep dream from which she was loath to wake. Her summer rolled on like the gently folding fields and pastures around her, like a lazily flowing stream on which she floated, enjoying the scenery as it passed by. She worked at the Hasty Taste and learned all the regulars' names. She cleaned the funeral home and met the families of the people they buried. She spoke words of comfort and received their hugs and patted their hands. She walked the Creeper Trail and learned to recognize the flowers. She made careful drawings of them and pasted them in her scrapbook—blue violets and wild columbine, fire pinks and foamflowers, stonecrop and winter cress.

She and Joseph walked together to Damascus and back on a sun-baked Saturday morning. She fished with him in his secret place on Glen Cove Stream and caught a good-sized trout with a lure from his tackle box. She wore his waders and nearly sank. They laughed like children.

Every Wednesday and Saturday she shopped at the farmers' market. Ruth taught her how to make a pie crust. Each Saturday evening she joined Ruth and Eden and Joseph for music in the park. She helped Ruth weed and prepare her gardens for the annual garden tour. On the Fourth of July she played games and dunked Joseph by throwing a softball at a bull's-eye, then sat beside him afterward and watched the fireworks change the dark sky into confetti.

She got a library card. She was invited to Venita's daughter's baby shower. She went to church. Joseph, looking a bit sheepish, testified for her at her traffic violation court date, and the case was dismissed. She had coffee with Pastor Hector three times, and the last time they talked about Jesus. She wrote in her journal about people she was getting to know and who was seeing whom and whose daughter was having a baby and recipes and quilt patterns, and she bought some watercolors and started painting again. These were real things of real life instead of pictures of foreign cities and people.

She sat among Joseph's family in their pew on Sunday mornings and ate with them afterward, and after a while she forgot she was only pretending to belong here. But every now and then something would make her remember why she had come. Something would tap on her heart and warn her to pull the shutters tight and batten down the doors. A storm would eventually come, the inner voice said, and when it did, she would not be ready with every door flung open like this and her arms stretched out wide.

chapter 45

H enry looked at Joseph with incredulity. "Strike while the iron is hot," he said. "The early bird catches the worm. Time and tide wait for no man. Do you know what all these expressions have in common?"

Joseph nodded wearily, but Henry didn't give him a chance to answer. "They all mean *get off your duff and make something happen!*"

Joseph grinned. Henry shook his head. "It's no laughing matter, son. This gal has been around nearly three months now. It's already July. It's obvious to everyone who sees you that you're two peas in a pod, and you haven't asked her out on a date yet?"

"We've done things together."

"Son, do I need to draw you a picture? Fishing is one thing. Walking is another. But when you fix yourself up and take a woman out for an evening on the town, you're stating your intentions. Isn't it about time you did that? You shuffle and stutter around much longer, and she's likely to up and leave or take up with somebody else while you're still picking your moment."

Joseph sighed. "All right. All right."

"What does that mean?"

"It means I'd already decided to invite her to dinner this weekend."

"Well, then. That's more like it. Where are you taking her?"

"The Pepper Mill," he began, but Henry was already shaking his head.

"No, son. You've got some lost time to make up for. I'm talking suit and tie and flowers and the nicest table at Caroline's and reservations at the theater afterward. And a walk in the park after that. I'm talking wine and dine. We need to get this party started, as the young folks say."

Joseph laughed. "Henry, I never knew you were such a romantic."

"Been married happily for forty-five years, boy. Learn from those who know. Now, I'm happy to do my part, but you've to got to do yours. When are you going to ask her?"

"Tonight," he said.

Henry gave a nod of satisfaction and slapped him on the back. "Don't mess this one up, now. You might not get a second chance."

Joseph hadn't been this tense since he was doing reconnaissance in Mogadishu. But now that he thought about it, even that had been easier. He'd had a weapon then. Now he had nothing but himself. Well, there was no use putting it off. He cleared his throat and approached the mission's objective. Eden, who knew everything, had told him she was here, in her favorite park, sitting beside the creek. "Hello, Miranda," he said.

She looked up with a smile that eased his heart, but her eyes were clouded with care today. Perhaps she would tell him about it later on.

"Hello, Joseph," she said. "I see you came again with gifts."

He twisted the top off a bottle of sarsaparilla, handed it to her, then sat down beside her and opened his own.

"Thank you," she said, taking a drink. "How was your work today?" she asked.

"About as good as it gets," he said. "We busted a car thief who's been plaguing us all summer."

He took a sip himself. He really didn't care for sarsaparilla. He'd be glad when they got past the impressing each other stage and he could go back to Mountain Dew.

"And still no more Travelers?"

He shook his head. He still had the feeling, but he had to admit there hadn't been any more trouble. "Nothing for months," he said. "I guess they moved on."

She nodded. "That's good."

He decided to get to the point. "Miranda."

"Yes?"

She lifted her pretty face to him, and suddenly he felt unsure. What if he was misreading everything? What if she wasn't interested in him at all? All his old doubts came back to haunt him. He might mess up a friendship. She might just say no. He hesitated a minute, then decided there was nothing to do but to press on through, although a felon with a gun wouldn't have seemed as terrifying as those cool blue eyes this minute. He started to ask, then choked. And he knew what the problem was. The evening Henry had pressed him to plan suited him about as well as a tuxedo did a monkey. He made a quick course correction and plowed on.

"I'd like to take you out for supper on Saturday," he said. "There's a place a little ways down the road that has the best barbeque north of Atlanta. And once a month the Grange sponsors a barn dance with old-time fiddling. What do you say?"

Her face turned pink. He wasn't sure what that meant, but at least she wasn't breaking out in hives—a bad sign.

"Would you go with me?" he asked, thinking perhaps he hadn't made himself clear.

She nodded and the tightness in his chest eased. "Yes," she said. "I'd love to. That sounds like a lot of fun."

He relaxed. Her face stayed pink, but they were both smiling.

"You look relieved," she said, teasing him.

He smiled. "I'm out of practice."

"Me too," she said, her mouth twisting in a funny grin.

They were silent for a minute, sipping their drinks. "Is something on your mind tonight?" he finally asked.

She hesitated, looked at him, then looked away, giving a slight shrug. So. She had decided not to confide. Well, that was all right. Maybe the pump needed to be primed.

"There's something I've been wanting to tell you," he said. "Something I'd like you to hear from me. I'd like to tell you about . . . about Sarah. About me . . ."

She looked him full in the eye then and set down her soda. "All right," she said.

He took a deep breath and started at the beginning. "We both grew up here. Knew each other since we were kids. We were high-school sweethearts. Everybody understood that we would be together for good. Some things just seem like they were meant to be, you know? My brother, David, was running wild around then. My pop had died, and David went off the deep end. Things weren't good between us. It seemed like every rivalry we'd had all our lives came up during that time. Poor Ma. I think it about drove her crazy.

"Anyway, I went off to college. David and Sarah had another year of high school. The first year everything was all right. When I came home for Christmas the second year, Sarah and I got engaged. She'd been going to the community college, but she was tired of school, she said. She wanted to settle down and have babies. The plan was that we would marry. I would finish college; then we'd come back to Abingdon and do just that. So after Christmas, I went back to Ferrum. She got a job at the chamber of commerce here in town doing something for the mayor. David had flunked out of the university and didn't go back after Christmas. When I came back the next summer, everybody knew about them but me. Have you ever had a time when nobody would look you in the eye?"

Miranda nodded. "Oh yes," she said softly. "I have."

"I knew something was wrong, but I had no idea. Even now I think back and can almost feel the sucker punch. She wouldn't see me. Wouldn't answer my calls. My ma finally put me on to the truth. 'Something's going on,' she said. 'You need to talk to Sarah.'

"But Sarah wouldn't." He shook his head. "I went to David and asked him if he knew what was going on. And that's when he told me."

Miranda looked pained as she listened. He could still feel the pain himself. "Anyway, David told me they'd been seeing each other. And that she was pregnant. It was his child. My brother's baby."

There was silence for a minute. He didn't feel as churned up now when he thought about it, but he didn't know exactly why. It seemed to have just become the event that had disrupted his life, the hinge of before and after. "I finally caught up with her, and I didn't even need to ask. I could see it all over her face. The guilt. I went off to the marines. I heard they got married. They moved up to Fairfax. They would bring the baby and visit Mom from time to time, but I didn't have anything to do with either of them for years."

"And then one day Eden showed up," Miranda said with a smile.

He nodded and chuckled. "In all her glory." He sobered after a second. "I was determined not to love that child, but what could I do?"

Miranda grinned. "She sort of worms her way into your heart, doesn't she?"

He nodded and smiled.

"So how are things now?" Miranda asked. "Between you and David and Sarah?"

"Strained," he admitted. "We never talked about any of it. I'm afraid now it's too late."

She shook her head. "I don't think it's too late," she said. "As long as they're both alive, it's not too late."

"I feel I shouldn't bring it up to him now. Like it's too much to add to his burdens, and it's petty compared to what he's going through."

She tipped her head and considered. "If the idea was punishment or simply confrontation, I might agree with you. But if the goal is reconciliation, I would say you're just in time."

He thought about that for a moment. It raised some uncomfortable questions about his motives and his desires.

"Thank you," he said.

She shrugged. "It's always easier to see other people's stuff than your own, isn't it?"

He nodded. He thought of all she'd been through recently. What she must be thinking about her mother's life. He wondered then what kind of girlhood she'd had with no father and a mother who had been through so much, and he felt a surge of protectiveness rise up in him.

He leaned toward her, and she leaned toward him. He kissed her softly on the lips. She kissed him back.

He heard heavy breathing. Panting, actually. Followed by a loud splash and cold water as Flick jumped into the creek, turned, and splashed toward them.

"Uncle Joseph! Miranda! Guess what? Guess what?" Eden flew down the hill on her bike and skidded to a stop before them, leaving a gouge in the grass.

"What?" Miranda asked a little breathlessly as they moved apart.

Joseph wiped away the creek water from his face and grinned at Miranda. She smiled back. So much for romance.

"What is it, bug?" he asked his niece. "What's so important?

Did one of your stories get accepted? Did Grady learn to dive?"

"No," she said, shaking her head with impatience. "It's way better than that. It's my dad," she said, her face breaking into a brilliant smile. "He's coming home."

chapter 46

Miranda was a little nervous about Saturday evening, but she told herself there was nothing to be frightened about. She chose her orange-and-pink tiered skirt and a peasant blouse and her pretty beaded shoes. She didn't know what people wore to barn dances, but the occasion seemed to call for something more festive than jeans, and besides, this skirt was perfect for twirling.

A knock came on her door at exactly six o'clock. She opened it, smiling expectantly. Joseph stood on the tiny stoop, looking handsome in jeans, boots, and a white cotton shirt. He was carrying a little nosegay of violets and lilies of the valley and ferns wrapped in a paper doily and tied with ribbon.

"Oh, they're beautiful," she said. "Come in."

He ducked his head, a little embarrassed, and Miranda had to hide a smile.

"The lady at the florist shop suggested them," he said.

"I guessed something like that. Somehow I couldn't imagine you going in and asking for a nosegay," she commented with a smile.

"Thank you. I appreciate that."

She grinned and put them in a vase.

"You look . . . *very* nice," Joseph said.

"Thank you," she said. "I wasn't sure what to wear to a barn dance."

"This'll do just fine," he said with an approving grin, and now she was the one blushing.

"Shall we go?" he asked.

She nodded, grateful to get out on the road where a natural conversation might occur.

They walked out the door and were driving past the park when Miranda noticed a morose figure sitting on the bench by the creek, kicking her feet back and forth listlessly. Flick sat beside her, watching her with an anxious expression on his doggie face.

"Is that Eden?" she asked.

Joseph briefly closed his eyes and shook his head by way of answer. He pulled the truck over and stopped. Eden looked up, and her face brightened immediately.

"What are you doing out here in the dark by yourself?" he demanded.

"It's not dark," she answered, unperturbed. "It's only six o'clock. Hey, Miranda."

"Hi, Eden."

"You didn't answer my question," Joseph said. Miranda thought his sternness seemed a little forced.

Eden breathed a huge sigh. "Grady couldn't play today, and Grandma's busy getting things ready for my dad to come, and there was nothing to do, and Grandma said I couldn't bother you and Miranda, because Miranda was getting ready for your date and you had to work."

Miranda looked at Joseph. He was trying not to smile.

"Besides that, Pastor Hector had to go to Roanoke today to a conference or something, and I rode my bike over to Mr. Applegate's to see if I could ride Susannah's horse, and he had up and sold it!" Her outrage was palpable.

"Wow," Miranda said. "You've had a really rotten day."

"Your mom and dad are coming home tomorrow," Joseph

reminded her. The look Eden gave them was as much fear as anticipation.

That did it. Miranda looked at Joseph. He looked back. They both sighed as his cell phone rang.

"Williams," he said. "Hi, Ma. No, she's not missing. She's right here. Uh-huh. I know."

Eden looked even more pitiful, if possible.

Joseph looked at Miranda. "It's fine with me," she murmured with a smile.

Joseph put the phone back to his ear. "No, Ma. We'll bring her with us. Yeah. I'm sure it's okay."

Eden was whooping with joy. She opened the door to the backseat, and she and Flick jumped in.

"He rides in the back," Joseph said firmly.

Eden seemed to know not to push her luck, and Flick was consigned to the truck bed, where he happily leaned out, getting ready to let the wind blow his ears.

"Where are we going for dinner?" Eden asked, her morose mood gone like a foggy morning. "This is the first time I've ever been on a date."

The Dixie Barbeque was everything Miranda had expected. It had a screen door that twanged, a loud jukebox, paper-covered tables with baskets of peanuts for appetizers, and the patrons were encouraged to toss the shells on the floor.

The food was delicious. The three of them put on huge bibs and used piles of napkins. Miranda and Joseph ordered rib platters, Eden chose the chicken, and they all had side orders of barbequed beans and corn bread. They shared a hubcap-sized piece of black-berry pie with ice cream and drank sweet iced tea. Eden put money in the jukebox and worked the word puzzles on the placemat while Miranda and Joseph talked. And talked. She told him about her childhood. Her father. Her meteor. Her scrap-book. He told her about his brother and the things they had done when they were boys. They covered high school, sports, jobs, with Miranda definitely having had the most experience in that area, and finished up with religion and politics. They agreed on most, disagreed on some, but those didn't seem worth fussing about.

It actually didn't inhibit Miranda at all having Eden with them. In fact, there was something about Eden's presence that made her feel more able to be herself. Or at least the person she wanted to be.

"What's a ten-letter word for rice wine?" Eden asked just as Miranda and Joseph were settling the problem of presidential politics.

"It's saké," Joseph said, barely breaking the thread of his conversation.

"That's not ten letters."

"Then the crossword's wrong," he said.

"The crossword is never wrong," Eden argued.

"Let me see," Miranda interjected. "Here. You're looking at thirteen across. This is thirteen down."

"Oh. How do you spell saké?" she asked.

"Let's go dance," Joseph said.

Eden dropped the puzzle in a flash. "I love to dance," she enthused. "Is it square dancing or line dancing or the kind where you put your head on each other's shoulders and hug?"

"Did you think we'd have this much fun on our first real date?" Joseph asked Miranda from the corner of his mouth. "Or do you think we'll have to save that title for another event?"

"This counts," she said, taking his arm impulsively. Eden took the other one, and the three of them headed for the barn dance.

It wasn't far away. They parked the car in a mowed field and walked over the stubble to the real live barn where the music had already started. There were two fiddles, a bass fiddle, a mandolin, a guitar, and people of all ages and shapes. The caller was just getting started. Tall and thin with cowboy boots, he looked the part with a western shirt, a bolo tie, and a ten-gallon hat.

"All of y'all get out on the floor," he called out. "I'll teach y'all a few simple steps, and then we'll practice with a dance. Those of you who know help those who don't, and let's all have us a good time." Before he was finished speaking, the fiddles started up, and Miranda and Joseph went and found a place by Eden, who was already learning the grapevine step from an older lady in a square-dancing skirt.

"Vine right and touch," the caller said. "Step right and touch."

The uneven line of people giggled and swooped. Some were very good, others not, but it seemed everyone was having a good time. They stepped, they turned, they stomped and slid. Miranda laughed. Joseph laughed. Eden seemed very serious, intent on learning the steps.

After a few dances, they purchased cold drinks for fifty cents apiece and picked cans out of a galvanized washtub filled with ice. Then the caller did some old-time square dancing, and the three of them did the do-si-dos and swung their partners.

They stepped outside for air a time or two, and finally the caller and the band announced the last one. It was "Save the Last Dance for Me," and Miranda was aware of Eden's eyes on her and Joseph as they danced, her hand on Joseph's neck, his around her waist. She glanced over once, but Eden was not laughing and silly. She held her chin in her hands and watched with a little smile.

They piled into the truck after taking a cold drink each for the road. Miranda kicked off her shoes. Eden flaked out in the backseat.

"She's going to be too tired for church tomorrow," Miranda said, then remembered David was coming and they probably would not attend. She wished she hadn't brought it up.

"We're near my place," Joseph said. "I'd like to show it to you if you'd like."

"You'll like it," Eden mumbled sleepily from the backseat. "It's really cool and he built it himself."

Miranda smiled and Joseph did, as well. It was the last they heard from her. She was sound asleep when the truck stopped beside the log house perched on the side of the mountain. Miranda got out of the truck and walked across the wet grass to the riverside in bare feet. Flick bounded down and into the water, obviously overjoyed to be home.

"Oh, it's absolutely beautiful," she said, looking down over the valley, barely outlined by moonlight. She was aware of Joseph standing very close behind her. His hands touched her arms, and she leaned back against him.

She almost told him then. It was right on the edge of her heart and ready to come spilling out. *I need to tell you something, Joseph,* she wanted to say. *I had a baby. When I was just fifteen.* She wondered if it would matter to him. If he would look at her differently after that, and somehow the wondering tucked the truth back into her heart.

He took her hand. "Would you like to see the house?" he asked. "I think we can leave her here for a minute."

She peeked at Eden, who was sound asleep.

"Flick," Joseph called. "Stay here."

Flick sat down obediently at the door of the truck, and Joseph went ahead to the porch and turned on the lights.

It was a beautiful house. Log and chinking with a tin roof, a wide wraparound porch, and planked floors. Inside was warm wood and color. There was a huge stone fireplace and a wood-stove.

"I can't believe you did all this," she said.

"It was a labor of love."

She looked at him. He smiled and she didn't see the bitterness she had expected. He held the door open for her, and they stepped back out on the porch. He turned out the light and closed the door. Flick was still guarding Eden. They stopped at the water's edge again.

"I'm ready to let it go now, Miranda," he said quietly. "I've been angry long enough. I want to forgive Sarah. I want to forgive my brother. I just don't know how to talk to them about it."

"Don't you think if your heart is ready, the opportunity will present itself?" she asked quietly.

He nodded in the darkness. "I suppose you're right." Miranda could tell he was smiling.

She could have told him then, as well, and on the way home, as the truck bumped down over the graveled road, she realized why she hadn't. She was afraid.

Finally they were back in town. He dropped off Eden first, stopping at his mother's house and carrying her in. He returned after a few minutes, locked the front door behind him, and drove Miranda home.

He walked her upstairs to the door.

She opened it.

He frowned. "Don't you lock your door?"

"In Abingdon? With you on the job?"

He smiled but then grew serious again. "Please lock your door from now on."

"All right."

He peeked in and apparently satisfied himself that there were no ax murderers in wait.

"It's been a perfect evening," she said.

He smiled. "As much fun as going to Caroline's for dinner and then the Barter Theatre?"

"Are you kidding? I wouldn't trade this night for anything. Not anything," she said, and she meant it from her heart.

He leaned down and kissed her tenderly. She touched his rough cheek, his warm chest. They broke apart.

"We'd better say good night," she said.

He nodded. "I'll see you tomorrow."

She went inside and didn't go to bed for the longest time. She looked at herself in the mirror and promised herself that no matter what happened, she would remember this day.

chapter 47

D riving into Abingdon in the back of Ruth's big car, looking at the back of Joseph's neck and looking across David
to her daughter, who chose not to sit beside her, Sarah was put
in mind of the Roman triumphs. They were parades of sorts,
during which the victorious general would march back through
Rome, his vanquished enemies driven before him in chains while
everyone saw their disgrace. The streets of this small perfect town
were not lined with jeering onlookers, but she imagined them so.
She pictured a great cloud of witnesses looking on their
destruction.

Her fears and anxieties of the earlier months had boiled down
to this bitter fatalism. It seemed that her and David's relationship
had taken the same path as his body. Both had been wounded and
raw but now had hardened into a ruined mass of scars.

David had not touched her since the accident. Even after
they'd moved into the apartment by the hospital so he could
practice real life. He had slept in the bed and she on the sofa.
"It's better that way," he'd said, and she didn't argue, remembering with shame the way she had blanched when she'd been
asked to care for his wounds. That was probably what he was

remembering, as well, fearing her cringe. They had lost each other. The sweet intimacy they had once enjoyed was gone, crushed as completely as David's body.

She remembered a Bible verse somewhere about being stricken, smitten of God and afflicted, and she realized that's what she felt had happened to them. From the first, as soon as she had lost David's baby, she had felt she'd come under the hand of God. She had been expecting the punishing ax to fall ever since. The only difference was that it should have fallen on her, not on her husband. It was her shame. She was the one who had lied and been false. It was her womb that remained barren and shut. Now David had been cut down, and that was her fault, too.

And she had lost Eden. The replacement child. Oh yes. Sarah's motive was clear to her now. She had never really wanted to know Eden. She had never tried to ask, *Who are you, little girl?* She had wanted only to make her be what she, Sarah, had needed her to be, and she had collapsed into helpless tears whenever Eden refused to be molded. And now it was too late to change, even if she somehow found the strength. She had lost another child, her daughter.

Sarah knew it the moment she saw Eden at the airport. She had thrown herself at her father, had wept openly and held him, but she would not even look at Sarah. Ruth had held Sarah's hand and whispered comforting words. *"She's a child,"* she had said. *"She doesn't understand."* Joseph had succeeded in giving them both stiff hugs without really touching them. And now as they drove through the streets, Sarah looked out the window at the town that had been so familiar, that had been her home for most of her life. Now the prospect of staying here seemed unbearable. But so did the prospect of going home. She feared what would happen when it was time to return to Fairfax. She could not imagine living with this silent husband and child so far away from warmth and help.

They arrived at Ruth's, and somehow the first horrible evening was over. Joseph finally left, and Eden finally went to bed.

Sarah asked her mother-in-law for another room, giving a simple explanation. "We sleep better separately."

"Of course," Ruth said, deep sadness in her eyes. "Take your pick, Sarah."

She chose the one next to Eden, even though the proximity was only physical. She'd tried two, five, ten times to converse with Eden, who still refused to even look at her and answered only in monosyllables.

Sarah lay now in the empty bed and rehearsed a speech. *You're doing nearly everything yourself now,* she said to the David in her mind. *Would you object to my going to my parents for a while? I haven't seen them for a long time. And I would like to go somewhere and rest.* He would be as happy here as anywhere, she thought. And Eden was happier here with Ruth, her new friends, and her father. Without Sarah.

It would be so simple to run away. She could go to her father and mother, and they would ask no questions. Perhaps she could go back to being a girl again and forget all this trouble.

She must have slept. She awoke in the dark, the only light a full moon that shone on the bed and on the floor. She opened the door and went next door, carefully turning the knob, then peeking in to look at her daughter. Eden was back in the play-room, hers again, and Sarah felt guilt for the summers she had shipped Eden here because she was tired. Tired from the exhausting effort of trying to make Eden be the child she never was and never could be. Eden lay sprawled across her bed. She saw the dark unruly hair and freckles and could not help but look down at her own tanned arm and imagine her own blond hair and brown eyes.

Whose child are you? she wanted to ask her daughter, and she felt a curiosity that had come too late. *Whose child are you? Not mine. Never mine, for all my desiring it.* But now she wondered who Eden was. What she loved and what she wanted. Now that it was too late to know.

She shut the door gently and went to David's room. She

opened it quietly and saw him carefully positioned on the bed, his wheelchair nearby. His Bible on the nightstand. She couldn't make out his face or features, but she could hear his breathing.

She stood in the hallway and listened, and it was almost as if she could hear the old house breathe, and she fancied a *what if*. It caught at her mind, and she held it with a longing she hadn't known she possessed. *What if* she could stop time, could turn back all their breaths until things were at the beginning place again. She could undo all this, but even as she thought it, she knew that would mean no sweet years as well as no bitter ones. She quietly closed David's door, then went back into her room and lay on the bed and knew that, even as she had named their daughter Eden, she had given voice to that wish. She had been searching all her life for the way back to that place. But she knew the truth now. There was no going back. This was their life, their broken life. There was no going back to Eden.

chapter 48

Miranda spent the morning before meeting Eden's father by watching the DVD Ruth had given her.

"It's of one of his conferences," Ruth said, "on finding your lost heart."

She turned up the volume on her laptop and watched him speak, reminding herself that the David Williams she saw here might not match the one she would meet this afternoon.

He was tall and slender, warm complected. She could see a faint resemblance to Joseph, though he was darker in complexion and not nearly as classically handsome. Still, there was something extremely winsome about his appearance. He had dark, longish hair, soft beard, gentle eyes, expansive gestures. But mostly, she supposed, his attractiveness was due to what could only be called his spark. He had a way of emphasizing what he said. Phrases would tumble out on top of one another as if he was too excited to slow down. She tried to follow what he was saying in addition to observing him. And again, she was struck by the fact that his face was unguarded and open. His eyes so warm and inviting. His gestures so inclusive, his words so full of hope.

David Williams thought God possessed the secrets to finding

that hidden treasure of the heart. And that He was willing to share them. A theory she had heard expounded on before, though the practice of it remained elusive, at least for her. And this man didn't sound like any religious speaker she had ever heard. He was actually interesting, but she was having trouble understanding him. She tried to hold in her mind all the things he was saying, to follow the flow of his logic, but even though she thought she might be a somewhat intelligent person—despite Mama's evaluations—there seemed to be too many words for her to process, and they were spilling over one another. She would grasp hold of one, and then it would slide away. They were slippery thoughts, these, and she felt as if she were trying to sew Jell-O to pudding. He talked about losing heart and wounded hearts and healing the heart and the enemies of the heart and the home of the heart. She liked that last part. The home of the heart, and she had a flash of insight that it might be the true destination she was seeking. And perhaps it was what her father had been looking for on all those journeys. But then the epiphany slid from between her fingers, and she was reminded again of those shooting stars. Before you really knew what you were looking at, they were gone.

She watched a few minutes longer, then turned down the sound. David continued to gesture and smile. She wondered if the opposite situation was true now. Perhaps he still said the same things but lacked the joy and life so obvious here. She realized with a surprising sense of fervor that she hoped not.

"This is our friend Miranda," Ruth said, giving Miranda the reassuring pat on the shoulder she probably needed herself. Miranda could tell Ruth was under a lot of strain, and she wondered again if it was a good idea for her to be here, but Ruth had called and invited her, and Joseph wanted her to come to the family supper, as well.

"I want you to meet them," Joseph said firmly, and she wanted to meet them, too. She wanted to have faces to put on these people who had tipped the first domino in Joseph's life. She reminded herself not to judge as she walked across the room to meet Sarah.

She had pictured someone coolly conniving. But Miranda's first glance at Sarah drew only compassion from her heart. She almost caught her breath at the sight of that drawn face and sad eyes. She was beautiful, but she wore grief like a garment.

"Hello," Miranda said with a warm smile.

"Hello," Sarah said and smiled back, but it was superficial, only a movement of her face.

"Where's David, dear?" Ruth asked her daughter-in-law.

"The last time I saw him he was out in the garden with Eden," Sarah said; then after another strained smile, she excused herself.

Ruth exchanged glances with Miranda but said nothing. "Let's see if we can find him," she said, and just then Eden came in.

"Miranda!" Eden gave her a hug.

Miranda squeezed her back. "Hey, kid, how are you doing?"

"Good," she said heartily.

Miranda was ashamed that she felt a loss. She rebuked herself for her selfishness.

"Grandma," Eden said, "Dad asked if he could have a glass of iced tea."

"Certainly. Why don't you make it for him, dear? I'm going to take Miranda out and introduce her."

As they walked out the back door and toward the pergola, Miranda tried to coach herself so she wouldn't stumble. *Don't look at the wheelchair,* she repeated to herself. *Don't look at his legs. Look at his face. Take his hand. Treat him as you would anyone else. Don't think about his past with Joseph. Don't think about anything but the conversation you're having right now.*

They approached the bricked patio where he was sitting. Miranda could see the back of his chair. His hair was still long, falling down into his collar. She and Ruth walked around, and she put a smile on her face. He looked older and more tired than the man she had watched speak so eloquently this morning. His face had new lines and he was thin, painfully so. She wondered again if he still believed God was good despite the devastation that had been wreaked on his own life.

"I understand you've been a friend to my daughter," he said gently after they were introduced, reaching for her hand and giving it a squeeze. "Thank you."

"It wasn't hard to do," Miranda said. "She's a wonderful girl."

"Grandma!" Eden called. "Telephone."

"Excuse me," Ruth said.

"Please, sit down," David invited, so she took a chair.

"I watched one of your conferences on DVD this morning," she said. "It was very . . . interesting."

He smiled and looked at her with interest then, and his face regained a tiny shade of animation. "A very noncommittal word. What about it bothered you?"

"I wouldn't say bothered." She searched her mind for the right word. "Confused would be more accurate."

"About?"

She tried to put it into words, then shook her head a little. "I guess about the whole idea that there's a grand plan. There seems to be so much . . . I don't know . . . *randomness* in the world. Sometimes I wonder why things happen the way they do." She was thinking about her mother and Beck Maddux and her baby.

David nodded thoughtfully and glanced down at his chair.

She felt a wash of shame. "I'm sorry," she said. "I didn't think."

"Don't think I haven't gone down that road myself," he said gently. "I've asked the questions, too."

"Have you found any answers?"

He shrugged. "I stopped for coffee after I left. What if I hadn't? I pulled off the highway and made a phone call. What if I had driven straight through? I got lost and had to ask for directions. What if I'd looked the airport up on MapQuest before I left home like my wife told me to? Any one of those things could have caused me to miss that SUV. Did God ordain it? Is it a result of an evil force at work in the world? Or was it simply an accident?" He shook his head. "I don't know and it doesn't help me to wonder. It happened," he said. "It is what it is."

"What about God?"

"What about Him?"

"Aren't your feelings hurt?" It hadn't been her intention to phrase the question that way, but now that she'd said it, it was exactly what she wanted to ask.

"Yes. That's a good way to put it. I think they are. Deeply. But I also have to believe He loves me and has a plan He's working out for good." He seemed as if he really meant it. Miranda felt deep compassion for him and not a little amazement.

"What about you?" he asked, bringing her to attention.

"What *about* me?"

"Where are you on your spiritual journey?"

The same question the pastor had asked her that night so long ago in Minnesota. She tried to come up with an answer now. She thought back on the talks she'd had with Pastor Hector, the people she had met. She thought of her mother and her father and her baby, and she remembered the feeling she'd had in the motel that night when she'd first arrived here and had prayed. The feeling that God was with her, guiding her. She remembered Mr. Cooper and his prayer for her, and she had the feeling somehow that she was walking along a path that had been prepared and laid out for her in advance. "I think I'm being pursued," she said and felt a little awe as she said it.

"Ah. The Hound of Heaven is after you."

She gave him a puzzled look.

"'I fled Him, down the nights and down the days; / I fled Him, down the arches of the years; / I fled Him, down the labyrinthine ways of my own mind; / and in the mist of tears I hid from Him, and under running laughter.'"

"A poem?" she asked.

He nodded and smiled. "Very badly recited, but, yes, it's a poem."

She smiled and considered what he had said. It was like the Hound of Heaven had been pursuing her with careful, studied persistence. "Yes. The Hound of Heaven is after me."

He looked at her kindly, the light still there, she could see, but burning very low.

"Will you let Him catch you?" he asked.

She thought, then leaned toward him to answer when voices interrupted.

Hector was here, and Henry and Vi. They leaned and hugged him, and Vi stroked his face. There were tears and kisses. Eden came with his tea, set it on the table, then stood at Miranda's side, and Miranda put her arm around Eden's shoulders. She looked at Eden's face as Eden watched her father, and there was concern mixed with the joy. Her happiness and security were fragile, Miranda could see. A stiff wind could capsize the ship.

"My dad's gonna be all right," she said, and it was obviously a question rather than a statement.

"Your dad is a wonderful man," Miranda said, meaning it from her heart. "His Jesus is helping him."

Had she said that? She was surprised, but Eden was comforted. The words seemed to bring her great joy. She threw her arms around Miranda's waist and squeezed. Miranda kissed her head and looked up to see Sarah watching them, obvious pain on her face.

"Joseph is on his way," she said. "Ruth wanted me to tell you."

Miranda nodded, embarrassed, feeling suddenly as if she had walked into a maze of relationships and divided loyalties and had complicated them further. She gave Eden a final pat, and the girl went over to stand beside her father.

"Don't hover, Eden," Sarah said sharply. "Give him room to breathe."

"She's all right," David answered, giving his wife a warning look.

Vi rescued her. "Miranda, would you come out and help me bring in my pies?"

She hurried to help, and by the time they'd transferred the four pies, Joseph was pulling into the driveway. Miranda fairly flew out to meet him.

He came around the truck, smiling, and took her hand. "Well, that's a nice welcome."

She smiled brightly. He gave her a wise look. "Is it that bad in there?"

"It's . . . strange."

He nodded. "Welcome to my world."

She said nothing more, even though she wanted to tell him all about it.

"Shall we go in?" he asked.

She nodded and they walked in together.

Things were better when dinner was served. Carol Jean arrived. The table was loaded with delicious-looking food, and finally they were all sitting down, a spot cleared for David's chair. They prayed. They ate. Miranda answered questions and made conversation. She watched Eden hang on her father and ignore her mother. She watched Joseph sit stiffly and saw the pain on Ruth's face. It was then that she realized something. Through the years she had thought her own family unique in their brokenness. Now she saw that they were not. And she knew then with certainty that if she could peer into Hector's past and into Vi and Henry's and even into Ruth's, she would find disappointment and failure there, too.

After supper she and Sarah were left alone together. Vi and Henry and Carol Jean had gone home. Joseph was finishing up a game of Rook with Hector and Eden and David. Ruth was doing the dishes and refused her help. "Go sit down and talk to

Sarah," she said, then whispered confidentially, "She could use some cheering up."

So Miranda had dutifully walked into the family room and sat down on the flowered sofa. Sarah looked up from the game show she was watching and turned off the television.

"You don't have to do that on my account."

"That's all right," she said, smiling stiffly. "I shouldn't watch so much. I got into the habit at the hospital. There wasn't anything else to do. Some of the other wives there did needlework, but I've never been good at it. How about you?" she asked.

Miranda felt sorry for her. She was obviously trying very hard to make conversation when she'd probably much rather be alone. "Some," she answered. Now did not seem the right time to talk about her hobbies. "I'm hoping to take one of Ruth's quilting classes. She taught me how to make a block, but I'm afraid that's as far as I've gotten."

Sarah smiled. "Ruth's a very talented and capable woman. She makes everything look easy."

Miranda agreed and wondered how it felt to Sarah to enter the family as she had and then try to follow in the footsteps of competent, kind Ruth.

"I imagine you're looking forward to getting back to your own home," Miranda said, "to sleeping in your own bed."

Sarah smiled but her eyes were veiled. "I am," she said.

"I've enjoyed getting to know Eden," Miranda said. "She's a wonderful girl. You must be very proud of her. She's so lively and full of creativity."

"She is a wonderful girl," Sarah said.

Everything seemed to have a subtext, an undercurrent. For now the tone was sadness. She was a woman of layers and moods, Miranda could see, and then she immediately rebuked herself. Sarah had been through horrors this past year. Anyone might have an emotional backlog after such an experience.

She tried one last time. "I know Eden is glad to have you here. She's missed you terribly."

374

Sarah smiled, a bit bitterly. "She missed her father," she said.

Miranda teetered then as she decided whether to let Sarah push her away or whether to keep trying.

"She missed you, too," Miranda said, determining to be kind. "Every child wants their mother."

Again Sarah gave her a look she couldn't read.

"Yes," she said. "You're probably right."

chapter 49

The next few weeks passed slowly for Miranda, probably since Eden was preoccupied with her father and no longer her constant companion. Miranda missed her, but the realization made her uncomfortable. She didn't like to become overly dependent on anyone for her happiness. They would inevitably leave, or she would, and then where would she be? But she had to admit she missed Eden's bubbling presence. She was energetic and creative and downright entertaining.

She saw Ruth a time or two. "Come and visit me," Ruth invited, but Miranda thought of Sarah and David there, trying to knit their fractured family back together, and decided it would be better to wait.

She saw Joseph more frequently. They took walks and talked, and the more she knew about him, the more she respected him. She rode along with him to his work once on her day off, and she saw the passion he had for keeping the town calm and safe. She saw the open cases on his desk. And the closed ones. He had tracked down one bunch of Irish Travelers—arrested one Pete Sherlock and three of his sons. He showed her his life: where he went to grade school, high school. He introduced her to old friends. She visited his home one Saturday, and he took her fishing, rafting on the river, and then they barbequed steaks. They hiked in the woods, and he showed her some elementary tracking principles. How to identify animals by the length and width of the tracks, the number of toes or claws, and whether or not there was a heel. He showed her how to tell whether the tracks were from a front leg or a back and how to determine the speed and type of gait.

"Follow the tracks, and you'll find out where the animal lives," he said, "in a tree or burrow, the water or deep woods. That's another clue to identification. Follow the tracks long enough and well enough, and sooner or later you'll find the animal itself."

She only wished the advice applied to people.

Joseph talked more about David, and she knew he had gone to visit his brother several times. "We've gotten so we can sit in the same room and not be tense," Joseph said.

She felt hope that there would be complete reconciliation between them soon.

As the days passed she knew it was her turn. It was time for her to share her life with him. She made a start by fixing him a dinner in the tiny kitchen of her apartment. They ate picnic style on a blanket in the tiny backyard. A meager effort, but even so, she was afraid. She was beginning to feel her feet dragging when she walked, tangling around the roots that were beginning to tie her to Abingdon. Part of her wanted to cheer, to say, *Yes, this is where I will put down my roots. This is where I'll bear my fruit.* But another part that sounded like her mother asked her who she thought she was. Reminded her that if she stayed here, paradise would no longer be perfect.

She saw David and Sarah several times but never together. She crossed paths with Sarah once when she went to look for Eden at St. James on food bank day. The food bank was closed, though, and as Miranda sat on the church steps enjoying the sun, Sarah came out, eyes red, obviously having been crying. Miranda assumed she'd been talking to Pastor Hector. She felt as if she were invading Sarah's privacy by witnessing it, but Sarah barely noticed her. Just said hello, then got into her car and drove away—not in the direction of Ruth's house.

Miranda saw her another time out on the trail, just walking. She had said hello and smiled warmly, but Sarah just acknowledged her and kept on going. Obviously now was not a good time for making friends. She felt a deep compassion for the little family.

It was a few days later that Miranda saw David. He came into the Hasty Taste for coffee one morning just after Joseph had finished his breakfast and left. David wheeled his way across the restaurant, stopping to visit with several people along the way. It seemed he knew everyone, and there was much pressing of hands and earnest conversation. He finally settled at a table. She took him a glass of water and greeted him warmly. He still looked subdued but not quite as strained as he had the first night at Ruth's house.

"I didn't know you were working here," he said.

"Temporarily. Elna is due back in a few weeks." Saying it made her realize the clock was ticking. Was her time in Abingdon drawing to a close? "I haven't seen Eden in a while," she said. "And I must say I miss her."

David smiled, and Miranda saw genuine love on his face. "That girl's the light of my life," he said.

She felt a flash of something then. A longing for her own child, she supposed, but she quickly realized the one had nothing to do with the other. She would not begrudge David his daughter's love.

"She and Grady had plans today. Grady's father is taking them fishing. I was invited to go, but I have something else I have to do. Have you met Grady's dad?" he asked.

She shook her head.

"He seems like a kind man," David said. "My mother thinks the world of him."

"Your mother is a very good judge of character," Miranda agreed. "Can I get you a menu?"

"Two, please," he said. "I'm meeting Hector."

She got the menus and another water. Hector arrived. She served the men their meals and kept their coffees full. They were talking intently, and she felt very glad that David had Pastor Hector to encourage him. She thought about the Hound of Heaven again. She had been feeling Him nudge her, gently pull her. Sometimes she felt as if He walked silently beside her, waiting for a chance to speak. Waiting for her to turn her gaze upon Him. She felt longing then, but it didn't last long. For instance, it seemed He was tugging right now, but she wiped tables and made a fresh pot of coffee and her mind was distracted.

Venita sidled up to her and nodded in David's direction. "They say that wife of his has run off. Sorry thing," she said, shaking her head in disapproval.

"Sarah left?" Miranda was shocked to the core. It almost felt like a physical tremor passing through her.

Venita nodded. "I heard she went off day before yesterday. Said she was going to see her folks—they bought a place down near Gatlinburg, but . . ." She shrugged and made a disgusted face.

"Maybe she'll come back," Miranda said and realized she really hoped so. "She's been through a very hard year. Maybe she just needs to get away for a little while and rest."

"Maybe," Venita said, but she gave her a skeptical look.

The two men sat talking for a long time. After Hector left, David stayed and pulled a thick stack of papers from the pack on the side of his chair.

"Do you mind if I take up space for a while?" he asked when she refilled his cup.

"Not at all."

He worked, reading and scribbling and shaking his head in frustration. She refilled his coffee until he told her he'd had his quota for the day. After an hour or so he came up to the register and paid his bill. The stack of papers was in his lap.

"It looks as if your project is a big one," she said.

"It's a book I was writing," he said, and he didn't look happy.

"Wow. I'm impressed."

"Don't be."

"What's it about?"

"It's about what I used to think I knew. David Williams expounds on the meaning of life." He smiled, and she saw a shadow of bitterness.

"I'd like to read it," she said boldly, surprising herself with her words.

He looked at her for a moment, then shrugged. "Take it," he said. "You'd be doing me a favor. Tell me what a fresh, un-indoctrinated pair of eyes sees."

"Seriously?"

"As a heart attack," he said.

She laughed. She liked David Williams very much. She felt a little guilty because of that fact, a little disloyal to Joseph, but again, what had the one to do with the other?

She took the manuscript gratefully. "I can't wait," she said.

"Take your time," he mumbled on his way out the door. "I'm in no hurry."

She finished her shift, went to the Laundromat, tidied her small apartment, and completed her funeral home chores. Joseph called at suppertime to postpone their plans for the evening. He was busy on a case. She told him to be careful, then feeling slightly uncomfortable, realized she was glad for the opportunity to read David's book. She took a blanket out in back of her apartment and sat on the grass to read. There was a slight breeze. Not enough to blow away the pages, but enough to cool her. She was quickly drawn into David's book.

As she read, the things she had heard a hundred times growing up suddenly stopped being dry facts and became a drama of cosmic proportions. There was the benevolent, righteous king. There was a near perfect member of the court, trusted as a son, who became evil through envy. There were treachery and revolt. A coup that ultimately failed, but not before battle and shouts and the sound of war. There was the aftermath, the violent expulsion of the rebels, who now ruled planet Earth where the good subjects fought bravely against them. There was the prince who had given his life to redeem the kingdom. And there was a promise that someday each' rebel would be hunted down and destroyed and that peace would be restored to all the farthest reaches of the kingdom.

Her eyes were damp and the light failing when she finished reading. The story was not complete, but her mind was full. She understood now. She had a choice. She could cast her lot with the resistance, or she could go on as she had and pretend she'd never heard.

She set the book aside finally and lay back on the blanket till it was dark. Gathering up the manuscript, she went upstairs to bed, but it was a long time before she slept.

She read David's book through again and took it back to him several days later. She knocked softly on the screen door. After a moment she heard the whirring of the chair's electric motor, and David himself came to the door.

"Welcome," he said. "Come in. I'm afraid Ma and Eden are over at the church, getting things ready for the Highlands Festival." He didn't mention Sarah, and she didn't ask.

"Actually, I came to see you," she said. "I read your book. Twice."

"Really!" He seemed surprised.

She nodded.

"Well, do you have time to tell me what you think?"

"I don't need time," she said. "I loved it."

He smiled. "Now, that's the kind of constructive criticism I can use. How about a glass of iced tea or a cup of coffee?"

"Sure. I'll have some tea."

He whirred into the kitchen, then returned with the two glasses tucked into a holder on the side of his chair. "Here you go," he said, handing her one. "Shall we sit on the porch?"

"That would be perfect. I think there's a breeze."

Miranda sat in one of Ruth's ladder-backed rockers, David in his chair.

"I've never heard anyone talk about all of this the way you do," she said. "It's not boring."

"That's high praise. Thank you."

She thought she saw a flicker of interest in his eyes. She looked down at the chapters and scanned the progression he had drawn. The cosmic battle. The expulsion from Eden, the struggle to find the way back—those chapters had caught at her heart.

"It was like you knew me," she said. "All the places I've gone and the things I've done to try to make things . . . I don't know, *right,* I guess."

"Did you succeed? In making them right?"

She shook her head. She thought of her child, lost to her. Her mother, never known. "But then the book just sort of *quit.*"

"You noticed that."

"Yes, I noticed, but you can't leave things there. It's like closing a story before the happy ending. Like ending a movie three-quarters of the way through, at the dark moment."

"The dark moment?"

"You know, the moment when the hero and the heroine are all upset with each other and the worst thing has happened and it looks like they'll never be together."

He nodded. Soberly.

She could see the sorrow in his eyes. And then she understood. His life had become the dark moment.

"I can't see my way past it," he said.

She took a deep breath. Who was she to counsel the counselor? But she felt she must try, so she spoke. "You know the way," she said. "You know it even in the dark."

He looked up at her, his eyes shiny with tears. "Do you think so?"

"I know it," she said, and she put her hand over her heart, as if making a promise.

They sat silently for a while. She set down her glass and stood. "Call me when you finish," she said. "I'd like to read the whole story."

chapter 50

By the last week of July, the town seemed to have shifted into high gear, and Abingdon's streets were full of bustle and activity. The Hasty Taste was busier than usual. Venita said the craftspeople and the first tourists were trickling in. Apparently the Virginia Highlands Festival was quite an event, with musical performances, a quilt show, arts and crafts, lectures, plays, spinning and weaving, nature tours, and food.

On Monday, just after opening, a heavyset woman, bright red hair with white roots, came into the Hasty Taste. She gave Miranda a worried look. Venita went flying out around the counter to hug her. "Elna! You're back! How are you, dear?" Miranda heard before their voices lowered in gossip or commiseration, . . . *knows it's just temporary,* and *don't you worry, another week will be just fine.* She didn't need a memo to know her tenure at the Hasty Taste was almost up. Venita made it official as soon as Elna left.

"We sure have appreciated your help," she said, "but Elna needs her job back."

She thanked Venita graciously, and they agreed her last day would be Friday. *And then what?* she asked herself as she went about her work. She supposed she could try to find another job, but she had come here to find her child, and she had gotten distracted by other things. That other thing came in just then and winked at her as he took his customary place. Henry joined him, and Miranda brought them their breakfasts without needing to take an order. She had a feeling she and Joseph were approaching critical mass, and she wasn't sure yet whether things would end in fission or meltdown.

He seemed a little unnerved, as well. As she cashed him out, Henry poked him in the ribs and said, "Remember what I said. Get the party started, son." It seemed to rattle Joseph. He fumbled with his wallet, and pictures and credit cards went cascading onto the floor. Miranda came around the counter to help pick them up. She leaned down, he rose up, and their heads bumped. Embarrassing for both of them. Endearing to everyone else, apparently.

"Ain't they cute?" Venita said to Wally, who answered with a grunt. Miranda said a quick good-bye and went back to work with burning cheeks.

She worked hard all morning, and when her shift was over she noticed a missed call on her cell phone. It was C. Dwight Judson, her erstwhile attorney. He was in and came straight to the point.

"I've heard from the attorney in Tennessee about the court order," he said.

A feeling of shock ran through her, as if the telephone in her hand carried a current. Her heart was beating like a hummingbird's. "Yes?" She held her breath.

"I'm afraid the court denied your petition. The records will remain sealed."

She was silent for a minute. She thanked him and ended the call.

She said good-bye on autopilot to Venita and Wally, then walked back to her apartment, got into her car, and drove. She passed farms and houses and had a mind to keep on driving. To drive and drive and drive and never stop until she was far away from anything that would ever remind her of her child again. She would not mind leaving the laptop or her few clothes, but faces flashed in her mind like slides on a blank screen in her heart. Over and over she saw them, and finally she turned the car around, and after another spell of driving she found herself at St. James church.

She parked the car, walked across the graveled parking lot, and sat down on the steps. They were warm from the afternoon sun. She took out her cell phone and, without the emotion she would have imagined, called Nashville information. The last she'd heard, Danny Loomis was still living in town, working for a trucking company. She had not spoken to him in eleven years.

"I'd like a number for Loomis," she said to the operator, "Daniel Loomis."

She wrote it on her hand, then dialed quickly before she could think.

A child answered on the third ring. A little girl, and she felt a thrust of pain.

"I'm trying to get ahold of your daddy," she said. "Danny Loomis?"

"He's at work. You want to talk to my mom?"

"Do you have your daddy's work number?"

"Just a minute." Heavy breathing, paper rattling, then the number read to her.

"Thank you," she said just as a woman's voice spoke in the background.

She signed off, then dialed again, quickly.

"Beauregard Trucking. This is Kip."

"I'd like to speak to Daniel Loomis."

"Just a minute." She was put on hold. The phone picked up after a few seconds.

"Loomis," the voice said. It didn't sound familiar in the least.

"Danny," she said, "this is Miranda. I mean, Dorrie Gibson."

A long silence, which she broke herself. "This isn't a social call," she said bluntly. "I'm sorry to bother you, but I need some information."

"Okay." He sounded cautious, and she began to feel angry.

"I'm looking for our child," she said.

A deep expulsion of breath. "Look, Dorrie, I can't talk about this now."

"I don't want to talk. I just want to know everything you know. Don't you think you owe me that?"

Another pause. "I don't know anything."

"Danny, someone got the original birth certificate. Was it you?"

A deep sigh, and her anger flared.

"You have it?" she demanded.

"Had it," he said. "I gave it to your mother."

Miranda felt stunned. She felt once more like the victim of treachery.

"All I know is that it was a girl. Your mother said she had a good home for her. Christian people. That's all I know."

"You told me you didn't know anything."

"That's what your mother told me to say. You know how it was, Dorrie."

She knew how it was, all right.

"Look, I've got to go," he said.

Her anger was replaced by desperation. "How much did she weigh?" she pleaded. "What color were her eyes?" She could hear herself almost wailing.

"I don't know. I don't remember. Look, I have to go. I'm sorry. I'm really sorry, but that was all in the past. Let's leave it that way."

And then he hung up.

She held out the phone and looked at it. Then she laid her head on her knees and wept. Deep wrenching sobs. And somewhere during her sorrow someone came near. She knew because she could feel it, a sweet presence, and then a warm small hand on her back. She could smell her. It was the sweet smell of childhood. Soap and sweat and grass.

"What's the matter?" Eden asked quietly.

Miranda couldn't speak. She shook her head.

"You want me to get somebody?" Eden asked. "Pastor Hector or Mom or Uncle Joseph?"

Miranda shook her head again. "Just you," she said. So Eden sat down beside her and slipped a warm hand into her own and stayed there without talking until Miranda's sobs became shuddering breaths.

⌒

By morning she had made a decision. She had to tell Joseph. And she would do it today. She would do it this evening, she decided, for they had agreed to go walking on the trail for an hour or so when he finished work. She would do it now if she could, so eager was she to have it done.

"We'll stop by the Dairy Freeze, and I'll buy you a burger for supper," he'd said when he called her last night. It was the perfect opportunity. Their long walk, surrounded by the beautiful mountains, would give her the courage that she needed.

The other decision she had made during the long sleepless night was to go public in her search. It was her only chance to find her daughter. As soon as she told Joseph, she would tell her other friends. She would ask the four pastors. She would put an ad in the newspaper if necessary.

She went to work as usual. She made coffee, filled the cream pitchers, and did the morning prep work, and while she was working, she slipped the picture of her baby girl out of her purse. She set it under the edge of the register so she could see it and be comforted. The tiny face peeked at her and made her smile. At six o'clock she unlocked the door. Joseph arrived a little after that and greeted her with a warm smile. She brought him his coffee, and he told her he was looking forward to seeing her tonight. She told him she was looking forward to it, too, and tried to ignore her churning stomach. No mature man would hold a fifteen-year-old girl's mistake against her, would he? And then she suddenly repented of calling her daughter a mistake. Now that she knew a little more, the child was real to her, not someone she had only dreamed of. Her child wasn't an *it* any longer. She was a *she*. She, Miranda DeSpain, had a daughter. A little girl.

Joseph and Henry ate. After a half hour or so Henry left and Joseph came toward the register. He took out his wallet and then she saw something that changed everything.

Joseph smiled at her, lowered his eyes to his wallet, withdrew a bill, and set it on the counter. Then he frowned, something having apparently caught his attention. She followed his gaze. He was looking at the photograph of her baby. Her heart began thumping. Why had she been so foolish as to leave it out? She prayed he wouldn't ask her about it now.

As she watched, he reached over and picked it up. And then the oddest thing happened. He looked at the picture, not as if it was unfamiliar and he was studying it or trying to make sense of something, but fondly, as if it were someone he knew. Even loved. A brief smile played on his lips, and then he did something that stunned Miranda even more. He tucked it into his wallet.

"Thanks," he said. "I'd hate to lose this. Where was it? Under the counter?"

She didn't answer, but suddenly she was seeing yesterday's cascade of photos and credit and business cards all over the floor as their heads bumped. She stood watching and thinking, her mouth slightly open. Was it? No. It couldn't be. She stood absolutely still, as if moving too quickly might banish the vague picture that was beginning to form. She nodded and smiled, as if she knew what he meant.

"I thought I'd picked up everything," he said, "but obviously I missed one."

"It's a good thing you saw it," she said. "I didn't know who it was." Truth. Clear truth.

He met her honest gaze. "Couldn't you recognize those cowlicks?" He set two bills on the counter and waved away the change.

"Such a sweet baby," she said, wanting him to say something to confirm what she already knew. What she supposed she had known at some level since their first meeting.

"She's still a sweet girl," Joseph commented, giving her another warm smile. "But then, you already know that."

She finished her shift somehow, her mind overwhelmed with what couldn't be. There had to be a misunderstanding. After work she went into her tiny apartment and shut the door. She thought. About Eden and Joseph and Sarah and David and what she knew and what could not be true. Sarah had been pregnant, hadn't she? With David's child? Then how could Eden be her own daughter? She didn't understand how it could be true, but she had a feeling it was. There was only one way to know for sure. With her hands shaking, she phoned Ruth's house and asked for Eden.

Eden's voice was innocent and out of breath. "Oh, hi, Miranda," she said. "Dad and I have been playing Ping-Pong. He can still beat me, even in his chair."

Miranda made some kind of response. And then she asked, trying to keep her voice casual. "Hey," she said. "I just realized there's something important about you that I don't know."

"What's that?" Eden asked, and once again Miranda was struck by the innocence of her voice, and she had the urge to stop right then. To say never mind and leave the question unanswered. But the scale had been tipped and the slide toward movement inexorable.

"When's your birthday?" she asked, and in the seconds it took for the answer to come, worlds could have been created and destroyed.

"I'm gonna be twelve," Eden said, "on December fourteenth."

chapter 51

Miranda spent the rest of the evening working out the how. Joseph came to the door at five o'clock, and she told him she wasn't well. If she told him the truth, he would think her insane or a liar. She must have looked authentically sick, for he gave her a concerned look and told her to get some rest.

She phoned Reverend Webb. He answered on the seventh ring, just as she was ready to hang up. His voice sounded frail, but she needed answers. She had waited long enough for them.

"Reverend Webb, this is Miranda DeSpain. I visited you the other day and asked you about Noreen Gibson."

"Yes," he said. "I remember."

"I forgot to ask you something then. Could I ask you now?"

"Yes. Go ahead."

"Mrs. Tallert said that Beck used to let Noreen and Bobbie go to church outings and trips. Do you remember what some of those were?"

"Oh dear. It's been a long time," he apologized.

"I know. That's all right," Miranda said and wondered if she should have bothered him. He became agitated when he couldn't remember things.

"Wait. Wait. There was a trip we took to Lewisburg to the state fair. I believe Noreen went to that."

"Uh-huh," she said.

"There were singings we went to from time to time at other churches. We went over to Hinton once and another time to Beckley."

She took a deep breath and asked the question. "Was there anything in Virginia, Reverend Webb?"

There was a silence. "I believe there was, now that you mention it," he said. "There was a camp the children used to visit. I believe Noreen went once. I can't remember the name of it, though, or where it was."

"Could it have been in Abingdon, Reverend Webb?"

"I suppose it could have been."

"Could it have been Camp Berachah?"

"It was!" he said triumphantly, his voice full and his memory sound now that he was on solid ground. "That was it. The valley of blessing. I remember because it was in the valley of blessing that Jehoshaphat cried out to the Lord with his enemies attacking, 'Lord, we don't know what to do, but our eyes are on you.'"

"You're sure about the name of the camp?"

"Oh yes. I'm sure. Now that you tell me, I remember it well."

She thanked him, her hands shaking.

"I've helped you, haven't I?" he asked.

"You certainly have, Reverend Webb. Thank you, again."

She hung up the phone and sat there putting the pieces together. When she was finished, she had a feeling she knew who the person was that her mother had trusted.

chapter 52

Ruth waved good-bye to Eden and David and watched as they proceeded down the hill together, David in his power chair, Eden on her bike.

"Are you sure you don't want a ride?" she'd asked.

"Ma, we've got wheels," David had joked. "We don't need a car." She had smiled at her son and kissed them both before they left. Eden and David had exchanged tolerant grins, and she had felt her heart lift. She had the sense that her son's spirit was beginning to heal just as his body had. Even in the absence of his wife.

Neither David nor Sarah had explained Sarah's absence. They had talked behind closed doors and then announced that Sarah was going to visit her parents. David and Eden would stay here if that was all right with Ruth, which, of course, it was. Eden's jaw had tightened when Sarah had kissed her good-bye, but she had become her sunny self again with her father. Her mood darkened only when Sarah's name came up or at certain random times when Ruth was sure she was thinking of her mother.

She watched David and Eden proceeding down the hill, David going entirely too fast for a wheelchair on the sidewalk, Eden sticking her hands out at her sides. She shook her head and turned away before she could worry herself into an early grave.

She hadn't seen much of Joseph during the past few days. He was busy with the festival. There was never much crime in Abingdon, but more people meant traffic and crowds, both of which were the police department's bailiwick.

She checked her watch and went back inside to fetch her purse. She was meeting with Johnny today to talk about the campground. She felt a pang of discomfort when she thought of Joseph and what he would say about the arrangements she'd made, but then she reminded herself that she was still the mother and he was still the son. She was a capable adult and could make her own decisions. And the truth was, she didn't want anyone, not even Joseph or David, not Hector, not anyone, not even Vi and Henry to point out the obvious flaws in her dream. She had always longed to see the campground open again. And now it seemed possible. She was not going to let go of that hope easily.

She closed the front door, climbed into her car, and made the short drive to the camp, passing under the sign with the same joy she always felt. It had been a valley of blessing, not only for her and her husband and her sons but for hundreds of children who had come there. She had a desire, a holy desire, she believed, to see it happen again.

Johnny and Grady were waiting on the porch of the lodge, sitting in new ladder-backed rockers. She parked the car and got out, waving a greeting their way.

Johnny rose up and greeted her with a hug. "Good day to you, Ruth. How are you?"

"As fine as this day, Johnny," she said. "Just look what you've done here!" She looked around with joy. The dock had been repaired, and the canoe was actually sitting on top of the water instead of hanging listlessly beneath it. She could see that the roofs on several of the cabins had been patched, and there were new gutters on a few places that had rusted through or fallen down.

"Come inside here and look," he said, opening the door to the lodge. She followed him through the dining hall and into the kitchen. "I've taken out this wall here where the dry rot was and replaced it. I put new pipes in this one here. There was a small leak. And I laid new vinyl on the floor." She looked down and sure enough, there were shiny new black and white squares under her feet.

"It's beautiful," she said. "How much do I owe you?"

He held up a hand. "Hold on," he said. "Let's look at the big picture. Will you have a cup of coffee?" he asked. He pointed toward the counter where he had set up a small coffeepot that was bubbling.

"I'd love a cup," she said.

Grady took the opportunity to go outside and play tetherball, also a new addition. Ruth took the cup Johnny gave her and sat down with him at one of the long tables in the dining hall where he had placed several folders.

"I've met with the subcontractors, and we've come up with a tentative plan."

She nodded.

He opened the folder and took out a detailed drawing, like an architect's plan. "These are the existing buildings," he said as she listened carefully, "and I've marked the areas that would need replacement or repair, and alongside I've put bids by three companies."

She briefly scanned the paper work and did some crude calculations in her head. Well, it was certainly more than she had on hand. She listened carefully as he outlined all of the projects and the work necessary. When he finished speaking he slid a piece of paper across the table to her. "Here's the final estimate, using the low bid for almost all of the contractors, except two that I felt did inferior work after checking their references."

She looked at Johnny. "You've done a very careful job here."

He lowered his eyes. "It was the least I could do. But before you move forward, it's time to count the cost," he said.

She met his gaze. "I think you're right," she said.

He nodded and handed her the entire sheaf of papers. "You

take these home and think about them. If you decide not to go ahead with it, there will certainly be no second guessing on my end. I'm grateful for having had the chance to know you and to stay here at this beautiful place."

"Johnny, I've already counted the cost. I feel settled in my mind that this is the right thing to do," she said, looking around her and smiling. "If I opened the camp again, would you consider staying on as caretaker?"

Again he ducked his head. "I'm not worthy," he said, and his use of the word surprised her.

"None of us is worthy, Johnny. That's the meaning of grace."

He raised his head and took a deep breath. "If the camp opens, I will stay," he said.

She nodded and rose to her feet. "Thank you for all your work," she said. "Call me when the papers are ready to sign." She was aware of his eyes on her as she got into her car and drove away.

Miranda breathed deeply and prepared herself. Fortune had smiled on her in at least one thing. She had seen David and Eden downtown. Ruth had been at home when she'd called, though she was breathless from having just walked in the door. She had told Miranda she was welcome to come and talk. Miranda walked to Ruth's front porch now and knocked softly on the door. No one answered, but the door was unlocked. She pushed open the screen door and stepped in. "Ruth?" she called softly, "where are you?"

She found her in the kitchen, sitting quietly at the table, a stack of papers in front of her. Her face looked a little melancholy, and Miranda wondered if she should ask the question she'd come to ask.

"What's wrong?" she asked.

Ruth looked up and shook her head. "Nothing, really. I'm

just thinking about the cost of love."

Miranda gave her a quizzical look and Ruth smiled. "I was thinking about David and Sarah and you and Joseph and Grady and his father, and it seems to me that in all of these instances there's a love path and a safe path."

Miranda sat down at the table and dropped her purse onto the floor.

"The love path is reckless and dangerous, and there are thorns and briers and a chance of complete destruction. The safe path is . . . alone. You don't have to trust or risk. Which would you choose?" she asked, staring directly into Miranda's face.

Miranda wondered if she somehow knew why she had come and was giving her some cryptic answer. "I don't know," she said flatly.

Ruth set the papers facedown on the hutch and smiled. "You didn't come to hear me ramble," she said. "You said you needed to talk to me. What is it?"

Suddenly Miranda was seized with insecurity. She suddenly saw it the way it would look to Ruth. To Joseph. They would never believe she hadn't known. They would think she had wormed her way into their family for the purpose of stealing back her child.

"Miranda?" Ruth asked.

There was no easy way. She looked up and let the truth come spilling out of her mouth.

"When I was fifteen I got pregnant," she said.

Ruth's face registered surprise, then compassion.

"My mother said the baby wasn't coming back to her house. She thought the best thing to do was to put the baby up for adoption, so that's what she arranged."

Ruth was looking at her intently and had become very still.

"I had the baby. They took it away. I was told nothing. Not the weight or length or even the sex. That was eleven years ago."

Ruth's face had blanched white.

"My mother died a few months ago and left me one clue. A

picture, taken when the baby was one year old and postmarked from Abingdon, Virginia."

Ruth's eyes were filling with tears. So were Miranda's.

"I came here to look for my baby," she said.

The two women faced each other across the table, and no one spoke for what seemed like a long time.

"And you found her," Ruth finally said softly.

"But I don't understand," Miranda said. "I can hardly believe it, even though I know it must be true. I don't understand how it could be. No one has ever told me anything, and I need to know. Would you please tell me the truth?"

Ruth wiped her eyes and nodded. She took a napkin from the holder on the table and gave one to Miranda. She began speaking quietly.

"My sons took it hard when their father died," she said. "Especially David. He had always been jealous and competitive of Joseph. Whatever Joseph did, he wanted to do. Whatever Joseph got, he had to have one, too. Natural brotherly rivalry but taken to an extreme. I watched them hurt each other, especially after their father died, but I didn't know how to stop them.

"When Joseph left for college, that's when the trouble came. I watched it, but I didn't know how to stop David. I didn't know if I should tell. I've always felt guilty for that. I should have done something." She paused for a moment, then went on.

"Joseph came home. Sarah was pregnant with David's child."

Miranda shook her head in confusion. Ruth continued talking.

"Oh, it was horrible—the hatred, the murderous hatred between them." She was weeping now. "Joseph went off to the marines, and I was so afraid he'd die with that hatred on his heart, but the Lord spared him. Not so with Sarah's baby," she said softly, and Miranda felt a chill.

"She miscarried in her seventh month. It was a girl. They named her and buried her up there in Fairfax. I wept and cried for them, for Sarah, especially. She was so wracked by guilt. Have you ever been torn up with guilt?"

Miranda paused, then nodded. Every day of her life as she wondered where her baby was.

"There was nothing I could do except pray. And I did. For all of them. I interceded before God and begged Him to make a way. And then one day the telephone rang. It was your mother." She smiled at Miranda.

"She said, 'Mrs. Williams, this is Noreen Gibson. Do you remember me?' And of course, I did. There are a few you remember, and she was one of them, with her sad empty eyes and hard heart. She'd been wounded, terribly wounded, we could tell, but she never opened up to us at camp. Which was why I was somewhat surprised to hear from her. But not so surprised really. The Lord takes His time, but He always gets His way," she said softly. "But it wasn't exactly what I'd expected. I thought perhaps she was calling to tell me of her spiritual journey, but it was another prayer she was answering. Noreen said her daughter was pregnant. She wanted to arrange a private adoption, and she wondered if I knew of anyone I would trust with her grandchild."

"She said that?" Miranda asked. "Those exact words?"

"Those exact words," Ruth affirmed.

"She cared about her," Miranda murmured.

"She cared very deeply," Ruth said. "And to me it seemed like a miracle." She smiled, almost laughed. "I called David and Sarah, and they could hardly believe it. Especially Sarah. 'He forgives me' was all she could say, and I knew she didn't mean Joseph.

"And then the baby came. Your mother called us as soon as you went into labor, and Joseph and Sarah went to Nashville. They brought her back home, and I went up to see them right away. Oh, what a precious baby! That sweet face, and so alert! She looked at you with those big blue eyes, and you just felt like she would give you a piece of her mind if she could talk." Ruth laughed. "That's how Eden always seemed to me as a baby, impatient that she couldn't tear around on her own." She shook her head. "What a character!"

She sobered. "The only darkness was the secrecy. No one should know. That was shame, you know. Sarah's shame. She didn't want anyone to know that God had taken her baby. And she especially didn't want Joseph to know. In time Eden knew. I knew. David and Sarah knew. Their friends in Fairfax knew, but everyone here thought Eden was the child that Sarah had borne to David. She didn't want Joseph to have the triumph of knowing.

"Your mother had asked me to send her one picture. That was all. 'Just let me see that she's all right, and I'll never bother you again,' she said. I didn't tell David and Sarah," Ruth said, "although I suppose I should have. I took the picture Sarah sent to me of Eden on her first birthday, and I sent it to your mother."

"And she hid it and saved it all these years. Then she died. And then I found it. And then I came," Miranda said.

"And then you came," Ruth agreed. "And now it will all come out." And she did not look sad at all but peaceful, even relieved.

chapter 53

Eden waited another twenty minutes for Grady, then went to find her dad. The festival had started, and he was sitting with Pastor Hector and Uncle Joseph in the park at the tables where all the grown-ups sat around, and they were laughing.

"Dad, have you seen Grady?"

"No, Eden, I haven't," he said.

"He was supposed to meet me here."

"He'll probably be along," Pastor Hector said. "He probably got distracted by something. There's a lot to look at." He pointed around him at all the booths with the paintings and pottery and the games and singers, and Eden supposed he was right. Still, she had a funny feeling that something wasn't right.

She was just getting ready to ask Uncle Joseph if he would drive her to the campground when he got a call that somebody needed to see him back at his office.

Eden went back home and asked Grandma if she'd seen Grady, but she said no. She went back out to the road on her bike and started out for the campground. She was about halfway there and really wishing she'd brought something to drink when a familiar car came toward her.

"Hi, Miranda!" she said.

"Eden, what are you doing?" Miranda looked funny. Surprised, but more than that.

"I'm worried about Grady," she said. "Can you give me a ride to his place?"

Miranda took a minute to think. "Did you ask your dad?" she finally asked.

Eden hesitated. She couldn't afford to have Dad say no. "It's okay with him," she lied, and she felt terrible, but just as strong was the feeling that Grady needed help.

"I was supposed to meet your uncle ten minutes ago," Miranda said. "But I suppose I could drop you off, go find Joseph, and then come back for you two. Are you sure it's okay with your dad?"

"I'm sure," Eden said. She was glad Miranda was quiet when they drove, and she scrambled out of the car as soon as it stopped.

"Go make sure Grady and his dad are there, then wave at me. I'm not going to leave you here alone."

Eden agreed and tore down the hill toward the RV park. "Grady!" Eden called. "Grady! You come out here!"

There was no sound, and as she came through the grove of trees, she saw nothing moving around the trailer. Mr. Adair's truck was gone, but Grady's bike was there, and if she listened real quiet she could hear snuffling. She went to the door and peeked in and sure enough, there was Grady, sitting at the kitchen table bawling like a baby.

This was serious. She heard a horn honk. She'd forgotten about Miranda. She ran back through the trees and waved good-bye, feeling a little guilty because Grady's dad wasn't actually there. It was the second lie she had told, but before she could reconsider, Miranda held up her hand and backed out. Eden hurried back to the situation in the trailer. Grady hadn't moved.

"What's the matter with you?" she asked.

He didn't answer, and he didn't even try to hide or pretend he wasn't crying, which meant things were pretty bad. Eden was really feeling worried now. There were too many people crying this week. First Miranda and now Grady. She was wishing she hadn't waved Miranda off. There weren't many times when she needed a grown-up, but sometimes it was nice to have someone who had a driver's license.

"What's wrong?" she asked, kinder now.

He shook his head and couldn't speak for the gulps and sobs. She went to the sink and ran a glass of water and took it to him. He took a few sips. She found a napkin and handed it to him.

He blew his nose with a big honk, and she was going to laugh, but when she saw his face she decided not to.

"I'm supposed to get things ready to leave," he said.

"You're leaving?" she asked with disbelief.

He nodded.

"When?"

"Right now. As soon as my dad gets back."

Eden hadn't paid a lot of attention, but she had thought that Grady's dad was working for Grandma. Another secret she wasn't supposed to know about. "What about the campground?" she asked, and Grady looked even more miserable. He shook his head again.

Eden suddenly got the feeling that something was seriously wrong. "Look here, Grady, you'd better tell me what's going on."

"If I tell you, you'll tell your uncle, and then my dad will go back to jail."

"Why would your dad go to jail?" Eden asked, feeling truly alarmed. "Has he done something bad?"

Grady nodded. "Real bad. And he's doing it right now."

Eden stared at Grady. She didn't believe what he was saying. Nice, kind Mr. Adair a jailbird? She tried to remember if she'd ever seen his face on a Wanted poster, but nothing came to mind.

Grady struggled for a minute, the tears back again. Finally he seemed to make up his mind. "Here," he said, going to the bedroom area and opening a drawer. "Look in here."

Eden looked in, and it took a minute for her to figure out

what she was seeing. She picked up the stack of cards. They were driver's licenses, all with Mr. Adair's picture but with different names.

"And here," Grady said, opening the broom closet and showing her a stack of license plates.

Grady looked miserable.

Eden didn't want to believe it, but she could see he was telling the truth.

"You said he was doing something bad right now," she said.

Grady nodded again.

"What is it?" she asked, and she had a really bad feeling about it, even before he answered.

"He's stealing some money," he said, "from your grandma."

Johnny smiled and held out a sheaf of papers for Ruth to sign. "These are all the contracts for the roofers and drywallers and plumbers and electricians," he said. "And one naming me general contractor. If you think I'm up to the challenge."

Ruth gazed intently at Johnny Adair. "I feel this is the Lord's project and that He has His hand on it. Don't you?" she asked, meeting his gaze.

He met her eyes and gazed at her steadily. "I have sensed that myself," he said.

"Well, then, He'll watch over every detail, don't you think?"

She reached for the papers he held out to her, and for the tiniest fraction of a second he didn't release them. They both had hold, and neither one let go.

"You wanted me to sign?" she asked.

"Oh. Yes." He let go.

She set the papers down on the table and signed each one by the yellow flag, then handed them all back, this time her check for the deposit on the work clipped to the top one.

He reached for the contracts, but now she held on a second too long as she spoke.

"That camp was a wonderful place, Johnny. It was a place where children and young people could decide what kind of lives they would live. Whether they would follow Christ into the wildness of His journey for them, sometimes leaving everything familiar behind, or whether they would not. I think we all have such a moment, don't you, Johnny? A time of decision. When we make up our minds what kind of person we're going to be. I think at those times we can't think too much. We have to just say yes and trust that if we do right, things will be right."

He met her gaze. His eyes were dark and unreadable. She let go of the papers, and he must have let go, as well, for they scattered to the floor. They both stared at them; then after a second he stooped and picked them up. He shuffled them together, his head and eyes lowered.

"I'd better get to the bank," he said, "before it closes."

"You'd better go, then," Ruth said and watched him walk out the door.

chapter 54

I didn't know what to do," Wally said, "so I came to you."
Joseph looked at the paper in his hand and felt sick. "You did the right thing," he said.

"It was just odd, you know, her giving me the social security number and then having them say it wasn't her."

"Yes, it is odd, but it's probably nothing," Joseph said, wishing he believed it.

"That's what I think, too. Like I said, she's a real nice gal. Just thought you ought to know."

"Thank you, Wally," Joseph said. "I'll let you know if there's a problem."

Wally shuffled off, and Joseph's head swam as he looked down at the paper. The owner of the social security number Miranda had given Wally belonged to one Dora Mae Gibson, the social security administration said. Joseph was confused. And he had a feeling that when the facts made sense, he would wish they didn't. Things didn't add up.

He checked his watch, then quickly, before it closed, phoned Tennessee's vital statistics department. He identified himself and waited while the clerk searched birth, marriage, divorce, and death certificates for Dora Mae Gibson. Death and marriage struck out, but birth yielded one return.

"I have a birth certificate on file for Miranda Isadora DeSpain. Mother Noreen Gibson, father Thomas Orlando DeSpain."

He thanked the clerk, hung up, then shook his head. Why did she use two names? Maybe there was an explanation, he thought, holding on to a thread of hope. The desperation with which he did so made him realize how much he had grown to care for her. Something was rumbling, though, and he remembered the feeling he'd had when they'd first met. JDFR. It just didn't feel right. That had been what his gut had told him, and gradually he had let his heart override it. He felt a heaviness in both now.

"Hey." Her voice drew him out of his brooding.

He swiveled his chair around. She was standing in the doorway, looking sober herself.

"David said you'd been called back to work."

He nodded, not sure what to say or how to proceed. She took the matter out of his hands.

"Joseph," she said, "there's something I have to tell you."

Her face was sober, her eyes full of tears, and he had an impulse to tell her no. To walk toward her and put his hand over her lips and say, *Whatever it is, it doesn't matter.* But he did not. "Tell me," he said.

She stood there in front of his desk like a child called before the principal.

"Sit down," he invited.

She shook her head and looked straight at him, and he felt grief mixed with love.

"Just let me tell it," she said.

"Tell it," he said and steeled himself to listen.

"I don't know where to begin, so I'll just start in the middle," she said.

He had to stifle a smile. It faded when she spoke her next words.

"When I was fifteen I had a baby," she said, her voice breaking with emotion.

Oddly enough, he thought of Eden. Of how he would feel if it were her standing before him in a mere four years, telling him this. His heart twisted with sorrow, and he nodded and waited for her to go on.

"My mother made arrangements," she said, and he remembered the story of Noreen and how his hand and Miranda's had clasped together tightly as they heard it together. "A private adoption was arranged, and I knew nothing at all until my mother died. She left an envelope."

She dug around in her purse and handed it to him. He took it from her and looked at it. He recognized his mother's gracious swirling handwriting immediately. He frowned, trying to make sense of what she was saying, of what he saw.

"This envelope?" he repeated dumbly.

She nodded, tears flowing freely now. "With a picture inside. Of my baby."

Why would his mother have a picture of Miranda's baby? The obvious interpretation made no sense. It didn't fit with what he'd been told, but he made the leap anyway, knowing that if his preconceived beliefs didn't fit with the evidence, one of them must be wrong.

Miranda watched him. She seemed to be waiting for him to say something. He looked back down at the envelope and went through that evidence now, taking reluctant steps with the determination of someone who knows a devastating truth must be faced. She had appeared out of nowhere at just the right time. She had sought out his family. She had certainly shown an excessive interest in his niece. And suddenly he remembered. As the last piece slid into place, he felt the same sense he always did on solving a small mystery. It was slight surprise mixed with vindication, as if a key was selected from a group, and amazingly it slid into the lock and the door opened. But this time it was mixed with sharp regret. He barely needed the confirmation, but he made it anyway.

He remembered standing at the cash register, and there it had been. The picture of his niece. He thought, seeing the scene in detail, remembering her responses and his rejoinders.

He looked at Miranda, still standing before him. She was watching his face, and her own expression was stoic.

He opened his wallet now and took out his small bunch of photos, and he knew what he would find, but he hoped, he prayed he would be wrong. There could still be another answer, his heart insisted, but his brain knew the truth.

The photograph he had taken from beneath the register was on top of the stack. He took it out and held it up to the light, and now, of course, he could see that it wasn't worn in the same pattern as the others, not curved from his wallet, but flat and shiny. He turned it over and saw Eden's age written on the back in his mother's handwriting.

Slowly he thumbed through his other pictures, his mind racing ahead and not wanting to come to the conclusion he had to face. With each picture he looked at and then placed on the bottom of the stack, he felt as if a hope was being set aside. He looked up again and saw Miranda watching him silently, her eyes pooled with tears.

He set down another photo, and just past the gap-toothed first grade picture, there it was. His own baby picture of Eden Elizabeth Williams. He set the two identical photos side by side on his desk and felt a grimness slide in alongside what he could only name loss and grief along with confusion. Why would his brother have lied? His mother? The ripples were seismic. He couldn't begin to understand the what, much less the why.

There was one last hope.

"What day did you have your baby?" he asked, desperately wanting the answer to be something other than the one he knew would be given.

"December fourteenth," she said, "nineteen ninety-five."

The truth fell on him like a weight. He had purchased compasses, lariats, radios, boots, and backpacks on that date for years. He still didn't understand the how of it all, but he knew what she was saying had to be the truth.

He sat in silence, one image putting all of this into question—the picture of Sarah, guilt-stained, pregnant with his brother's child.

"But Sarah was pregnant. She and David—"

"Lost their baby," Miranda finished softly. "At seven months. Just before my mother called her long-ago camp counselor and asked if there was anyone she would trust with her grandchild."

Some emotion washed over him—something between anger and grief. At his mother. His brother. At Sarah again. He stared into the past and his eyes finally came to rest on Miranda.

So now he knew what she had really wanted with him.

She opened up her mouth to speak again, but his telephone rang. He picked it up, taking the way out provided. He did not want to hear any more. He had already heard enough.

It was Loni, the dispatcher, calling from downstairs. "Lieutenant Williams," she said. "I think you'd better come down here. Your niece just called and, well, just come down. I think it might be urgent."

"I've got to go," he said, leaving Miranda watching him with a grieved expression on her face.

He took the stairs three at a time and listened to Loni's terse report.

"How long ago did she call?" he demanded. Loni looked a little bit afraid of him.

"About ten minutes ago. She called in all of these plates and asked me to check them. I thought you ought to know."

"Did you call her back?"

"I tried, but there's no answer."

"What was the number of the phone she called from?"

Loni read it to him. "It's a cell phone. I called the company, and it's issued to a John Adair."

He ran the name through his mind. It was Grady's father.

Loni continued. "The billing address was Number 8 Crabtree Drive, North Augusta, South Carolina."

"Murphy Village," he said with growing alarm. "He's a Traveler. I should have known." He berated himself for not looking further into his niece's friends. "Did you run the plates?"

"I'm doing it now. The first three are stolen."

He phoned his mother on his cell, cutting short any preliminary courtesies. "Where does Grady's father live?" he asked without preamble.

His mother hesitated.

"*Now*, Ma. I don't have time to explain, but he's not to be trusted, and Eden might be with him."

"Oh, Lord."

"Where does Grady's father live?" he repeated. "I need to know now."

"Down at the campground," she said. "He's been doing some work for me."

He hung up the phone and ran to the car. He had no time for anger now. He screamed down the highway, siren blaring, called for backup, and drove into the campground, knowing already what he would find. He drove past the lake to the RV hookups on the other side. Empty, but there were the tracks again. The RV and the truck. And Eden's bicycle hidden in the brush.

He radioed Loni again as he tore out of the campground. "Put out an APB with all the stolen plates," he said. "For Virginia, North and South Carolina. A green Dodge Ram and a Jayco fifth wheel. And start an Amber alert."

He had no idea where Adair was going. He could only think of one possibility. If he was a Traveler, they always went home after they'd finished the long con. He put on the siren and headed for Highway 81 and the Traveler village in South Carolina.

By the time Miranda finished repairing her face in the

washroom and stepped outside the police station, Joseph was gone. So. This was how it was to be.

She took a deep breath, got in her car, and drove back through town. She stopped suddenly when Hector bolted into the street in front of her, David following in his chair.

"We need your car," Hector said. "Ruth called David. She was hysterical. Something about Grady's father and skipping town and Eden being with them. Eden was last heard from at the campground."

"Get in," Miranda said. She and Hector transferred David and stowed the chair in record time. She drove through the crowded streets as fast as she could. They had just turned onto the road to the campground when Joseph's car approached in its own cloud of dust, headed back the way they'd come. He stopped and rolled down the window just long enough to tell them to go home and he'd call them, then sped off again.

"I'm not going home," Miranda said, swinging the car around in a screeching U-turn, spewing gravel and dust and barely missing the ditch.

"I'm not, either," David said.

"I'm with you," Hector said.

"Fasten your seatbelts, then," Miranda said, gunning the engine to keep Joseph in sight. She had just found her daughter. She was not going to let some two-bit con man take her away.

chapter 55

E den made her citizen's arrest when they stopped for gas in
Bristol. It had been kind of exciting bumping down the
road. Finally they had stopped, and she had climbed out of the
cramped cupboard where Grady had stowed her, and she used her
radio to call Uncle Joseph before making the collar. "We're at a
Sheetz station right by the mall," she said. "I'm going to take
him in."

"You'll do nothing of the sort," he hollered, but she turned
off the volume. Sometimes a person just had to do their duty, and
hers was plain. She opened the door of the camper and walked
right up to Mr. Adair as he was pumping the gas. He looked
surprised, but she couldn't waste time on explaining things.

"Mr. Adair," she said, "I'm going to have to make a citizen's
arrest on you."

He looked at her seriously.

"You have the right to remain silent," she said. "Anything you
say can and will be used against you in a court of law. You have
the right to speak to an attorney, and to have an attorney present
during any questioning. If you cannot afford a lawyer, one will be
provided for you at government expense. Do you understand
these rights, Mr. Adair?"

"I believe I do," he said. "I've heard them before."

She nodded. She felt kind of sorry for him.

He put the gas nozzle up and reached for his wallet. "I need to pay for this gas."

"Go ahead," she said. She went with him, though, just in case he decided to bolt.

"Do you mind if I move the trailer so folks can use the pumps?"

"I don't mind," she said. She climbed into the backseat of the truck behind Grady. He looked like he might cry again.

"I'm sorry, son," Mr. Adair said, and he really did look sorry.

He pulled the trailer to the side of the big parking lot. "Do you mind if I get us some doughnuts and milk while we wait?"

"Send Grady, if you please, sir."

"A good suggestion," he said. He handed Grady ten dollars, and he hopped out of the truck.

"Get me some with sprinkles," Eden said, "and chocolate milk, please."

Mr. Adair put on the radio, and they listened to the *Old Time Gospel Hour* out of Lynchburg while they ate the doughnuts. They were finishing the last one when Uncle Joseph drove up. He looked about as mad as she'd ever seen him.

She hopped out of the truck and walked over to greet him, but he just said he would deal with her later and went over and started talking to Mr. Adair. Then Miranda drove up with Dad and Hector, and Miranda grabbed her and kissed her and said, "Are you all right? Are you all right?" And Eden said, "Of course I'm all right. Now let me go so I can turn over my prisoner."

She finally got untangled and went back to the truck where Uncle Joseph was with Mr. Adair. She officially passed custody to Uncle Joseph then and tried to tell him that she'd already read Mr. Adair his rights, but he just told her to keep quiet, and he went on and told them to him again. Then he put the handcuffs on Mr. Adair and sent her back to stand with Miranda and Dad and Pastor Hector. Dad had to hug on her, too, and she was missing everything, but finally she had them all calmed down enough to watch what was going on.

Uncle Joseph sent Grady first and was just leading Mr. Adair around the truck and camper to put him in the police car when Eden thought Miranda might faint. Grady came first, and Miranda said hey to him, and then Mr. Adair came in front of Uncle Joseph, and Miranda's face looked white as a sheet, just like she'd seen a ghost.

Mr. Adair smiled sort of sad-like and said, "Hey, Mirandy."

Eden was surprised, because now that she thought about it, she didn't think Miranda had ever met Mr. Adair. But what Miranda did next surprised her even more.

"Hello, Daddy," she said.

chapter 56

R uth was as exasperated as she'd ever been in her life. "Henry, maybe you can talk some sense into him. I've tried and so has Hector, but he has them both in jail and says he won't let them out until everything is sorted out."

Henry looked weary, and Ruth supposed it was understandable. None of them had gotten much sleep last night. She had spent hours the night before sorting things out with Miranda and Johnny, but to tell the truth, she felt invigorated. David and Sarah were here, too, Sarah having decided that her daughter's almost abduction merited a return trip home. They had brought Eden down to the jail at her insistence, and actually, they both looked livelier than they had in weeks. Ruth herself had taken charge of Grady until all this was sorted out.

"Now, tell me this again?" Henry said, and Ruth went through it for the third or fourth time.

"I called the bank yesterday, and they said Mr. Adair never cashed my check," she said. "He deposited it back into my account."

"Then why's he in jail?" Henry asked.

Hector spoke up, sounding apologetic. "There are a few other warrants. Something about some heat pumps."

"He paid them all back," Ruth said. "Call and ask them. He told me he stopped by each house yesterday on his way out of town and left each of them a check in their mailboxes. What they paid and extra for their trouble."

Henry looked interested. "Were the checks good?"

Ruth hesitated. She actually hadn't thought about that. "I'm sure they were," she said firmly. "But a simple phone call can verify that."

"Even if he paid them back, what he did is still against the law," Henry said, shaking his head.

Ruth was exasperated again. "Well, at least let Miranda out. She had no idea her father was doing anything illegal. In fact, she says she didn't even know he was here. She says she hasn't seen him in years, and I believe her."

Henry looked incredulous. "Joseph has Miranda locked up?"

"Big as you please," Ruth said. "I've tried to tell him he should let her go, but he won't listen to a thing I say."

"Where's Eden?" David asked. "She was here a minute ago."

"She borrowed my cell," Hector said. "She's calling Miranda's attorney for her. Said she wasn't allowed to make her one telephone call."

David grinned. Ruth smiled, too, then turned serious again. "Really, Henry, can't you do something?"

"I'll talk to him," he said, "but don't expect too much. When he gets like this, there's no reasoning with him. He's out for revenge."

David and Sarah looked sober at that. All of them were quiet.

Henry took Grady aside and spoke to him, found Eden and questioned her, then went to Joseph's office. Ruth followed him and listened from the hallway. Joseph was at his desk, glowering, filling out the arrest report, she supposed. Reports, plural.

"Joseph," Henry said, "I've got four upstanding citizens out here who think you've got one too many people in that jail."

"She played me for a fool, Henry."

"I don't think so, but even if she did, that's not against the law."

"What makes you think she wasn't in on the scams?"

"For one thing, none of the victims say anything about a woman. There's no evidence linking her to the frauds. Which might not even be frauds, because they did sign contracts, and he has returned the money, according to a reliable witness. And he redeposited the check your mother gave him. He may have slipped by you this time, my friend."

Joseph suddenly looked more tired and puzzled than angry. "I completely read her wrong, Henry. How could I have done that?"

"Did you really?" Henry asked. "Maybe she's telling the truth. I mean, what's she really done?"

"Came here under false pretenses. Used me to get information about my family. Lied to me about her father and helped him perpetrate a fraud."

"I'll admit it looks suspicious," Henry said. "But just because one woman couldn't be trusted doesn't mean they're all liars." He paused, letting that sink in.

Joseph said nothing, but Ruth thought the bullish look on his face softened a little.

Finally Henry spoke. "You do what you think is right, Joseph."

Ruth smiled triumphantly from her listening post. There was no other charge that Henry could have given Joseph that would accomplish what she wanted more effectively. Joseph would do what he thought was right, even if it meant his own hurt.

Henry left, giving her a wink as he did so. Ruth went out to the waiting room and told the others it would only be a matter of time. "Let's all go home now, so he can save face," she said. God loved humility but not humiliation.

chapter 57

M iranda sat in the holding cell, thankfully by herself. She sat on the thin mattress and looked around at the concrete fixtures, but oddly enough, the overriding emotion she felt was an absurd urge to laugh. The Hound of Heaven had chased her right into this cell and now sat patiently waiting for her decision.

She had spent the long night dozing and reading from the New Testament the female guard had supplied her when she requested a Bible.

To him who is thirsty I will give to drink without cost from the spring of the water of life was scribbled inside the front cover. Oh, she was thirsty. She knew that now, and she knew she would not leave this place without making the transaction she had been running from all her life.

Her thoughts slid to Joseph, and she felt sadness but not the tearing despair she would have thought. She understood why he was angry. She had kept him in the dark for too long, and when she had finally presented him with the truth, it had been immediately peeled away to reveal what seemed to be a layer of falsehood beneath it. She didn't know if he would forgive her or not. Judging from her present surroundings, things didn't look hopeful. But still, against all logic, hope was exactly what she felt. And it had nothing to do with Joseph. Or even Eden.

She heard clanging and buzzing from the hall and then footsteps. She looked up to see Pastor Hector's face regarding her with raised eyebrows and a slight expression of amusement. "Would you like a visit from your clergyman?" he asked.

"Absolutely," she said, and the guard unlocked the door and admitted him.

"Sit down," she said, scooting over on the mattress. "Welcome to my home."

He shook his head. "I'm still trying to figure out how things came to this," he said.

She sighed. "I didn't know my father was here."

"I know," Hector said. "I believe you."

"You do?"

"Absolutely," he affirmed, and she felt the sweetness of grace.

"Do you know about Eden?" she asked.

"Ruth told me," he said. "I hope it's all right."

"It's all right. I would have told you myself."

"What are you going to do? Will you tell her?"

"I don't know."

He nodded and didn't attempt to persuade her one way or the other.

She cleared her throat and brought up the matter which was most pressing on her mind. "I think I would like to become a Christian."

His brown eyes became even warmer. "All right," he said.

"What should I do?"

"Tell Jesus."

She took a deep breath and was beginning to feel anxious when she remembered what the pastor had said to her that night at the church so long ago. *"Just open your heart and ask Him to come in,"* he had said. So that is what she did. The words were simple, but as she prayed them she felt a deep peace rise up and spill over the edges of her heart.

"Amen," Hector said.

"Amen," she echoed.

Hector took out his handkerchief and blew his nose. She helped herself to some of the tissue the guard had left her.

"Is this a jailhouse conversion?" she asked, breaking the sober moment, and they both laughed.

More clanging and buzzing and footsteps. The guard again.

"You're free to go," she said, opening the cell door.

"Wow," Miranda said, giving Hector an amazed look.

"He sets the captive free," Hector quipped.

Hector stayed with her until she had checked out of the jail. A female officer gave her back the envelope containing her belongings. Inside was the picture of her baby—Eden, she knew now. She also knew who had put it there. She took it as an indication that she would not be seeing Joseph again.

"What's going to happen to my father?" Miranda asked the officer.

"That's for the judge to decide," she said.

"Can I see him?"

The officer shook her head. "Visiting hours are this afternoon from two to four."

She said good-bye to Hector, then went back to the little apartment. She didn't feel that she could still call it home. Ruth called and Miranda thanked her for her efforts. They promised to talk again soon. She slept for a few hours, scrambled a few eggs, then sat down at the table to think.

There were decisions to make. She sat there and thought about them. There was Joseph. She would at least try to talk to him and attempt to explain. There was her father, and here she would have a chance to forgive. There were David and Sarah. And there was Eden.

She prayed for the third time in her life. "Father, God," she said, "guide me as I walk through this day," and as she said amen, she knew He would. It was that simple. She showered and washed her hair and changed her clothes and went to the jail to see her daddy.

The same female guard patted her down, ran the metal detector over her, and let her in. She sat down on a hard plastic chair and waited for her father to come in. He finally did, looking old and lined and sad and tired. Her heart caught, and she suddenly remembered, no felt again, how she had loved him.

"Well, I suppose our bonding is complete now," she said with a smile. "We've spent the night in the same jail."

"Your mama would skin me alive," he said, but he wasn't smiling.

"That she would," Miranda agreed.

He sat down across from her and ran his hands through his hair. "This is all my fault. I never should have come here, but I felt I had to find you."

She blinked in disbelief. "You came here to find me?"

He nodded. "Bobbie told me you were in Abingdon, so I suggested to Mikey, my business partner, that we head over this way. But it was a mistake. All I've done is bring bad things to good people."

"But why?" she asked.

"Why what?"

"Why did you want to find me?"

He ducked his head and ran his hand through his hair again. Sighed deeply. "Miranda, I'm not proud of the life I've led."

"Is it true what they're saying, Daddy? Are you one of the Travelers?"

"No, but I had one as a cellmate in prison."

"You were in prison?"

He nodded and his face looked worn again. "I did some time for writing bad checks. When I got out I didn't have any money, and Mikey took me home with him. Said we would hit the road and make some money. I had to get Grady back," he said. "His mama was no account. He was staying with her sister, who wasn't much better. That was five years ago, and I've been riding along with the Travelers ever since. But you know, I just had a feeling my luck was running out. Either that, or I've developed a conscience in my old age. I knew it was wrong to steal from folks, and I didn't like it. That's why I came to find you. I had a feeling things were falling apart, and I didn't want Grady to go to some foster home."

He looked so weary, Miranda reached across and took his hand. It was callused and strong, and she remembered something else then.

"But you did a good thing, Daddy," she said softly. "I know what you did for Mama. You saved her."

He looked surprised.

"I've been to Thurmond," she said.

He looked pained and sorrowful. "I wish you hadn't had to know that."

"I think I want to know it all now. The good and the bad. I don't want to live in a fairy-tale world anymore."

"He was a terrible man, your mother's daddy. He did terrible things to her. I took her and her little sister and got them away. But your mama, she never got over what her daddy had done to her."

Miranda thought of her mother's closed heart and knew it was true. She had never gotten over it.

"When did you figure out Eden was yours?" he asked Miranda.

"You knew?" She was incredulous.

"Of course I knew. The minute I laid eyes on her, I knew. She's the spittin' image of you when you were that age. Full of vinegar, too. Just like you were." He smiled and they were silent for a minute, both of them remembering. "You were a fine little girl, Mirandy, and now you're a fine woman. Don't let anybody tell you different."

She wanted to ask him why he had left, why he had never called. But she didn't. He had done what he had done. Her choice was to forgive or not.

"I love you, Daddy," she said.

"You know I love you, Mirandy." He looked sad again, as if he wanted to say more.

"I forgive you, Daddy," she said.

He brushed tears from his worn face with an equally worn hand. "I don't deserve it."

"That's true," she said. Then they looked at each other and smiled, and she liked him so. She loved him and she liked him and she wished, she hoped, she could know him.

"So what's going to happen to you?" she asked.

He shrugged. "I'll probably do a little time. Ruth came to see me," he said, shaking his head in disbelief. "She's going to go ahead with the campground and said the job of caretaker is still mine if I want it."

"Do you?" she asked.

"How would you feel about that?"

"You assume I'm going to be here."

"Yes," he said, smiling, "I was assuming that."

"I'd like it," she said quietly.

Her father blinked back tears.

"I'd like it very much," she said.

"Take care of your brother for me?"

She smiled, having already worked that relationship out as she lay in her cell. "So I've got a little brother," she said.

"More than one, but that's another day's story."

"What about his mother?"

"Rita? No account," he said. "I've got legal custody. Papers are in the dash of the truck. And I'm making you his legal guardian until I get out of here. If you'll take him. He's a good boy, Mirandy."

"Of course I'll take him," she said. "I'll have my attorney draw up the papers." She wondered what she would do with a child. She wondered how long her daddy would be in jail.

Her father smiled, apparently easy in his mind now. "What are you going to do about Eden?" he asked.

"I don't know," Miranda admitted. "What do you think I should do?"

He looked at her seriously, then answered her softly. "I don't know, but I believe you'll do what's best for her."

She was silent for a minute, and when she spoke she could hear the loss she felt come out in her voice. "I hate to think of her growing up and not knowing me or you or anything about us."

Her father smiled at her, as if remembering something pleasant. "Mirandy," he asked, "do you still write everything down in those notebooks like you used to?"

She smiled and nodded.

"Give them to her," he said. "The whole unvarnished story. Not the sanitized version. Gather it all up, the old parts and the new parts. The parts you're proud of and the parts you're not, and put them all together in a book. It will be your gift to her," he said, "and you will know the right time to give it."

Miranda listened, and what her father said sounded good and right to her. She nodded. "Thank you, Daddy," she said.

"You're welcome, baby."

She told him good-bye and started to leave, then stopped and came back just as he was turning to go out the door. "Daddy," she called.

He turned back.

"Are we really Basque?"

He smiled and shook his head. "Sorry, darlin'. But it was a sweet story, wasn't it?"

chapter 58

S arah hung up the telephone with trembling hands. Ruth and David both stood watching her.

"What did she want?" David asked.

."She wants to meet. Now."

Sarah watched Ruth's face go pale, and David's—she couldn't read David's. She realized then it had been so long since she'd wondered how someone else was feeling that she was poor at seeing the signs. "How are you, David?" she asked.

He looked up in surprise at her question. "I feel sad," he said. "Sad for everyone."

She nodded. Ruth excused herself and went into the kitchen.

David wheeled his chair toward the door. "I'll go with you," he said, and Sarah surprised herself again. "No," she said. "If it's all right, I'll go alone."

David looked questioningly at her. She met his gaze, and he must have seen something there that cheered him, for his eyes regained a little of their light.

"All right," he said. "I'll be praying."

She nodded and left, choosing to walk down the hill to the church. She had plenty of time, and it would give her a chance to compose herself. She saw Miranda from a distance, a solitary figure sitting on the steps of the church, and oddly enough, she felt compassion for her. And for Eden, as well.

"Thanks for coming," Miranda said as Sarah approached.

"Sure," Sarah said.

She sat down on the steps a comfortable distance away. Miranda gave her a level glance, like a boxer inspecting his opponent before a match.

"Ruth told us," Sarah said. "I know who you are."

"Good," Miranda answered, not seeming to be disturbed by that fact in the least. "Then we can get down to business."

Sarah felt a slight shock of fear and realized again that this woman could take everything away from her by simply telling Eden the truth. Her daughter's heart was already cold to her. This would be the final blow. And along with the fear, Sarah felt anger and surprise that she cared. She had thought she was beyond caring, that she had given up, but perhaps she'd been as wrong about herself as she'd been about everyone else.

"Exactly what *is* our business?" she asked, her tone arching with her eyebrows, and she could have been mistaken, but she thought she saw a gleam of appreciation in Miranda's eyes when she heard the grit in Sarah's voice.

"Eden is our business," Miranda answered. "I need to know something. What exactly are your intentions?"

"What are yours?" Sarah shot back.

"I asked you first."

Sarah smiled without really intending to.

Miranda did, as well. "I suppose that did sound childish," Miranda said.

Their smiles faded and Miranda came quickly back to the point. "Are you back for good, or will you return to your parents?" Miranda asked.

And there it was. The question Sarah had been asking herself since she had made the breakneck drive yesterday evening. It was the question in Ruth's eyes and in Eden's and in David's. *Are you here for good? Will you stay?*

Miranda took her pause for an answer. "Because if you don't want Eden, I'll take her."

Sarah was truly shocked at the bald declaration. "I do want her!"

"Do you? Do you really? Do you want *her*? Because I like *her*. I like her the way she is. I like her stories and her jokes and her cowlicks and her freckles. I like her schemes and her adventures and the way she's always up to something. I like those things about her, but I get the feeling that you love her in spite of those things. In spite of who she is."

Sarah hung her head, then raised her eyes to Miranda's. "I suppose I deserved that," she said.

Another level look from Miranda.

Sarah did not flinch or look away. "I have behaved horribly toward Eden," she said. "I haven't accepted her for who she is. I'd like to have another chance, but I know it may be too late."

Miranda's face softened a little then, but Sarah didn't stop. "You asked me what my intentions are. I'll tell you. I intend to go back to my husband and my daughter. I intend to ask them both to forgive me, and then I intend to make a start at doing things differently."

Miranda sniffed. "Go on."

"If they'll have me, I intend to go back home with them, and then I intend to take Eden out of the private school and let her go to the one down the street with her friends from the neighborhood. I intend to cancel after-school swimming and gymnastics and study group. I intend to watch spy and adventure movies with her instead of making her watch *A Little Princess*, and I intend to see if she would like to take riding lessons with me. And I intend to buy some material and make her a horse shirt for every day of the week."

Sarah was crying now, and Miranda was wiping away tears with the palm of her hand. She looked so much like Eden that

Sarah felt a stab of love for her. "Those are my intentions, at least to begin with. I know I won't do it perfectly. We won't do it perfectly as a family. But I intend to try. If I get the chance."

"She needs you to love her," Miranda said. "Not the way she *should be*. The way she is. I need to know that you will try. Or I won't be able to let her go."

Sarah's heart lurched with hope. "I will," she said. "I'll do my best."

Miranda said nothing back, just continued to look at her, and after a minute or two Sarah got up and walked away.

Miranda didn't have long to wait before seeing Eden. She went to the little park to recover from the meeting with Sarah, and there was Eden sitting by the creek, dipping her feet into the water, just as Miranda liked to do.

"Hey," she said.

"Hey," Eden answered, looking a little shy, definitely an unusual state for her.

"Where's Grady?"

"He's with Grandma," Eden said. "And it's a good thing, because I've been wanting to talk to you. Alone."

Miranda's heart beat faster. "Well," she said, "I'm finally out of the slammer now. Let's talk." She sat down beside Eden. "What's on your mind?" she asked.

"I've been thinking," Eden said.

Miranda felt a rumble. Eden was bright. Very bright, and no one had been able to keep a secret from her for long. Joseph knew now and so did Ruth. So did David and Sarah. And Eden, how should she put it, followed events closely. Ruth said Eden knew she was adopted. It was only Joseph they had kept the secret from. She was afraid Eden knew the truth.

She was *afraid* she knew the truth. And she realized it had happened again. Her heart had decided before her brain had known. For all their flaws and faults, Sarah and David were the only parents Eden had ever known. Ruth was her grandmother.

Joseph was her uncle. This was her life, and to take it from her now would be cruel. This fragile family needed at least a chance before another blow crushed it lifeless. She remembered what her father said. *"You'll do what's best for her."* She felt tears begin to rise. How easy it would be to steal her away, she realized. How very easy.

"Suppose a person knew something," Eden began, looking at her seriously. "Supposing they knew something that would change . . . everything."

Miranda nodded.

"What should that person do?"

"What do you mean exactly?"

"Well, should they tell what they know? What they think they know?"

"Is it something bad, like what my dad did?"

Eden looked at her with scornful disbelief. "It's a felony to knowingly conceal a crime."

"Right." Miranda grinned. "I forgot who I was talking to. Well, is it a secret that could hurt someone? Is somebody being hurt or abused? Is it something like that?"

"No!" Eden looked frustrated and then gave her a meaningful look. "It's just a guess about something. Something I—something the person is not supposed to know."

There it was. It was in her hand, and she could do whatever she wanted. Here was the power, the decision that had been taken away from her. She thought of David then, of Sarah, of Eden. She thought about families and how flawed they were and how strong. She thought, oddly, about Beck Maddux, and she knew then that she was not like him. He had taken and taken and still stayed empty. She would give and be full.

She put aside her hesitation and spoke with authority she hadn't known she had. "Eden, sometimes we can find out things that are too big for us to carry. Is there anyone else who knows this person's secret?"

Eden met her eyes without blinking. "I think so," she said.

Miranda took her hand. "Then maybe she should let that person carry it for her for a while."

Eden's neck turned red, and before Miranda's eyes, hives appeared. A tear escaped and rolled down Eden's cheek. She wiped it off in obvious annoyance.

"Will she ever know?" she asked, her voice sounding tight.

"I think so," Miranda said, her throat hurting, too, from the effort of keeping back tears. "But not for a while. Not until she grows up. Maybe then."

Eden threw herself against Miranda's chest, and Miranda hugged her long and fiercely.

"I love you, Miranda," Eden said.

"I love you, too, baby. I love you, too."

After a moment they broke away. Eden wiped her eyes on the back of her hand, and Miranda knew she was angry that she had cried.

"You'd better get home," Miranda said. "Your mom and dad are waiting for you."

Eden gave her one last look, then got onto her bike. She rode a short way, then turned and looked back.

Miranda waved and blew her a kiss. Eden turned and rode away, and Miranda watched until she turned the corner.

She went back to the apartment and lay on the bed in the dark. She could leave now. She could leave, and no one could blame her. Ruth would take care of Grady, and then she would not have to see Joseph again or her father or anything that would remind her of what she had almost had and lost. She remembered the prayer she had prayed in the jail cell, and it seemed like months ago. She sat up and prayed again that she would know what to do. Part of her cried out to run, but another part, just as obstinate, sat down and refused to budge. It was funny what made her decide. The little spiky rock, the meteor her father had given her, was on the bedside table. She picked it up and ran her fingers over the sharp surface. She thought about a meteor, flaring swiftly across the sky, illuminating and taking the breath away for one brief moment on its journey. She set it down and went to the window and looked out at the night sky. It was full of bright stars, shining softly, giving light, and she knew then the difference between the two.

chapter 59

The next week went quickly for Sarah. She and David made arrangements to return to Fairfax, and on Saturday morning they were ready to leave. Ruth was in the kitchen, no doubt packing a staggering lunch for them to take on the plane. The two of them and Miranda sat on the porch waiting. Sarah felt the cool breeze on her face and realized it would be fall soon. And for the first time, perhaps in her life, she felt a sense of purpose and hope. It was tapping insistently now, like a chick on its shell, telling her that perhaps there would be good things in store, and perhaps she was worthy to receive them.

She had failed. She no longer tried to hide it, and it was odd, but there was freedom in admitting it. Who would have thought? She had always avoided looking at the ugly places inside her for fear they would overwhelm her. But somehow bringing them out into the light had drained their poison.

"May I stay?" she had asked David that night a week ago, when she'd returned from the confrontation with Miranda.

"Are you sure you want us?" he had asked, and she accepted the gentle rebuke the question contained.

"I want to want to," she had said, and he had smiled and said that it was enough for a start.

They had even made their peace with Joseph. He had come to them last week, and they had cried and wept together. They had forgiven and asked forgiveness, and what had been festering and full now felt cleansed and empty, ready to be filled with new things. She did not feel guilty anymore. And she did not expect perfection, even from herself.

They would never be a display model of perfection, her family, but they were here. The picture might be scarred and marred, but it had not become blackened ash. Its restoration was a bigger job than she could manage. In fact, everything was bigger than she was, and with the inability to control had come a blessed sense of—dare she name it—relief? For the first time in her life she seemed to be inside her own skin instead of gazing at herself and her life as part of a critical audience. She would do what she could and walk by faith regarding the rest. She was small. She was creature, not Creator.

And her husband was not a god. He was a man. He was made of flesh, the same as she was, and now he was the one who needed her. But she loved him. She loved her husband. The truth of that settled down and stayed as all the flotsam floated away. She loved the vital *who* of him and not merely his physical body. She loved her husband, and she loved their daughter. It felt good and right, and she knew it was enough for now. She remembered wondering if he would ever laugh again, really send joy out as waves of sound, and even about that she felt hope.

The car was loaded with their suitcases. Eden and Grady were in earnest conversation over by the garage, even though Grady would be going to the airport with them. Eden said she needed to make sure Grady knew all the things he was supposed to do until she came back. She was handing him a stack of Wanted posters. He looked a little overwhelmed.

David reached up and took Sarah's hand and laced his fingers through hers as they said good-bye to Miranda.

"I've been thinking about the last chapter to your book," Miranda said.

"I'm all ears," David said.

"I think I know what the ending should be."

"Tell me."

"You can't go back to the garden," Miranda said. "It's never going to be perfect here again. And if you waste all your energy trying to make believe or to look for the perfect place or the perfect person or the perfect life, you'll miss the good while looking for the perfect."

Her thoughts exactly, Sarah realized, and she looked at Miranda with a tender feeling.

"There's going to be a perfect place," David said, smiling, "where the sick will be healed and the dead will live and the lame will walk again, but we're not there yet."

"Not by a long shot," Miranda agreed. "But there are good things here." She looked over at Eden.

Sarah was quiet, seeing the love in her eyes.

"Here," Miranda said, reaching behind her and handing Sarah a large box wrapped in brown paper. "It's for Eden. When and *if* you decide the time is right." Her eyes glistened with tears.

Sarah received the gift for what it was, a sacrifice of love. "I will give it to her," she said, taking it into her hands. "I promise."

"Take good care of her," Miranda said solemnly. "Let her run around. Let her be herself. Let her be creative and imaginative. Enjoy her." A blessing, a benediction, a charge.

Sarah nodded, now with tears in her own eyes. "I'm going to try my best," she said, and she meant it. She felt she had been given a great gift, that something precious and almost lost had been restored to her. She didn't intend to make the same mistakes twice.

"I don't suppose you have anything in that little black bag for me?" David said, a wry smile on his face.

Miranda laughed, then sobered. "Oh, how I wish I did."

David shook his head and smiled. A real smile, Sarah could see, that began in his heart and overflowed onto his face. "I already have everything I need. Thank you for all you've done."

Miranda shook her head. "To quote my little brother, 'It weren't nothin'.'" By now everyone's eyes were damp, though they were all smiling.

Sarah looked across to where Eden was talking to Grady. She was punching him on the shoulder, her sign of deepest endearment.

"Joseph already stopped in to say good-bye," David said. "He said he was heading down to the old campground to do some repairs. Just thought you might want to know."

"Oh," Miranda said.

"Have you talked to him?" David pressed.

Miranda nodded and answered vaguely, "We straightened everything out."

"Everything?" he pressed.

She shrugged. "He asked me if I was going to stay or leave and told me to let him know when I had an answer."

David was looking at Miranda intently. "And do you have one?" he asked her.

"I don't want to leave," she said.

"So don't," David said.

"Well, it's funny, but all these years when I've felt like I ought to stay someplace, all I wanted to do was leave. And now I feel like I ought to leave, but all I want to do is stay."

"Why do you feel you ought to leave?" David asked.

She shifted uneasily and glanced toward Eden. "I just thought it would be easier for everyone."

"I'm all right with your staying," David said. "How about you, Sarah?"

Sarah looked at the hope on Miranda's face and felt the seesaw of emotion. She could send her away and be safe. Or she could take a risk and love. She needed only a moment to make her decision, for the truth was, Sarah's heart, for the first time she could remember, was full, positively overflowing, and she knew that she was safe, that she had no need to grasp and hold things so closely that they suffocated. In that moment she felt she would love nothing better than to know Miranda was close, building a life with people she loved, able to be a part of theirs someday.

"Yes, it's absolutely all right," she said. "It's the right thing to do."

David smiled sardonically. "Besides which, if you leave, I think my brother will probably grow moss waiting for you to come back."

Miranda shook her head, and her face darkened with regret. "I think he might prefer it if I left."

"Oh, please," David said. "I haven't seen him so smitten since Daisy Ferguson in the second grade."

Sarah saw a twinkle in his eye that hadn't been there three months ago. A smile played on his lips.

Miranda's face lit with hope, and she looked so much like Eden that Sarah grinned with recognition.

"Do you think so?" she asked.

"I know so," David assured her.

"Joseph has learned a lot about forgiveness," Sarah confirmed.

Miranda looked joyous and childlike. "Well, then, maybe I'll be seeing you," she said.

David nodded and smiled. Sarah felt something true and right settle down into its proper place in her heart.

Eden came toward them then, sniffling furiously and looking determined not to cry. She went to Miranda. The two of them looked at each other for a moment; then Eden flung herself at Miranda, and with her arms encircling her waist, she buried her face near her heart. Miranda's hands hesitated over Eden's head for a minute, then finally closed over her curly dark hair. She laid her own head on top of Eden's and rocked her softly from side to side. Both were crying. David was crying. Sarah was crying, and for a split second, Sarah wondered whose resolve would crumble first. She hesitated, vacillated. Was it wrong not to tell?

Miranda made the decision for them all.

"Good grief, Charlie Brown," she said, giving Eden a last squeeze and a smacking kiss on the top of the head. "We're acting like we'll never see each other again."

"You're not leaving?" Eden tipped her head up and looked at Miranda with joy.

Miranda blew out a little puff of air and shook her head. "Just between you and me and the cat box, your uncle Joseph sorely needs somebody to straighten him out, and I intend to have a go at it."

Eden grinned. David grinned. Grady grinned. Sarah felt her face lighten with her spirit.

"So you'll be here the next time I come?"

And in that second between Eden's question and Miranda's answer, Sarah wondered if she would take the opportunity to give herself an emergency exit.

"I will be here," Miranda said firmly, meeting her daughter's eyes without a blink. "I will be here whenever you need me. You will always know where to find me."

Eden gave her one last hug, then slung her backpack down onto the ground. She unzipped it with practiced precision and drew out her Kenwood police radio. "Here," she said, handing it to Miranda with a mischievous smile. "You can borrow it until Thanksgiving. That way you can keep up with him better."

Miranda laughed. She held out her hand. Eden slapped it, and then they linked fingers. "Friends forever?" she asked.

"Friends forever," Eden answered.

Then Eden turned toward Sarah, and Sarah saw relief and peace on her face, and in that moment Sarah wondered what she knew. She wondered, for a fraction of a second, if she had known all along. She wondered until Eden came and stood quietly beside her and took her hand, then reached across and took David's, and they were joined again, a threefold strand that would not be easily broken, no matter what came against them.

"Let's go home," Sarah said firmly. And they turned to leave.

After a few seconds David paused and wheeled halfway back around. "Remember," he said, calling back to Miranda, "the luckiest people are the ones who don't walk away."

"That's easy for you to say," Miranda quipped, then looked horrorstruck, realizing what she'd said.

And as Sarah watched, David stared at her for a moment, then threw back his head and laughed, a sound of pure, sweet joy.

chapter 60

Joseph drove into Camp Berachah and parked his truck. Flick jumped out of the back and ran down toward the water. Joseph got out and walked onto the lodge's porch, then sat down on the steps and looked around. The early morning air was moist, the grass green from last week's rains. He could hear the breeze shushing through the leaves of the trees, and the sunlight sparkled off the waters of the lake. He remembered his boyhood, his father, and he felt a sense of connection to him that he hadn't felt in many years. He supposed it had to do with making his peace with David, with letting go of the bitterness and coming back to God.

He felt joy that he had work to do. He had a small piece of the earth to subdue, and he would try to do it well. He thought of himself as a servant of God now, a messenger, not to put too fine a point on it. Oh, he knew he was just a creek that flowed into the ocean, but he took a clean, quiet pleasure in knowing he would do his part, sure and true. This was his post, a humble place, but his few miles of earth to tend and guard and keep, and oddly enough, sitting here on this porch that his father had built, he had the feeling that this place was where he belonged—here in this very spot—and that once again he would hear it ring with joy and laughter.

He got up and walked around the campground and inspected the work that Tommy DeSpain had done. It was all solid construction. The craftsmanship was fine. He walked past the chapel and the cabins, the teepees, down to the dock, then to the house where his parents had raised him and his brother. It needed a new roof. The foundation was good. It would need painting inside and a good cleaning. But nothing was beyond restoration. This he knew for certain.

He opened up the lodge, went inside, found the coffee, and put on a pot. He went to the shelf in the corner and took out the Bible that was there, then sat down and read, the only sound the gurgling of the coffee and the turning of the tissue-thin pages. The book of Romans. He read it carefully, following each thread of logic, seeing again the inescapable conclusions of lostness and law, then allowing himself to be carried along on the current and speed of the apostle's relentless, methodical ascent to the ringing declaration of mercy and grace. *What shall we say to all this?* he read, and he could almost hear Paul's voice, booming. *If God be for us, who can be against us? He who did not withhold or spare His own son but gave Him up for us all, will He not also with Him freely and graciously give us all other things?*

He bowed his head and prayed, then raised it and opened his eyes. The windows were bare. The sun streamed in like liquid gold. He sat quietly and watched the room fill with light, the smell and sound of his bubbling coffee rousing him from his thoughts. He set aside his Bible, poured himself a mug of the strong black brew, then walked back to the lake. Flick bounded along beside him. There was a good place for a garden there in that sunny spot. He would plant one next year. It was time something grew again in this rich dark earth.

He prayed the Lord's Prayer, then added one of his own. And he had a feeling that today he would know her answer. Whether she had left. Or whether she had stayed. He had gone past the small apartment last night to speak to her, but it had been dark. He had gone home and prayed and trusted now that the answer would be right.

⌒

Miranda watched them drive away and then quickly, before she lost her bearings or resolve, she got into the car. She drove to the campground, through the gate, and was not surprised to see Joseph there, sitting on the edge of the porch, watching and waiting. And she dared to hope he was waiting for her.

She parked the car and stepped onto the crunching gravel. He got up and started toward her. As the distance between them closed, she could see his usually flinty face was soft, and it wore an expression of joy. He began walking quickly, eating up the ground with his long strides. She began to run, and finally he was here, and she threw herself toward him. He caught her neatly, stumbling only slightly as she landed in his arms. The two of them laughed as they balanced each other, and she realized how right and natural it felt to have his arms around her.

"You're still here," he said after a moment during which their attention was otherwise engaged.

"Yes," she said simply, kissing him again.

"Are you staying?" he asked, his face clouding with doubt.

She sniffed and pushed away from him slightly. "That doesn't sound very proper to me at all."

He looked a little unsure. "What do you mean, not proper?" he asked.

"I mean my mama always told me, 'Don't make a commitment to a man who's not willing to make a commitment to you, Dora Mae.'"

He looked relieved, grinned, and pulled her back close to him. "Would you like something in writing?"

"Well, I would like to at least know I have a little job security.

I happen to be unemployed, and these temporary jobs are wearing on my last nerve."

"I have an opening for a file clerk," he said with a grin. "At least until next summer when the regular clerk comes back. If you want it, I'll have the paper work ready for you first thing Monday morning. As for the other, I was thinking of a more romantic setting."

"No way," she said, and she was amused to see him again look uncertain.

"No?"

"No," she said. "Not Monday morning. You need to take some time off. When was the last time you took a vacation?"

He relaxed, smiled in amusement as she teased him, and slipped his arm around her waist as they walked back up to the lodge.

"You know what's wrong with you?" she said authoritatively. "You need to take a trip."

"Is that so?"

"That is so. Have you ever been to the Northwest? You would love it! There are mountains and lakes and woods and the ocean, everything you could possibly want."

She kept talking, and he kept listening, nodding his head from time to time, a smile playing on his lips, and as she kept step beside him, he steadily led her home.

Dear Reader:

Eden. We all long for it, whether we have ever set foot in a church or experienced anything even close to it in this life. If we're human, there seems to be a desire hardwired in each of us for perfection, especially in our closest relationships.

The characters who populate the fictional world of *In Search of Eden* are on the quest for redemption, meaning, and love. Miranda believes if she can only undo the mistakes of the past by finding and reclaiming her lost child, her heart will finally be full. Miranda's mother, Noreen, seeks to find perfection through flawless performance—and by trusting her heart to no one. Joseph, a small-town cop, refuses to accept anyone who is flawed, including himself.

In the beautiful Blue Ridge Mountains of Virginia—as near to Eden as any place I can imagine—in a quaint, historic town, these characters learn what pastor and author David Seamands so eloquently explains: "Life can never be fully perfect again . . . at least not here on this planet and in the sense it originally was. . . . Here and now, life can be perfect only in a new and different sense, in the way of God's freely given grace." Only as the characters in this story learn to accept and forgive one another and finally themselves do they find the peace and safety they're seeking.

I hope as you read this book you'll be captivated by the journeys of the characters and enriched by their stories. But I also hope we can all stop working so hard to make everything perfect, including ourselves, and instead love and be loved by the bumpy, imperfect people around us.

In Him,
Linda Nichols

Discussion Questions:
In Search of Eden
Linda Nichols

1. What did the epigraph "He will make her wilderness like Eden, and her desert like the garden of the Lord" say to you before you read the story? What does it mean to you now? Have you ever had a wilderness or desert experience that God turned into a garden of Eden?

2. Nurse Wanda, disregarding the instructions given by her patient's mother, allowed the young girl to see her baby for a few moments before it was taken away by the adoptive parents. Discuss Wanda's action. Was it right or wrong? Why? What would you have done in the situation?

3. Discuss your reaction to Dorrie's mother, Noreen. Did she do the right thing in making adoption arrangements? Were there any other options? Was it right for her to never tell Dorrie anything about the baby? Did your opinion of Noreen change at any time? If so, when and why?

4. Noreen said Dorrie inherited her wandering spirit from her father. Do you think it was an inherited characteristic? If not, where did it come from? What events influenced or molded Dorrie's character?

5. Miranda (formerly Dorrie) felt an enormous amount of guilt regarding her child, that somehow she'd abandoned her or him. Was that a credible feeling? Do you know of anyone who has given up a child for adoption? If so, how does she now feel about her decision? Discuss the various emotional

ramifications of making such a decision—or having it made for you.

6. Eden knew she was adopted. Was it right that she had to keep it a secret? Was Eden right in her assessment that her mother wished she'd never adopted her? Discuss their relationship. How and why was it different from Eden's relationship with her dad?

7. For eleven years Joseph held bitterness against David and Sarah for their act of betrayal. How did this change him? Why was it so difficult for him to forgive them? Do you know anyone who is still holding a grudge for an offense committed years ago? If so, discuss how it has affected that person's life.

8. The reader is given hints that all is not well in Grady Adair's life, but Eden took him at face value and became his friend. Discuss what it must have been like for this young boy to pretend everything was all right when he knew his dad was scamming gullible old folks. Have you ever been loyal to someone you knew was involved in wrongdoing? Either by choice or by force?

9. Ruth Williams had suffered the loss of her husband and then the heartbreak of her two sons' estrangement, yet she was a strong Christian. She put on the armor of God in prayer daily. So why, then, was she vulnerable to Johnny Adair? What does that teach us?

10. Miranda decided not to tell Eden that she was her biological mother. Was that the right decision? Imagine yourself in her position. Could you have done what she did after finally finding your child? Can you think of any better solution?

11. For Miranda, the literal meaning of the title *In Search of Eden* means a search for her child. What deeper meaning might it have for her? For Joseph? For Sarah? For other characters? What does *Eden* mean to you? Are you in search of Eden?

12. Noreen is an example of someone who is a nominal Christian yet lives in misery. She reflects with pride at one point

that she has been scrupulous all her life about obeying the law. Joseph is also dedicated to the law. Do you see any applications here in a spiritual sense? What are the consequences of living by the law instead of by grace? How are these characters' choices different, and to what extent are they able to receive grace?

13. Miranda's counselor encourages her to enjoy God's good gifts in His presence. Miranda realized some people are like the frightened dog who fearfully protected its food. What caused this distortion of God's character? Do you struggle with the concept of God as a Giver rather than a taker? What does John 10:10 say about this?

14. Was life on planet Earth more like Eden in days gone by? Were times then better or easier? Are certain places more like Eden? How about Christian communities or sects who withdraw from the world and live separately? Do you feel they are legitimate or false?

Be the first to know!

Want to be the first to know *what's new from your favorite authors?*

Want to know all about *exciting new writers?*

Sign up for BethanyHouse newsletters at
www.bethanynewsletters.com
and you'll get regular updates via e-mail.
You can sign up for as many authors or
categories as you want so you get only
the information you really want.

Sign up today!